continued . . .

Thief of Light

Denise Rossetti

BERKLEY SENSATION, NEW YORK

THE BERKLEY PUBLISHING GROUP
Published by the Penguin Group
Penguin Group (USA) Inc.
375 Hudson Street, New York, New York 10014, USA

Penguin Group (Canada), 90 Eglinton Avenue East, Suite 700, Toronto, Ontario M4P 2Y3, Canada
(a division of Pearson Penguin Canada Inc.)
Penguin Books Ltd., 80 Strand, London WC2R 0RL, England
Penguin Group Ireland, 25 St. Stephen's Green, Dublin 2, Ireland (a division of Penguin Books Ltd.)
Penguin Group (Australia), 250 Camberwell Road, Camberwell, Victoria 3124, Australia
(a division of Pearson Australia Group Pty. Ltd.)
Penguin Books India Pvt. Ltd., 11 Community Centre, Panchsheel Park, New Delhi—110 017, India
Penguin Group (NZ), 67 Apollo Drive, Rosedale, North Shore 0632, New Zealand
(a division of Pearson New Zealand Ltd.)
Penguin Books (South Africa) (Pty.) Ltd., 24 Sturdee Avenue, Rosebank, Johannesburg 2196,
South Africa

Penguin Books Ltd., Registered Offices: 80 Strand, London WC2R 0RL, England

This is a work of fiction. Names, characters, places, and incidents either are the product of the author's imagination or are used fictitiously, and any resemblance to actual persons, living or dead, business establishments, events, or locales is entirely coincidental. The publisher does not have any control over and does not assume any responsibility for author or third-party websites or their content.

THIEF OF LIGHT

A Berkley Sensation Book / published by arrangement with the author

PRINTING HISTORY
Berkley Sensation trade edition / November 2009
Berkley Sensation mass-market edition / February 2011

Copyright © 2009 by Denise Rossetti.
Cover art by Jim Griffin.
Cover design by Judith Lagerman.
Interior text design by Laura K. Corless.

ISBN: 978-0-425-23984-1

BERKLEY® SENSATION
Berkley Sensation Books are published by The Berkley Publishing Group,
a division of Penguin Group (USA) Inc.,
375 Hudson Street, New York, New York 10014.
BERKLEY® SENSATION and the "B" design are trademarks of Penguin Group (USA) Inc.

PRINTED IN THE UNITED STATES OF AMERICA

10 9 8 7 6 5 4 3 2 1

1

Choose.

When the Lady's dark velvet voice spoke in Erik's dream, the power of Her will vibrated deep in his bones. He struck out, jarring his arm as his fist hit the wall next to the bed.

But he didn't wake.

Anger and dread banged about in his chest. "Choose?" he rasped. "Choose what?" Gritting his teeth, he tried to lever his eyes open, but they were sealed shut. The goddess had him cornered in his own body.

Twenty years ago, My Lord and I gave you a great gift. Or had you forgotten?

Erik stiffened.

A Voice so enchanting, so compelling, it captures the beating hearts of all who hear it. And what did you do with this blessing, hmm?

The Lady's tone dropped to the ear-aching pitch of thunder in the mountains. *You made of it a curse. In your vanity and your lust, you spoke a command to an unwilling soul.*

"You don't need to remind me, Great Lady. I know what I did." Every muscle in his jaw—his neck, his shoulders—locked tight.

Do you, indeed? A huff of displeasure. *We see little evidence of this.*

Out of the corner of his eye, Erik saw the movement of a graceful, star-dappled hand, the palm so big he could have curled up in it to sleep.

Or to die.

In the waking world, men trod warily around Erik Thorensen, with his massive shoulders, his chest muscled like a warrior's. The Dark Lady could snap him in two with the flick of a thought.

Should he risk it? Hell, why not? All he had left to lose was his life.

Bracing himself, he said, "Why not see for Yourself?"

An impatient exclamation, and the Lady was rummaging around in his head, turning his soul inside out to look at the underside, inspecting all the dirty little nooks and crannies. When Erik groaned in involuntary protest, She withdrew, but without haste.

Another voice, so deep as to be almost below the threshold of human hearing, rumbled, *Well?*

The Lady turned to Her Lord. *No better and no worse than many others.* Either the goddess shrugged, or every star in the cosmos shifted in its cold bed. *His soul remembers, but his conscious mind chooses to forget.* Her voice dropped. *He doesn't think of her if he can help it. Only in his dreams.*

Nightmares, more like. Erik squinted into the sparkling nimbus that marked the presence of the Horned Lord. He caught the impression of a vast, nebulous figure, antlers spanning the stars. Without being obvious, he tried to angle himself toward that huge male presence. His heart hammered in his chest, fast heavy beats that hurt.

"I can't—" Hiding from the gods was useless. He'd learned that lesson at seventeen. "I have to live in my skin, face myself in the mirror, day after fucking day." Vaguely, he was aware his cheeks were damp. Must be sweat.

He raised his head, resentment burning a sullen hole in his belly. "It's the way I function, stay sane." Fuck it all to hell. Say it. "What use is a broken tool, even to the gods? My Lord, when I was a boy and You gave me the Voice, You said You had a task for me."

Dead silence.

The Lord's rumble of anger thundered through every cell in Erik's body. He grunted, squeezing his eyes shut, willing himself to endure.

But the Lady sounded amused. *Only you, Erik. Only you would dare. Little one, you cannot bargain with Us.* The sensation of Her smile tingled over his skin, both fond and terrible. *The day will come, my dear, when you encounter one you cannot charm, cannot control.*

"So?" he panted, still fighting for breath. "Doesn't matter about anyone else. I have my own rules, and they work for me." Cautiously, he sat up. "I live. Exist."

Last chance, growled the Horned Lord. *Choose.*

Erik set his stubborn jaw. "I want my life to have been worth something. Whatever it is You want, I'll do it. Just tell me."

You misunderstand, purred the goddess. *You've already committed yourself to Our service. The promise you made as a boy cannot be undone.*

"Then what—?" He shook his head. "Never mind. What is it I have to do?"

The Pattern is what it is. Beyond even Our touch, said the Lord. *You will know your life's work when the time is right.* The weight of the god's attention was like a solar flare crisping his skin.

"Soon? It will be soon?"

I am not in the habit of repeating Myself.

Erik resisted the impulse to roll his eyes. "It's all a trifle . . . cryptic." Nothing like going in blind.

Enough! The goddess moved abruptly, and a freezing wind ruffled Erik's hair, chilling the sweat on his chest. *You cannot know more of your destiny without affecting the balance. It is a different choice We offer you tonight.*

Shit, shit, shit. Despite himself, Erik's hands shook. He laced his fingers together into one big fist, the knuckles white.

Listen well, Erik Thorensen. If it is truly your desire, you will never again compel another with your Voice. We will take it from you.

His heart leaped. Gods, yes! No more rules, no more boundaries, no need to censor every word he spoke, constantly alert lest he . . . slip.

Again.

Inexorably, the Lady continued. *By your own actions, Erik, you besmirched the blessing of the Voice. You used it to steal a soul dear to Me.*

Judge and jury.

The blessing and the curse cannot be separated. If We take the Voice, you will lose everything. No more of the music, my dear, the music that makes your soul soar.

Executioner.

He couldn't make a sound, but a full-body shudder raised all the fine hairs on his skin. Because the music was all he was—Erik Thorensen, also called Erik the Golden—that, and the easy, unruffled charm he wore like armor.

When he concentrated, the Voice flowed out of his deep chest like a stream of purest, golden air. It made people think of silk or the best chocolat liqueur from Concordia or the glorious, sliding friction of sublime and endless sex. It was a miracle, that Voice. The rest of the time, he was still a damn fine singer, if a trifle run-of-the-mill.

"No." All he could produce was a hoarse rasp. "No."

Despite the way he'd corrupted the gods' gift, music brought his soul as close to the warmth of human connection as any artifice could do. His magnificent baritone gave him passion that was real, more satisfying than any sex he'd ever had. It kept him sane, focused on the here and now. Without the Voice, there'd be nothing left that was *Erik*. He'd be a shell that walked and talked, a big golden body women would desire for its own sake. Nothing more.

Hell, there were dark nights of the soul when he suspected he'd already reached that state.

A huge forefinger stroked the length of his naked spine from nape to buttocks, excruciatingly lightly. Erik shivered.

You're lonely, murmured the Lady. *Aren't you, little one? And yet women tumble in and out of your bed, smiling as they leave.*

"Yes," he said. "But it means nothing. *They* mean nothing."

You don't enjoy sex? asked the Horned Lord. *How is this? You control the women, the bedsport. You get the release you need, and all of it on your own terms.*

"True, my Lord, but I want . . ."

What? A growl like thunder. *More?*

Erik gritted his teeth. "I presumed."

You wield your charm like a weapon. The threatening pressure of the Dark Lady's disapproval rolled heavily down his spine, bringing with it a drifting scent of ice and ancient stone and warm woman. *What need do you have of anything more?*

Pressing his lips together, Erik shook his head.

Answer My Lady's question, rumbled the Lord. *Or would you prefer I peer into your miserable soul Myself?*

Fuck, he'd never survive it.

Erik cleared his throat, the heat rising in his cheeks. "There is no one who cares for me, who knows me. The real me." Humiliation washed over him, a warm, greasy wave. He clamped his mouth shut.

Audiences adore you. You have friends, said the Lady. *Grayson, for example.*

"I suppose so." Erik ran a hand through his hair. "Gray's a good man, but we're not close, not really."

It helps if you don't hold people at arm's length.

Hell, She was *teasing* him.

"I have to," he snapped. "In case I—" He broke off, sucking in a rasping breath. "It's the price I pay for the Voice. For the music."

She'd have to be your match, Erik. So she can fight you every delicious step of the way.

"What? Who?"

The woman whose love you crave, the lover whose trust you desire. The very thought of her makes you hard with longing, doesn't it?

"Don't be stu—" Erik bit his tongue in the nick of time. "She doesn't exist. Anyway, she'd have to know. And once she did . . ." He dropped his head, breathing hard. Then he shrugged. "Ah well."

The Lady's tone softened, became almost regretful. *A moment ago, you chose to keep the Voice, the power to compel any woman to your will. Why not use it?*

Insult the Dark Lady and he'd be dead before he hit the floor. But couldn't She see? Or was She testing him? "Great Lady, You know as well as I do that love compelled cannot be real. How would I know the difference between what she gave me and what I just . . . took?"

You are finely caught, are you not? The Horned Lord sounded thoughtful, and not particularly displeased. *Use the Voice to command what you so deeply desire, and by its very nature, you can never be sure you have it. Neither trust, nor love.*

Correct, said the Lady. *And yet, We offer you a choice. Think again, Erik. Shall We take the Voice from you?*

The Lord's deep tones: *Be very certain, Erik. All or nothing.*

Silence fell, so profound Erik thought he could hear the small bright tinkling that was the crystal song of the stars. Or it could have been the mental speech of the gods.

"Without the music, I am nothing, no one," he snarled. "I'll keep the Voice—the blessing and the godsbedamned curse."

2

On the stage of the Royal Theater, a chorus of devils and angels sang their hearts out, but Prue McGuire listened with only half an ear. She didn't particularly enjoy opera.

"A demon king?" she'd snorted to Rosarina as they settled into their seats before the curtains opened. "The plot doesn't make sense." Frowning, she scanned the program. "Why does he carry her off when she wants to go with him anyway? It's plain silly."

Like the experienced courtesan she was, Rose had given an elegant shrug. "Who knows?" Her beautiful lips curved. "It's opera."

As the queen and her entourage swept into the Royal Box, Prue put her head next to her companion's. "I got us a discount," she murmured over the sound of the applause.

Rosarina patted her hand. "And these excellent seats in the bargain." She surveyed the dozen or so exquisite young people in their box with maternal pride. "Well done, dear."

"It was an investment," said Prue. "We'll get more clients out of this, you'll see."

"Not that we need them." Her friend and business partner waved a graceful hand. "But never let it be said I argued with a bookkeeper about profit." Casting Prue a twinkling, sidelong glance, Rose flicked the playbill with one finger. "They say the Unearthly Opera Company's really very good, and this Erik the Golden is something quite exceptional." The twinkle became a naughty grin. "In every possible way."

"Rose!" She did her best to look scandalized.

"Don't *Rose* me, you wicked woman." A slim finger tapped the dimple quivering in Prue's cheek. "Not with a dead give-away right here." The orchestra struck up and the curtains swished open. "Shut up and enjoy, sweetie."

But Prue spent the first scene writing a tutorial on compound interest in her head. She'd rather die than admit it to her friend, but she'd come to find teaching the apprentice courtesans even more fulfilling than balancing the ledgers.

And every extra cred went into her strongbox. For peace of mind and her daughter's future. Despite herself, her breath caught.

Never again.

With some difficulty, she wrenched her mind away from the brutal slum the people of Caracole called the Melting Pot—the way her nerves had quivered at every shift in the shadows, the hilt of a small kitchen knife cold as death in her palm, her daughter's tiny fist clutching her sleeve.

The music was catchy. Tapping her fingers on her knee in time, Prue pulled in a deep breath, forcing herself to relax. It was over. Finished a lifetime ago. Slowly, she exhaled, stealing a glance at Rose's perfect profile.

By the Sister, she'd done better than merely survive! In Rosarina, she had a dear friend and a partner both. Prue smiled her satisfaction. Every courtesan at The Garden of Nocturnal Delights was the owner of an independent business with but a single product—themselves. How she loved it when it all came together for them, comprehension dawning on those beautiful, clever faces. Rose wouldn't tolerate stupidity, no matter how gorgeous the package it came in. Still, compound interest . . . Not the easiest of topics . . .

So when the demon king appeared in a clap of thunder and a cloud of smoke, she was completely unprepared.

⌒∞⌒

When the lights came up for intermission, she was still trembling on a deep, visceral level that dismayed her more than anything had in years. Erik Thorensen had come striding out of fire and brimstone and clasped the shrinking heroine to his chest. And yes, he was a marvelous-looking man, his hair loose on his shoulders like dark-spun gold under the stage lights, the neatly trimmed goatee a shade darker. His eyes were such a vivid blue they pierced Prue all the way to her soft, silly soul. He was big too—so big only the athleticism of his tall, muscular frame prevented him from looking blocky. Gods, exactly the physical type she preferred, right down to the mischievous glint in his eye.

But Prue had spent almost two decades surrounded by the most beautiful people on the world of Palimpsest. She was accustomed to perfection, even to the delightful frisson of sexual dominance Erik projected so effortlessly. He was a fine actor.

But merciful Sister, that voice!

He'd glanced directly at their box and his face had lit up with a grin that had pure devil in it. Then he'd opened his mouth. From the first effortless bar, her foolish heart had tumbled into his keeping. Every note was round, rich, deeply masculine, filling the auditorium as if supported on smooth columns of air. Utterly enthralled, Prue had found herself leaning forward, her mouth hanging open, trying to breathe him in, keep him forever, hers alone. She felt feverish, tingling, her breasts tight and her sex swollen and slippery, as if he were stroking her naked body with velvet.

Even worse, the costume, in an old-fashioned style still worn only by the oligarchs on Green IV, suited him to perfection. A pair of over-the-knee boots emphasized the power of thighs and buttocks encased in tight cream breeches. Prue's mouth watered.

The tenor hero had pretty well disappeared in comparison. During one of his uninspiring arias, she managed to tear her eyes away and glance to her left. "Gods," gasped Rose, a flush mantling her cheeks. Her hand closed hard over Prue's forearm, the fingers digging in. "Have you ever—?"

"No." Every face in the theater was rapt. "Sshh. He's starting again."

The tenor had won the duel that ended the act, and the demon king lay wounded, his pain and heartbreak throbbing in a cascade of low, exquisite notes. Tears prickled behind Prue's eyes. Godsdammit, he was good! No, not good—superb, superlative, magnificent.

All through the thunder of the applause, the stamping of feet, the shouting, she sat frozen, putting herself back together, a piece at a time.

She could do better than this. She wasn't some silly girl to lose her head and heart to a handsome singer. She was Pruella Takimori McGuire, business manager of The Garden of Nocturnal Delights, a woman for whom numbers held no terror. Rose's friend and silent partner, Katrin's mother. That helped, the thought of Katrin, serious and steady, only nineteen, but so deeply in love with her Arkady. He was a good boy. That had her grinning ruefully, trying to relax.

Unfortunately, the second act was even worse. Or better.

Erik was surveying his makeup and costume dispassionately in the mirror when someone scratched on the door. "Ye there?" said a voice straight from the slums of Sybaris.

"Of course." Setting the powder puff aside, Erik grinned at his reflection, though it turned out more like a grimace. "Come in."

He'd woken half off the bed, half on, rubbed raw in some tender internal place he couldn't touch, couldn't soothe. He still had the sense of a dark, towering wave, gathering on the horizon, looming closer . . . His destiny or his death? Unless they were one and the same.

Fuck premonitions. He'd made his decision, hadn't he? Chosen the nearest thing he knew to substance, the only way to fill the emptiness and anchor him in this life. What was done, was done.

The door opened the merest crack, and a small, skinny

figure eeled into the room. Florien shot him a flat, dark glance from under a tangled fringe, and Erik suppressed a sigh. The boy had filled out some since Cenda and Gray had rescued him from the stews of his home world, but he still reminded Erik of an alley cat—wiry and half-savage, poised to claw or flee as the case demanded.

"What is it?" he asked when the boy showed no signs of breaking the silence. In the mirror, Erik tried a suitably diabolical leer. Better.

"Twenny minutes."

Erik raised a brow. "For . . . ?"

Florien's mouth barely moved, as if he begrudged each word. "T' secon' act curtain. Ranald sed t' tell ye." He turned away.

Lord's balls, how old was the lad? Ten? Possibly a little more. Did he ever smile?

On impulse, Erik said, "How do I look?"

The boy paused, grubby fingers gripping the latch. Erik rose and struck a pose, one hand on the hilt of his sword. He creased his face into a ferocious frown and scowled. "Evil, like a demon king?"

For a split second, Florien froze, then he relaxed, tilting his head to one side, though the effect was more calculating than engaging. He scanned Erik from head to heels, and all the considerable territory in between. "Nah," he said eventually. "Them britches is too tight."

Erik grinned, thinking of the party of pretty women gracing the best box in the theater. "Oh, I don't know," he murmured.

Unobtrusively, he wrinkled his nose. How long since the lad had taken a bath?

"C'mon," he said, clapping a hand on Florien's shoulder. The boy shifted uneasily, the bony joint both hard and fragile, lost in Erik's big palm. Erik removed his hand. "Let's go stand in the wings and I'll show you how to case a crowd."

"Nah," said Florien. "I'll show ye."

As they walked down the narrow passage, the building swayed beneath their feet, almost imperceptibly. Apparently visitors became accustomed to it soon enough, while the locals didn't even notice. Smiling a little, Erik shook his head. Caracole of the Leaves was amazing. A subtropical city of canals and clean blue water, of shining pagodas and elegant vice.

A population of a hundred thousand souls cradled on the gargantuan, platelike leaves of a titanplant, a marine organism built on a scale so enormous it boggled the mind of an offworlder. Each Leaf was a living island, hundreds of feet thick, anchored to the seabed by huge cable stems. Even during the fury of the summer storm season, their ponderous weight restricted movement to a gentle swell.

Down here, in the warren of poky rooms beneath the theater, he was still aware of the salty tang of the ocean, but what he found hard to credit was the deep green smell tickling the back of his nose, vast and vegetative and somehow serene. If it weren't for the evidence of his senses, he wouldn't have believed it, but he'd always been extraordinarily sensitive to airborne odors.

In the wings, Florien concealed his skinny person in a swathe of red velvet curtain, his eyes huge.

"Right then, lad. Tell me what I should know." Erik nodded at the chattering audience, perfectly illuminated by Technomage glowglobes in fancy sconces. His brows rose. Queen Sikara IV of the Isles clearly had an excellent relationship with the local Technomage Tower. Either that, or she was made of money.

"T' queen's up high." Florien pointed. "Got a fancy box done up wit' velvet an' gold tassel things." He twisted to grin at Erik over his shoulder. "An' did ya see t' doxies? Over there. Right pretty, yah?"

Erik sighed. A childhood in the festering slums of Sybaris was its own education. In any case, he'd noticed them immediately. How could he not? "Wonder where they're from," he murmured, thinking aloud.

"Place called T' Garden, Ranald sed."

Erik indulged himself in a long, luxurious survey. "Not doxies," he said finally. "Though I grant you they're gorgeous. Those are courtesans, my boy, the best-quality companions money can buy—entertainers, musicians, more than just a willing body to—" He stopped and cleared his throat.

They were so beguiling, seated there, displayed for a man's

inspection like flowers ready for the plucking. Dark and fair, tall and dainty, male and female. Turned up high for intermission, the lights gleamed on thick tresses streaming over creamy shoulders, silver cuffs on strong masculine wrists, perfect complexions of every hue, straight noses and mouths made for kissing deep.

Courtesans. Gods, the tall one in the rich burgundy gown would be a perfect match for him. The way she threw her head back when she laughed, that glorious bosom. A creature of the senses, a woman who loved her bedsport, he could tell from here.

The Garden obviously catered for every taste. Beside the dark beauty sat a small, curvy woman, not spectacular, but pretty enough. She reminded him of one of his mother's hens, all smooth brown feathers and soft breast and propriety. She had a sweet, lush mouth and tip-tilted eyes, though he couldn't make out their color from this distance. Erik's lips twitched. A woman who looked that proper simply begged to be debauched.

The murmur of feminine voices and the clatter of heels announced the arrival of the dancers behind him. A heavy combination of stage makeup and sweat drifted past his long-suffering nose.

The gods knew, never before had he contemplated paying for sex. It hadn't been necessary. Besides, the idea hadn't appealed, too sleazy, too . . . soiled. Money was its own means of compulsion, almost as repugnant as the commands he refused to utter with the Voice. Hell, you couldn't buy the connection he craved.

But these women were all class and elegance, and suddenly, a straightforward transaction didn't seem like such a bad idea. Independent courtesans of this quality made their choices with eyes wide open. No complications, no aftermath, and he could do what he liked, the way he liked it.

There'd be no trust, but there'd be no compulsion either. A purchase was a purchase. He might feel a little uncomfortable, a little dirty, but he could live with that. The stain on his soul wouldn't be permanent.

And he could let go.

The need to control the physical act was woven deep into the fabric of his soul. Who knew whether it had come before the gods' gift or as a consequence of it? Either way, the fucking irony hit him between the eyes.

Because he'd be paying good creds for an illusion. There was no way he could open his mouth and *command* with the Voice, the way his dark desire for possession urged him to do, the words emerging from somewhere deep and dominant, the most primitive part of what made him male.

But if he wished to orchestrate a woman's pleasure until she writhed, sobbing and pleading for release, a Garden courtesan would oblige him with sublime artistry—enough that he might even believe her.

Gods! Erik's mouth went dry and his pulse began to surge in his ears like a mighty wind battering at a wall. He reached down to tug at his breeches, now tighter than ever. Five minutes to curtain.

Cursing under his breath, he laid a palm over the center of his chest, feeling the small, hard bump beneath his shirt—a stark reminder of what a man could and couldn't do and still meet his own eyes in the mirror each morning. He'd worn it every day since the year he'd turned seventeen, a part of his ironclad personal code, first on a thin, plaited strip of leather, then a silver chain, now a gold one.

Because he'd made a rule to preserve his sanity—Erik's first rule—Erik's *only* rule.

Don't use the Voice to speak.

Singing? Well, that was a different matter. But speech? Gods, no! It was the only way to be safe.

He could count the exceptions on the fingers of one hand. There'd been the time a ham-handed acrobat had dropped a flaming torch in the timber theater on Green IV. The place was so ancient, only the varnish held it together. If he hadn't used the Voice to quell the mass panic, the gods only knew how many would have died in the rush for the exits.

Lightly, he squeezed the boy's shoulder. "Will you run a message for me?"

"Yah." Florien listened, then repeated it word perfect in his thick slum accent. He squirmed through the pack of dancers, avoiding their casual, affectionate pats with a toss of the head.

Gods, the discipline had been so hard at first! Anger, lust, fear—any strong emotion and the Voice surged out of him in a rushing tide he couldn't hold back. Impulse and instinct became Erik's sworn enemies.

In his mid-twenties, not long after he'd joined the Unearthly Opera, he'd come across a shabby man teetering on a windowsill on the top floor of the highest tower on Concordia. The instinctive command had burst out of him. "*No! Don't jump.*" He'd walked closer. "*I forbid it.*"

As the Voice echoed around the room, the man withdrew his legs without comment and swung around. In complete silence, he'd shuffled past Erik and out the door, leaving the sour stink of his terror sweat behind. His eyes had been horrible, somehow empty, but also brimful of an agony too great to be borne.

Erik had stumbled to the window, struggling to hold on to his lunch. Because he knew, with absolute certainty, the man would be driven to find another way, slower and crueler than the shattering impact and quick obliteration he'd planned. Why the fuck had he meddled?

Well, hell, he had to give the Lord and the Lady Their due. As the years passed, the Voice brought with it a crash course in stubborn. He'd learned what honor was—the hard way. So he clung to whatever remnants of decency he could, even when his deepest desires flayed him with specious arguments. *Just this once. It won't hurt. Say it, say it.* It drove him fucking mad.

He'd gone for years now without a lapse, but Lord's balls, one of these days, the strain of it would kill him, just wear him out.

Depression darkened his mood, the fit of his breeches no longer a problem. It didn't matter how he twisted and fought, the gods had him tight by the balls. *You are finely caught, are you not?* Whatever his mysterious task might be, the sooner it came the better. Damn Them and their cryptic utterances!

The orchestra struck up and the dancers swept past him in a tight phalanx. The tenor came on from stage left, seized the soprano and embraced her with clumsy enthusiasm. Erik filled his lungs. The demon king was on.

He spent the rest of the opera angling his Voice toward that box, subtly, carefully, but nonetheless . . . What was the harm? He was only singing after all, just taking the air and molding it into notes, one after the other, bar after bar.

But he couldn't shake the tingling sense of the little courtesan's tip-tilted eyes dwelling on his body.

3

After the grand finale, he lost count of the curtain calls. The Unearthly Opera Company bowed again and again, hands linked, beaming. Erik stepped forward, gazing out into the darkened auditorium, savoring the expectant hush, the faces turned up to his like night-blooming flowers. This—*this*—was what kept him sane.

The blessing of the music. The audience. *Connection* . . .

After what he'd done—

Don't go there, not now. With the ease of long practice, he jerked himself out of the murky waters of memory.

After he'd . . . left home, it had taken him quite some time to realize it was when he sang that the Voice was truly the blessing the Lady had named it. An instrument of joy. Nothing more, nothing less. A few hours respite from the daily grind, smiles for tired faces. Sometimes, he thought it was like flying, feeling all those souls shake loose and soar free beside his. Together, they ranged the gamut of human emotion—from despair to triumph, hate to love.

Deliberately, Erik emptied his mind of all the distractions, settling himself for his favorite encore. *Great Lady*, he thought, as the first notes of the lullaby floated free, *this is the most*

*beautiful thing I can make for You. Take it as yet another down
payment on my bloody penance.*

He didn't even realize he'd made a choice until he was on
the final verse and the woman seated beside the dark beauty
used her fingers to wipe the tears from her cheeks like a child.
Next to such perfection, she was decidedly plain, but she kept
drawing his gaze. Why that should be, he had no idea, but
something about her hooked him at a deep, primeval level.
Perhaps it was because she was so small, so feminine, sitting with her spine ramrod straight in the indomitable way of
bossy women the worlds wide. Her very posture constituted
a challenge to his masculinity, his charm. She seemed so perfectly contained, the temptation to unravel her was irresistible.

The decision made, Erik relaxed into the music, smiling
on the inside. She wouldn't have a chance. He'd wrap her up,
envelop her, overwhelm her with pleasure 'til she screamed.

Speculations rioted in his brain: What perfume did she
wear? He loved the way women smelled. Was her voice light
or deep? How would she look when she laughed? Or when she
was poised on a pinnacle of pleasure, lost to propriety, gone
beyond rational thought? He had to know.

Oh yes. *That one.* He'd never seen a courtesan quite like
her before. A refreshing change. She'd do very well, very well
indeed.

By the time it was all finished, the lullaby, the applause,
the bows, he was alight, every vestige of depression washed
away by the stimulation of performance. This was what filled
the empty places—the thrill of it, the rush. How could the
gods think he'd give it up?

∽

By way of an encore, Erik the Golden sang a lullaby unac-
companied, his voice a thread of dark gold woven around the
weeping heart.

> *Storm clouds gather, love,*
> *In your eyes, in your pretty eyes.*

Prue had always loved the "Lullaby for Stormy Eyes," but
she'd never heard it sung this way, like an exquisite, aching

elegy. As the last notes fell away to a throbbing hush, she scrubbed at the tears on her cheeks.

The world seemed to hang suspended for a moment, as if the Sister Herself held Her breath. Someone clapped, hesitantly, then someone else. Suddenly, the Royal Theater was buried under an avalanche of noise—shouting, stamping, clapping, cheering. People stood and yelled at the tops of their voices. It made Prue's head swim.

Erik Thorensen bowed again and again. He looked straight at the courtesans' box, his eyes bright. Prue felt the impact of that glance as though he'd pressed his mouth between her open thighs, though she knew he had to be looking at Rose, because all men looked at the Dark Rose. They couldn't help it.

A final bow and he blew a kiss in their general direction. Then he strode offstage and the lights went up. Prue pulled in a shuddering breath, folding her hands in her lap.

"Gods, that was wonderful. Here." Rose sank back in her seat and thrust a handkerchief at Prue. "Blow your nose, you great softy." She frowned, reaching out to undo the top two buttons of Prue's one and only evening gown.

"Rose, what—?" Prue batted at her hands, but Rose persisted.

"We're going to a party." Briskly, Rose smoothed the fabric open, exposing the upper swell of Prue's plump breasts.

"Rosarina!"

A dark brow arched and Rose's strange, long-lashed eyes gleamed, dark and mysterious as moonslight on the sea canals of Caracole. Her lips twitched. "Erik the Golden just sent us an invitation to Her Majesty's reception. Did I forget to tell you?"

∞

Death Magick wasn't all doom and gloom—a common, if ignorant assumption. The Necromancer's lips twitched as he leaned back into the velvet embrace of his seat. Of course, a little terror, judiciously applied, was very sweet, but it wasn't as if he was incapable of appreciating life and laughter.

Beauty.

His thoughtful gaze dipped below him to the left, to the dozen or so courtesans preparing to leave their private box,

highlighted like a bed of exquisite blooms by the glowglobes.
He moved on, to where the last two had risen to shake out their
skirts. They were deep in conversation, their heads together in
the manner of old friends, comfortable in each other's space.
The taller had a sweep of shining midnight hair, spilling soft
and straight and thick all down her back, the other appeared
to be short and softly curved, her hands gesturing busily as
she spoke. From this angle, all he could see of her was one
creamy rounded cheek, a determined little chin. Her hair was
a gleaming nut brown, lightly confined in a net of gold, her
gown a simple, severe black.

Then the tall woman turned her head. She was laughing,
her face alight with pleasure and humor, and despite himself,
the Necromancer's brows rose. He'd never seen a woman more
alluring, and Shaitan knew, he was immune to feminine charms.

Interesting. This had to be famous Dark Rose herself. The
copper-satin skin, the lush mouth, the magnificent body clad
in a simple burgundy gown of such surpassing elegance that it
enticed even as it concealed.

Her establishment was well named. The Garden of Nocturnal Delights was the most exclusive, expensive courtesan
house in Caracole of the Leaves. Indeed, on Palimpsest itself.
The Necromancer had never been to The Garden. Money was
not an issue, but he had no need for the pleasures of the flesh,
and no interest either, not from the moment he'd discovered
the sublime taste of soul-death, the screaming, writhing,
astonishing intensity of it, filling him, exalting him, sending
him to the stars. Sex paled in comparison.

The Necromancer's fingers flexed on the arm of his chair.
He prided himself on his precision, though no audience had
yet survived the performance to applaud his skill. The whores
were in his line of sight. It would be child's play to reach out,
choose one—it made no matter which, the tall or the short—
and then . . . Oh yes. He'd take her spinal cord between his
invisible fingers and *squeeze*, oh so slowly. Those pretty eyes
would open wide while her mouth contorted with agony and
fear and her friends panicked all around her.

He'd drink her down at his leisure, sip her soul as if she
were an aperitif. She'd squirm like a fish on a cruel hook,

but by the end, he'd have her—everything she'd ever been, everything she'd ever known or thought or imagined or done.

His.

Tapping a forefinger against his lower lip, the Necromancer considered his options.

⟨∞⟩

Erik's lips quirked as he bowed and murmured greetings. The reception had started well. The elegant, chattering crowd milled around right on the stage, the good citizens of Caracole clearly titillated by their glimpse of the glamour behind the velvet curtains.

His blood still ran hot, rushing and tumbling through his veins. Where was she, his little courtesan? Lord's balls, what he needed now was a soft body and a horizontal surface. No, fuck that, he'd have her standing up, against the wall, the door. Who cared? After the first urgency was out of the way, they'd negotiate the rest. He'd torture them both with pleasure for the rest of the night.

No sign of the women yet, though he knew the boy had conveyed his invitation. Gods, tonight it was actually good to be alive!

"Erik, perhaps you would sing one more for us?" A pause. "*Erik?*"

It dawned on him he'd been peering over the queen's elegantly coiffed gray braids toward the wings. Heads were turning in the same direction, one after the other.

A tall, graceful woman gowned all in burgundy emerged from the shadows. Erik's gaze darted past her. Yes! The dark beauty paused by the curtain to whisper to the neat figure at her side.

"Delighted, Your Majesty," said Erik promptly. "Would you care for a love song? Something light and charming?"

Queen Sikara looked him up and down with a shrewd twinkle, her approval so endearingly frank, he couldn't possibly take offense. There'd only been time to remove the makeup, peel off the false beard and doff the jacket, so he was still clad in the dress shirt, now a trifle limp and sweaty, the breeches and those ridiculous boots.

"Excellent," said the monarch with decision. "Whenever you're ready." Which meant, *Now, idiot.*

Smiling inwardly, Erik bowed and went to find the accompanist he preferred. By the time the man had tuned his lute, the crowd had thickened, buzzing. Inconspicuously, Erik flipped open the buttons at his throat and sucked in a succession of slow, deep breaths. He wasn't nervous, that rarely happened these days, but he was keyed up, tense in a way foreign to his usual composure.

It was true what the Lady had said, the women did come and go in an endless procession. Sometimes, when all went well, there was more to the act than physical gratification—the merest flicker of connection, a pale shadow of something real. Just for that fleeting instant, the touch of it would soothe the hollow ache in his soul.

He still hadn't been able to get a closer look at his quarry, though he was preternaturally aware of her standing near one of the fake pillars stage left.

He'd have to be careful with her. It would be so easy to take both her wrists in one big hand and hold her helpless while he suckled her pretty breasts and she bucked and squirmed with the pleasure of it. Her skin would be warm, cream and honey and salt on his tongue, and she'd make wonderful noises. He might even use the flat of his hand, but carefully. Her plump little bottom would flush the prettiest pink while she sobbed with mingled shock and delight, and when he stroked her, she'd soak his fingers . . .

Right. Erik pinched the bridge of his nose. Focus on the music.

He loved the song he'd chosen, a lilting melody in an ancient form called a *canzonetta*. The rest of the work it came from was lost, the story of an unrepentant roué and his descent into hell. Only this and a few other fragments of genius remained.

The first notes rang out, building a perfect framework, all he had to do was slide into it and over it, as warm and smooth as heated caramel. Seduction, pure and simple—and when sung with the Voice, well nigh irresistible. But seduction with music was permissible, a spoken command was not. Erik touched his talisman as a reminder, took a breath and let the notes flow forth.

Come to the window, oh my treasure.

Casually, he strolled a little closer, watching her out of the corner of his eye, enjoying the warmth and weight of the crowd's attention. Hell, he couldn't quite see her face.

Oh, come and soothe my pain.

When he leaned carefully against the first of the fake columns, it creaked a bit, but it held. Women smiled and nodded in time with the music, their eyes intent. Brightly colored gowns swayed toward him, rustling like blossoms trembling beneath the caress of a summer breeze. No one spoke or even coughed. They were his, all of them in the palm of his hand, including the one he wanted most. Shit, it was fine! The best feeling in the world.

If you refuse me comfort . . .

Slowly, he turned his head. Ah. She was pretty enough, in a plump, round-faced sort of way. Nothing out of the ordinary, yet he liked the fresh, clear-skinned look of her. It gave her an air of grave innocence that was oddly tempting. Still, it was odd. He'd never had much of a yen for small brown hens before.

. . . I will die right before your eyes.

Her eyes were her most distinguishing feature—almond-shaped under strongly marked brows. But they weren't dark as he'd expected. They shone a pure blue green, bright with interest and open admiration. Like most of the females standing around her, her mouth hung slightly open, her lower lip sweet and full, so cushiony, he had to smile as he sang the next line.

Your mouth is sweeter than honey.

She had a dimple, quivering in one soft cheek. What other parts of her would be tasty? Dimpled? His hungry gaze traveled over a rounded bosom, the hint of cleavage in the modest black gown.

Your heart is sweet as sugar.

He couldn't be much more than ten feet away now. Erik straightened, pushing away from the pillar. He took a step closer. Another.

Ah, my delight, don't be so cruel.

He drew the last syllable out forever, making the air throb with unrequited passion.

A storm of applause rolled past Erik and away.

She blinked, once, twice, as if emerging from a dream. Her mouth shut with an almost audible click, while those vivid eyes scanned him from the top of his blond head to the soles of his boots in a single comprehensive glance. No longer clouded with desire, they were intelligent, measuring. The dimple flashed in her cheek as if at a wry, private joke.

She turned away.

Well, hell. What was that about?

When a tall, saturnine man tapped him on the shoulder, Erik said, "What?" with a good deal less than his usual easy charm.

The man inclined his head. "I am the Queen's Entertainment," he said, as if it were a matter of grave import. "At other courts, I would be known as the Master of Ceremonies. Her Majesty wishes me to convey her apologies and her thanks for your performance."

The man indicated the queen, who was leaving the theater surrounded by a gaggle of serious-looking people, including a man and a woman in elaborate uniforms. "She's been called to an emergency meeting of the Cabal. Trinitarian corsairs again, I'm afraid. I'm sure you understand."

Erik raised a brow. "Not really."

The Queen's Entertainment huffed with impatience. "Her Majesty wishes you to enjoy your stay. Allow me to introduce you to a number of nobleladies who have expressed the desire to meet you."

Erik stared at the courtesans, now the center of a chattering, laughing group. "That's the one I'd like to meet."

The man's gaze followed Erik's, and his expression lightened. His mouth trembled on the brink of a smile before he got it back under control. "The Dark Rose?" he said. "She's not a noblelady, though Her Majesty did offer to elevate her."

"What? It's the other— Hell, never mind." Erik took the man's elbow in a grip as unbreakable as it was friendly. "Introduce me."

4

The Necromancer's lip curled. Killing a single doxy, no matter how bedable, was nothing—a mite, a speck, in comparison with the dark triumph ahead. The Royal Theater and the thousand people in it meant no more to him than a nest of bitemes. Already, he held the queen and her Cabal in the palm of his hand, though they were blissfully unaware, the fools.

A satisfied breath whispered out of him. Life didn't get much better than this.

The Technomages now . . . The Necromancer rubbed his chin. On every known world, the political landscape was a three-way struggle for power between State, Science, and Magick, though in Caracole, Sikara was canny enough to hold her own.

Whereas on Sybaris, the State was nonexistent and the wizards were as weak as water, Technomage Towers everywhere. But the Technomage Primus of Sybaris had come all the way from her home world to find him. Exactly as he'd intended she should. His smile congealed. A pity she was such an irritating woman. If he could refrain from killing her before their work was done, it would be a miracle. Nonetheless, just as he'd planned, he had a tame Scientist of his own now, puddling about in the secret laboratory he'd built for her in his grand palazzo.

That left only the Wizards' Enclave. The Purists might pose a problem, they weren't all stupid—Magick was their business, after all—and he'd heard rumors . . .

The Necromancer frowned.

He'd missed the fire witch by the merest fraction, Shaitan take it.

Knowing she must be an integral part of the great Pattern, he'd scryed for the shape in blood still warm, seen it swirling, swimming out of the murk of causality, shifting and blurring. At the moment, all he had was an inkling, he couldn't make out the precise shape, the formless stuff of the universe too vast and complex for him to quite comprehend.

Yet.

One day, he too would see it clearly, every curve and node intimately known, mastered. *His.* He'd be a god, more than a god . . . Death Incarnate, the end of it all, the black hole at the center of existence . . . He'd take the universe apart, dismantle it, piece by piece, until its workings were exposed like a stripped clock and there was nothing left to defy him, nothing he did not control.

Rising, the Necromancer walked slowly to the door and paused to look back at the animated throng on the stage. He didn't regret missing the party; such human foolishness had always bored him. But there was something there, hovering like smoke around the crowd, the merest taste of it in the air. He inhaled.

Yes, Magick.

But different, elusive. Intriguing.

His gaze flicked over a pair of soberly dressed Purists, a man and a woman. Bartelm was staring across the stage, looking down his high-bridged nose as if something rotten had appeared right underneath it. Old Nori's hands were clenched around the handle of her cane. The Necromancer knew the flavor of their wizards' Magick almost as well as his own. It wasn't them.

No, it felt . . . decidedly odd.

Interesting.

Someone laid an affectionate hand on his shoulder. "Come,

old friend," said the queen. "Don't concern yourself, Entertainment will make our apologies. Time for the Cabal to go to work."

The Necromancer bowed his head lest she see the disgust and contempt in his eyes. His skin crawled. She couldn't keep her hands to herself, the silly bitch.

"Yes, Majesty," he said dutifully.

∞

Erik the Golden worked the crowd like a master, she had to give him that. Rose herself could have done no better. Every now and then, his deep chuckle would ripple beneath the shriller sound of feminine laughter, and all the hair on Prue's arms would rise. The singer had the philanderer's gift of immediate empathy, his head bent attentively as he conversed with an elderly, well-dressed couple and their plump, flustered daughter. Prue watched out of the corner of her eye as he set the girl at ease, made her smile and flush with pleasure.

Nothing was as flattering as genuine interest. Nicely done.

A final bow and Erik detached himself, tapped Entertainment's bony shoulder and nodded in Rose's direction.

Praise be to the Sister, now he was no longer singing, the spell of that sumptuous voice had broken. She couldn't believe it—Prue McGuire, *languishing* over a pair of pretty blue eyes and a feckless grin. That way lay disaster.

Never again.

She shook her head. His voice had been a dream, nothing more, but wisps of its sensual beauty lingered like a lover's touch, a deep internal stroking. She could only be grateful that as Erik had finished the song and strolled closer, the mists had cleared and she'd *seen* him.

A great golden bear of a man, glowing with confidence and strength and health. But just a man, no more. Funny, she could imagine him working the land, those massive shoulders flexing as he tossed bales or whatever it was farmers did, mud caking his big boots. There were shadows beneath those bright eyes. The singer was tired, but still exalted by the performance, riding high on the applause, the approval. She could see the shine of it all over him. Ah well, she'd allow him his professional pride. He deserved it.

Her equilibrium restored, Prue blew out a breath, smiling a little. Nonetheless, she wasn't inclined to add to Erik's high opinion of himself. Every woman at the reception was more than prepared to do that in her stead. Life with men and women whose livelihood depended on their charm and physical beauty had taught her all there was to know about self-absorption. He was undoubtedly more than a little spoiled, Erik the Golden.

Charmers might be a waste of time, but business wasn't. Over there, gathered around a decidedly gothic wishing well, were three merchants Prue dealt with on a regular basis. An excellent opportunity. The temperamental artist responsible for The Garden's famous gourmet cuisine was dissatisfied with the quality of the fresh produce in his kitchen. Sometimes he threw objects. Sharp ones.

Prue's heart lightened. A problem she could fix right now. Unobtrusively, she detached herself from Rose's side and drifted toward the merchants, happily preoccupied with the coming battle of wits. But as she did so, the tide of conversation ebbed and the men strolled away to reveal two Purists, absorbed in a serious, low-voiced discussion. The dignified, dark-skinned Bartelm Prue knew by sight and reputation, the most senior wizard in the Enclave. The other, a crone who appeared to be older than Time, was not familiar.

"Imagination," Bartelm was saying as Prue approached. "Nori, this is foolish. I've never—" His head jerked up and his gaze collided with Prue's. For an instant, his eyes went wide, then his lips tightened and he gave a short, curt nod.

"Good evening," he said. "Mistress . . . ?" A snowy brow rose.

"Prue McGuire." Prue offered her hand. "Financial manager of The Garden."

The wizard took a half pace backward, leaving Prue's hand to dangle unwanted on the end of her arm, but after an instant, he recovered himself and extended his fingertips, the merest disdainful brush.

It was so breathtakingly rude Prue could feel the heat rise in her cheeks, her eyes narrowing with irritation and hurt. But before she could speak, Purist Nori said in her creaky voice, "I'm sorry, Mistress McGuire, but it's difficult for us."

"Difficult?"

"To touch," said the old woman, more gently.

"I don't understand. You were presented to the queen." More than a little puzzled, Prue turned to Bartelm. "You kissed her hand, Purist. I watched you do it."

Bartelm's dark eyes studied her, uncomfortably keen. Eventually, he said, "We are so old, Nori and I, that Magick is pretty well all that holds us together. Do you believe in Magick, Mistress McGuire?" He stroked his grizzled beard.

"Do I—?" Prue stared, bemused. "Magick isn't part of my life. I don't think about it much, to be honest."

Old Nori folded arthritic hands on the head of her cane. The papery skin of her cheeks wrinkled as she smiled. "So busy," she murmured. "Always working, always *doing*."

"I'm a practical person," said Prue, rather nettled. "I have a business to run. I don't believe in things I can't see, and I certainly don't have time for dreaming, for nonsense like—" She broke off, folding her lips tightly together.

Merciful Sister, when would she learn to keep her mouth shut? She'd just insulted one of the most powerful wizards in the Enclave. Prue cast a sidelong glance at old Purist Nori. Not to mention the wisest.

She wouldn't blame them if they turned her into a scuttleroach—not that she believed they could. Her imagination supplied the image of a very surprised scuttleroach with a Prue face, waving its feelers in a frantic semaphore from the floor.

Godsdammit, laughing would only make it worse! Prue bit her lip.

"So I see." Bartelm's voice was very dry. "That must be why your barriers are so strong."

"Barriers? Purist, what—?"

"I've never seen an untutored shield like it," said old Nori. "Have you, Bartelm?"

"What, *exactly*, are you talking about?" said Prue through gritted teeth.

"You have a natural resistance to Magick, Mistress." The old man's dark lips curved very slightly. "Nonetheless, Magick believes in you, even if you don't reciprocate. Now, if you will excuse us . . ."

"Of course." Prue gave the Purists a polite nod. Gods,

Bartelm couldn't wait to get away from her! Then she looked more closely at Purist Nori. The old witch was swaying, her gnarled fingers clenched on the head of the cane. Instinctively, Prue leaped forward, putting her hand under the old woman's elbow. "Let me help—"

"No!" The word emerged as a near screech. Nori scuttled backward with remarkable rapidity. Her sunken chest rose and fell like a frightened bird's. "I'm fine." She gave a travesty of a smile, her lips bloodless with what looked like shock. "Bartelm," she said in a hoarse whisper.

"Yes." The wizard slipped his arm around the old woman's skinny waist. "Good-bye, Mistress McGuire. I doubt we'll meet again." Without further ado, the two Purists hobbled away. They didn't look back.

Prue's brows drew down, her heart fluttering in her chest. That was . . . downright peculiar.

From behind, Rose's distinctive throaty laugh rang out. "Ask her yourself," she said. Prue stiffened. She knew that tone. What mischief was her partner up to now?

A moment later, two big warm hands enveloped hers, and a wine cup was pressed into her palms. "Here," said a deep, calm voice. "You look like you need it."

Prue looked straight into a chest a mile wide, clad in fine linen. Not for the first time, she wished the gods had seen fit to grace her with a tall, statuesque frame like Rose. She had to lift her gaze to meet his guileless eyes.

"Talking with wizards is a chancy business," said Erik the Golden. "Requires alcoholic support." Those sea blue eyes were dancing, though his mouth was grave. How did he do that?

"Thank you," Prue said politely, and sipped.

Inwardly, she sighed, cursing Rose. Best get it over with, she thought. Godsdammit.

"What did you want to ask me?"

Erik smiled. "I'd like to visit with you, Mistress Prue, spend some time." The smile became a trifle feral, his teeth very white. "As soon as possible. Tonight."

Prue set her jaw. Rose and her devious sense of humor! Killing was too good for her.

"Make another choice," she said, flapping a vague hand at

Rose and the courtesans practicing their small talk. "There's no lack of variety. Or beauty."

"I've made my choice."

"Unmake it."

"No."

They stared at each other. Prue's fingers tightened on the wine cup. His lips were beautifully shaped, a generous mouth, rich with promise. The mouth of a man who understood pleasure, the giving and receiving of it. A woman could lose her soul to a man with a mouth like that.

"Rose has a strange sense of humor. She misled you, Master Thorensen. I am not a courtesan. Therefore, I am not available for, ah, visiting."

The singer didn't miss a beat. "Doesn't matter." He favored her with a slow, sweet smile. "And call me Erik."

"Master Thorensen—"

"Erik."

"All right then. Erik." Prue breathed hard through her nose. "I'm a busy woman, I don't have time to argue with—"

"Good." He set his hands around her waist and boosted her up to sit on the coping of the wishing well, his body screening her from the thinning crowd. The wine in her cup barely sloshed. The movement put them eye to eye.

Prue gasped. His fingers tightened on her waist, holding her steady, burning through the fabric of her gown.

"You enjoyed the song, Mistress Prue. I saw your face."

"Well, of course I did," she said crossly. "You're very good, and what's more, you know it. Take your hands off me."

Unperturbed, he said, "I know my worth, like any craftsman worthy of the hire. But you changed your mind about me, Mistress. I saw you do it." He released her, only to take the cup from her slack fingers and set it aside. "That doesn't happen to me . . . often."

"You're crowding me." Prue had the sensation of sinking, as if that blue gaze were a bottomless lake, the water closing over her head, so that she drowned by inches in slow, dreamy eddies.

Desperately, she tried to picture a scuttleroach with a blond mop and the bluest of blue eyes, but she couldn't quite manage it.

"My apologies." He moved back the merest fraction. "You've taken me in dislike, sweet Prue." One corner of that sinful mouth tucked up. "I'm desolated."

"For the Sister's sake, I don't have time for games. I have a business to run, a life to live."

"No fun? No light and shadow? No one to love?"

"I am perfectly happy. Thank you for your concern."

"You're a challenge, Mistress Prue." A fingertip brushed her cheek, feather light, and the sensation made the side of her face tingle, her lips quiver. "You have a dimple. Right . . . here. Just the one." His eyes blazed into hers like the blue at a fire's core. An infinitesimal pause and his chest expanded under the linen of his shirt. "*Let me kiss it.*" The timbre of his voice thrummed in the air between them.

Gods, the sheer command in that voice, the richness of it, the *rightness*!

Automatically, Prue tilted her head to one side, offering her cheek. Then she blinked. What the—? She stared, dumbfounded. "Are you mad? No."

Under her astonished gaze, the blood drained from Erik's face. "Fuck," he whispered. One hand crept up to touch some small object he wore on a chain under his shirt. He shook his head, like a man emerging from deep water. "I didn't mean it, Prue. Forget I said it."

"Yes, you did mean it, but forgetting's not a problem. Happy to oblige." Prue hopped off the wishing well, but in her haste, she stumbled, her flailing hand clutching at Erik's sleeve.

Immediately, he had her secure, held tight against his magnificent chest, his arms banded around her, his nose buried in her hair. She had to be imagining the trembles that rippled through his big frame. Or perhaps she was the one shaking deep inside.

Pulling back, he grinned at her, and the strange moment passed as if it had never been. But Erik the Golden had spent his life onstage. Now his face expressed no more than pleasant amusement spiced with a wary masculine interest, though he was still very pale.

"You smell wonderful," he murmured. "What's the perfume?"

"Soap." Prue's voice cracked a little. "Let me go."

"Of course." Erik steadied her and stepped back. He bowed, surprisingly graceful for such a big man. "Good evening, Mistress Prue. We'll meet again."

Turning, he sauntered away into the crowd, leaving her to stare at the powerful muscles of his buttocks flexing under the cream breeches, the long legs encased in supple black leather all the way to midthigh.

Godsdammit!

Prue snatched up the wine cup and drained it in a single reckless draught. Then she slammed it down so hard the wishing well rang with the impact. Ignoring it, she set her jaw and went in search of Rose.

⁂

It took an age to move through his guests and admirers, nodding and smiling, accepting compliments with grace, signing programs. Reaching the sanctuary of his dressing room, Erik ripped the door open, marched straight up to the far wall and slapped both palms against it with stinging force.

What the fuck was wrong with him? What had happened to his so-called ironclad discipline?

Fucking unbelievable. Years of grim control gone in a single instant. A softly rounded woman with hard, aquamarine eyes and a sweet, vulnerable mouth, and he'd crumbled, the Voice spilling him out of him on a tide of sheer *want*. A man who could *command* anything of anyone.

Erik the Golden sank into the chair in front of the mirror and regarded his reflection with horror. Pale and rigid, his eyes blue and glassy, but only those who knew him well would know he'd looked into hell and seen himself looking back. With a curse, he used his sleeve to wipe the cold sweat from his forehead.

Unbidden and unwelcome, Inga's pale face swam out of memory before he could prevent it, her wheat gold hair stained dark with water, tangled with the bright slime of aquatic weeds . . .

Dropping his head into his hands, Erik tried to get his scattered thoughts in order. What, in the gods' names, had he just done?

He couldn't believe it. He'd blurted out the command as if he were still the thoughtless, arrogant lad he'd been so long ago. He'd used the Voice to compel Mistress Prue McGuire.

Let me kiss it.

Shit. The only saving grace was that it hadn't worked.

Erik's thoughts shuddered to a halt.

It hadn't worked.

5

The Necromancer turned his key in the well-oiled lock and slipped into the vaulted, shadowed space of his own entrance hall. The sweetish smell of furniture polish assaulted his nose. Of his efficient, unobtrusive staff, only Nasake lived in, a man so deep in the Necromancer's thrall he no longer had a will of his own. It was simpler that way.

Alone in the dark, he bent to massage his aching knee, cursing as the movement put an unwelcome strain on his lower back. The chairs in the Cabal Chamber weren't made for a man his size and shape. Not surprisingly, the exercise of death Magick wasn't particularly conducive to glowing good health. The body he'd been born with was wearing out.

Another problem to be solved, another opportunity to be seized. He'd have to give it some thought.

The palazzo was so quiet, he could have been the only other living soul within it, but he knew for a fact that wasn't true—on two counts.

Firstly, he didn't have a soul, not within the strict definition of the term. In fact, it could even be said he was no longer alive—within the strict definition of the term.

Beneath his feet, in the special chambers he'd had constructed for her in the basement, the Technomage Primus of Sybaris was still awake and working. He could sense the glowing ember of her life, the warmth of it like a match struck and held aloft in the inky darkness. He could choose to cup it in his palms to feel the heat—or he might snuff it out entirely.

The Necromancer sighed, knowing he should go down but conscious of a certain, irritating reluctance. The woman was useful and he couldn't doubt her brains and drive, but, by Shaitan, she tried his patience! How could someone so intelligent be so obtuse? In her first few days at the palazzo, he'd had to discipline her numerous times. He enjoyed the process for its own sake, as he always did. Every creature's pain was unique, but there was a special flavor to human hurt, somehow bright and metallic and sparkling. But still . . .

For the first month, he'd maintained a vast, spectral presence, dark and eyeless beneath a hooded cloak, the way he'd first manifested before her. She'd been so proud then, so armored in her power as the Technomage Primus of Sybaris. At her core, she'd always despise the Magick she wished to master. She thought if she could measure it, dismantle it and put it back together, it would be hers to wield as a weapon. Foolish woman.

His mouth twisted with satisfaction. He'd taught her a little since then, though she was remarkably stubborn, the habits of command deeply ingrained. Now she knew if she patronized him, in even the most oblique way, unimaginable pain arrived right on the heels of her indiscretion. But though the Primus had grown wary of his temper, she was still utterly convinced of her own superiority.

Deep in thought, he walked across his study and pushed aside a set of bookcases. It wasn't like him to entertain doubts, but he wondered if he should recalculate. Perhaps he'd been careless, allowing her to see the body he wore, but manifesting as a dark god grew tiring after a time, and he'd slipped, grown lazy. Not that it mattered, of course, because the Primus was as good as dead. He passed a hand over the small door he'd revealed and the runes on its surface twisted into being, glowing a vicious shade of acid green, spiced with the clotted reek of old blood.

It was a powerful spell, its intricate coils a trap for a hungry demon. Creating the Doorkeeper had cost the Necromancer the lives of a small, dusky-skinned child and a blue, aquatic creature called a seelie, and he himself had been drained, weak and pale for a day after. The child was no matter—slum dwellers bred fast. Sacrificing the seelie had been the true price.

They were so rare, the seelies of Caracole, their deaths inexpressibly sweet to his palate. His loins clenched as he thought of it, the sensation like the sexual fervor he dimly remembered, but—oh gods!—infinitely better.

"Silly as a seelie." That's what the city folk said of the stupid or the slow, the little creatures long faded to the status of legend, the stuff of old, half-forgotten stories.

But they weren't myth; they were oh-so-delightfully real.

The Necromancer nodded pleasantly at the Doorkeeper's horned face, even as it snarled and bared its fangs. "A good evening to you too," he murmured, starting down the long stairs.

The Technomage was seated at her console, but her head jerked around as the door opened and her stylus clattered to the desk. The Necromancer smiled. "Good evening, my dear," he said, because he knew it galled her to be so addressed.

"I got another one," she said curtly, rising to pull the cover off a large tank at the far end of the long room. "Finally."

Saliva pooled in his mouth and it was a moment before he could speak. It had been so long. "You mean Nasake got it."

"No." Something sparked in her rather prominent blue gray eyes. "I was bored, so I made a number of modifications to your trap. All Nasake did was pull it up from the canal. He's as dumb as a beast, that man. I don't know why you keep him on."

"Blind loyalty is useful," said the Necromancer absently, trailing a finger over the glass of the tank.

The seelie within recoiled, its whiskers vibrating with terror. Bubbles clung to its long blue fur as it twisted away. You couldn't say seelies were pretty, not by any stretch of the imagination, but they had their own bug-eyed, whiskery charm. With their long tubelike snouts and webbed fingers and toes, they were perfectly adapted for life underwater. The Necromancer had a seelie-fur rug next to his bed. He relished the luxury of it under his bare soles first thing in the morning.

There was something . . . *visceral* . . . about his connection with the half a dozen creatures who'd died to make it.

Gods, he really must take care to savor this one, not gulp it down like a raw apprentice with his first blood. He pulled his gaze away to study the diagram revolving slowly on the gray screen, and his brows rose. "Ingenious."

The Scientist's breast expanded under her white coat. The garment was beginning to look more than a little gray and limp, but the numeral one embroidered on the collar was still crisp and dark. "Not difficult," she said, "given your trap wasn't a very sophisticated apparatus to begin with."

After a split second, she realized what had come out of her foolish mouth and froze, waiting for her punishment. Really, she was doing very well. Progress.

"No offense taken," said the Necromancer, waving a hand. "In fact, I think a reward is in order. You deserve a name."

Her lips thinned. "I already have one."

"A number is not a name."

"It's all Science gives us. Perfectly sufficient."

"In a Technomage Tower perhaps, but not in the real world. Let me think . . ." Out of the corner of his eye, he watched the seelie cast back and forth, back and forth, while he pretended to consider. *No escape, little one. You're mine.*

"I knew a whore once," he said at last. "She was called Dotty, and she was a good whore." Actually, she had been. She'd been kind to a hungry little boy, long ago, in a different life.

"Well, Dotty, what else have you been doing?"

He thought he heard the Technomage's teeth click together. Certainly, her jaw bunched.

"I've done some calculations. I need to tell you . . ." The pause was so fractional, he barely caught it. His interest sharpened. ". . . something."

The Necromancer smiled. "You're worried I won't like it. Your concern does you credit." Spreading his robes, he seated himself on the Technomage's chair. "Go ahead, Dotty. Don't keep me in suspense."

The low heels of her sensible shoes clattering on the flagged floor, she strode back to her console and tapped a key. Columns of figures scrolled across the screen. His eyes aching, the Necromancer averted his gaze. His vision wasn't as sharp as it used to be.

The Technomage opened and closed her mouth. Then she said, "You have to stop killing seelies."

∽

"You," said Erik, snagging Florien's collar as the last of the dancers trotted toward the water stairs in a drift of perfume and tired chatter. "With me."

Florien looked from the fragile-seeming skiff rocking in the inky waters of the canal to Erik's face and back again. He scowled. "Kin we walk?"

"No. This is quicker." Erik glanced up at the big red moon called the Brother, high in the night sky. "It's late and I have things to do tomorrow."

A puzzle to solve and a woman to pursue. Were They toying with him, the gods? It wouldn't surprise him, not after last night. He'd been so perilously close to the edge, he'd very nearly dared Them to get it fucking over with and kill him. A life for a life.

The Sister, nearly full and silver blue, hung just above the rooftops, her pale glow softening the harsh martial light of the Brother. The Sibling Moons, Palimpsestians called them. The other main source of light was the single Technomage Tower near the spaceport, glowing like a blunt needle on the mainland, miles away. The tiny shape of a flitter buzzed across it like a mechanical insect as he watched. Interesting. Queen Sikara must be a canny politician to hold the Scientists to the one Tower. On Sybaris, where Florien came from, the Technomages were all powerful.

The combined moonslight gave shadows a strange blurred double edge and did extraordinary things to the already exotic architecture of the Royal Theater. Erik tilted his head back to stare up at it. Gods, it was an edifice, a monument to elegant excess, story after story climbing up to bulk against the star-spangled sky. For all the world like a towering layer cake.

Erik liked it. He liked the extravagance of Caracole, and he rather suspected Caracole approved wholeheartedly of the Unearthly Opera. He'd have to see about extending the run.

"Hold on tight," he said, scooping up the boy with one arm.

Florien cursed, but his fingers crooked into claws on Erik's forearm, all save the smallest finger on one hand. The burly skiffwoman roused herself from a doze in the stern and rose, balancing easily as the narrow craft bobbed. She stretched, working the kinks from her back, and her dark eyes flickered over Erik. She grinned, showing a missing tooth. "Where to, pretty master?"

With an effort, Erik returned the smile, passing the boy over as she reached out a calloused hand to steady his descent. Florien subsided with a gasp and fell silent, but his eyes were everywhere. Alley cat. Erik suppressed a sigh as he settled himself, his weight making the skiff dance in the water.

When he gave the woman the address of the boardinghouse where the Company was accommodated, she grunted and pushed off into the current. "Which way?"

"Pardon?"

"You wanta go by the Meltin' Pot?"

"What's that?"

The skiffwoman's remaining teeth shone as she guided the craft beneath a graceful humpbacked bridge. "Market, taverns, doxyhouses," she said. "Rough as guts. Still kickin'." She glanced up at the Sibling Moons. "Even now."

"Yah." Florien sat up straight.

The water slid by, dark silk brushing the hull. A cool breeze ruffled Erik's hair, moist and salt-laden. With it came the familiar deep green smell of massive vegetation, but now it was laced with the faintest odor of rot, like a scummy pool. Foul. Grimacing, he cursed his sensitive nose, not for the first time.

"Why not?" he said. "And do you know a place called The Garden?"

"Yeah." The skiffwoman glanced from Florien to Erik and back again. "On the Leaf of Pleasures."

"Take us past it."

The woman cocked a brow. "That'll be extra. 'Nother half-cred."

"Thet's cheatin'." The lad glared. "Twice t' goin' rate."

She chuckled. "Not against the tide, it's not."

As they slipped beneath another bridge, the ornate buildings began to give way to humbler structures. The skiff-woman poled them steadily toward a mass of lights that threw long flares across the night-dark water. New smells assaulted Erik's nose—stale beer, unwashed humanity, grilled meat. The buzz of noise became a roaring hum, underpinned with the occasional shriek and crash, someone playing a jig—badly.

Dark silhouettes moved across arched bridges or clustered outside brightly lit buildings that were clearly taverns. Skiffs darted across the water like so many improbable insects.

The lights blanched the boy's fascinated face to the white of bone. "Kin we stop?"

Behind them, a man's voice bellowed a curse, cut off by an almighty splash. A woman screamed a string of imprecations.

"No, we cannot," said Erik sternly, but he made a mental note. Later. Alone. He turned his head to hide his grin as the din receded in their wake.

"The Garden," grunted the skiffwoman, indicating with her chin.

Erik stared ahead, over the prow of the little craft, his eyes widening. Lord's balls, but that was pretty. So that's where she was. It figured. Low in his belly, everything went tight and hot.

The moonslight illuminated the roofline of a wide, two-story building, the eaves tilting up at the corners in graceful, somehow feminine curves. It was set a little back from the canal, surrounded by gardens. He could see the curve of a flagged path lined with poles bearing fat orange lanterns like ripe manda fruits, each with its strange double shadow stretching behind it. Pale blossoms gleamed, silvery fronds shimmering in a dance beneath the moons. Exquisite perfumes drifted across the water and he sniffed appreciatively.

"Looks expensive."

"Yeah," grunted the skiffwoman. "'Tis."

Prue's gown had been plain, but the fabric had had the sheen of the best silk, the upper curve of her sweet breast gleaming like pale honey against the black.

Other lights came into view, glowing through the foliage,

warm and welcoming. Smaller pavilions, about half a dozen of them. Water gurgled in the canal, a quiet counterpoint to his thoughts.

He'd spent all his adult life practicing the most severe self-discipline imaginable, and tonight, he'd ruined it all, destroyed everything, the effort of all those years. So easily, so wantonly, and for no reason he could discern. The Voice had surged out of him like a force of nature. He'd had no warning, not the slightest idea.

And if that wasn't enough to have him reeling, Prue McGuire had actually *resisted*. Godsdammit, how was it even possible? The shock of that mangled half-sentence on her lips had brought him to his senses faster than a dash of icy water.

Two completely unprecedented events.

Which left him with a number of possibilities.

Was it some kind of dreadful game and he a mere toy for the amusement of the deities? Had the Great Lady overridden his choice and taken both blessing and curse after all?

But that didn't seem likely. The gods had some purpose in mind for him, he believed that absolutely. He'd waited all his adult life for it. The Lady might be terrible in Her justice, but She wouldn't play him false. He'd still entranced the entire Court of Caracole with the Voice. Nothing unusual about that, it happened every night he sang.

So it had to be her—Mistress Prue McGuire, with her vivid, level gaze. For an instant, his mood lightened. Once he got his full growth, he'd discovered seduction was as effective as the Voice—it just took longer. And it had the added benefit of allowing him to live inside his own skin.

But Prue had resisted both. Erik rubbed his forehead. Why? Godsdammit, *how*?

Only one way to find out.

His chest tightened and automatically, he touched his fingertips to the talisman under his shirt. He'd have to do it again—compel someone—but how could he do that and be sure to do no harm? Because to be a true test, it would have to be something deeply against the victim's will.

His eye fell on the boy's grimy little fist, clutching the side of the skiff for dear life.

Oh yes.

First, make absolutely certain of the child's feelings. "Florien," he said casually, "when we get to the boardinghouse, I want you to take a bath. Immediately."

Florien's head jerked up and his mouth fell open. "Wot?"

"A bath," said Erik patiently. "I can smell you from here." It was true, he could.

"Ain't havin' no fookin' bath. Cenda made me take one las' week, 'fore we got on t' starship." His face stiff with indignation, the boy leaned over the side of the boat and spat into the water.

"Fine." Erik leaned back. *We'll see, my lad, we'll see.*

6

From one of the small pavilions in The Garden, the notes of a flute stole across the water, clear and bright as the chimes of a glass bell in the softness of the night air. Erik smiled, pleasantly surprised. The "Lullaby for Stormy Eyes." How flattering, someone had been listening. But when a female voice joined in, dancing a graceful minuet with the flute, the smile faded.

With a sigh, the skiffwoman rested her pole and let the current carry them back a little way while she listened.

It wasn't Prue McGuire, he knew that at once. This was the voice of youth, all promise and inexperience. The flute player could do with tutoring too. Not to mention a better instrument.

Very softly, Erik hummed along, considering the new and interesting options the gods had just set before him. The Lord and Lady could be unpredictable, but They generally played fair. They recognized the stubborn grain deep in his soul, disguised by his veneer of placid good humor.

The skiffwoman bent to the pole again, and The Garden slipped away around the bend, the music fading in the slap of water against the hull, the whisper of a sea breeze. Erik tried to recall the last time a woman had rejected him out of hand.

Really, there was only Inga—and she'd been in love with Jarner Andersen at the time.

He swore under his breath. So he'd slipped tonight. Though he'd used the Voice to compel, thank the gods there'd been no consequences. Prue McGuire was hardly likely to throw herself in the river. He released his hard grip on the side of the skiff, flexing his fingers to get the numbness out.

He'd only met the woman a few hours ago. All he'd intended was a night of casual pleasure. Instead, she'd changed his life—and he didn't think it was for the better. Uneasily, he recalled staring at his reflection in the mirror, that dark tide of premonition washing over him. Coincidence be damned. He frowned.

One you cannot charm, cannot control. The Lady's amused voice echoed in his head.

Erik set his jaw. Well, hell, charm certainly hadn't worked. Nor had the Voice.

All the fine hair on his body rose. His pulse sped up. Shit.

Prue McGuire was a direct challenge, a gauntlet thrown down by the dark goddess. She had to be.

Did She have a serious purpose or was She simply amusing Herself? Ha! Typical female. His lips twisted in a sardonic smile. Fleetingly, he wondered how the Horned Lord fared with His Lady. Was He as helpless and hapless as any human male?

Godsdammit, if there was anything that riled him, it was being played—even when the player was an immortal Being of immeasurable power. Erik Thorensen was his own man, not some kind of game piece to be moved about at will.

Prue had the potential to be almost anything—challenge, riddle, passing fancy, the heart's desire. *Divine retribution.* Chills raced up and down his spine.

Erik tilted his head, baring his teeth at the star-dappled sky, fathomless as the Lady's beautiful eyes. *So it amuses You to challenge me, Great Lady, to make me dance to Your tune? Well, I'm picking up the gauntlet. Let's see if I can charm sweet Mistress McGuire into bed on my own merits, and what wicked things I can persuade her to do once she's there.* He frowned, thinking it through.

And if she turns out to be susceptible to the Voice after all, well then—I won't use it. I swear on Your name.

Rolling his shoulders, he relaxed. Slowly, his lips curved. It wasn't going to be such a hardship. Unraveling Prue would be fun—for both of them. She'd be his match in determination, if not in guile. The grin widening, he imagined them tumbling back and forth across a big bed, tussling about who'd go on top, carefree and laughing. He hadn't done that with a woman in years. Forever.

Her piquant face was so expressive, so easy to read. He found it almost cute the way she didn't have enough experience to conceal how much he attracted her. The delicate flush on her cheek, her dilated pupils and her breasts swelling beneath smooth black silk—they all said one thing. Such a contrast to the snippy words coming out of that sweet carnal mouth. Oh yes, Mistress Prue was deliciously susceptible, despite her wariness.

When he was long gone, playing other theaters, other worlds, they'd both have some sweet memories to warm the nights. A pleasant interlude. Nothing more, nothing less.

With a soft thud, the skiff grounded at the water stair nearest the boardinghouse. Still smiling a little, Erik dropped an extra coin in the skiffwoman's calloused palm, despite Florien's audible huff of disgust.

Keeping a big hand on the boy's shoulder, he closed the door quietly behind them. "The bathhouse is just down the hall."

"Nah, I tol' ye, I—"

"*Florien.*" Erik snagged the child's dark gaze with his own. Held it. "*Go take a bath. With soap. Wash everywhere—hair included. Then come to my room and show me.*" He hadn't spoken loudly, but the Voice echoed eerily off the walls.

Florien stared, his brow knitted. Then he blinked as if waking from a deep sleep. "Fook it. All right."

He wandered off down the passage, casting Erik a final reproachful glance before he disappeared through the door at the far end.

Erik sagged against the wall.

You didn't take it from me, Great Lady. Your blessing, my curse. Climbing the stairs to his room, he sank down full length on the too-short bed. *Thanks—I think.* He threw an arm over his eyes.

How long did it take to wash one skinny little body? By the time Florien stuck a wet, tousled head around the door, Erik had given up on the bed. He was pacing the floor—two long strides to the window, two strides back.

Without a word, the child held out his hands for inspection. "Kin I go t' bed now?"

"Wait." Erik cleared his throat. "Your hair's wet. Come here." With one hand, he grabbed a thin shoulder, with the other, he snatched the threadbare towel from the dresser.

"Hey! Mmpf!" The boy's protest sounded muffled under the vigor of Erik's rubbing.

Erik paused. "You all right?"

Florien emerged pink and rumpled, his hair standing up in soft spikes. He checked the condition of both ears with careful fingers, shooting Erik a look of frank dislike. "Yah."

He slid out the door so rapidly Erik was left standing in the middle of the room, blinking, the towel clenched in his fists. He blew out a long breath. The gods be praised, the Voice hadn't caused the lad any damage, changed him in any fundamental way. Florien had done exactly as he'd been told—and no more. Smiling, Erik bent to unbuckle a boot. The boy's shirt and trews had been both familiar and filthy. He'd simply put them straight back on his clean body.

Well then.

The first boot hit the floor, then the second. Gratefully, Erik wiggled his toes and stretched until his shoulders creaked. His lips curved in a wicked grin. Tomorrow the real challenge.

Little Mistress Prue.

∞

The Necromancer raised his brows. "I must stop *what*?"

"Killing seelies," said the Technomage. She clenched her hands together, her spine rigid with tension.

"And why is that?" asked the Necromancer, rather enjoying himself.

Her shoulders still tight, the Primus indicated her screen. "I've been collecting data, doing projections. They were rare to begin with, but over the years, you've reduced the population to below a viable level."

"They've just learned to avoid the traps, that's all. Clever little things." The Necromancer glanced fondly at the swirl of blue fur in the tank. He could *taste* the terror. Luscious. "There are plenty more of them, I'm sure. Where did you put that bucket?"

The Scientist ignored him. She picked up a thick bundle of transplas sheets and thrust it in his general direction, her cheeks flushing pink with agitation. "No, no, you're wrong," she said. "Our research on Sybaris shows that such interference has unpredictable results. I need more data." She took two steps closer to the tank. "Let me talk to the Primus in the Tower here. I can keep this one alive for—"

The Necromancer's patience evaporated. He struck out, a whiplash of power curling around the Technomage's waist, jerking her off her feet. Her shoulder struck the tank with a jarring thud, so that it rocked, the seelie thrashing in distress. As he watched, she slumped slowly to the floor and her eyes rolled up in her head.

Huffing with irritation, the Necromancer bent to check her pulse. Fine. The stupid woman was fine. A mild concussion probably and some residual nerve pain.

He straightened, surveying the limp body thoughtfully. The Technomage Primus of Sybaris was a godsbedamned nuisance, not a doubt of it, but no investment came without cost. His gaze traveled from the diagram of the seelie trap on the screen to the little heap of blue misery in the corner of the tank, and he smiled.

What else had his Scientist been doing?

Stepping over her sensibly trousered legs, he crossed to the console and began to rummage.

∞

In her suite on the upper floor of the Main Pavilion, Prue laid the ink brush down with a sigh. Ruefully, she massaged the tight muscles at the back of her neck. Likely she'd transferred at least one smear of ink. She always managed to get the stuff all over her fingers. With considerable satisfaction, she surveyed the big ledger on the scarred surface of her big desk. Done, by the Sister! When the Queen's Money sent his tax collectors, all would be in perfect order at The Garden of Nocturnal Delights.

And she still had time for a bite of lunch with Rose. Smiling, Prue patted the pocket of her working trousers, cut in the flowing Trinitarian style, loose and sensible. Paper crackled beneath her fingers. They could adjourn to the sitting room, brew a soothing tisane of mothermeknot tea and open Meg's letter together.

The smile became wistful. How lovely it would be to travel to the country, spend some time with Meg. Together with John Lammas, her childhood sweetheart, their former housekeeper had bought a tavern in the small village of Holdercroft, way out on the Cressy Plains. The Garden still limped along without big Meg's calm efficiency, but it was churlish to begrudge the woman her happiness. If only it wasn't so godsbedamned difficult to find someone even half as good.

Her brow furrowed, Prue ran a finger over the battered cover of the ledger, trying to recall which merchant had supplied Meg with the last consignment of top-quality mothermeknot. Every female of child-bearing age on Palimpsest drank the contraceptive tea. The women of The Garden went through bushels of it. With an inward grin, she wondered if Meg still bothered. Somehow, she thought not.

Someone knocked.

Sweet Sister! Now what? If Cook had thrown another tantrum—

"Enter!"

Young Tansy popped her head around the door.

"Mistress Prue?"

Tansy was smiling, her lovely face, pretty as a flower, glowing with ill-concealed delight. It was hard to be angry with the little apprentice, which of course, Tansy knew full well, the imp. Prue rested her head against the high back of the chair and tried to look stern. "What is it?"

"Mistress Rose says she'll meet you for lunch downstairs, in the courtyard of the Sweet Manda. Fifteen minutes all right?"

Prue's eyes narrowed. "What's going on?"

Tansy primmed up her mouth, her doe eyes dancing. "Nothing, Mistress."

"Tansy . . ."

But the girl shook her head. "Fifteen minutes." She scampered off down the stairs.

By the time Prue reached the small pavilion known as the Sweet Manda, she was torn between curiosity and irritation. For that very reason, she spent a few moments talking to the luxuriant touchme bush that marked the fork in the path. The fringed silver blossoms chimed a happy greeting, bending to stroke her cheek and gift her with delicate wafts of perfume. Equilibrium restored, she took two steps forward and froze.

Sweet Sister in the sky!

She knew the voices. This was The Garden's music class; she'd heard them many times before. Every Garden courtesan could play an instrument or sing. But never so assured, so precise, their voices blending in a miraculous four-part harmony that soared and swooped with sheer joy. The touchme bush swayed in time, tinkling almost below the threshold of hearing, but Prue couldn't have moved to save her life.

Some innate sense of self-preservation told her to turn and run, because a dark part of her soul recognized his touch, his gift.

So abruptly it almost hurt, the liquid Magick stopped midbar. "No," said Erik Thorensen's rich, dark baritone. "Tansy, you're too damned good. You came in a beat early there and the altos tumbled along right behind you." A pause and she could imagine him smiling, those blue eyes bright with concentration. "Again, from the beginning of the verse. I'll count you in. Ready? One, two . . . three!"

Appearing beside her, Rose whispered, "He's so good with them, Prue. You should see their faces. Come in and sit with us."

Casually, Prue laid a hand over her solar plexus, where the nerves quivered like flutterbyes in a panic. Then she turned her head to skewer her best friend with a glare. "I'm not talking to you."

"Take a peek." Unabashed, Rose winked. "Go on, you know you want to."

Prue growled under her breath, tempted beyond measure. Slowly, she stepped up to the flower-laden lattice that screened the courtyard and peered through. She inhaled sharply.

Erik the Golden leaned against the wall of the pavilion,

one booted heel propped against the edge of a garden bed. Praise be to the Sister, he was in profile to her, so she was spared the impact of those eyes. The top of his shining blond head almost brushed the eaves of the small building. Prue knew women who would kill for hair like that, thick and wavy, burnished with the very slightest hint of auburn. Gods, he was big, and yet, he managed to be as supple, as full of grace, as the melody, one hand moving gently in the air marking the time. Must be the stage training, thought Prue, furious with herself. All that practice at showing off.

She drew back a little, narrowing her eyes. What *was* it about him?

Scattered around the garden like exquisite blossoms, some standing, some seated on jewel-toned cushions, were some of the most gorgeous young people on Palimpsest. Compared with such an extravagance of beauty and youth, Erik Thorensen looked more than a little worn, crinkles showing at the corners of those blue, blue eyes. He was talking to the two boys singing tenor, completely focused on something to do with tempo. The usual easy charm was eclipsed by concentration, grim lines bracketing his mouth, as if he were in the habit of clenching his jaw.

Quietly, Prue released a long breath. Why had she let him disturb her so? Over the years, some shatteringly beautiful, sensual men had worked at The Garden. Yes, the singer was good-looking, but he paled in comparison with those perfect specimens of manhood. Physical beauty was an accident of genetics. Furthermore, it was a commodity. How you used it, what you traded it for, depended on who you were—on the inside. She shot a glance at Rose from under her lashes, and a rueful smile tugged at her lips. Prue knew her dearest friend through and through, but even a woman as good, as fundamentally decent, as Rose used her loveliness as currency. She could no more help it than she could stop her lashes fluttering.

On Erik's count, the group inhaled as one and the music rose again. Every face was rapt, intent on him, be-spelled by the sheer force of his personality, the beauty they created together. It would be like flying to sing with them, caught up in something ineffably lovely, exquisitely ephemeral.

She'd never even been able to hold a tune, never had any sort of artistic gift. Despite herself, Prue's eyes prickled with tears. Blinking them back, she spun on her heel and hurried away down the path. Rose caught her arm before she'd taken three paces, and fell into step. Wisely, her friend didn't make a sound until they reached the door of Prue's suite.

Rose cleared her throat. "Prue. Sweetie . . ." Discomfort sat strangely on those perfect features.

Prue stared. Was that . . . *apprehension*? Oh, gods . . .

"What have you done?" she hissed.

Rose flushed. "It's only a few weeks. Truly, you won't know he's here." The flush intensified. "Much."

"Rose." Prue gripped her friend's arm. "*Tell me.*"

"He's agreed to provide intensive vocal coaching. Think of the publicity, the cachet it gives us, Prue—our courtesans, students of Erik the Golden, the most famous singer in the known worlds."

Prue snorted. "Aren't you exaggerating, just a trifle?"

"Well, he's reasonably famous." Rose's smile widened. "And he says Tansy is something quite exceptional. He's going to do special work with her."

"Lucky Tansy," said Prue. She'd meant the words to sound derisive, but to her dismay, they came out wistful instead.

Rose shot her an uncomfortably shrewd glance. "For some reason, I trust him," she said. "With our youngest too. Don't you think that's interesting? Prue, why don't you—?"

"Enough!" Prue threw up her hands. "Leave me out of this. How much are we paying the amazing Erik for the benefit of his wisdom?"

Rose studied her jeweled slippers. "We drew up a short-term contract. Here." Extracting a rolled-up sheet of gilded parchment from one capacious sleeve, she loosed the pink ribbon that bound it.

Merciful Sister!

Prue had no difficulty making out Rose's familiar scrawl, another signature in a bold, slashing hand, the space for her own name as co-owner of the business.

Her heart turned a hard, painful somersault in her breast. Who had he asked for? Rose, it had to be. All men wanted the Dark Rose, and as a stranger, Erik wouldn't know she'd retired.

Between her teeth, Prue said, "What—no, *who*—did you sell him?"

"Actually," said her friend, taking a prudent step backward, "you."

7

"*What?*" Prue's shout echoed down the hall. For a single delirious instant, every cell in her body leaped to attention, all hot and glowing.

Rose waved the contract under Prue's nose. Godsdammit, the woman was choking back laughter! "Not your body, silly, your head. Here, read the thing."

Rapidly, Prue scanned the parchment. Oh, of course. How ridiculous she was. Her heartbeat slowed from a gallop to a lurching jog trot. She raised her eyes. "He needs a bookkeeper?"

"Apparently." Rose shrugged. "But it's completely up to you, sweetie. You don't have to sign."

Little Tansy had looked exalted, out there in the courtyard. They all had. Prue might hold facile charm in contempt, but she respected talent, and she'd never for an instant thought Erik Thorensen was a fool. "He's already told them, hasn't he?" she said, tracing the bold brushstrokes with a fingertip. "About the music lessons?"

Rose nodded.

"They were thrilled, I'm sure. He's made it impossible for me to refuse. Very clever of you both."

"It's only a few weeks," said Rose, almost pleadingly. "Then he'll be gone."

Prue tossed the contract to the desk and took a few restless steps to the window. Without turning, she said, "You never met Chavis, did you?"

"No. And I haven't heard you speak of him, not in all these years." A hesitation, then more gently, "Katrin looks like her father, doesn't she?"

"Yes." Prue stared out into the garden below, unseeing. "Tall and fair. But she's not as beautiful as he was." In the shadowed reflection in the windowpane, Prue caught the bitter twist of her own lips. "Too much like me."

A rustle of skirts, Rose's hands on her shoulders. "Prue, love, don't—"

"Looking back, I know he wasn't a bad man, just weak. So pleasing, full of light and laughter. And he made a dead set at me." Prue fixed her gaze on the feature rock that marked the gentle curve of the path. Usually she loved its intriguing contours, the striations of green and shining gold.

She ignored Rose's murmur, the comforting press of her fingers. "I was stupid, yes, but I was only eighteen and he was ten years older. He had me tied in knots—flattered, besotted." Dipping forward, she rested her forehead against the cool of the glass. "It's funny what things you remember. He could juggle, Chavis. It was his party trick." Her eyes burned.

"When my parents refused permission, I . . . I ran away with him to Caracole, and we got married. At least"—she pressed her lips together—"I think it was a real Bonding. It may not have been. I no longer care."

Resolutely, she turned and met her friend's concerned gaze. "He left us flat, Rose, that's how much we meant to him. Katrin was so small, she could barely toddle. He took everything, the bastard, not just our savings, but my clothes as well, every stitch. Gambling debts, I suppose. He always loved the deep play. When I couldn't pay the rent, the landlord put us out. I had nothing, not a single cred. *Nothing!*"

She bared her teeth, the breath sawing in her lungs with remembered terror. "We spent three nights on the streets in the worst part of the Melting Pot. It was—" She swallowed the lump in her throat. "I never thought there were things worse than dying, but gods, what I saw . . . But I did it, I kept us safe. Katrin and I, we survived. The gods help those who help themselves, I always say. Chavis didn't do so well. They found his body in the canal a month later. Knifed."

With a murmur of pain, the other woman tried to envelop her in a hug, but Prue held her off. "Rosarina," she said steadily, "don't match-make for me, don't you dare."

"I'm not matchmaking, not really." But Rose didn't look away, didn't have the grace to look in the least guilty. "But you haven't— Not for such a long time. Who was the last? I can't even remember his name. It's not natural."

Prue tilted her chin. "Neither have you," she pointed out.

Rose refused to be diverted. "Yes, but I'm perfectly happy; you're not." Her lips quirked. "Dearest, you can't fool a courtesan of my experience. I saw your face. You want him."

"Do not."

Rose laughed outright. "Do too."

"This is childish. And pointless."

When Rose crossed her eyes and poked her tongue out, Prue couldn't help but giggle. "Oh, *you*!" she said, giving her friend the finger.

They collapsed, laughing, against each other's shoulders.

"Excuse me. Mistress Rose?"

Their heads jerked around.

"I brought him, like you asked."

That was self-evident. Framed by the doorway, Erik the Golden loomed behind little Tansy, his eyes bright with interest as he glanced from Prue to Rose and back again. He'd obviously heard the hilarity, but what about the conversation that had preceded it?

Fighting a furious blush, Prue wiped her eyes and marshaled her forces.

"Thank you, Tansy," said Rose, still smiling. "Better run to the fighting salle now. Walker and the others will be waiting."

Erik patted the girl's shoulder. "You did well today, sweetheart," he said, and he sounded absolutely sincere. Pink with pleasure, the apprentice bobbed a curtsey and trotted away, her step light.

One dark gold brow rose. "You have a fighting salle?"

"Indeed we do," said Prue crisply. There'd been a sword

duel in the *Demon King*, choreographed with great skill, Erik Thorensen moving through the steps with such grace and masculine power. She could imagine him in the airy space of the salle all too clearly, stripped to the waist, that magnificent chest gilded with sweat, muscles bunching and flexing with the rise and fall of the blade.

She squeezed her eyes shut for an instant, opened them again. Sanity prevailed. Gods, a real swordsmaster like Walker would carve an actor, a *fake*, to bloody ribbons. With some difficulty, she suppressed the curl of her lip. "Our gardener also happens to be a swordsman of note. All Garden courtesans learn the martial arts from Walker, both theory and practice."

How she knew, Prue had no idea, but she was certain Erik wanted to laugh. "So you're not entirely defenseless?" he said, his rich voice a melody that washed over her in a wave of warm honey.

Prue's lips drew back from her teeth. She still couldn't believe what had happened last night—his gall or her own stupidity. Thank the Sister she'd regained her senses in the nick of time. *Let me kiss it.* She suppressed the impulse to shake her head in amazement. "No," she said, "we are not."

After a short silence, Rose said smoothly, "I'll leave you two to discuss the contract." She glided toward the door, paused and offered her hand. "A pleasure doing business with you, Erik."

"Likewise, Mistress Rose." He raised it to his lips and kissed it, a real kiss, Prue noted, not just a polite brush of the lips.

Setting her jaw, she said, "Be seated, Master Thorensen, and tell me why you want a bookkeeper."

⌒∞⌒

In the courtyard of the Sweet Manda, surrounded by smooth, healthy flesh and shining hair, the implied promise of pleasure, it had crossed Erik's mind to wonder if he'd made a mistake about Prue McGuire. Why would the Dark Lady choose a no-nonsense woman like Prue to test his control? He'd been inclined to put last night's thoughts down to wounded vanity, the astonishing challenge her resistance posed to both his masculinity and the strange powers the gods had given him.

But the goddess had made no mistake.

Her hair lay loose over her shoulders in a gleaming ripple of brown, held away from her face by a couple of simple braids. To his delight, it was soft and thick, with an enchanting wayward curl, making her look softer, younger. The effect was enhanced because she'd been laughing when he walked in, her eyes narrowed, sparkling with merriment like those of a mischievous child.

The delightful gurgle of it was infectious. When Mistress Prue laughed, she gave it all of herself, helpless with amusement, the dimple quivering. Like warm fingers, the sound slid into his trews and curled around his balls, until they drew up in anticipation. Once a man got past the barriers, she'd be a generous lover, abandoned in her pleasure. Gods, she might even strike a spark in the emptiness that was his soul.

She wore loose trousers and an over-tunic in a blue so dark it was nearly black, the outfit obviously intended for comfort while she worked. She probably thought the getup modest, but any man's gaze would be drawn to the way the fine fabric pulled against the rounded curve of buttock and breast—unless he were dead, of course. Judging by the warmth and tightness in his trews, he'd be very much alive for some time yet.

To the seven hells with a bookkeeper, I just want you.

Instead, he fell back into role. He said mildly, "You called me Erik last night."

"I may have done." Seating herself behind the desk, she tapped the parchment, all traces of humor hidden from him. "Are there no bookkeepers in Concordia, Master Thorensen?"

Godsdammit, she was a prickly little thing. He'd hoped the music lessons would win her over, especially as Rose had been perfectly amenable. He should have known better. The Dark Lady's challenge wouldn't be worthy of the name if it was easy.

"Not one that I trust."

She didn't give an inch. "Why?"

"I'm a singer, Mistress Prue, not a mathematician." He rearranged his features into a pleasant smile, which appeared to soften her not at all.

This wasn't strictly true. Erik didn't particularly enjoy it, but he was perfectly capable of keeping the Unearthly Opera's accounts himself. In fact, he'd done so for years.

"I have a man," he said, inventing as he went along, his mind racing. "There are things he does I don't understand, but they don't seem to . . . ah . . . add up . . ." Spreading his hands, he trailed off, doing his best to look confused and suitably helpless. "I worry that he's cheating me. This is all confidential, of course."

It didn't seem possible, but the set of her shoulders grew stiffer. "Of course."

Lord's balls, but she had herself on a tight rein! Something small and petty within him capered with delight and he gave up trying to quash it. Because he'd lay odds it was something to do with him. At some deep, instinctive level, she'd already accepted she was prey, because the mere fact of his presence had her off balance.

Strangely content, Erik shifted his weight carefully in the spindly chair and looked around him with interest. The room was clearly an office, furnished with purpose-built shelves and cupboards with deep, sliding drawers. There were two other doors, one half-open. Through it, he could see a pleasant sitting room, cheerful sunlight spotlighting the rugs, spilling over one end of a large, squashy sofa. He wondered if she was tempted to curl up and take a nap there when work grew heavy. His lips twitched. No, not the conscientious Prue. She'd have to be persuaded. Difficult, but he was sure the right man could do it.

He watched in silence as Prue picked up her brush and moistened it in the water jar before loading it with ink from the ink block. She was aware of his scrutiny, that much was obvious. Little by little, the honey of her cheek flushed a darker pink, but she didn't look up from her task. When she was satisfied, she signed the contract, every letter small and precisely formed, finishing off with an unexpected flourish at the end. She didn't lack for nerve.

Erik smiled. *Got you!*

Prue set the brush aside and raised those amazing, tip-tilted eyes to his. "When I engage to do something, Master Thorensen, I do it thoroughly. No shortcuts. You should know that before we begin."

"Excellent, Mistress Prue," he said affably, assailed by delicious visions of the *thoroughness* of her surrender, the throaty, helpless gasps, the evidence of control shattered, burned away in erotic fire. Gods, he was going to enjoy it, relish every smooth, round morsel of her.

Hauling in a breath, he settled himself. "I'm all in favor of *thorough*," he said. "I think we'll suit, don't you?"

Ignoring his remark, she laid her hands flat on the big ledger in front of her and leaned forward. Ink stained the first two fingers of her right hand. He found it oddly endearing. "Bring the books and all the relevant receipts, bills and documents tomorrow." She shifted her gaze to a point on the wall over his left shoulder. "Good day, Master Thorensen."

"I haven't finished." Because he hadn't. There was still the greatest mystery of all—how had Prue McGuire resisted the Voice?

"I'm sorry, but I'm a busy woman. I have work to do." She gave the leather-bound volume a brisk pat.

"So I see," he said. "What is it you have there?"

"It's The Garden's tax records. The Queen's Money demands them once a year. We're not only ready, we're a whole month early." She smiled, an almost feline expression of satisfaction and pride.

"Congratulations," he said. "Paying tax gets you excited?"

Her lips twitched, the dimple flashing in her cheek before she could master her response. Inwardly, Erik crowed with triumph. "I lead a simple life," she said.

Slowly, he rose and held out a hand. "Will you show me the ledger?"

"No." She didn't miss a beat. "The Garden's accounts are none of a stranger's concern."

"I won't be a stranger for long, Prue." First, make absolutely certain she wouldn't do it, then . . .

Oh, gods.

"I'd like to see a sample of your work," he said.

She shook her head, her hair shifting like a gleaming brown shawl on her shoulders. "You'll see it soon enough." Reaching for the ink brush, she effectively dismissed him.

Erik hauled in a breath and rested both hands on the edge of the desk, looming over her. "*Open your private ledger,*

Prue, and show me." The words thrummed in the air, deep and thrilling, sheer command echoing off the walls.

Prue's head jerked up and her mouth fell open.

Those brilliant eyes clouded while Erik stared, his pulse hammering a mad tattoo. "*Show me.*"

She frowned. "It's wrong." Her knuckles went bone-white on the leather of the book. "I c-can't." Hauling in a huge breath, she rubbed at her eyes like a fretful child.

Erik could hardly bear to watch.

Another sharp inhalation. But this time, when she looked up, her gaze was once again as clear and hard as aquamarine. She laid her palms flat on the ledger, her lips thinning. "Very persuasive," she said with scarcely a tremor, "but none of your godsbedamned business."

Erik's head spun—with relief? Disappointment? He wasn't sure. All he knew was that this time she might have wavered, felt the force of the Voice. And he felt like shit.

"I see that now," he said softly. "Forget it, sweetheart. I was out of line."

No more than a heartbeat and she snapped back to her old self. "You seem to be out of line a good deal, Master Thorensen." She shoved the ledger into a drawer and slammed it shut.

Yes, she might want him, but that didn't mean she liked him.

More than a little piqued, Erik walked around the desk until he stood at her elbow. "Where I come from, we shake hands to seal a bargain." He waited, his hand outstretched.

She thought about it for an endless moment, her teeth sunk into a plump lower lip. It gave her a curious air of innocence and seduction combined. Erik's belly tightened with the desire to take control of that bite. And then kiss it better.

Finally she took his hand, her flesh warm and her grip firm.

Erik enveloped Prue's hand in both of his and drew her gently to her feet, her sweet breasts almost brushing his chest. She smelled intoxicating, the scent she'd said was soap combined with something uniquely fresh and female. And a touch of ink. "I'm not so bad, Prue," he said with a crooked smile. "I wish you'd trust me."

Her cheeks turned pink. "There are very few people I trust."

And wasn't that the ring of truth he heard? Clear as a bell, right there.

When he lifted her hand to his lips, he did it slowly and in silence, so she could pull away if she wished, but apart from a subtle intake of breath, she didn't move. When he pressed his open mouth to her knuckles, she trembled. Erik turned Prue's hand over and kissed her wrist, where the skin was thin and the blood beat hot.

This time, the gasp was audible. "Erik!"

She tugged, and reluctantly, he let her go.

Judging by the feminine panic in her eyes, the expression on his face must be more predatory than reassuring. Completely intrigued, he watched her work to master her reaction and set it aside. The Dark Lady was clearly more devious than he'd ever imagined.

"I'll see you tomorrow," she said coolly. "You have ink on your chin, by the way."

Erik chuckled, his blood bubbling. "Do I? A small price to pay for something so delicious. Good morning, Mistress Prue." Bowing, he turned on his heel.

8

By Shaitan, he'd waited long enough! Determined to pace himself, the Necromancer had made the wait an exercise in self-control, torturing himself all through the night with anticipation. As a result, he was light-headed with need, the blood fizzing and tumbling through his veins. These days, that sort of sensation was as near as he came to actually living.

Rolling up the sleeve of his embroidered gown, he paused, remembering a small boy in a slum, desperate to *know*, so focused on his ambition that he didn't care what price he paid or how much it hurt. His lips curved in a slow smile. The beauty of necromancy, the perfect glory of it, was that these days others paid the price on his behalf.

If there were minor inconveniences—he smiled at the bucket standing in the corner of his study—such as carrying a thrashing seelie in a bucket of cold water up a long flight of stairs, well, he could rise above them.

Because every seelie brought him one step closer to full knowledge. It was as if the little creatures possessed some sort of key, an instinctive connection to something far greater than their own small, blue-furred selves—something universal, so grand it defeated even the compass of a divine intellect. There was a system to everything, an internal logic, a great Pattern. He believed that, absolutely.

Whatever it was, that piece of the puzzle, the Necromancer wanted it.

What's more, he was going to have it, even if it required the death of every seelie on Palimpsest. A small cost, infinitesimal really, when the rewards were so great. The power to set a lever to the fulcrum of the cosmos and shove it the slightest bit off-kilter, just to see what happened.

Almost ready. His breath coming faster as greed clawed hard at his guts, he fixed the other sleeve and scooped up the length of oiled cloth Nasake had left on the desk. Then he reached into a bucket and drew out the squirming seelie, grimacing with distaste as its webbed fingers wrapped his bare forearm in a desperate, clammy embrace.

"Come, little one. Meet your destiny." Settling into the carved chair near the window, he spread the cloth over his lap. Keeping a firm one-handed grip on the seelie, he placed a gentle finger on the ridge between its protuberant eyes. The animal quivered, making a thin noise, a cross between a hoot and a bleat.

Smiling, the Necromancer murmured, "Let's see what you have for me." The sound of his voice triggered a pleasant upwelling of terror.

Outside, the scent of flowers mingled piquantly with the clean, briny smell of the creature in his hands. Beyond the low wall at the end of the formal garden, canal water lapped and gurgled in a cheerful song. Snatches of distant conversation drifted by, a skiffman and his client, negotiating a fare, someone selling vegetables.

Such an ordinary day to unseat the gods.

He began gently, stroking his fingers through plush, cobalt fur, admiring the patterns he drew in the deep pelt. The seelie froze, panic coming off it in waves. The Necromancer shut his eyes, sending out a tendril of dark power, probing for the right spot.

Ah yes! There!

With a spectral thumb and forefinger, he tweaked.

The seelie gave a bubbling shriek, writhing on his lap. The

hot fire streaking along her neural pathways melted whatever meager shields she had.

So it was a female. And she had young. He could see an image of three kits in what passed for her mind, all big eyes and soft baby whiskers, huddled in a woven nest deep in a forest of floating weed. It was dim and cool down there, hundreds of feet below a floating Leaf as big as a city block. For all he knew, those babies were directly under the room where he sat, here on the Leaf of Nobility. Or it could be the Pleasure Leaf or the Monarch's Own Leaf that blotted out the sunlight. Huge as they were, each Leaf was only one part of the gargantuan titanplant on which the city was built. The gods knew how old it was. Centuries? Millennia?

Well, it didn't matter, did it? Because he was right and the Technomage Primus of Sybaris was wrong.

There were plenty more seelies where this one came from.

The seelie's terror increased exponentially, almost as if she could read his mind. Abruptly, she was fighting, jerking and thrashing on the oiled cloth. One of the stubby claws on her hind leg caught in the fabric of his flapping sleeve, the raspy sound of the rip very loud in the quiet room.

The Necromancer spat an obscenity, something he did but rarely. He was particularly fond of this gown. Abandoning Magick for brute strength, he dug in with both thumbs.

Mortal terror exploded in the Necromancer's head as the seelie convulsed. Drinking it in, he let the power of it snatch him up and away like a fever rampaging in the blood. Every cell in the creature's body shrieked a desperate, screaming protest. His nostrils flared. He panted, hanging on, riding the crest of it, filled, exalted, whirling high among the stars.

Caracole of the Leaves lay beneath him as if sealed in a bubble, a toy created solely for his entertainment. There were the canals of clear blue water, the pierced white towers and graceful, curved rooflines. A hundred thousand souls going about their petty business—sniping, scrambling, cheating, dying. Such puny little lives, rocking on the bosom of the ocean, so futile, every one of them dying from the moment they were born.

In this moment, he was a god. No, greater than a god, because he was without worshippers, beyond the constraint of expectations. The dark Magick of Death set him free to do his will. It would take so little to awaken Caracole to terror, to uproot the Leaves like a kind, but ruthless, gardener, sweep all the little people away, relieving them of the burden of existence. A kind of weeding. He smiled at the conceit. Ah, the screams would deafen the heavens.

As he eased his grip, the seelie took a shuddering breath. She was strong, this one. Absently, he stroked her flank, his good humor fading, overtaken by a greater purpose.

Because with a shift in perception, there before him was the weft and warp of existence, known only to the gods, and now to him. He had but to stretch out his hand. If he tugged that strand, knotted it *here* . . .

This required finesse. Carefully, precisely, the Necromancer applied a Magickal tourniquet to the seelie's spinal cord, paralyzing her limbs. That was better, now he needn't rush. Somehow, he was convinced if he fumbled this, performed with anything less than perfect grace, there'd never be another opportunity so fine. Stupid, but there it was.

Disciplining his breathing, he closed his eyes and compressed the seelie's lungs. As the little creature screamed in bubbling silence, he slipped into the dark, bloody stream of her instinctive fight for life and let it carry him back to the foundation of all that was.

The Pattern glittered in the void, flirting with him like a capricious jade, advancing and retreating. Sternly, the Necromancer insisted, bearing down hard on the flailing soul in his grip. The shape of it swam slowly toward him, clearer than ever before.

Exalted, he drank it in. A Pentacle, a five-pointed thing of beauty, imprinted on the watching stars. So that was it.

A frown gathered, a tendril of disappointment unfurling within him, followed swiftly by contempt. Very pretty. Was this the best the gods could do, this . . . *prettiness*? Where was the glory? The power? Where was Death?

A long-tailed comet flashed by and the Pentacle burst into flame with a melodious roar, seeming to leap toward him out of the soft dark.

Despite himself, the Necromancer flinched. The seelie moaned.

By Shaitan, a taunt! He growled under his breath.

He'd heard the whisper of a name. Deiter of Concordia.

Deiter had the fire witch, Shaitan take him, the only true fire witch born for centuries. The Necromancer had become aware of her existence a fraction too late. Hell, the entities that called themselves the gods were rubbing his nose in his failure like a naughty puppy in a puddle of its own pee.

The fire subsided with a good-humored crackle, to be followed by a breath of fresh air. Literally. He could smell its light, sweet perfume, track its laughing presence as it swooshed around the Pentacle, tumbling and swirling with delight.

Faugh. Air Magick. He recognized the cloying feel of it. His gorge rose.

Irresistibly drawn, the Necromancer reached out to rend and crush, his spirit a great dark cloak smeared across the infinite, star-filled sky. A fireflake danced out of the Pattern, flashing under his guard to sting his soul like a cheerful wasp, right on the most tender spot.

Seemingly in his ear, a woman's voice said, "Oh, got it! What was—?" And she was gone.

He reared back, fighting for composure, gulping at the seelie's life energies. Nothing, it was less than nothing. The fire witch hadn't seen him, not truly. How dare she challenge him? Shaitan take the bitch.

He'd find her and he'd pull her to pieces, one screaming gobbet at a time, and then he'd rip the Magick out of her bones and sinews, make it his own, take the Pentacle, the Pattern, and smash and tear and stamp . . .

The seelie's heart and lungs collapsed. With a long, rattling shudder, her life force faded to an ember, wavered for a split second and winked out.

The Necromancer howled. Surging out of the chair, he hurled the limp body against the wall with all his strength. As it hit with a flat squelch, a wave of dreadful weakness roared over him. He fell to his knees on the rug, clinging to consciousness, the acid of his own fear filling his mouth. Dissolution hovered, the Magick of Death, uncompromising in its finality, its indifference. He knew he should welcome it, but he couldn't. He had so much still to do. The gods damn this worn-out body to hell!

∽

She wasn't waiting, she was *working*. Prue rubbed her brow with fretful fingers. Sister save her, why couldn't she concentrate? A rueful grin tugged at her lips as she gazed at the laundry bill on the desk. Sheets, pillow slips, napkins—they couldn't compete with the memory of those eyes, blue as chips of a noonday sky. Nor with that magnificent chest. She'd been damn near mesmerized by the almost imperceptible rise and fall of hard slabs of muscle beneath fine linen, the collar open to reveal a wedge of skin tanned to a light gold.

Godsdammit, she wasn't dead. There was no reason she couldn't admire him like the piece of work he was. Even though, now that she came to think of it, Chavis had had finer, more regular features.

Erik's pulse had beat in the tender hollow at the pit of his throat. So soft, so vulnerable compared with the hardness of the rest of him.

Her lip curled. Vulnerable? There was nothing vulnerable about Erik Thorensen. His eyes might be the most beautiful clear blue imaginable, but they were hard and wary. There were times, when he forgot to smile, that the singer gave her the chills.

He should have arrived by now to drop off the Opera's account books before singing class. She drummed her fingers on the desk and glared at the door. Tansy and the others would be waiting. Perhaps he'd changed his mind? She wouldn't put it past him.

No, that was unjust. Small-minded, even. Music was his gift, he'd be steadfast in this, if nothing else. Ah, hell, she hated being in such a muddle, not knowing what to think, how to feel . . .

Well, no one would know the extent of her foolishness, not even Rose. With a long sigh, Prue let herself slip into pure indulgence. Closing her eyes, she lifted her wrist and nuzzled it, smelling her own skin. He'd branded himself on her consciousness—the firm brush of his cheek, his mouth warm and pliant. What had he felt, for the few seconds his lips had caressed the flutter of her pulse? Experimentally, she kissed the exact spot and an arrow of sensation speared through her belly, made her nipples crimp. So delightfully wicked, so stupid.

So damn good.

Someone coughed.

Prue's eyes flew open. She froze, caught in a ridiculous posture. Sniffing her own arm, for the Sister's sake!

A skinny urchin of indeterminate age leaned against the door frame, observing her with a dark, interested eye. "Yer Prue McGuire?"

Prue clasped her hands together on the desk and straightened her spine, ignoring the heat in her cheeks. "I am." Under one arm, the boy carried a box about a foot square, made of red leather. She nodded at it. "You have something for me?" It would be a relief not to see the singer. She wasn't disappointed, not in the least.

"Yah." Taking his time, the boy placed the box on the precise center of the desk. He scanned the room, his eyes missing nothing. "An' there's a message."

"Yes?"

"Erik sed he's sorry fer t' mess."

"Pardon?"

"He sed he's sorry fer t' mess an' yer trouble." The lad spoke a little louder, enunciating each word in the strange slum accent as if to the simpleminded.

Prue blinked. "I heard you the first time." She'd braided her hair so tightly this morning, her head ached. "But I'm not sure I understand. What mess? You mean the papers in the box? Is that what Master Thorensen actually said?"

The boy shrugged. "Near 'nuff." He made for the door.

"Wait!"

He paused, caution in every line of him. They stared at each other like duelists at dawn.

"Are you hungry?"

The child shrugged, but his face brightened. "Yah." His shirt and trews were scruffy and creased in the manner of all small boys, though his face and hands were clean enough.

"Give this"—Prue scribbled a note—"to Katrin in the kitchen."

He crumpled it in a hard little fist. "Who's thet?"

"My daughter." The inevitable smile of pride curved Prue's lips. "Also the pastry cook, and a very fine one too."

The boy's head bent as he scanned the note. His neck was heartbreakingly scrawny. "Wot's it say?"

"Feed this child."

"Not porridge? Hate t' fookin' stuff."

Prue shut her mouth with a snap, though she was sorely tempted to laugh. "That's all you'll get if you don't watch your language. Tell me . . . do you work for Master Thorensen?"

"Fer Erik?" The boy's skinny chest expanded. "Yah." A pause. "Sorta."

"You know him well?"

A wary look. "Sorta."

"What did he really say?"

The child shot her such a knowing glance that when she flushed, it felt like they shared a dirty secret. "He sed, 'Florien, take t' box t' t' lady wit' t' brown hair an' t' pretty eyes on t' second floor.' An' then he sed, 'An' make sure she knows I 'p-poligize.' But that was more a mumble, yer know?"

Automatically, Prue nodded. "Yes, I know." She eyed the red box as if a corpsebird had laid its wrigglers in there. Pretty eyes? He thought she had pretty eyes?

When she looked up, the child had disappeared, without either farewell or thanks.

Prue shoved her chair back and rose to pace. The box glowered at her from the desk. She scowled right back. Mess? What mess?

On impulse, she pushed up the window to let in the air. A light breeze whispered past, cooling her heated face, playing with the stray tendrils that had escaped the braid. With it came a thread of music, a lilting soprano singing a country air. Tansy.

The girl started and stopped three times, improving, getting a little farther each time. On the fourth attempt, Erik's voice slid in beneath hers, a deep, ardent counterpoint that both supported and flattered Tansy's newly minted talent. Prue leaned against the sill, listening to them soar together, smiling. Beautiful, simply beautiful.

The box.

There's no one else to do it, she told herself. *This is what you do, what you're good at. The gods help those who help themselves. That's if they even exist. Get it over with.*

Prue sat herself down, removed the lid and set it to one side with steady hands. Working quickly and methodically, she began sorting papers into neat piles on the desk—receipts, wages, takings, bills. A crease formed between her brows. In the normal course of business, she found bringing order out of chaos a soothing process. Erik Thorensen's accounts had exactly the opposite effect.

By the time Rose popped her head around the door, Prue had gone beyond bemused to downright irritated. "What did you say?" She pushed the hair out of her eyes. Gods, her stomach felt hollow! A little more and she'd stop and eat.

Rose flopped into a chair, groaning. "Remind me why we promised Walker he could teach quarterstaff. Ow." Wincing, she massaged the back of one long thigh. "I'm black and blue. He only let me go when I pleaded starvation. Want to break for lunch?" Her gaze lit upon the desk cluttered with papers, the brand-new ledger open at a pristine page. "Ah," she said. "I see Erik delivered the Opera's accounts."

"No, he didn't." Where was the receipt that matched this invoice? Paint, timber, canvas. Must be for scenery. "He sent the oddest child. With an offworld accent and a foul mouth." Oh, there it was! Pouncing, Prue unpeeled the page from its neighbor. She wrinkled her nose. Someone appeared to have used it for a tablecloth.

Rose said dryly, "At least he succeeded in getting your attention."

"What?" Prue's head jerked up. "Oh, love, I'm sorry. I've nearly finished this pile. Can you wait another five minutes?"

Rose gave a wry grin. "Never mind. I'll nip down to the kitchen for a tray if you promise to eat with me when I get back."

"Of course," said Prue absently. "Thanks." For the Sister's sake, was that a four or a seven? She held the document up to the light, squinting.

She barely heard Rose's chuckle, or her quiet curse as she rose and limped gracefully to the door.

Prue furrowed her brow, concentrating fiercely. Releasing a gusty sigh, she massaged the back of her neck with her non-inky hand. One more column of figures to total.

A man cleared his throat.

"Sweet Sister!" Prue lifted her head so fast, it spun. Erik was propped up against the door, watching. "What are you doing here?" Though why she was foolish enough to ask she didn't know. The gods had created Erik the Golden for the sole purpose of tormenting her.

All sweet reason, he nodded at the heavily laden tray he carried. "I ran into Mistress Rose on her way to the kitchen."

Prue bet he had. Every dish was piled high. Leaning back in the chair, she raised her brows. "I'm not that greedy, Master Thorensen. There's enough there for a family of six."

Erik opened his eyes wide. "Hmm. So there is." He paused for a single beat. Then another.

Perfect timing, she couldn't fault it.

"A lusty appetite—that's what you need." His eyes danced. "For lunch, that is." Grinning like a boy, he heeled the door shut behind him. "And I'm your man."

9

"No," Prue meant to say, but what came out was an ungracious, "If you wish." To the seven hells with ingrained courtesy and all the ridiculous habits that went with it.

Erik favored her with another sunny smile. "Why, thank you, Mistress Prue. I do wish."

He strode past her and into the sitting room. By the time she caught up with him, he'd unloaded a delicate tisane pot and cups on the low table. Rose kept that set for only the most exalted clients. Prue gritted her teeth. Her so-called friend would be smiling with glee, undoubtedly surrounded by reliable witnesses. Boiling in oil was too slow.

Prue watched Erik lay out the dishes one by one. This was a gourmet picnic, everything of the very finest, nothing like the mundane lunch she and Rose would have shared. There were small, savory quiches, golden three-cornered spicepuffs, a plate of Katrin's exquisite pastries, including a couple of individual curdle pies made to Meg's recipe and piped with meanders of clotted cream. Even a bowl of summer fruits on ice, manda segments bursting with juice and a selection of fat, ripe berries, ranging from purple to crimson to blush pink, all dusted with powdered sugar.

"There." Carefully, Erik placed a crystal bud vase in the center of the arrangement. It contained a single perfect dark rose, the satiny, near-black petals half-open.

Prue regarded it with misgiving. The Garden of Nocturnal Delights was a small, self-contained world, worse than a village for gossip. The rumor mill would have her bedded and Bonded with the singer before he'd brushed the crumbs from his stubborn chin.

Gods, what would Katrin be thinking?

She hadn't realized her eyes were shut tight until a big hand enveloped hers.

"Are you all right? You're very pale." A firm grasp on her elbow, a gentle tug. "Sit down, Prue."

Gathering her wits, Prue sank into the armchair near the fireplace.

Erik poured tisane into one of the elegant cups. "Drink." He molded his warm palm over her fingers until she had the cup securely in her grasp.

Gratefully, she sipped. "Have you had good houses this week?" she asked stiffly.

Erik had been piling delicacies onto a pretty dish. "Eat and I'll tell you."

Prue looked at it blankly. "That's too much for me. You have it." She leaned forward to hand the plate back. "I'm not very hungry."

"I'd lay odds you haven't eaten since early morning."

"I was busy."

"With my account books, I know. But for now, you're going to eat every scrap. If you don't"—his teeth gleamed very white— "I will sit you on my lap and feed you with my own hands." He refused to let her look away. "I trust you believe me?"

Her mouth dropping open, Prue stared, a vision flashing before her mind's eye, clear in every devastating detail.

Herself, curled up like a happy child, safe in Erik Thorensen's arms, smiling as he popped a delicious morsel into her mouth. The tender, lustful gleam in his eye as he nuzzled her neck. Her lashes drooping with pleasure, her body boneless, buttressed by all that easy strength.

Oh, gods! A few, precious moments of utter relaxation. Nothing else to do, nowhere else to be.

If she defied him . . .

For a split second of insanity, the temptation was so great her whole body trembled, flushing with heat. Then she came to her senses.

"That won't be necessary." She took one of the spicepuffs.

"Pity."

Caught midbite, Prue choked on an unwilling huff of amusement. Erik chuckled as he refilled her cup. With perfect self-possession, he began talking about the Unearthly Opera Company, his voice deep and unhurried, strangely soothing. Slowly, she allowed herself to settle back in the chair.

If he gave up music, he could make a living as a story-teller, she thought dreamily, her lips twitching as he described missed cues, wardrobe malfunctions, triumphs and disasters. Worlds and people she'd never seen and never would see. A life she found difficult to imagine but all too easy to envy— sailing across the cold reaches of space in a Technomage star-ship, watching the gossamer-thin slingshot sails deploy, their star-shine the faintest gleam in the endless dark.

His voice gave her the same feeling of sensuous comfort as a dark blanket made of soft, plushy velvet.

Rising, he removed the plate from her unresisting grasp. "Well done, love," he murmured.

Prue sat up straight. "Are you, by any chance, *patronizing* me, Master Thorensen?"

"Erik," he said, unperturbed. "And no, you've done very well." With a grin, he waved the empty plate about under her nose.

So she had. Prue took a moment to tilt her head back against the back of the big chair. On a sigh, she said, "I should get back to work." Even to her own ears, she sounded reluctant.

"Not just yet." A fleeting touch on her arm. "Mistress Prue, I—" Erik broke off to clear his throat. "I owe you an apology. The Opera's accounts are in a terrible state. I knew that when I asked you to look at them."

Prue snorted. "You made the right decision—either your bookkeeper's cheating you or he's not right in the head. I haven't decided which yet."

"True enough." Erik's lips curved as though at some secret joke. "The man's a fool, that's for sure." Slipping a hand inside his shirt, he withdrew a small, flat package wrapped in a square of unbleached linen and laid it on her knee. "I want you to have this—by way of apology." The charming smile reappeared.

"If it's a gift, I can't accept it."

A brow rose. "Can't or won't?"

"Both."

Erik dropped to one knee on the rug and unfolded the linen covering himself. A flick of his fingers and a cascade of shimmering jade silk flowed over her lap.

Oh. *Oh.*

"It's a ring shawl," he murmured. "I chose the color for your eyes."

Unable to resist, Prue lifted the fabric to her cheek, the weave so fine the whole length of it could be threaded through a woman's ring. It smelled like a cool, soft kiss with a strange, spicy scent, citrus mixed with something musky.

She'd never had anything so lovely, presented so charmingly. *Never would have again.* To her fury, tears prickled behind her eyes. Blindly, Prue shoved two handfuls of fabric toward him. "No," she said. "I can't."

She heard him take a deliberate breath, as if he were about to launch into song.

"*Prue.*" Only her name, but Erik's voice dropped an octave, thrilling through every nerve, the impact like the echo of distant thunder, making her tremble right down to the marrow of her bones.

"Yes?" she whispered through dry lips.

"*You must have a mirror. Tell me where it is.*"

She was drowning in the blue of those ocean eyes, just as she had the first time she'd met him. Prue struggled, but in the end, it was simpler to tell him what he wished to know.

"Bedchamber."

"*Put the shawl on and go see how pretty you look.*" Erik bent and pressed his lips to her cheek, right over the dimple.

Prue's head whirled, her senses overwhelmed by the warm, masculine scent of his body, starched linen and a hint of leather.

Shakily, she rose, Erik standing so close their arms brushed. He steadied her, then stepped back. "Go on," he murmured.

Sister, what could it hurt? It was the least she could do, after all. Her brow furrowed, Prue walked the few steps into the adjoining bedchamber, her thoughts muzzy and confused. Vaguely, she wondered if she'd overeaten.

Shivering, she shook out the shawl and draped it over her shoulders, stealing a moment to feel the fineness of the fabric between finger and thumb. When she looked up, her mouth dropped open in a soundless exclamation. Sister save her, it was true. The deep, vibrant jade made her eyes glitter like best-quality aquamarines, the ones the nobleladies of Caracole prized so highly. Her skin glowed, honey and roses, and her hair gleamed a rich, glossy brown.

Embroidered the entire length of the shawl was a stylized school of seelies gamboling among the waves beneath the silvery light of the Sister's sickle. Wonderingly, Prue rubbed a forefinger over the indigo silk the unknown artist had used for their pelts. As a child, she'd loved the old tales, and her favorites had always been the ones about seelies, with their bulgy eyes and naïve wisdom. "Silly as a seelie" went the saying, but in the stories, the seelie was the only character who saw what was truly just and right.

Thank the Sister her head was clearing. Gods, he was clever! He couldn't have made a more perfect choice. Unable to bear the sight of her reflection a moment longer, Prue spun around to face him. She tilted her chin. "I still can't accept it. Now what?"

Erik Thorensen gazed down at her, as calm as ever. "Welcome back, Prue," he said. Which was decidedly odd, even on this strangest of days.

He took a light, two-handed grip of the shawl around her shoulders and gave it a little shake, pulling her slightly closer. "Do you like my gift, Prue?" The unsettling twinkle had returned to his gaze.

A hot chill ran straight up Prue's spine and down again. She moistened her lips. "It's beautiful," she said. "How could I not?" When she shrugged, moving within the constraint of the jade silk held taut by his effortless strength, she had the mad urge to rear back against it, to fight. He'd pull her right into his broad chest, his hard thighs. In every fiber of her being, she *knew* it. And she wouldn't have to think anymore.

Gods, she was losing her mind!

But instead, he turned her swiftly to face the mirror, her spine flush against his chest. "Look, sweet Prue."

When she opened her mouth, he placed a stern forefinger on her tingling lips. "Sshh." Her head didn't reach his shoulder. Towering above her, all charm and personality, his eyes danced, a bold, devilish blue.

"Watch." He raised the edge of the shawl and settled it over her hair, adjusting the folds on her shoulders. "See, you can use it as a head covering, the way Trinitarian girls do."

"Is that where it—?"

"Quiet. The color deepens the color of your eyes. Gorgeous. She said it would, the stallholder, when I described you." His lips curved with satisfaction.

"But Erik, how mu—?"

"A bargain. Let's try it this way, like a good Trinitarian wife." He drew a fold across her face. "Gods, that's erotic. One look at those eyes and a man'd kill to see the rest."

Sister save her, she couldn't keep up! Her frantic breath warmed the silk against her lips, her pulse a nagging beat that tightened her nipples and pattered low in her belly, between her thighs. Gods, it had been forever since she'd felt the sharp bite of desire! But why now? And for the Sister's sake, why this man?

Erik whipped the shawl away and draped one end around her neck, tossing the other over her shoulder. "A winter scarf, or"—his voice dropped—"a belt."

His long arms wrapped around her from behind, cinching her in a long swathe of fabric, once, twice, three times. He handled her with confidence, but so deftly his touch was barely there.

"It's too long," she said stupidly.

"No, it's not, you're small."

Their gazes met in the reflection, and Prue's heart turned over. His lips curved, slowly, oh so slowly. Holding her breath, she watched Erik the Golden smile for the first time without reservation, slow and very sweet. It broke over his face gradually, like sunrise stealing over the city, transforming him, softening the hard angles and planes. He seemed to hover on the brink of joyous laughter.

And yet, and yet . . . She knew she wasn't perceptive. It was why she managed the business of The Garden and Rose the people. But something about this beautiful man made all the hair stand up on the back of her neck.

"Erik, I . . ." She ran down, unable to think of what she'd been about to say.

"I bought it for you because I imagined you wearing it and the thought gave me pleasure. Also because I feel guilty about the state of the Opera's accounts. But mostly because I knew you'd like it. It's not a bribe, Prue, or a price." His long fingers spanned her waist and his cheek nuzzled hers, his breath warm and sweet. "It's a gift, freely given. Please, don't spoil it."

"I don't wish to be ungracious. Let me think about it and I'll tell you tomorrow." She'd speak with Rose, they'd work out a strategy between them.

"There's only one problem with that."

"What?" Prue glanced up in the mirror and fell into endless blue.

"I thought I was a patient man," said Erik Thorensen. "I just discovered I'm not."

Hooking his fingers into one side of the makeshift belt, he tugged. The silken clasp tightened and he pulled her around, right into his chest. Off balance, Prue flailed, clutching two fistfuls of shirt.

Spreading a broad palm over her back to keep her steady, he bent his head. His mouth landed on hers so sweetly, so softly. How strange! She'd been sure she'd be consumed, that Erik Thorensen would devour her and she'd be lost forever in his strong blond beauty. Instead, it was a real first kiss, almost awkward, his lips warm and smooth, learning hers little by little—a nibble here, a nuzzle there. An unhurried lick over her bottom lip and she couldn't help the hum of pleasure, deep in her throat.

Only a kiss, nothing more. An experiment of sorts, an indulgence, then she'd come to her senses and return to the work she was meant to do.

One arm slid around her waist and down to her buttock, hauling her flush into a wall of hot muscle, his erection prodding shamelessly into her belly. With the other hand, he cradled her skull, tilting her head at the perfect angle for his marauding tongue.

Erik the Golden kissed the way he sang, with consummate artistry and overwhelming passion. Sweet Sister, his timing was uncanny! Every time Prue feared she might pass out with the sheer wicked pleasure of it, he'd pull back just enough to let her breathe, whether she wanted to or not.

With every deft stroke, he stole another degree of control from her, until she was lost indeed, hanging in his arms, kissing him back with everything she had. He tasted so dark and sweet. The very air they exchanged was spiced with his potent masculinity. Dizzily, Prue wondered if she could simply lie in his arms forever and breathe him in. Nothing could hurt her then.

The room spun as he picked her up and strode out of the bedchamber.

What? Prue levered one eye open.

"Sshh," he murmured into her mouth. "I've got you."

With a booted foot, he pushed her big office chair around and sank into it, Prue curled close in his lap like an astonished kitten. "I thought you'd feel safer here," he said calmly enough, though his chest rose and fell with his quick breaths. "Away from the bed."

The dazzle of sparks in her blood died away to a slow splutter. Gods, she was wrapped around him like a lover vine in high summer!

She sat up, fumbling with the shawl, trying to rip it off.

Wincing, Erik shot her a pained look. "Stop wriggling." He untangled her, taking his time. "You'll damage the silk. Not to mention me."

Kissing him had felt so good, so wonderful, and now look at him—smiling to himself as if he thought she'd believe him, all confident charm and golden good looks—leaving her perched on his knee like the silly girl she'd once been. Surely she'd learned her lesson? For a split second, she was back in the Melting Pot, in the fetid dark, listening to heavy footfalls pass her hiding place, praying that Katrin wouldn't cry.

Neither she nor her baby had had the power to hold him. Both of them burdens Chavis couldn't wait to shed. *She hadn't been enough.*

The memory sent her scrambling off Erik's lap in a graceless rush. Using her anger as a shield, she faced him, gripping her hands together. "Merciful Sister, Erik, this isn't a play. Who writes your lines?"

10

Erik's smile evaporated. "Prue, don't be frightened of what you want."

"Frightened?" It was a relief to feel the strengthening rush of anger. This was familiar ground. "I know all about men like you, Erik. I will not be manipulated. Or charmed, or patronized."

Erik rose to loom over her, and suddenly, he seemed more dark, more deadly than golden. "Who was he?"

"What? Who?"

"The man who did this to you, hurt you so badly."

Stupidly, she wanted to cry. What was the use of denying what was clearly so obvious? "No matter, he's long since dead." Squaring her shoulders, she looked Erik in the eye. "In a strange way, I owe him everything I am. Because of our child, I had no choice but to go on." She shrugged. "So here I am. A self-made woman, I suppose you'd say."

He went very still. "You have a child?"

"Katrin." He didn't know her nearly as well as he thought he did. Prue gave him a thin smile. "She's nineteen. My darling."

He was folding the jade shawl with smooth, efficient moves, avoiding her eye.

"When does your engagement in Caracole finish?" she asked coolly. "I can send the Opera's accounts after you easily enough." There, that should do it. Her shoulders slumped.

Erik crossed the office to place the small square of fabric on a shelf. Sister, he knew how to move, all long-limbed, dangerous grace! When he turned, the light from the window turned his hair into a glorious nimbus. "Tickets sales have been so good already, I've extended the run. Signed the contract this morning."

He came to stand before her and the twinkle was back in his eye. "I'd better get back for rehearsal." Nudging her chin with his fist, he said, "Shut your mouth, sweetheart. Another two weeks, pretty Prue. I look forward to meeting your Katrin."

Swiftly, he pressed a kiss to her cheek, the one with the dimple. "See you tomorrow." He strode from the room.

∽

Scarcely daring to breathe, the Necromancer crumpled, waiting it out, his cheek pressed ignominiously against the silken rug. It was almost an hour before he felt able to move and another fifteen minutes before he could get himself propped up in his chair. His chest aching, he tugged the bell pull that would summon Nasake.

"Take a message to the rest of the Queen's Cabal," he said. "I'm working from home today." He gestured at the lax bundle of blue in the corner. "Get rid of that."

His dark eyes flat and dull, the man bowed, expressionless as always.

"Wait."

Nasake straightened, the seelie's corpse dangling from one hand. "Master?"

"Hand me that bundle of transplas from the desk. Oh, and Nasake?"

"Master?"

"You may have the creature. Do with it as you will."

The corners of Nasake's lipless mouth lifted. He bowed. "Thank you, Noblelord." He passed over the transplas, gathered up the bucket and the seelie and left as silently as he'd arrived.

Unseeing, the Necromancer gazed down at the sheet of

transplas he'd taken from the Technomage's console. It trembled so much, he had to brace it against his knee before he could bring it into focus. The Scientist had drawn a plan for some other kind of trap, from several different angles, complete with captions, footnotes and tables. With a sigh, he closed his eyes. He couldn't be bothered with Technomage nonsense now. Something was nagging at him and he'd learned never to discount his own instincts.

What, in Shaitan's name, had he missed? As if the fire witch hadn't been irritating enough, the taste of air Magick still lingered in his mouth. Reaching for the carafe of wine on the desk, he paused.

The *familiar* taste of air Magick.

Where?

His heart thudding, he disciplined himself to think. Somehow, somewhere, he'd touched it. Recently. He went out so seldom, reserving his energies for his high office and his dark Magick. Only when the queen insisted, did he—

The Royal Command performance!

He had a sudden, vivid recollection of gazing at the party in full swing on the stage, the monarch's hand overly familiar on his shoulder. Bartelm and Nori, the Purists, other people milling about—the beautiful whore from The Garden with her little brown-haired friend, a gaggle of merchants and noblelords and ladies, the big blond singer, working the crowd. Come to think of it, the man was quite good. The Necromancer had felt the tug of something that might once have been feeling.

He'd fumbled his play with the fire witch, through no fault of his own. So be it. He wouldn't make the same mistakes with the air witch; he'd readjust, switch strategies. The dark fates were working with him now, because she had come to him, here in Caracole, he could swear to it. Again, he recalled the elusive, intriguing taste of Magick in the air that night. The gods were thumbing their divine noses at him. A direct challenge.

Yes!

The transplas fluttered out of his slack fingers and skated across the rug. Godsdammit! His back protesting, the Necromancer leaned forward to retrieve it and froze halfway, staring at the drawing.

It wasn't so much a trap, as a reservoir.

Uncaring of his dignity, he lurched forward to his knees on the rug, the gown billowing around him.

By Shaitan, a reservoir for Magick! His brain racing, he devoured the explanatory notes, skipping the data tables he didn't understand. Stumbling to the desk, he picked up the wine jug with a hand that shook. When he poured, a few ruby red drops spilled like blood. It took him almost an hour to work through all the sheets, but in the end, he had the gist of it.

A glass of wine in his hand, the Necromancer sat on the rug in his study, glowing with satisfaction. Perfect! More than perfect! The solution to all his problems in a single elegant package, profoundly selfish, profoundly evil. It had a sublimely wicked symmetry he adored. He couldn't fault it.

He'd *own* the air witch, her Magick, her soul—her body.

The Technomage Primus of Sybaris had made good use of the time she'd had the fire witch under her control. Her analysis of the physical nature of fire Magick was brilliant, he had to admit, though it was nothing if not abstruse. Metabolic rate? Membranous exchange?

No matter.

Because his pet Scientist had devised a method to harvest Magick. And if she could siphon it *from* one individual, then the converse must also be true—she could transfer it *into* another.

His breath caught, thinking of the possibilities. He couldn't imagine life as a female, had never even contemplated it, but he wouldn't quibble if it meant being healthy and flexible again. It might even be . . . piquant, despite the obvious disadvantages. Wistfully, he remembered the splendid breadth of the singer's shoulders, the muscle in his thigh. Now there was a magnificent male animal. Ah well, it couldn't be helped.

Gods, he hoped it was the tall whore.

⌘

Erik lay back in the skiff, gazing up moodily at the Sibling Moons. They might wear different faces on different worlds, but They were bloody everywhere, the gods. The Lady and the Lord—the Sister and the Brother. Prue swore by the Sister, and he'd noticed men in Caracole swore by the Brother, as he did by the Horned Lord.

His lips curved in a tired smile. Another full house, another dozen encores. One woman had climbed onto her seat, reached up under her gown and flung some filmy piece of nothing toward the stage. Falling short, it had fluttered into the orchestra pit to drape like a bizarre flag of surrender over the drummer's bald head.

Surrender.

Gods, he couldn't decide whether he was an utter bastard or a lunatic or both. Scowling, he thumped his clenched fist against the side of the craft, scraping his knuckles. He'd pushed Prue ruthlessly this morning and she'd fought with everything in her. The strength of her resistance still astonished him, but watching her bright face cloud had made his heart twist.

Fine. He'd established the facts. Mistress Prue McGuire might be the most bloody-minded subject he'd ever had, but godsdammit, the Lord and the Lady hadn't taken the Voice from him. She'd gone under. Only for a few moments, true, but she had.

He exhaled. Never again. By the Horned Lord, he'd never use the Voice on her again. He'd taken an oath. From now on, she'd come to him of her own free will, or not at all. *Let me kiss it.* He'd been shocked to the core, the words spilling out of him without conscious volition. Erik gritted his teeth. All right, he'd simply exercise greater discipline, scrutinize every impulse, stifle every instinct. *I swear it.*

The Dark Lady's deep, silvery laughter echoed in his head.

"You wanta go by the Meltin' Pot?" asked the skiffwoman, the same one he'd had the first night. She'd got into the way of waiting at the water stair outside the theater. "Bettsa," she'd said. "Call me Bettsa."

"Yah!" Florien sat up straight.

Erik frowned. What was the lad doing here? He'd been so preoccupied he hadn't noticed Florien sneak on board. "No," he said repressively.

Florien patted the pocket of his grubby trousers. "I'll teach ye t' Sybarite shell game."

"No!"

Bettsa chuckled and poled out into the current, working with the outgoing tide.

Prue's plump little tits had pressed so hard against the fine fabric of her tunic, he could close his eyes now and recall the precise shape of her nipples. He might have another two weeks available for the seduction, but he had no intention of waiting. Her tongue had been like velvet twining and flirting with his, her whole lush body pressed ardently against him.

A little more patience and he'd have her. Without the Voice.

He no longer doubted the Dark Lady was personally responsible for designing Prue McGuire, because everything about the woman appealed to him more and more. The hell of it was that he *liked* her—admired her intelligence and determination, enjoyed her acerbic humor. Life with Prue would never be boring.

She'd stood before him, swathed in jade silk, her eyes shining with challenge and deeper down, a yearning that tore at his heart. She worked so hard, practical Prue, always responsible, always respectable. But he'd seen her laugh 'til the tears ran down her cheeks, felt her heat, her passion, her longing.

If things had been different, if he hadn't . . . done what he'd done. Prue might very well have been born for him—so fragile, so strong, so right. The goddess was clever, he had to give Her that. But it could never be. All he had was a few short weeks.

If only she'd trust him. The breath caught in his throat. Gods, the games they could play!

He'd always been a self-assured lover, confident of his ability to please. If he tended to be a trifle dominating, well, he knew exactly how far to go. The trouble was, once he started with Prue McGuire, he wasn't sure he'd be able to stop until he'd taken complete control.

Prue might be shocked by some of his darker desires at first, but she wouldn't flinch or squeal, she'd look him straight in the eye and defy him, say she felt nothing, pretend she wasn't trembling with the need to fly free while his mastery kept her safe. He didn't doubt he could persuade her—eventually.

In the process, he'd warm his cold, empty soul, like a man crouched before a blazing fire. It might be a fleeting sensation, but gods, it was going to be good, very, very good.

What could he give in return?

Pleasure. Oh yes, he'd pleasure her until she begged him for the release only he could provide. In the heat and the pleading, she'd find surcease too. Maybe even peace.

Temptation whispered to him, hot and sly. *You can have everything,* it said. *Her body, her mind, her soul—all yours if you use the Voice. The more she desires you, the more susceptible she becomes.*

He'd be able to watch those fine lines beside her eyes smooth out as she lay asleep on his shoulder, but he'd never know for sure . . .

She'd only trusted a man once. The bastard coward.

Compel her with the Voice and he'd be an even lower form of life. Scum.

As if the thought had conjured it, the wind shifted, filling the air with a stench so vile he coughed.

"What's that gods-awful stink?" he croaked.

The skiffwoman's shoulders bunched as she hauled on the pole. "What stink?"

Cursing, rubbing his sensitive nose, Erik peered at the grand palazzos slipping by, their lights shining across the water. The air was full of the smell of slime and rot and slow dissolution, corruption on a vast scale. Bile filled his throat, burning and sour. "Gods, woman, what's wrong with you? Can't you smell it? Like a swamp stuffed with corpses."

He saw the whites of Bettsa's eyes in the moonslight as she shot him a startled glance. She raised her head and sniffed loudly. "Nothin'," she muttered. "Ain't nothin' 'cept the turn of the tide."

"Florien?"

Slowly, the boy shook his head. "Nah." A pause. "Mebbe a little."

The wind changed, giving Erik some respite. "Where are we?"

"The Leaf of Nobility." The woman spat over the side.

"Erik?" Florien stretched out a hand, then dropped it. "Ye sick?"

Gritting his teeth, Erik settled back in his seat. The stench had dissipated, drifting away on the sea breeze. "I'll do." But the apprehension in the boy's thin face was so clear, he forced a smile and ruffled Florien's hair. "I hate marsh smells," he said. Which was the absolute truth.

They reminded him of death.

◦⌒◦

Prue padded down to the cavernous kitchen, wrapped in her shabby old robe. "You still here, sweetie?"

"Mm," said a voice from deep inside the huge pantry. "Put a kettle on, will you?"

A moment later, Katrin emerged with a plate of small cakes. Smiling, she bent to drop a kiss on her mother's cheek. "Love you, Mam."

"You too." Prue gazed up at her calm, capable daughter, and her heart turned over with love and pride. "Long day?" she asked.

Katrin busied herself with a tisane pot and cups. She shot Prue a cautious glance from under her lashes. "Not really. I came in at noon, which was just as well, because Cook needed the help." Her gaze became speculative. "I fixed a special lunch, in fact. For two."

"Oh." Prue grabbed a washcloth and swiped it over an already spotless bench. "Erik Thorensen stayed on. We were discussing his accounts." She sat down at the sturdy wooden table.

Katrin joined her, pouring the tisane with a steady hand. "He's the singer?"

Prue nodded. "Rose arranged a deal. He gives music lessons and in return I sort out the Opera's accounts."

"Tansy thinks he's wonderful. Is he?"

"He's certainly an excellent teacher. And his voice is incredible. I've never heard anything like it. But he has no head for business."

Katrin chuckled, reaching for a cake. "Not your type then."

Before Prue could gather her wits, Katrin raised a hand, forestalling the reply. "On second thoughts," she said, wrinkling her nose, "don't tell me anything, I don't want to know."

"Fine with me, sweetheart." Prue smiled, uneasily conscious of her glowing cheeks. "You never have before." She changed the subject. "Tell me, did Arkady get the lease on the shop?"

Katrin's face lit up, her blue gray eyes shining. "Oh yes! Mam, it's in such a good place. And there are rooms upstairs, a bit shabby, but we don't care."

Prue wrapped her fingers around the warmth of the cup and listened to her daughter's enthusiastic chatter. Memories paraded by—a chubby baby with a gorgeous gurgling laugh, a quiet little girl with fair curls waving around a serious face, the tip of a pink tongue slipping out when she concentrated. All those years when she'd been everything to her child— father as well as mother, disciplinarian and teacher, comfort and refuge. Source of hugs and kisses.

Her baby. She resisted the impulse to shake her head in wonderment, hardly able to credit the passage of time. The presence of this tall, graceful young woman, now poised on the verge of a separate life, was a precious, bittersweet gift. Thank the Sister, Arkady was perfect for her darling—steady and solid, but with an underlying sweetness of spirit she couldn't help but like.

Half an hour later, she went up to bed, smiling. Her heart might ache a little, but she felt restored to the Prue she knew.

11

Godsdammit, he hadn't come to see her! She'd wasted the
entire morning grimly ignoring the vocal glory drifting up
from the courtyard of the Sweet Manda. Of course, if she
hadn't flung the window wide in the first place, no effort
would have been necessary, but well, it was a warm day.

With a huff of irritation, Prue regarded the figures marching
in the neat columns down the page before her. She had to admit
to a certain degree of surprise—the Unearthly Opera wasn't in
the dire financial straits she'd feared. Far from it, in fact.

She tilted her head, listening. Ah, Erik must be leaving.
She heard his velvet baritone raised in farewell, his quick step
on the path leading to the water stairs.

Good. The hollow feeling in her midsection was hunger,
nothing more. She'd have a bite to eat and finish preparing her
tutorial on trading in commodities. Excellent. Truly.

Rising, she crossed the room to fetch her notes from the shelf,
but when she looked down, it was jade silk she was holding, her
fingertips stroking to and fro. Prue froze, the embroidered seelies blurring. She sniffed the tears back, blinking hard.

Oh, what the hell. Her head held high, she marched into

the bedchamber, slinging the shawl across her shoulders as she went.

For a long time, she stared at the figure in the mirror. With trembling fingers, she opened the first three buttons on her tunic and folded it open. Then she pulled a pin from her hair, followed by another and another. Breathing hard, she raked her hands through her braids until her hair curled in wild profusion around her flushed face and tumbled down across the vivid silk.

"Well, well, look at you," said an amused voice from the door.

Prue whirled to face Rose.

Her friend sauntered forward, graceful skirts swishing with every step. "You look gorgeous, sweetie." With a grin, she fingered the edge of the shawl. "Wear it tonight and leave your hair loose. I'll send Tansy up to brush it for you."

Prue narrowed her eyes. "I'm not going out tonight."

"Yes, you are." Rose sank onto the bed and lounged back against the pillows like a copper-skinned houri. "Erik Thorensen wants to return our hospitality. We're going to the Royal Theater and then having supper with him."

"For the Sister's sake, it was lunch on a tray!" Prue shrugged out of the shawl. "You go if he's that worried about it."

"Not without you."

Prue set her jaw. "Don't force my hand, Rose. I won't be blackmailed."

Rose's sculpted lips thinned. "Are we partners in The Garden or not?" she demanded.

"Of course."

Rose sat up. "This is business," she said. "Erik wants to extend the contract, and that's something we have to discuss with him together." She leaned forward to catch Prue's hand in both of hers. "I'm sorry if you don't like him, love, but we can't afford to be throwing away the opportunity. Anyway, you have to be there if we're going to beat him down to something we can afford. I'm too soft."

Prue scanned her friend's perfect features. *Soft* wasn't the word she'd have chosen to apply to Rosarina. *Devious* was more like it. Behind that lovely face was a mind so subtle and complex, it would frighten the life out of The Garden's clients—if only they were aware of it. Fortunately, they had no idea. Everything Rose said sounded reasonable, but then it always did.

Hesitating, she was lost.

"That's settled then," said Rose. "Was it Erik who gave you this?" When she lifted the silken fabric to rub it against her cheek, Prue's fingers curled into fists.

"Yes," she said curtly. "But I can't accept it. I'm going to give it back."

"Really?" Another rub and a low purr of pleasure. "I'll take it off your hands."

"No!" Prue reefed the shawl out of her friend's grasp. She took a calming breath. "No, I'll return it myself."

A dark brow arched. "Excellent. Bring it with you this evening." Rose dropped a kiss on Prue's cheek as she passed. "I'll send Tansy with lunch. She can help you pick a gown."

Prue opened her mouth to protest, but save for a drift of Rose's distinctive perfume, the chamber was empty.

∽

The tall, carved doors of the Royal Theater stood open to the night as the audience dispersed, their faces transfigured by pleasure and excitement. Another magnificent success. The Unearthly Opera had done a different piece tonight, romantic, even humorous in places, but once again, the soaring splendor of Erik's voice had reduced Prue to tears, though she'd fought it with everything in her. He made her cry, he made her laugh. He made her *want*.

Godsdammit, she was a level-headed, adult woman. She *knew* what he was—and she'd never been so fascinated by a man in her life.

When a salt-laden breeze whispered around the foyer, Prue shivered. She stepped behind the shelter of an ornately carved pillar, rubbing her arms.

"For the Sister's sake, Prue, you're freezing. You brought the damn thing with you. Put it on!" Rose pulled the wadded-up shawl out of Prue's hands and flung it around her shoulders.

"Ladies," came a velvet purr, and there he was, bowing with a flourish. "Sorry to keep you waiting. You look beautiful, both of you." Erik's gaze moved from the silk fringe Prue was twisting in her fingers up to her face, and his eyes danced. But all he said was, "Shall we go?"

Rose took the arm he offered. "You were wonderful tonight, Erik," she said. "Superb."

Prue could have sworn he preened. At the snort she didn't bother to suppress, Erik lifted a brow. "Did you enjoy yourself, Prue?"

"Of course," she agreed calmly. Credit where it was due. "You were even better than I remembered."

His grin of pleasure was so unstudied, so spontaneous, she was ensnared before she knew it. A tremor of excitement coiled up from the base of her spine. Unconsciously, she leaned a little closer, absorbing his body heat. Erik slipped his arm around her shoulders and snugged her into his side. "Warm enough?"

Before Prue could speak, Rose exclaimed, "Oh look, there's Noblelady Izanami!" She waved at a tiny woman dressed with the severest elegance. "I have to talk to her about deportment classes for her daughters. My dears"—she patted Erik's arm—"you go on without me. I'll catch up."

A quick smile, a swirl of skirts and the Dark Rose was halfway across the foyer, Noblelady Izanami turning to greet her with a smile, her hands held out in welcome.

"I've got a skiff waiting," said Erik, guiding Prue in the direction of the water stairs. "Come on."

"But—"

He shot her a glance brimful of wicked mischief. "Scared?"

Prue gave a huff of laughter. "That's the oldest trick in the book."

Erik lifted her hand and kissed her knuckles, his lips soft and warm. "I'm afraid I've sunk to desperate measures, Mistress Prue." One eye closed in an unrepentant wink. "But I'll take my punishment like a man."

Prue shook her head. "Now you're being silly." But something warm and foolish melted all through her from the inside out. "Godsdammit," she said. "I give up. Take me to dinner and be done with it." She threw a dark glance at Rose's unresponsive back. *You'll keep, my dear.*

He'd hired one of the fancier skiffs, with a leather seat and an awning to protect against the weather and provide some privacy. He also appeared to be on the best of terms with the skiffwoman. Prue sighed. Was there a woman alive immune to that easy charm?

"You're still cold, sweetheart. Come here." Disregarding her protests, Erik tucked Prue under his arm, opening his coat and wrapping it around her. His big body seemed to envelop and overwhelm hers with heat and hardness, the uncompromising density of male muscle and bone.

"Not a word until we get there, all right?" His breath stirred the hair at her temple.

Prue shrugged within the circle of his arm. "Fine." Idly, she watched the long ripples slip by, burnished by the lights streaming from the buildings on the banks. Erik sighed and rubbed his cheek against her hair. He drew her fractionally closer, his powerful thigh sealed all along hers.

Sister, it was so good to relax into this comfortable silence, no demands, no arguments, no games. Prue's lashes fluttered down. She didn't need to be anyone she wasn't. He'd seen the worst of her, after all. With the rhythmic splash of the skiffwoman's pole, random thoughts floated in and out of her head, until finally, one stranger than the others snagged her attention.

He was coddling her, courting her as if she were precious. Like a lover. Even more astonishing, she was permitting it.

How long had it been since she'd been cared for this way? Prue frowned, but she couldn't really bring any occasion to mind since she'd left her home and her parents, so long ago. She swallowed, her pulse accelerating. No wonder his touch was like a drug, soothing and stimulating all at once.

Blankly, she stared at the fine palazzos on the banks of the canal. How amazing. She thought she'd armored herself against him, but Erik the Golden had slipped past her defenses.

Slowly, Prue pushed away from the heat of his body, her heart thudding. Remembering the dark, hot spice of his mouth, the unyielding press of his muscled torso against hers, none of that served any useful purpose. She'd had her moment of self-indulgence. Another taste and it would be too late. Erik Thorensen bore all the hallmarks of a powerful addiction. And when he was gone, she'd be desperate with longing for what she couldn't have.

He brushed his fingertips over the dimple in her cheek. "Prue?"

She ignored him.

The skiff floated past the Leaf of Nobility, toward a long, low building glowing with lights. The tinkle of glassware and the low buzz of conversation drifted across the water. Prue stiffened, her eyes widening. She knew this place. Exquisite food and wine, secluded booths meant for seduction, hideously expensive.

Merciful Sister, she couldn't afford to turn her whole life upside down—not to scratch an itch. Prue counted her breaths, shoring up her resolve. Better to make the break tonight rather than later. Logic said it would hurt less . . . Her body ached as if she'd been beaten all over with sticks.

Rose managed these situations with perfect grace and poise. Invariably, the lover kissed her a wistful, lingering good-bye, going his way with precious memories. It didn't have to be ugly, not between adults.

As Erik handed her out of the skiff, she summoned up a smile.

Two reckless cups of wine later, she'd relaxed enough to hold up her end of the conversation. She'd never have thought it. Chavis had loved to hear himself talk, but part of Erik's charm was his ability to listen. In the candlelit booth, his eyes shone with what seemed to be genuine interest as she described how she and Rose had made The Garden of Nocturnal Delights the foremost training house in Caracole.

By the time they'd discussed a new musical curriculum for the apprentices, her brain buzzed with possibilities and her plate was empty. She refused more wine, noting that Erik drank very little.

He insisted on ordering a sumptuous sugary dessert, so she made him share it, their spoons tinkling together in a companionable sort of way. Erik leaned back, smiling as he watched her chase the last morsels around the dish. "Good?" he asked, his gaze on her mouth.

Carefully, Prue laid her spoon aside, the happiness leaking out of her. It was over. "We should go back," she said.

The lazy smile disappeared. "You sure?" She couldn't read his expression.

"Yes."

The skiff was nearly at The Garden before she managed to assemble a suitably dignified speech in her head.

"Erik." She put a hand on his sleeve. Although she'd cleared her throat, she still sounded hoarse and raspy, as if she were coming down with the winter ague. "I think you know what I'm going to say."

"No." The tone was uncompromising.

Bracing herself, Prue turned to confront him, while he loomed over her in the small craft. With as much poise as she could muster, she said, "Please, believe me. This is the best thing—for both of us. It isn't going to work."

A tingling silence. "You won't bloody let it." Temper deepened his voice, clipped his words.

How did Rose *do* this? "There's no place in my life for a man like you. I'm not your type." The laugh strangled in her throat. "I know I'm not."

"Like hell." His voice dropped to the intimate velvet purr she loved. "Come on, pretty Prue. All I want is your company. What about lunch tomorrow? I'll bring the tray, I promise."

Prue gave a shaky laugh. "When you talk like that, you could charm the birds from the trees."

Erik's mouth went tight and hard. Turning his head, he met the fascinated gaze of the skiffwoman. "As fast as you can, Bettsa."

The woman muttered something under her breath that sounded like, "Daft buggers."

Without another word, Erik withdrew his arm from around her shoulders. Prue shivered, huddling into the silk shawl. Cold seeped into her bones, her heart.

At the water stairs of The Garden, Bettsa steadied the skiff while Erik handed Prue out. "Wait here," he said to the skiffwoman, his tone curt. "I shan't be long."

"There's no need," said Prue. "I'm perfectly capable of walking to my own front door."

"I'm sure you are." Erik took her arm in a steely grip and guided her up the path. "But I'm not so easily dismissed."

Prue stopped just inside the buttery pool of light spreading from the wide-open doors of the Main Pavilion. "Here, take this." As she went to slip the shawl from her shoulders, the movement pulled at the fine hair on the nape of her neck. "Ow!" Her eyes watered.

"Stand still." A pause while Erik's fingers lifted a braid aside. "Your hair's tangled in the hook-and-eye things on your collar." A big hand on the back of her skull urged her closer to his tall, blurred figure. "Bend your head forward."

Perforce, she did. Until her nose was buried in the open vee where his shirt was unlaced, his long fingers tugging gently at her hair. Her face heated, sheer mortification combining with the sharp physical pain. Desperately, she tried not to inhale, but it was impossible.

Merciful Sister! No man had ever affected her so profoundly. She'd had lovers over the years, all decent men, a couple of them almost as handsome as Chavis. She was a healthy, adult female, in charge of her own life. She'd walked away from every one of those relationships when she felt the time was right. Besides, she'd had her priorities straight—her daughter and her work.

But this? It was like a summer storm, all sultry heat and flashy lightning, whirling in her head until she couldn't think straight. She hadn't felt so off balance since she'd been eighteen, head over heels in love with Chavis. Sister save her, only a few moments more. Frantically, she cast about for some kind of distraction.

"Tell me you can't juggle." The instant the words were out of her mouth, Prue stiffened, utterly appalled.

"I can't juggle," said Erik equably enough, his hands still moving in her hair, separating one lock from another. "Why?"

"Chavis used—" She broke off.

He froze. "Chavis? That was his name?"

Prue bit her lip. "Have you finished?"

"Nearly. This one's completely knotted." The ice had thawed. "When you do something, you really are thorough, aren't you, sweetheart?" Now his voice had a beguiling lilt that invited her to share the humor of the situation. How in the gods' names did he do that?

"Here, better hold on." Picking up her clenched fist, he laid it high on his chest, over his heart. Thud, thud. Thud, thud.

Prue clung to the rhythm, acutely aware of the inviting expanse of golden, hair-dusted skin. The slightest tilt forward and she'd be tasting him whether she wished to or not. She set her jaw.

Somewhere in a far-off, crazy part of her brain, she wondered if his nipples were sensitive. Some men loved being touched there. Or licked. Broad or small, pink or brown? If she uncramped her fingers, slid her palm down a few inches . . .

She'd lost her mind.

"Nearly done," he said, his lips so close to the shell of her ear she felt the warm whisper of his breath.

A muttered curse, another cautious tug, the lingering brush of his fingertips against the pulse fluttering in her throat. "There."

"Thank you." Gathering her courage, Prue pushed the hair off her face and raised her eyes.

Cradling her cheeks, Erik stroked his thumbs over her eyebrows. Despite herself, Prue leaned into the touch, her lashes fluttering down.

"You're not really going to give the shawl back, are you?" he asked softly.

Prue met his gaze without flinching. "No," she said. "I changed my mind. I'll keep it as a souvenir."

"Let me show you something." Erik drew the shawl from her shoulders, took her hands and draped the folded length over her wrists.

She stared. "What on earth are you doing?"

"A ring shawl this length can also be . . ." Slowly, carefully, he wrapped the fine fabric a couple of times around her joined wrists, leaving the ends to dangle. He raised his eyes to hers, his face illuminated by the light from the windows, a world-weary angel with a devilish sparkle in his eye. ". . . a way to show you trust me."

Impossible.

It was so loose, she'd be able to shake it off in an instant.

If she wanted to.

Erik reached out and picked up one end of the tie, leaving plenty of slack. "You see?" he said simply.

Prue flushed from toes to scalp in a scalding tide of heat. His eyes blazed into hers. For a single glorious instant, she was beautiful, desperately desired, needed in a way that was entirely new.

Safe.

It was so ridiculous she almost laughed in his face. Except that she could barely speak. "I don't understand. W-what do you want?"

She watched him weigh the words before he spoke. A lock of golden hair fell over his brow as he bent his head and she'd almost lifted a hand to brush it back before she remembered. *Tied.* Surreptitiously, she pressed her thighs together, trying to quell the liquid burn of desire.

"Isn't it obvious?" That beautiful smile. "You."

The sensuous spell broke with an almost perceptible snap. When Prue gave the shawl a brisk tug, he released her. Her hands shaking, she unwound it, folded it up. "I can't afford games. I can't afford pleasure. I can't afford *you.*"

At the door, she turned back. He hadn't moved. "But thank you for your gift. It's truly lovely." She forced her trembling lips into a smile. "Good-bye."

She reached the top of the stairs before the first tear fell.

12

The grand palazzos baked quietly in the afternoon heat, their white, pierced towers and curving roofs glittering with gold leaf and fretted bronze. Small blue waves cavorted and kissed in the canal. A single skiff poled unhurriedly around the bend. A perfect summer's day. It would have been idyllic, thought Erik grimly, if not for the appalling stench that drew him reluctantly, but irresistibly forward.

He didn't have a clue what he was doing, but he couldn't leave it alone. Last night, he'd watched Prue's small, straight-backed figure all the way into the Main Pavilion, jagged, sharp-edged thoughts whirling about inside his aching skull like storm-tossed debris.

He'd been enjoying the hunt for its own sake, so arrogant, so certain of his prey, that he'd fumbled it. The only one he couldn't charm, couldn't control, as the Dark Lady had foretold. When he'd blundered back into the fancy skiff, he'd nearly tipped Bettsa into the canal. Once the craft stopped wallowing, he'd asked her to take him to the Melting Pot. A midnight supper of hard liquor sounded fucking fine. He'd flexed his fists. With a brawl if one was in the offing.

Halfway there, the appalling marsh-stench returned, doubling him over, but leaving Bettsa unaffected. Perfect. Now he had a matching set of miseries, inside and out—and he had not a shadow of a doubt they were connected. Such an exquisitely awful coincidence could only be the work of the gods. Gritting his teeth, he'd ordered the skiffwoman to take him back to the boardinghouse instead.

The night had been virtually sleepless, interminable, the smell befouling his nostrils, Prue's words echoing over and over, a death chant at the funeral of pleasure. *I can't afford you. I can't afford you.* He clenched his fists. The Dark Lady might think She'd proved a point, but he wasn't done with Prue yet—hell, no.

A maid at the boardinghouse had been happy enough to find him a large square of linen and saturate it with the sweet perfume of Lady's lace, imported from Sybaris. Now he held it clamped to his nose as he negotiated the web of bridges that connected the Leaves of Caracole. Across the Roisterers' Bridge to the Melting Pot, then the Bridge of Empty Pockets off the other side. After that, he lost count, but the sea breeze was his guide, and as it shifted, he'd wait, drop the handkerchief and sniff. Then he'd cough and walk on.

The Processional Bridge, broad and sedate, brought him out on the Leaf of Nobility proper, and he paused, half-expecting some officious servant to run him off. Nothing. Nothing but the tall palazzos and their elegant gardens shimmering in the sun.

The odor in the air grew stronger, dragging him down a narrow, twisting alley that led between the buildings, skirting the back walls of courtyards and trellises. A servant's track. At the far end, an unremarkable wooden gate gave onto the small water stair.

He could swear he could see it, hovering over the water, a gray, green, purple miasma of death. Erik's legs gave out from under him. He collapsed on the stairs, fighting to keep what little remained in his stomach.

Smell, the most primitive sense. It sped directly to his hindbrain, bypassing his rational faculties, triggering . . .

Ah, gods! He pressed the heels of his hands to his eyes, but the memories sprang forward like clawed beasts, terrifyingly swift—mercilessly insistent.

He'd hauled Inga out of a brackish eddy where the water swirled in a slow, muddy meander, her tall, slender body surprisingly heavy. "No! *No!*" His protest had been a scream to the cloudy sky of Concordia. When he'd gripped the girl by the shoulders and shaken her, her head lolled as if her neck was broken, clotted hanks of her hair falling against his forearms with a cold, unpleasant splat.

But he ignored it all, throwing her down on the bank, spreading his big-knuckled boy's hands across her diaphragm, pressing, pressing . . . A torrent of brown water spewed out of her pale lips, but she didn't move or open her eyes.

The fetid odor of the swamp, of slow, soft rot and dissolution, sinking to the bottom in a silty cloud of mud, putrid, stinking . . .

Sitting on the top stair, Erik dropped his head between his knees, breathing hard. Deliberately, he superimposed Prue's lively features over Inga's pallid face. But that served only to make it worse. Instead of obliterating Inga, Prue seemed to sink into the other woman until rosy lips faded to gray, bright eyes dulled and they were one. Dead, dead, *dead*.

Ah, fuck, not Prue . . .

Godsdammit, he wished he could have seen her this morning, touched her hand, steadied himself. Shuddering, he gazed into the sparkling blue water. Because he was going to have to go down there, and he wasn't sure he had the courage to do it. But they were all linked somehow—this death-stench, the task the gods had given him, Inga and Prue.

The moment he'd reached The Garden that morning, he left the singing class flat and pelted up the stairs to her office. But her door was locked. "Prue!" he'd yelled, giving it a healthy thump.

A short silence, the creak of her chair. "If that is you, Master Thorensen," came her voice, perfectly composed, "go away and leave me work. I'll send the completed books to you by messenger." The rustle of paper as if she'd slapped something down hard on the desk.

He'd made a rude gesture at the unresponsive door, but

then he'd put his hands on his hips and stared at it, imagining her working on those damned accounts. His lips quirked with grim amusement. Once he'd had the idea, it had taken him most of a night to create the crazy effect, and to make separate copies of what was serious and essential, but he'd chuckled as he'd worked. He'd never had to cook the books before.

Mistress Prue and the dark goddess would find it took more than a curt dismissal to get rid of Erik Thorensen.

Now, he pulled off his boots and shrugged slowly out of his jacket. On second thoughts, he removed his shirt as well, ripping out the laces to tie his hair back and tucking his talisman and its chain into the pocket. He couldn't risk losing that. The source of the corruption was under the water stair, beneath the Leaf. Praise be to the Horned Lord, the water was clear and calm. He was big enough and strong enough for this, surely? Fencing with his friend Gray kept him fit and made him a competent enough swordsman for the stage. He could hold his own in a barroom brawl or a knife fight.

But swimming? He hadn't swum much since he'd left the place of his birth, New Norsca, on Concordia. On the other hand, he sang opera for a living. He could hold his breath longer than anyone he knew.

Barefoot in his trews, Erik padded across to the nearest garden and leaned over the wall. Gazing about, he noted the lush vertical lines of daffydillies and the graceful fronds of a widow's hair tree, bending at the exact angle to brush the dimpled surface of a small, irregularly shaped pond. A dense bank of delicate plants starred with small pink flowers tumbled over the edge and drifted across the water in a sprawl of lace.

Very pretty.

He shoved the bundle of his clothes and boots under the twisted roots of the widow's hair tree, behind the bright trumpets of the daffydillies. A middle-aged woman leaned out of a second-floor window and shook a cloth; Erik froze and her gaze passed right over him.

Without giving himself further time to think, he turned, walked rapidly down the water stairs and kept going, straight into the canal and the death mist in the air.

Warm and silky, the water caressed Erik's body, plastering

his trews against his skin. But as he stroked around behind the stairs, it grew darker and the swamp stink intensified to an almost unbearable level. When he stopped to tread water, a stealthy chill grabbed him by the ankles. Enough light penetrated to create a flickering world of broken reflections. Directly before him was a dark, ragged arch, three times taller than he.

Wonderingly, Erik swam closer, reaching out with curious fingertips. The surface was as tough as the bark of an ancient tree, striated and knobbed, pitted in some places with crevices so deep Florien could have squeezed right into them. And all of it was wet and shiny.

When he examined his palm, it dripped with an eerie green light. Phosphorescence.

With an exclamation of disgust, Erik wiped his hand on his trews.

This was stupid. Going in there, following that dark, noisome tunnel to the gods knew where . . . it was crazy. Lord's balls, this was the living flesh of the titanplant!

So what if he was the only one who smelled the rot? He'd go to the queen, to the proper authorities, and force them to believe him. They'd do it properly, bring torches.

Something soft and wispy brushed past his knee and Erik damn near swallowed his tongue. He thrashed in the water, peering down. When it didn't come again, he drew up his legs to extract the small knife he wore in a sheath against his calf.

Four feet away, a head broke the surface. A tubelike snout whiffled. "Hoot?"

The little animal disappeared in a neat swirl.

"Hoot?"

Erik spun around. Gods, there was another one behind him! Or perhaps it was the same one. He gripped the hilt of the knife.

Out of the corner of his eye, he caught sight of a sleek blue body barreling through the water at extraordinary speed. Breaking the surface, it soared straight over his head, brushing the underside of the stairs, before it dived neatly back into the water. In its wake trailed a formless melody of hoots expressed in a sweetly minor key.

Now there were six of them surrounding him, no, eight.

Possibly ten. Their heads bobbing, singing their strange, double-throated song. Occasionally, one would break formation to gambol across the water, as if with an excess of energy.

They looked just like the creatures on Prue's shawl, the one he'd used to—

Erik lowered the knife. "Seelies," he gasped. "You're seelies."

He could scarcely credit it, but it looked like the biggest one nodded. Its dark, bulging eyes stared into his for a heart-stopping moment. "Hoot!"

There was no time to fight, even to take a real breath. A wall of blue fur surged forward, jammed itself tightly around Erik's body and propelled him forward toward that hideous opening—at first slowly, then faster and faster, until the dark closed in all about him and the stench.

Erik struck out, his massive shoulders bunching, but he had the sensation that for every seelie he struck, another replaced it, then another and another, until he was submerged in blue fur, flying through the black water, the tunnel growing closer and closer until it brushed his hair and his thrashing feet.

His lungs squeezed with agony, just as they had when he'd nearly died of the lungspasm as a child. *Can't breathe, can't breathe.* His whole body became a litany of babbled prayers and demands. *Lady, Great Lady, don't kill me again. Not yet, not 'til I've finished whatever the hell this is.* His vision filled with spots, the blood thundering in his ears.

His head broke the surface and he whooped in grateful gulps of air. One seelie inserted itself under his left arm, holding him up, while a second pushed and pulled him toward a ledge, nudging and hooting the whole time.

"All right." Erik collapsed, his lower body still in the water. Stubby, clawed web-paws wouldn't leave him be. Urgently, they tugged, leaving scratches and bruises. "*All right!* Gods, if it had been anyone but me, they'd be drowned, you fools." He rolled over.

The eerie glow of phosphorescence showed the roof of the chamber some twenty feet above him, the walls made of that same barklike material. It was more a hollow than a room really, but huge, roughly circular, the water lapping dark as ink. Inside the Leaf of Nobility! Erik glanced upward. This echoing, stinking space was but a small irregularity to the titanplant, with its leaves hundreds of feet thick. He gave a tired grin. All those fine noblelords and ladies above, if only they knew! With a snort, he hauled himself onto the ledge.

Experimentally, he reached behind him and prodded the wall. His finger sank into the knuckle and one of the seelies gave a hoot of distress. A half dozen of them floated before him, their whiskers twitching with agitation.

Unconsciously, Erik lowered his voice to a melodious rumble. "There's something wrong, isn't there?"

The largest one answered, a continuous trill of notes, finishing on an amazingly complex chord. How did it do that?

"Is it what I can smell?" He touched his nose and made a pantomime of sniffing and coughing.

The chamber filled with loud, emphatic hoots. Dark water turned white with the thrashing of little bodies.

Erik tugged at his hair, needing the pain. No, he thought carefully, he wasn't mad, he was sitting in a hollow space inside a gigantic Leaf conversing with creatures out of legend. And he was probably going to drown at some stage of the proceedings.

His other life was locked away in a shining bubble, small and bright. Gone beyond his touch. Prue McGuire and her vivid aquamarine eyes. Himself standing center stage, looking out over the footlights, hearing that special hush, the one that meant you held all those hearts in the palm of your hand.

Gods, he loathed small places, too damned big to tolerate confinement. The weight of the entire fucking Leaf was leaning on the back of his neck, the wet-rot stench corroding his nasal passages, making his chest ache. Fuck, he *hated* this!

Get it done. Get it done right.

"You want me to see it?" he sang back, using the same tonal pattern.

The big seelie turned a complete somersault out of the water. "Hoot, hoot, *burble*!" it sang. Then it sped over to Erik's ledge and tugged at his foot.

"Wait, wait." Erik kicked it off. "We have to do this carefully. Do you understand, *carefully*? Or I'll drown."

"Hoot?"

The big seelie stared at him, doubt in every whisker twitch, its protuberant eyes extraordinarily expressive. If it hadn't possessed so much natural dignity, it would have looked cute. *I bet the Lady loves you,* thought Erik, not without envy.

Dripping, clad only in his trews, he hauled himself to his feet and gave the performance of his life.

This is how it has to be, he sang in the Voice, *this way. You see?*

With his mind, he formed pictures as clearly as he could. Himself breathing deep, sinking beneath the water, the seelies guiding, not pushing, letting him come up for air when he signaled. Then he sang it all to them, again and again.

By the end, the little creatures were caroling a hooty descant, virtually dancing on their tails in the water.

Despite himself, Erik laughed aloud.

The seelies froze, seemingly entranced.

Then the big one grabbed Erik's ankle and pulled him under. But when he jackknifed for the surface, it released him immediately. Erik trod water, expanding his massive chest, sucking in air until he felt giddy, fizzing with the gods' gift.

With a final inhalation, he dived for the bottom, accompanied by a retinue of seelies. A nudge on his shoulder and they had him headed into a different, shorter tunnel, back under the monstrous weight of the Leaf. His guts lurching with apprehension, Erik peered ahead. Pressure echoed in his ears, the world gone all silent and drifty. The seascape was patterned in degrees of shadow, no light, only gradations of gray and black. Traces of luminescence clung to what he could see now was a forest of stems, of weeds and vines.

And beyond . . . one of the gigantic stems of the titanplant itself.

A monstrous, dark shape, as big around as three palazzos together, bigger than the largest Technomage Tower he'd ever seen. In awe, he tracked the length of it as it fell away below, to disappear into the utter black of the deeps. Then back up again, to where it joined the underside of the Leaf of Nobility.

Sinuous silver shapes, some with gleaming teeth or long ropey tentacles, darted about on the periphery of his vision. As soon as the seelies approached, they faded gracefully away, but he had the sense of them, their endless, voracious patience.

His lungs beginning to burn, Erik pointed at the cable stem, and two seelies thrust themselves beneath his arms, accelerating until weeds battered at his face and shoulders with the force of their passage.

Close up, he could *see* the putrescence. Tentatively, he reached out, tumbling forward with a startled grunt when his arm sank into the soft mass as far as the shoulder. Particles of rotting flesh circled away on the slow currents, clinging to his hair, his shoulders, like evil, slimy snowflakes.

Gods, he was *inside* the guts of a giant corpse, like some small, filthy scavenger, watching it dissolve into a foul mush.

With a flurry of kicks, he backpedaled, his vision hazing with revulsion as much as with lack of air. Urgently, he gestured. *Go back, have to go back.*

Between them, Erik and the seelies got him back to the hollow chamber. For a long time, he lay sprawled on the ledge, his chest heaving. The moment he struggled to his elbows, the leader seelie tapped him on the ankle. "Hoot?" It looked over one blue-furred shoulder, in a different direction. "Burble?"

"Shit, not again?"

"*Hoot!*"

Wearily, Erik pumped himself full of air. But this time, it wasn't quite so bad. The seelies took him so deep, his ears began to ache, but then they brought him back up again, allowed him a snatched breath and hustled him across the canal, looking both ways, so like a set of blue-furred sneak thieves he had to smile.

He was so turned around, he couldn't work out which Leaf this was, but once underneath, it was clear enough what they wished him to see. A huge cable stem green with health, firm and resilient to the touch; the water clean and clear; sparkling shoals of fish and bright, floaty things with long, drifting skirts. Animals that looked like flowers. Flowers that looked like animals. So many species, he couldn't count them all.

When he finally lay sprawled and waterlogged across a set of unfamiliar water stairs, the sun on his face was such a benediction that tears sprang to his eyes. He bowed his head. *Thank you. My Lord and Lady. Just—thank you.*

"Hoot!"

Sitting up, he tried to shake the water out of his ears. "Yes," he said. "You did well. Relax, this is finally it, the task the gods set me. I'll find someone who can fix your problem."

The round blue faces didn't look convinced. Tube-snouts quivered as they gave voice. "Hoot, hoot, burble?"

From around the bend of the canal came a burst of laughter, the splash of oars. Two crafts came into view, more like barges, certainly too large to be properly called skiffs. "Hoot!" A series of swirls and ripples in the water and the seelies were gone.

Erik stood and stretched. Gods, every muscle in his body ached! The claw marks on his arms and shoulders stung like a bitch. Sourly, he glanced over his shoulder at the stairs he'd have to climb, the bridges he'd need to cross to get back to the Leaf of Nobility and his clothes.

When someone whistled, long and loud, he pushed the wet hair out of his eyes. Perhaps a lift? The words died on his lips.

13

"Well, well, if it's not a merman," laughed a man with a face like a dark, mischievous angel. He looked vaguely familiar. When he made a motion with his hand, the barge slowed, blue water rippling about its gilded sides. "The perfect appetizer for a sunset dinner cruise. Hop on board, my friend."

The grin widened as he looked Erik over, taking his time. His bold stare lingered over Erik's chest, the golden fur there glinting in the late afternoon sun. Then it swooped down to his big bare feet and lifted again, taking a lengthy stop midway. "My, my." Coolly, his brows rose. "There's plenty to go around."

Erik glanced down. Not only was he stripped to the waist, but his trews were so wet they were essentially transparent. Every contour, every pubic curl, every muscle, was revealed in a way more salacious than honest nudity. Gods, there was a limit to public performance!

A grinning crewman gathered up a rope while other well-dressed passengers crowded to the rail, and Erik remembered where he'd seen that handsome, wicked face. At The Garden. As if in confirmation, through the smattering of applause, the cheers and the catcalls, he heard a woman's distinctive throaty laugh. Rose!

With a growl of fury, he launched himself into the water in a long, flat dive, going deep, using the tremendous power of his lungs to stay under, all the way to the other side of the canal. When he finally surfaced, the barges were disappearing around the bend, laughter drifting behind them like confetti. He was only a few hundred yards from the small water stair on the Leaf of Nobility.

Shivering, he retrieved his belongings from behind the clump of daffydillies and dressed. He had an hour before the overture began at the Royal Theater.

Swearing, Erik broke into a jog trot, then a flat-out run.

It wasn't one of his most inspired performances, but he got through it and gave the people their money's worth. Pacing himself, he brought to bear all his technique and experience, saving the Voice for last. So the demon king's death brought the house down, as usual, but he had to revert to "The Milkmaid's Jugs" in his own perfectly adequate voice for the first encore. But even that turned out well, the audience clapping along to the risqué, jogging rhythm of the chorus.

By the time he came to the "Lullaby for Stormy Eyes," Erik felt sufficiently restored to impose his will on the air, to use his blessing to shape the aching beauty of the melody. As he sent the notes arching forth into the hush, in his mind's eye, he saw Prue's vivid, tip-tilted eyes, turbulent with emotion, none of it good. And all of it directed at him.

His whole body seething with impatience, Erik bowed and bowed. With a final wave, he sprinted offstage and down to his dressing room, ripping off his sweaty shirt as he went. Five minutes later, he was standing at the top of the theater's water stair, scanning for a skiff.

Florien materialized at his elbow in that uncanny way he had. "We goin' back t' t' boardin' house now?"

"You are." Where the hell—? There! Spying Bettsa's skiff bobbing about on the canal, Erik waved her over. "I'm not." He fished out a couple of oct-creds and saw the boy's face brighten.

Florien reached out a small paw, casting him a sidelong

look from under inky lashes. "Ye're goin' t' *her*, ain't ye? T' bossy one, at t' Garden?"

Well, hell. With coins in his pocket, the child would be off to the Melting Pot, no question. The gods alone knew what might happen to him there—or the damage he might do.

Erik frowned, thinking furiously. "None of your damned business."

He grabbed the boy's chin with hard fingers. Gods, he had no time to waste, not with this strange urgency blowing through him like the hot breath of a furnace, but the Voice wasn't the only way to compel, and he had to see the boy safe. "I will have your promise to take a skiff back to the boarding-house and go straight to bed. No . . . detours. Understood?"

"Yah," said Florien easily. Erik growled under his breath.

Moving swiftly, he left the boy standing and then spun around a few steps down, so their faces were level. "Do you know what a man's word is, Florien? What it means?"

"Mm."

"When you give your word, you carry through. You put your honor at stake."

Florien shrugged. "Fine."

Bloody hell! Breathing carefully through his nose, Erik said, "Think carefully, lad. If you shake my hand, I give you my trust in return for your promise. It's a precious gift." Despite himself, his lips twisted. "You may not want it. If you don't, it's your choice. I'll take another skiff and pay Bettsa here extra to march you into the boardinghouse by the collar and hand you over to the landlady." He held out his hand and waited.

Leaning on her pole, Bettsa gave a rough chuckle. "Pleasure."

Erik watched the child think it over. Abruptly, Florien drew a breath and whipped his right hand behind his back. The one with the crooked finger. His cheeks flushed a dull red and his flat, dark eyes glittered with what could have been rage or tears, or both. He shook his head, his fringe flopping.

Gods, he'd forgotten. Surely Gray had told him the child's mother had broken it? Or was it his father? Poor little bastard. "No problem. You've got two hands. Use the other one."

Florien searched Erik's face, the first time he'd held his gaze voluntarily for more than a few seconds. Something swam behind the flat, dark eyes. "Ye'd trust me t' do as ye say, just 'cos we shake hands?"

"Yes."

"Yer funeral then." With a jerk, the boy thrust out his left hand.

Gravely, Erik swallowed it up in his and administered a firm manly squeeze, gripping it left-handed to match. Then he clapped Florien on the shoulder, remembering at the last moment to pull the blow. Even so, the boy staggered a bit. "Fair enough." He dropped the coins into an eager little palm.

Bounding down the stairs, he stepped into the skiff, causing it to rock dangerously. Bettsa gave a hoarse chuckle. "In a hurry, are we?"

His blood bubbling, Erik grunted something unintelligible as she maneuvered them out into the current. Prue would try to throw him out, but he'd refuse to go.

Gods, he needed her, needed to hold her, bury his nose in her shining brown hair and hear that brisk, sensible voice break a little as she said his name. He exhaled, trying to contain his impatience. Because now it was about so much more than his own desires.

What would she say? Even now, with the bruises stiffening up, he could scarcely credit what he'd seen, but every time the wind veered, he could smell the reek of it in the air. Fuck, seelies and tunnels and chambers in the Leaf and rotten cable stems. He knew what he had to do, but Prue would know how to go about it, with her clever, practical mind.

He wanted to be inside her more than he wanted to breathe. Not that there was any chance of that.

The moment Bettsa grounded at The Garden's water stair, he was off, thrusting a whole cred into her hand. "Go back to the boardinghouse and check on the boy. Don't let him see you."

"I know boys. He'll do it." The skiffwoman shrugged. "But hell, it's your money." With a grunt, she shoved off.

The fat orange lanterns he recalled lined the path to the Main Pavilion. Light streamed out of the tall, arched windows on the ground floor, together with drifts of laughter, the tinkle of glasses. The double doors were open wide, and Erik strode through without breaking step.

Some sort of party, or soiree, was in progress, and he paused on the threshold of an elegant room decorated in cream and gold, and faced with mirrors. It took him a moment to separate the well-dressed reflections from their flesh and blood counterparts. He growled under his breath. Some of them had been on that godsbedamned pleasure barge. The center of a laughing crowd playing dice, Rosarina smiled as she caught his eye. Unobtrusively, she lifted her gaze toward the elaborate molded patterns on the ceiling. Long lashes swept down in an unmistakable wink.

Erik nodded his acknowledgment, spun on his heel and took the stairs two at a time. By the time he reached the landing, he was moving so fast, the paintings on the brocade-papered wall passed by in a lush blur of color.

Panting, he skidded to a halt outside a familiar door. "Prue!" he pounded with a big fist. "*Prue!*" His voice cracked with urgency.

☙

The hairbrush fell from Prue's fingers, bounced off the corner of the dressing table with a clatter and landed on the rug. She didn't hear it.

One moment the bottom had dropped out of her stomach, the next, she was flying to the door. Sweet Sister!

"What? What's wrong?" She wrenched it open. "Are you all—?"

Erik surged into the room like a storm front made of muscle and male need, gathering her up in the process. The door banged back with the wind of his passage, turbulent air swirling around the room.

"Prue," he muttered into her hair, his arms tight around her like bands of iron. "Oh gods, Prue."

She gasped as her feet left the floor, and then she had no breath for anything else because he backed her into the wall of her office, bent his head and sealed his mouth over hers, robbing her of breath.

"Wha—?" she panted into his mouth, her mind going blank with shock.

He had her pressed between his huge body and the wall, both equally unyielding, but for some foolish reason, she wasn't afraid. He left her no time to think—only to feel. Hot and glorious, fury filled her veins, tangling with the ferment of frustrated desire, setting her free. How dared he? Without compunction, she nipped his lower lip, licked away the bead of blood.

Erik only grunted, tilting his head to improve the fit. His tongue coiled around hers in a mind-numbing dance of lick and suck, push and pull. Prue gave as good as she got, refusing to yield, fighting back, her fingers twisted hard in his shirt.

She'd never met a man this way before, as if she knew him on some level of the soul, had never even imagined such a match between passions was possible, his physical desperation triggering hers until her conscious self exploded in a raging red blur of fiery need. The vicious power of it blew through her, a deep, vibrating chord sung by a choir of bass voices, all primeval and male. Gods, the thrilling sounds he made, deep in his throat, the delicious, solid weight of him crammed against her!

The Prue McGuire she knew went away, leaving only the quintessential female—flying, soaring high and free. She fumbled one hand into his hair, the way she'd longed to do from the first. Thick and soft, it feathered across her knuckles. Every sensation was magnified, from the warmth of his strong, hard skull against her palm to the cool silk of the tips brushing her knuckles.

When he slid a hand under her nightgown, over her knee, her thigh and onto her bare buttock, she used his strength as a support, wrapping her leg around him as if he were a tree.

Erik murmured and hitched her higher, his eager, burning length pressed against her. Ah, sweet Sister, it was good! She dug her fingers into his shoulders, her entire body a wet, empty space, yearning to be filled. A light breeze slid over her skin, caressing with fluttering, gossamer fingertips, driving her insane.

"Yes," he groaned, dusting searing kisses down her throat, nipping at her breast through the gown. "Fuck, yes!" Taking the golden flesh of his throat between her teeth, Prue worried at it, glorying in the strong arms that held her.

Erik pushed with his hips, sliding up, then back, and Prue cried out with the tingling pleasure of it. When he repeated the action, he hit her clitoris at the top of the stroke. Even through the nightgown, the intensity of the spasm had her choking back a scream. She buried her head in the curve between his neck and his shoulder.

"Gods, Prue." Words surged out of him. "*Let go and lie back.*" The order was a deep, commanding vibration filling her head, making her brain spin, the tone she found so difficult to resist.

His voice dropped even further, drowning out the struggling whisper of reason inside her. "*Trust yourself to me.*"

Prue spread her arms wide against the wall and gave herself up. She caught a glimpse of Erik's set face, his eyes burning like molten sapphires. Gods, he felt huge, mouthwateringly hard. When she tightened her legs about his hips, his cock leaped against her and she shivered with pleasure.

Erik froze.

The breeze died.

Prue cranked her eyes open. "What?" She wriggled, glorying in her power as a woman, the response he couldn't hide.

He didn't move. Sweat stood on his brow, the sexual flush fading from beneath his golden tan until his face was as white as her gown. He licked his lips. "I—I shouldn't."

Prue stared, numb with shock. She couldn't speak.

"Not this way." His whole body went rigid, as if he were dealing with excruciating pain. Very slowly, he stepped back, taking her weight, lowering her gently to the floor, pulling the gown down over her hips.

Then he turned his back, rearranging himself in his trews.

A creeping cold overtook her senses. "*Get out.*" The words came out of her mouth in a thin, strained whisper. She wanted the snug comfort of her bed, so she could wrap her arms about herself and weep under the covers like a child. Instead, she extended one hand behind her, resting her chilly fingertips against the wall. Because that was what Pruella Takimori McGuire did. Hold on to what was real. Go on living.

After an eon, he turned. "I can't," he said, "not yet. I can't explain what happened just then, Prue. But it's not you, it's me."

Why didn't she just hand him her beating heart on a plate? It would be so much simpler. He could dig his strong thumbs into the skin and peel it like a ripe manda fruit.

Prue bared her teeth. "Haven't we all heard that one before?" If she could have trusted her legs, she would have stalked to the door and flung it open.

"You're wearing the shawl." With a twisted smile, he nodded at the length of jade silk, still clinging to her shoulders.

Prue wrenched it off and flung it at his chest with all her strength. "There! Now you have everything that's yours. Go."

Erik's mouth worked as though he tasted something foul, but his fingers closed hard on the silk. "I have to talk to you."

"There's nothing to say." Prue gripped her hands together 'til her knuckles creaked.

Abruptly, he collapsed into her office chair. In the full blaze of the lamplight, his face looked drawn and tired, the strong bone structure exposed. He was going to be a very handsome old man, Erik Thorensen—if a woman didn't kill him before he reached his dotage.

Shaking out the shawl, he held it up between them like a shield. "I need to talk to you. About . . . the seelies."

"*Seelies?*"

He rested his head in his hands, pinched the bridge of his nose. "I've had an interesting afternoon, Prue. Swimming with seelies." He looked up, his blue gaze very direct. "I need your help."

Prue goggled. The last few minutes of madness had swept every thought from her head, but now, clear as a bell, she heard Rose's sensual chuckle. "Gods, sweetie, you should have seen him, standing there dripping wet. Only the Sister knows who put him through the wringer, but she's smiling through happy tears, believe me. If I could, I'd stand him on a pedestal in The Garden, stripped, and people would pay just to look." She'd gone on and on, damn her, describing every delicious swell of muscle, every long, graceful limb—especially the one between his thighs.

"You must be mad," Prue hissed. "Why would I help you do anything? Look at you!" She flung out an accusing finger. His shirt hung half off his shoulders—had she done that? Mercilessly exposed in the lamplight were deep reddish gouges on his shoulders, bruises, what could have been bite marks on the flat slabs of his pectorals. A gold chain winked cheerfully against the carnage.

"She must have been a wild one. I see why I got boring so fast."

He set his jaw. "It wasn't a woman. It was seelies."

"And I'm the Grand Pasha of Trinitaria." She gave him her back.

Fabric rustled. She didn't hear him move, but suddenly a wide chest filled her vision, sprinkled with a silky mat of red gold fur. "Take a good look, Prue. No human did this." He spun about so that her nose was an inch away from the strong knobs of his spine. Six parallel scratches ran down one shoulder blade, more desecrated the smooth, beautiful swell of his left bicep. They couldn't possibly be fingernail marks; they were too broad, too deep.

With a startled exclamation, Prue dragged his arm closer to the light. "This one's already infected," she said. "Serve you right if I left it to rot." Cursing herself for being soft and stupid, she scorched him with a glare. "Don't move."

Darting into her bedchamber, she rummaged in the dresser until she found the small vial of healall potion she'd bought from the healer in the Wizards' Enclave when Katrin began her martial arts lessons. Hopefully it was still potent.

"Tear a piece off your shirt," she said as she returned, bottle in hand.

"What's that?" Erik ripped a sleeve straight off the shirt and handed it over.

"Something to stop the infection." Prue slammed a pad soaked in the stuff onto the wound.

"Fuck!" Erik jerked, then froze. "It burns," he said through gritted teeth.

She'd thought she'd enjoy inflicting a little pain, a petty revenge for the body blow he'd dealt her. Instead, she had the same light-headed, trembly sensation she'd had the time Katrin sliced her palm open with Cook's favorite carving knife.

"Really?" she said, hoping her voice didn't shake. "That means it's working. Hold still."

Slowly, she circled his massive body, dabbing here and stroking there, feeling confused and even a little queasy as his jaw grew tighter and tighter and his great fists clenched.

She finished, standing directly in front of him, doctoring a shallow slice on his chest. "What's this?" She flicked the pale object dangling from the golden chain. It looked like a piece of old bone, pearlescent and twisted into a flowing curve.

"Nothing," he said curtly. "Nothing of importance to anyone but me."

Prue bit her lip. She gazed at the almost glowing thing as it rested against a tawny expanse of hard muscle.

Sister, he did have beautiful nipples, though she would never have thought she'd notice such a thing in a man. Disks as dark and smooth as the formal velvet worn at the Queen's Court, nestled in that tempting sprinkle of hair. With tightly ruched peaks that made her mouth water.

Godsdammit, she was pathetic!

Prue slapped the vial down on the desk. "You're done."

"No, I'm not. Don't you want to know what happened?"

"No," she lied.

14

"Prue." When long fingers cradled her jaw, she jerked her head away. Erik sighed. "I know you hate me right now, but I don't have anyone else to turn to. You have to hear me out."

Oh gods, no more, no more! She couldn't take it. "Did you think The Garden was unprotected?" she said. "I'll have you thrown in the canal. You can swim back to the theater."

"You could try." Cautiously, he flexed one arm, the muscles moving fluidly under the skin. He sent her a grim smile. "But the process will be loud and noisy. Not to mention embarrassing."

He took a restless turn or two around the room while she watched in baffled fury. After a moment's pause, he said in an entirely different tone, "I'm sorry, I know this sounds bad, but I'm starving. I haven't eaten since last night. Can I— Godsdammit, never mind."

Prue ignored the question. "Seelies?" she said. "That's a new one. You really must think me a fool."

Erik closed his eyes for an instant. His throat moved as he swallowed. "I'll show you tomorrow if you like, my word on it."

Her head whirling, Prue tugged the bell pull. The taste of her grief and humiliation was so vile, so strong, her stomach roiled with it. Ruthlessly, she forced it down. She'd survived those terrifying nights on the slum streets, she'd created a new life and nurtured it to bright young adulthood, she'd built a business. There were worse things than rejection by a man as worthless as he was talented.

Prue and Erik stared at each other in silence over the length of the room, her angry stare tangling with his steady blue one. She couldn't read the expression on his face; it was as hard as granite and just as impenetrable. But a pulse ticked in the base of his throat, and after a few minutes, he crossed to the window and leaned his forehead against the glass, gazing out into the double-shadowed garden.

When Tansy popped her head around the door, they were still standing in the same places.

"Mistress Prue?"

Godsdammit, why did it have to be Tansy? Prue bent a stern gaze on the little apprentice. "Ah, Tansy. Bring a meal, party leftovers is fine. And a fresh tisane with two cups."

Tansy's doe eyes went very wide as she took in Erik, looming silent and half naked by the window, Prue in her nightgown, her feet bare. But that was all—Rose's apprentices were well trained.

She bobbed a curtsey. "Yes, Mistress Prue."

"And Tansy?"

"Yes, Mistress?"

"This is my business and mine only. Understood?"

Another curtsey, another "Yes, Mistress." A final flickering glance at Erik's magnificent body and the girl trotted away down the passage.

Without a word, Prue went to her bedchamber and fetched a robe. She had two, but she passed over her shabby old friend in favor of a splendid, deep-sleeved creation of terracotta brocade, with lapels and frogging in a deep, glowing cream. It had been a natal day gift from Rose, whose taste never erred. Prue tied the sash with a warrior's resolve.

"In here." She marched into the sitting room, the skirts swishing imperiously behind her, and took the armchair near the empty fireplace. Erik followed slowly, sinking into the embrace of the sofa with a stifled sigh. He had the jade shawl bunched in one fist.

"All right," she said. "Talk."

He cleared his throat. "I hardly know where to begin."

Prue drummed her fingers on the arm of the chair. Sister, he looked weary! Worn to the bone.

"Do you know what a death swamp smells like?" he said eventually.

There was a knock on the outer door, a couple of brisk raps. "Come in, Tansy," called Prue, still attempting to comprehend the question.

Erik was facing the door and when his expression went completely blank, she shot out of the chair, her heart hammering with a dreadful premonition. A tall young woman stood on the threshold, a covered tray in her hands and a bundle tucked under one arm.

"So you're Erik," said Katrin. "I thought it was time we met."

⌒⌒⌒

Erik's chest ached—inside and out. If he hadn't been so ravenous, he would have stretched out full length on the floor and sought the welcome oblivion of sleep.

"Yes," he said, rising to take the tray and place it on a low table. The Voice had come out of fucking nowhere, completely beyond his control. Prue had done it to him—*again*. "I've been wanting to meet you too." The shock of hearing the command echo around the room, of realizing how he'd failed, had destroyed his erection more effectively than an iced bath.

"But Katrin, what—?"

"Don't blame Tansy, Mam." Katrin bent to peck her mother on the cheek. "I was in the kitchen finishing up a cake and I didn't give her a chance."

The girl was at least six inches taller than Prue, still coltish in a way he was certain Prue had never been. As a mature woman, Katrin would be calm and queenly rather than sparkling with life and energy like her mother. But with their heads together, he could see the resemblance between them—those exotic almond eyes, the stubborn shape of the chin. Her hair down in a wavy, glorious profusion, Prue didn't look much older, but he knew she wouldn't believe him if he told her.

She was still pale and shaky. Gods, he was a bastard. He might as well have taken his big fist and rammed it into her stomach.

Katrin ran a considering gaze over his torso, lingering on the scratches and abrasions, but all she said was, "Catch," as she tossed the bundle in his direction. It turned out to be a cotton bathrobe, large enough to fit even him.

Prue was fairly vibrating with agitation, Katrin as calm as milk. But the girl's gaze was narrow with the unflinching judgment of the young. Erik was glad to shrug into the robe.

But when she removed the cover from the tray, he could have kissed her. "You did this?" he asked, surveying the platter of bread and meat and cheese, the pastries and fruit. There was a jug of wine and two cups. His belly growled so loud the girl grinned.

"I like to feed people," she said, watching him lean forward to grab a plate and load it up.

"Katrin's our pastry chef," said Prue. *Not a courtesan*, her level stare conveyed.

Erik nodded, his mouth full.

"Sister save us, when did you last eat?" asked Katrin, fascinated.

He chewed and swallowed, busied himself preparing another slab of bread and cheese. "Last night." He darted a glance at Prue. "With you."

"But why?" A pause. "And what happened to you?" Katrin's cheeks pinkened. "Especially your, um, chest?"

But before he could reply, Prue patted her daughter on the hand. "Thanks, love. Better go now."

"Yes," snarled Erik. "I might sully her ears."

"In that case, I'm sure I should stay." With complete composure, Katrin sank to the rug and leaned back against her mother's knee. Prue's objections sailed over her head. Literally.

Two pairs of tip-tilted eyes gazed at him expectantly, one set wide and blue, the other bright with suspicion and blue green as a wave shot with summer sun.

He cleared his throat and began. "There's a place on Concordia called Morte Swamp. Centuries ago, there was a dreadful battle there. Thousands were slain, some by cold steel, others dragged down by the weight of their armor and the evil of the bog. It stinks," he said baldly. "Even now. Worse than anything you can imagine."

"But what has—?" Katrin's brow wrinkled.

"Sshh." Prue laid a hand on the girl's bright hair.

"I haven't been there since I was a lad, the night I ran—" He broke off. "Last night, as the tide turned, I smelled it again. This afternoon, the seelies showed me the source of the stench."

"*Seelies*?" Katrin gaped, then she giggled. "Have you been drinking?"

"Begin at the beginning," said Prue. "And don't leave anything out."

By the time they'd finished with him, he felt as if they'd turned his skull inside out and scoured it clean, but only crumbs remained on the supper tray.

Prue rose to pace, her movements jerky. "No one in their right mind would make up a story like that." She cast him a narrow, sidelong glance. "Maybe.

"Why are you the only one?" she went on. "To smell the . . . smell. Especially if it's so bad."

"I don't know." He met her skeptical gaze. "I nearly died of the lungspasm as a lad. I've been incredibly sensitive to air-borne odors ever since. Drives me crazy sometimes."

"Hmm." She didn't sound convinced.

Katrin's eyes shone with excitement. "What are we going to do, Mam?"

Prue came to a halt. "I don't believe what I can't see. Prove it to me." She challenged him with her level blue green stare.

"In the morning," he said. "First thing, I swear. And when I do, Mistress McGuire? What then?"

"This is the business of the Queen's City," she said with decision. "He'll know what to do, how to fix it." Her voice rose. "He's a client of ours. I can contact his office and arrange an appointment."

With a sigh, Erik rose and planted himself in front of her. "For tomorrow?"

Prue stepped neatly around him. "Don't be ridiculous. More like a month, a fortnight if we're lucky."

"Prue." Erik snagged her elbow and she froze, glaring. "I don't have that sort of time, neither does Caracole." Slowly, he released her. "Tell me, in the old stories, what did the seelies do?"

"Do? What do you mean, *do*?"

"Mam, don't you remember? You used to read me *The Spotless Seelie.*" Katrin smiled across the room at her mother. "And that other one, about the seelie who lost his polishing cloth. He asked everyone in the sea if they'd seen it, and it turned out the leviathan was using it to mop up her tears because she was so sad and lonely. And they became lifelong friends. Remember?"

Prue's tender smile illuminated her face in a way he hadn't seen before. Suddenly, Erik was acutely conscious of standing alone in his skin, his abrasions singing an unlovely chorus. "Explain," he growled.

"Seelies are supposed to keep everything in the sea nice and clean," said Katrin. "Like little blue gardeners, I guess, weeding and pruning and taking the rubbish away."

"Well, they aren't, are they? Not under the Leaf of Nobility, at any rate." All the small hairs rose on the back of Erik's neck. "It's dying," he said slowly. "The whole Leaf is dying from underneath, that's what they were trying to tell me."

"Assuming you're in your right mind—" Prue stopped and started again, horror dawning in her face. "There are over seventy palazzos on that Leaf."

"How many people?"

"Gods, hundreds." Helplessly, she shrugged. "Maybe a couple of thousand in round figures. I don't know. Those places need a lot of staff."

"What if it's spread to other Leaves?"

Now she blanched. Katrin came to stand beside her, and they stood, hand in hand. Prue wet her lips. "Disaster," she whispered. "A hundred thousand people live in Caracole. Sister save us."

"Right." Erik ran a hand through his hair. He'd do what he had to, he thought grimly, because this had to be the destiny for which the gods had saved his life. Even the divinities would agree the ends justified the means, as they had in the theater on Green IV. He hadn't been shamed by his actions then, he'd been proud and grateful.

"Let's try someone else. What about the Queen's Entertainment? All I need is a few minutes alone with him and he'll get me a private audience with Sikara." He paused. "I guarantee it."

"You'll have to fight your way through the crowd in his

antechamber first," said Prue dryly. "Everyone wants to perform at Court."

"Brother and Sister preserve us." Katrin made the two-handed sign of the Sibling Moons. "What are we to do?"

Prue stared at her daughter. "The moons," she whispered. "The *moons!*" Running to the window, she threw it open and lunged forward. Automatically, Erik reached out a long arm and grabbed a fistful of the back of her gown, acutely conscious of the rounded rise of her sweet bottom.

As suddenly as she'd flung herself forward, Prue retreated and whirled around, her small hand clamped onto his forearm. "The Open Cabal! That's it!" She was practically jigging with excitement.

Nonplussed, Erik glanced at Katrin, but Prue reached up and wrenched his jaw around, capturing his undivided attention. "The day after Sibling Full Moons, the Queen's Cabal sits in open session. Any citizen may speak before them. See?"

The sense of relief was so heady he had to touch her cheek. "Clever, *clever* Prue." Because he couldn't resist the triumph shining in her vivid little face, he picked her up and swung her around, a sweet night breeze dancing all about them like a giddy child. He was sure he heard her chuckle, a deep, delicious sound. The dimple quivered.

On the next breath, she went rigid in his arms. In complete silence, he lowered her to her feet and stepped back.

Clearing his throat, he said, "I'm not a citizen of Caracole."

"I know," she said, "but I am."

"You'll come with me?"

Once again she studied him, her expression unreadable. "Show me a seelie and I'll vouch for you."

"Done. As soon as it's light tomorrow." Erik held out his hand and after a short, stinging pause, Prue placed hers in it. But when he drew it to his lips, she wrenched herself free.

"No," she grated. "Don't."

Crockery clinked as Katrin hefted the tray. "Would you hold the door for me, please, Erik?"

"Of course."

As he strode into the office toward the outer door, their voices dropped to a low feminine murmur behind him.

The farewells made, Katrin walked past him into the

passageway. Then she gestured with her chin. "Out here. And shut the door."

Erik did as she asked, bracing himself.

"Rose likes you," she said abruptly.

"Good." Erik raised a brow. "And you?"

"I saw Mam's face just then." She was a little pink, still young enough to be uncomfortable with the rudeness of plain speaking. But she wasn't her mother's daughter for nothing. She stiffened her spine. "What have you done to her?"

Godsdammit, he couldn't prevent the betraying flush either.

Immediately, Katrin went bright scarlet. "Actually, I'd rather not know." Her nose wrinkled. "Gods!"

Stepping forward, she shoved the edge of the tray into his stomach, not gently. "Rose says you're strong enough to hold your own. Mam's awfully bossy, you know."

He had to smile. "So I've discovered."

"Yes, but it's all on the surface." The girl's intensity was palpable. "Underneath, she's . . ." The blue eyes filled with tears. She dragged in a hasty breath and took the plunge. "Do you love her?"

The spiky feeling in his guts had told him that one was coming. "What? Katrin, how could I possibly know that so soon?" He thought he managed it creditably enough, but in the back of his mind, he heard the Lady's huge dark laughter.

"Keep your voice down!" She glanced at the door. "That's how it was with me and Arkady. One look and—*boom*!"

"Arkady? Who's—?"

"Never mind," said Katrin fiercely. "I have to go. Don't hurt her, that's all. Please don't hurt her."

"I'll do my best not to, I swear." But he was speaking to the girl's back as she hurried toward the stairs.

When he went inside, Prue was standing in the middle of the office, her arms folded. "What was all that about?"

"You. How old were you when she was born?"

"Eighteen. And you have no right to discuss me with my daughter." Turning, she walked toward the bedchamber, hips swaying enticingly beneath the gown. Was she doing it on purpose? "Be here early tomorrow. You have a seelie to show me."

Erik glanced out the window at the moons high in the sky. "That's only a few hours. Not worth going back to the boardinghouse." He fiddled with the tie of the borrowed robe. "It's been a hell of a day. I'd like to stay."

Prue lost a little of her high color. "I don't want you anywhere near me," she said through her teeth.

"I know that. There's a lock on the door to your bedchamber, isn't there?" When she gave a curt nod, he said, "Use it."

Her chin went up. "Why should I?"

"So we can go seelie hunting at dawn?" He let out a gusty breath. "Prue, I'm so bloody tired, I'll sleep on the stairs if I have to, but I'd prefer the couch."

Twice now he'd compelled Prue without intending it— *twice*. He felt hollow inside, scraped raw by an appalling realization. Once he might pass off as an inexplicable lapse, bad luck, a moment of madness, but not twice. Something about Prue simply pulled the Voice out of him. It flowed forth, borne on the tide of his desire. The Horned Lord knew what he might command her to do the next time he kissed her, when he finally got her beneath him.

The fact remained he could no longer trust the discipline that had served him all his adult life. Shit, the Dark Lady had him exquisitely trapped. With Prue, he'd gone way beyond anything as pale as *like* or *respect*, into a realm of ironclad purpose and possessiveness. By all the gods, he was going to have her! But as himself, and himself alone. Walking a tightrope made of razor wire would be simple in comparison, but otherwise, he'd never know if she truly consented.

In the process he'd do his best to heal the wounds he'd inflicted. Erik met a murderous glare that informed him in no uncertain terms how much ground he'd lost and how badly he'd hurt her. His gutsy Prue.

He watched her watching his grip on the open front of the robe.

"I've already said what I had to about . . . what happened. I'm not going to make it worse." He steadied himself. "I know I'm a bastard, but I swear it wasn't what it seemed. I swear. I don't expect you to forgive me. Just don't . . . shut me out of your life. Please? Give me a chance?"

Prue shook her head. She walked straight into her bedchamber and closed the door firmly behind her.

Erik pressed his fingertips to the wood, then his forehead.

"Divine retribution, that's what you are," he said. "The challenge I still can't resist. Gods, I'm a fucking fool!" But he didn't speak above a whisper.

Wearily, he kicked off his boots and curled up on the couch, trying in vain to accommodate his length. After an hour of tossing and turning and cursing, he rearranged himself on the floor, a couple of cushions under his head. Just before the dark tide of sleep washed over him, he reached out for the jade shawl. Bunching it in his fist, he held it to his nose and inhaled. Reminiscent of the warmth of her body, the fresh smell of the soap she used. Gods, that was better!

He slept.

∽

She must be mad.

"Your shoes, Prue," said Erik patiently, setting aside the towels. "Take them off."

They sat side by side at the top of The Garden's water stairs, alone in the early morning hush. Behind them, flowers tilted their pretty heads to the rising sun, emitting drifts of perfume, sweet or spicy, according to species. Before them, the water flashed and sparkled, so brilliant in the new light that it hurt the eyes. In the pavilions, the human occupants of The Garden slept the sleep of the well satisfied.

Erik bent and slipped off one of Prue's slippers. He rubbed her foot in his big warm hands, and it felt so good, she let him continue for a few moments before she came to her senses and jerked away. Her heart was beating its way up into her throat, choking her. How, in the Sister's name, had sensible Prue ended up here—going seelie hunting with a singer? It was insane.

"Can you swim?" he asked.

"Yes." She cleared her throat. "Well, I'm competent, I suppose."

His lips twitched. "I expect no less of you, Mistress McGuire." He slid an arm around her waist, hugging her into his body.

Prue shivered, so preoccupied with what was to come she absorbed his warmth without thinking. "It's going to be chilly in there."

"I know, but we need to do this now, before anyone's up to

ask questions." He turned his head to gaze into her eyes, and she got lost for a minute in his serious smile. "Ready?" The stubble on his firm jaw glinted red gold in the sun.

All he wore were his trews, muscles sliding fluidly under the smooth planes of his upper body. And the strange talisman around his neck on a golden chain. The bruises were flowering nicely. Why she should find the cup of his navel, surrounded by hard muscle and a swirl of silky hair, so irresistible, she had no idea. It was infuriating, and more than a little unnerving. Perhaps it was because she'd woken in the night and tiptoed to the door of the sitting room, drawn by the low rumble of his even breath. The light of the full moons pouring in through the window spotlit his massive form as if he were on a stage. He'd been stretched out on the floor, the contours of his long body like the rough undulations of a mountain range. One hand had been splayed over the jade shawl lying next to him, every fingertip in contact with the fabric.

It took her back to Katrin's baby days and the blanket she'd adored.

Ah, now she was getting maudlin!

Rising, she left him, marching down the steps to where the water splashed and gurgled. "Let's do it then."

15

"That's my Prue." Her spine prickled with the heat of his grin.

Before she could retort, he'd launched himself past her into the water in a long, flat dive. Surfacing with a strangled yell, he pushed the hair out of his eyes and stroked back to the stairs, his face alight with excitement, the strength of his features only emphasized by his water-darkened hair. He still looked brutally tired. Prue's heart lurched. Not only maudlin, but a fool in the bargain.

She didn't want to think anymore. She was as ready as she'd ever be—wearing her oldest nightgown because he'd warned her it might be messy under there, her hair braided and tied back out of the way. *Sister save me, I've lost my mind.* Prue sucked in a breath and leaped.

The cold struck her like a fist in the chest, but as she trod water, watching Erik cast about under the stairs, her blood began to pump, her skin to tingle.

He reappeared at her side with a couple of easy strokes. "It's behind," he said. "Just like the other one."

"All right," she said breathlessly, sculling around the base of the stairs, acutely aware of eyes as blue as the water, watching her every move.

At last he said, "You're a bit more than competent, Prue." Something warm bloomed in her chest.

Beneath the stairs, water lapped at the tough outer skin of the Pleasure Leaf. Wonderingly, Prue touched it, solid as a building. She couldn't make a mark on it, not with all her strength.

Erik slid his arms around her from behind, giving her the shelter and support of his body. She wasn't fool enough to reject it. Their legs brushed under the water, her nightgown billowing. He inhaled deeply, expanding his chest "There's nothing wrong here, thank the Lord and Lady. No stink, no rot."

"The seelies?" She peered around.

"Through there." He pointed to an opening about ten feet in diameter in the Leaf. "With any luck."

Prue's mouth fell open. "You mean we—? Gods!"

"If it's like the Leaf of Nobility, that passage leads down to all kinds of hollow chambers, inside the Leaf itself. I'll go through and check first. Then I'll come back for you."

"But—"

"Shush," he said sternly. "I can hold my breath much longer than you can. You wait here, understood?"

Prue clutched his shoulders, the density of bone and muscle chilled and hard under her fingers. He was so big and strong, so vital, he seemed indestructible. But he wasn't, no man was. "You'll be careful?"

"Of course." He gave her a crooked grin. "Especially seeing you still care." With both hands he grasped her head, pulled her forward and kissed her deep and hard, his lips cool, but his tongue hot and deft. She was still gasping with outrage when he released her, jackknifed into the water and disappeared down the tunnel. Her final view of him was the flex of powerful buttocks and the pale flutter of the soles of his feet, kicking.

As the seconds ticked past, the cold rose out of the depths, climbing up her legs, caressing her belly, her breasts with slow, deadening fingers. Prue clung to the walls of the Leaf, her nightgown tangling around her legs like a shroud. First, she counted the seconds in her head, then out loud, her hoarse whisper no more than a thread among the lapping of the wavelets.

She reached a hundred three times before she broke. Merciful Sister, he had to be dead, trapped in some small, horrible space, those beautiful eyes gone wide and dull, his lax limbs bumping against the walls of the tunnel as the current rolled—

He burst out of the dark opening like a Technomage starship barreling toward the heavens on a plume of flame. Then he had the nerve to laugh out loud, a sound of sheer joy that echoed around the shadowed space.

Prue thumped him hard on the chest with her fist. "I thought you'd drowned!"

"Don't be silly." Erik dropped a kiss on her nose, then drew her close before she could gather her wits sufficiently to hit him. "This tunnel's quite short. Hold on to me and you'll be fine."

Prue searched his face, the moving shadows flickering over his features. She could do this, of course she could. He'd keep her safe. "Give me a minute."

Closing her eyes, she breathed deep, filling her lungs, calming her racing heart. Gradually, she became aware of Erik's hands soothing up and down her spine in a hypnotic rhythm, his muscled chest, pressed against the softness of her breasts, vibrating with a deep, wordless croon. She suspected this was how he might communicate with nervous horses and small children, but if truth be told, she didn't care, the comfort was too great.

With an effort, she raised her head. "Ready."

"On a count of three then. Hang on tight, and let me do the work. It's not far, Prue, I promise, but you mustn't panic."

"I don't panic." She glared.

"I knew that." Another smile, a brief kiss pressed to her lips. "Here we go. One . . . two . . . *three!*" His arms banded around her.

Together, they sank through the shadowed water and entered the tunnel. The light vanished, and Prue clenched her teeth so hard her jaw ached. In the darkness, Erik was her only reference point, and she burrowed into his warmth and strength, feeling the flex and release of his mighty muscles, his legs moving against hers as she added her kicks to his. She had the sense of an immense weight pressing down on her, her body brushing against a smooth, unyielding surface.

Just as her lungs were beginning to labor, they broke through into open space.

Whooping for breath, she clung to Erik's shoulders. His palm cupped the back of her skull. "All right?"

When she nodded, he loosened the arm he had around her waist. "Look, Prue," he whispered, awe coloring his voice. "Look!"

Secure in his hold, she leaned back, staring. Her jaw sagged. The world was made of a shifting twilight, illuminated by flashes of the most shockingly vivid yellows, blues and greens, as if the sea gods had decided to manifest their essence as captive light. The chamber was no more than thirty feet across, roughly oval, its sides curving in a pattern that was too organic to be completely regular. Every now and then, there were other dark openings, ledges and indentations.

"Oh," she breathed. "*Oh*. What's that? The colors?"

"Healthy phosphorescence." Erik's voice was hushed. "I think the titanplant produces it."

Prue slid out of his grasp and stroked toward the nearest wall. Skeins of opalescent color shimmered in the flesh of the titanplant. When she reached out in wonder, it coated her fingertips, sliding down over her hand and wrist in a wash of glowing, vibrant beauty. There was no physical sensation, as if she truly bathed in light. Her eyes prickled with tears.

She met Erik's gaze across the water, his eyes dark. "You look like a goddess, Prue," he said softly.

"Don't be stupid." She shook her head. "Anyway, I don't believe in the gods. They've never done much for me."

The air tasted warm and moist and briny, pressing against her, making her acutely aware of the life pulsing beneath her skin, the wet nightdress molded to her body. But she was no longer cold.

Prue swallowed. "Seelies?" The word came out in a husky whisper.

"I'll have to call them." He glanced around the chamber. "C'mon. Over here." Taking her hand, he drew her along the wall toward an indentation that formed a spacious ledge about three feet deep and quite a bit longer. "Up." Without warning, he set his big hands to her waist and boosted her forward onto the ledge. When she teetered, he chuckled and spread his palms over both cheeks of her bottom for the final shove.

Ignoring the murder in her glance, he hoisted himself up beside her with easy strength. Water streamed off his head and shoulders, making him look darker, sleeker, but no less powerful. As he moved to lean against the back wall of the ledge, the charm around his neck glowed pale amid the wavering shadows.

All the fine hairs on the back of Prue's neck stood up. What was it Purist Bartelm had told her? *You have a natural resistance to Magick, Mistress.* She'd always been so practical, so grounded in reality, in the cold, hard beauty of numbers. The old wizard had been right, she didn't really believe in Magick, though she knew on an intellectual level it must exist. Any time Katrin had been sick as a child, she hadn't hesitated to send for the healers from the Wizards' Enclave, but that was only because she wasn't quite poor enough for a visit to the charity clinic in the Technomage Tower. Whether it was the herbs or the Magick or the resilience of youth, the child had always recovered. Prue frowned, remembering. Now that she came to think of it, the healers invariably asked her to move to the other side of the room. One man, less tactful than the others, had said outright her presence interfered with his concentration.

The melody began deep in Erik's chest, so soft and blurred it was scarcely there. His gaze still fixed on the water, he reached out and drew her into the shelter of his arm. Hot chills danced up and down her spine. Slowly, it grew and grew, a song without words, but clear and pure, each rich, arching note shaping the warm, salty air into something of ineffable beauty. The phosphorescent lights glowed and pulsed like a living rainbow.

Prue resisted the urge to settle her head against Erik's shoulder. *Come to me.* The call echoed back and forth off the walls of the chamber, an irresistible summons. *Come, come.* But that wasn't all it was. There was the promise of comfort threaded through it, of love and laughter, a sense of coming home.

Safe harbor forever.

He was warm, so very warm, and he was stroking her arm,

again and again, the lightest absentminded brush with his fingertips.

The tears welled up and spilled over. It might be Magick and it might not, but she knew she'd never have this again—this moment of crystalline, perfect beauty. A single gift to last her entire lifetime. Prue drew gradually closer until every inch of her side was in contact with some part of him. She pressed her open palm over his heart, feeling the steady beat of his life, his broad chest rising and falling with the formless melody.

When she inhaled, she seemed to taste the salt on his skin.

The song swelled, the echoes joining in, until her head was ringing with it, the vibrations thrumming in her very bones.

"Hoot!"

Erik lifted Prue's hand from his chest and kissed the palm. Then he squeezed it gently, once, twice. When she looked up, blinking, he smiled, still singing, and nodded toward the water.

"Hoot!"

Prue's head whipped around.

Something cut through the water, moving sinuously in and out of the glimmering shadows. Two somethings.

Her heart trying to beat its way out from behind her ribs, Prue reared up, peering.

A round blue face popped out of the water, almost under her nose.

At her stifled shriek, it disappeared just as promptly, leaving only a glittering swirl behind.

Erik chuckled, but almost immediately, he resumed the song, this time with words. "*She won't hurt you. See how pretty she is, pretty, pretty Prue.*"

Gods, how silly did he think she—

Cautiously, a tubelike snout broke the water. The seelie sculled about on its back, watching her out of huge dark eyes. It was smaller than she'd expected, about the size of a medium dog.

Prue froze, her eyes wide with wonder. A myth, a story for children, there in the blue-furred flesh.

"Burble, hoot, hoot, burble," it sang, and she realized what the echoes had been.

She glanced at Erik and stopped, transfixed. His posture, his face, everything about him spoke of pure joy, not something as weak as mere happiness, but fulfillment of the soul. He looked as if some god had lit a candle inside him. Here, under the Pleasure Leaf, with the seelies—with *her*, Prue McGuire—he was fully present in a way she hadn't seen before.

Her foolish heart squeezed with longing.

On the other side of the chamber, a second seelie arched out of the water in an exuberant leap.

Erik switched the beat to something irresistibly toe-tapping, and the seelies began to dance—there was no other word for it—just the two of them, an exhilarating pas de deux of twists and rolls and near misses in the air that had her gasping. Prue laughed aloud, clapping her hands, fizzing with delight.

It finished too soon, the seelies slowing the pace and Erik subsiding to a hum and then a murmur, and finally, silence.

Wavelets gurgled and lapped against the walls of the chamber.

The seelies bobbed in the water, an arm's length from the ledge. "Thank you," said Prue in a shaky whisper. "Oh, thank you."

Two sets of protuberant eyes regarded her unblinking. She could have sworn they looked . . . anxious.

"Hoot?"

"I gave my word," said Erik. "I'll do it. And she'll help."

"Oh yes." Prue leaned forward. "I promise too."

"Burble! Hoot!"

And they were gone.

Erik and Prue stared at each other in silence. Eventually, he reached out to wipe the moisture from her cheek with a gentle thumb. "Shall we go back?"

She shook her head. "I need . . . a little time."

Erik settled more comfortably against the wall behind them and held out a hand. He didn't speak.

Never again, she'd never have this again. Reality was waiting, with all its familiar, depressing problems—her own inadequacies as a woman, shown so clearly by the way he'd turned away from her last night. And on top of it all, the Open Cabal yet to face. No one would believe them.

She knew it was weak, cowardly even, but she refused to think of it, to end this precious time out of time, caught like a teardrop trembling on the lashes. *Merciful Sister, just a few more moments.*

Prue placed her hand in Erik's and crept closer. When she nestled into his shoulder, he sighed and turned to rest his cheek on the top of her head.

She wasn't sure how long they lay there. It felt like a dream of peace, so drifty and disconnected she couldn't tell whether she'd actually dozed off. Imperceptibly, the gentle touch caressing her skin became an integral part of the languid, floating sensation. Feather light, his fingertips traced the outline of her shoulder blade beneath damp fabric, explored the hard, delicate shape of her spine, traveled to the nape of her neck and soothed.

Prue sighed with pleasure. A minute hesitation and Erik shifted his attentions to her throat, the shell of her ear. When he smoothed her hair back, she lifted her face toward the caress like a child.

But she didn't open her eyes because something inside her was unraveling and he mustn't see.

A tender fingertip wandered over her eyebrow. "Prue." The word was so soft, it was more a vibration in his chest than an actual sound. "Please don't cry."

She made a negative sound. *I'm not.*

Warm lips brushed one eyelid, then the other. "I'm sorry," he said. "So very sorry."

Prue screwed her eyes shut tighter. "Don't . . ." But what she really meant was, *Don't make this real, don't spoil my beautiful dream.*

"Sshh." The kisses were light as air, there only as fleeting, tingling sensations—on her dimpled cheek, her jaw, her nose, her closed eyes. That warm mouth touched hers, nuzzling to and fro. Delicately, he brushed his tongue over the cushion of her lower lip, making her quiver.

She didn't open her eyes, not even when he shifted her gently in his arms and dusted kisses down her throat, lingering over her thundering pulse. All she wanted was to pretend in the dark behind her eyelids, to willfully believe in his tenderness, to imagine he really loved her. When he brushed the swelling undercurve of her breast with his knuckles, she drew a deep breath, her nipples tightening in shameless response. When he sealed his mouth over one, she arched and a low moan escaped her. Sweet Sister, so hot and strong and gentle, all at once, the stubble on his cheek a delicious rasp through the fine fabric.

"Aren't you even going to look at me?" Deft fingers loosened on her laces, exposing her quivering breasts to the salty twilight atmosphere of the chamber. An instant's silence while she listened to his rough breath. "Gods. Gorgeous." Currents of heated air swirled around her, fondling her breasts, licking at her nipples. Without looking, she knew they were standing long and proud, begging for his attention.

Prue threw one arm over her eyes. *It's only a dream, a dream of what love can be. A memory you can keep forever.*

"If you want me to stop, sweetheart, you have to say so." She heard his breath whistle between clenched teeth. "Now." Everywhere his flesh touched hers she could feel what his control was costing him, his flesh unyielding, like a big piece of sun-warmed timber.

Don't wake, don't open your eyes and spoil it. It's a *dream, a beautiful dream.* Hair like damp silk whispered across her sternum and broad palms stroked over her ribs to frame her aching breasts. Erik's assault was exquisitely gentle—she would never have thought such a big man capable of so light a touch—but inexorably thorough. He didn't miss an inch of skin, not with fingers, lips or that hot, clever tongue.

It wasn't until he was nibbling around her navel, while his thumbs flicked back and forth over her tormented nipples, that it dawned on her he'd pushed the nightgown right up to her waist. Returned abruptly to reality, she opened her mouth, but whatever she'd been about to say strangled in her throat as he shifted and all the air whooshed out of her in a gust.

16

In a single smooth movement, Erik slid down between her legs. With a faint splash, he slipped into the water up to his waist. His long fingers gripped her buttocks, lifting her to his mouth as if she were a ripe fruit. He was humming, a wordless croon that had no real melody but was redolent of masculine purpose. Possession.

The floaty, trancelike state disappeared, grounded abruptly in the physical here and now. The echoes of Prue's scream overlapped, bouncing off the walls of the chamber and gradually fading away to soft, frantic sobs.

He didn't gobble, he was precise, almost finicky, as though he was restraining himself, holding back. His breath vibrated against her excruciatingly sensitive flesh as his tongue flicked back and forth across her clitoris with pinpoint accuracy, driving her crazy.

She'd had a lover do this before, but only one, and although he'd certainly appeared to enjoy it, Prue had been too embarrassed to relax, and climax had eluded her. In the end, she'd pretended rather than disappoint him.

Now though, she was too wild, too frenzied, for anything that coherent. Gods, she had no idea! If she'd been able to think, she would have been amazed at the range of demanding noises that came out of her mouth, the pleas, the whimpers. The salty breeze that swirled around the chamber seemed no more than an expression of her need. Her eyes flew open. Fumbling, she sank the fingers of one hand into his hair.

"Ow." Then he chuckled, a low wicked sound that screwed the tension up another unbearable notch. "Gods, you taste divine." He licked his lips.

When her hips surged in instinctive response, he grinned. Even in the shadows of the chamber, she could see the feverish glitter of his eyes, the high spots of color on his cheekbones. "All sweet and salty. And in here"—he slid a gentle finger inside, massaging the clinging walls of her sheath—"you're absolutely fucking perfect, so hot and wet." A second finger joined the first, and he purred with approval when she ground down against them, her head thrashing. "All mine. Mine to pleasure, mine to fuck."

Slowly, he rotated his wrist, finding a sweet spot deep inside she hadn't known she had. This time, when he sealed his lips over her dripping folds, his intent was clear. The flat of his tongue rubbed over her clitoris, again and again, strong measured sweeps, pushing her up and up, building a coil of tension that tightened inexorably deep in her pelvis.

Drumming her heels on his back—how had her legs got there?—she tried to speak, but she'd forgotten how. Finally, she gasped, "P-please. Make me—" He wrapped his tongue around the throbbing bundle of nerves that was her clit and gave it a tweak. Prue had no breath left to shriek. She bucked under his hands.

"Ah, you beg so beautifully," he murmured, pushing those diabolical fingers a trifle deeper. "What was it you said?"

"Erik." She dragged in a breath. "Damn you to hell, *do it!*"

"Yes." A split-second pause. "*Yes!*"

If she hadn't been so ready, it might have hurt. Instead, the strong suction felt glorious, exactly what she needed to tip her over. The tension trembled for a terrifying instant, vibrating like a single note sustained almost beyond bearing. Then it shattered. Erik, the chamber, the water—Prue herself—everything exploded in a burst of white-hot release.

Fragments of pleasure rained down, continuing to sear her with tiny licks of lightning, so that she shuddered with the aftershocks, over and over. Vaguely, she wondered if she would ever breathe normally again, let alone walk, talk or function. Every bone in her body had been reduced to the same consistency as overcooked noodles.

Gradually, the hardness of the ledge beneath her hip made itself known, growing lumpier and more insistent by the minute. Oh gods, how was she going to face him? She must be sprawled with her knees wide and her gown hiked up around her waist, no better than the cheapest dockside tart.

Her heart still thundering, Prue struggled to her elbows, dreading it.

Her feet dangled off the end of the ledge, submerged in water up to the ankles. The nightgown covered her knees, though her breasts still played peekaboo with the unlaced bodice. He must have . . .

Treading water a few yards off, Erik regarded her steadily, a small smile curving his firm mouth. The stubble darkening his jaw gave him a rough, piratical air.

"Uh." Prue drew a breath and tried again. "I—I don't know what to say. Why I—" She shook her head.

"Was it good, Prue?"

The flush burned all the way up her throat to her cheeks. Her head still spinning, she sat up, busying herself with retying her laces, ignoring the tremble in her fingers. "You know it was."

His teeth gleamed. "I didn't speak out of turn either. Total control." He sounded inordinately pleased with himself, though she couldn't imagine why.

It took all her courage to say it. "What about you? Did you—?" Not that she cared.

Erik's smile went awry. "I'm fine," he said brusquely. He gave a short bark of laughter. "You'd think water this temperature would make some bloody difference, wouldn't you?" Shaking his head, he sank, leaving only a trail of bubbles. A few seconds later, his sodden trews landed on the ledge beside her with a wet splat.

Surfacing, he rubbed one eyebrow. "Went off like a starship rocket right behind you. Haven't done that since I was a lad." Arching his arms over his head, he threw himself backward, his body a bulky length of golden, hair-dusted muscle, all grace and strength and water gleaming.

Doubtfully, Prue regarded the dripping garment beside her. "You can't walk back through The Garden naked," she said when he surfaced in a flurry of spray, shaking the hair out of his eyes.

"Ah, that feels good." He grinned. "Don't see why not. Shouldn't be anything out of the ordinary."

Prue thought of Rose. *I'd stand him on a pedestal in The Garden, stripped, and people would pay just to look.* She wouldn't put it past her friend to do just that. Despite the flutterbyes still dancing a saraband in her belly, the thought had her stifling a chuckle. "Sorry. Couldn't answer for your safety."

Erik laughed, the bright sound ringing around the enclosed space. He swam to the far end of the chamber and back again, using a powerful, overarm stroke. Sister give her strength, she wouldn't look! Not that there was much to see, unless she really concentrated, just the gleam of taut, muscled buttocks as he dived, water caressing the long line of a brawny thigh. And once, as he arched his body, a glimpse of the darker fur at his groin, his cock a pale length nestling there.

"We used to swim in the river, my brothers and I."

Prue tilted her head. "You had brothers?"

"Three." His lips curved. "Gods, we were a handful. Poor Ma."

"Your father?"

In the twilight illumination, his eyes looked black. "He was a fisherman. His boat went down in a storm when I was six."

"I'm sorry." Prue curled her legs under her. Asking was stupid, when every tidbit only intrigued her more. Hell. "Where are you from?"

"New Norsca. On the northern continent of Concordia. It's beautiful, Prue, mountains all the way to the sky, magnificent fjords. Cold as a bitch in winter." Returning to the ledge, he crossed his arms and rested his chin on them, gazing up at her.

"And you went *swimming*?" His body really was like music, a perfect lilting flow from the width of massive shoulders to a strong, trim waist to the high, arched rounds of his buttocks shimmering under the water.

"In summer." His smile became a reminiscent grin. "Naked as the day we were born." He slanted her an unreadable look. "Haven't done it in years until today. You?"

"Don't be ridiculous," she said. "What do you think?"

"I think it feels fucking wonderful." He reached up to pluck at the gown. "C'mon in. Dare you."

When she batted at his hands, he just laughed. "Live dangerously, Mistress McGuire. I've seen it all anyway."

In the end, he simply hoisted himself onto the ledge beside her with a twist of powerful shoulders and reefed the nightgown off over her head, despite her protests. "Take a breath, sweetheart." He scooped her hard into his chest and tumbled them both off the ledge.

The water closed over their heads and they sank slowly, Prue's hands clutching Erik's shoulders, his hands gripping her waist. Their legs tangled together. Tendrils of her hair escaped the braid to writhe around her face, but she didn't notice. Underwater, it was a dim, silent world, where their eyes met in wordless communication, and all she could hear was the beat of the blood in her ears. Erik tugged her flush against all that cool, slick hardness, and she tilted her head so her lips met his.

The kiss was cool and unhurried, an exploration of what felt like familiar territory, already dearly beloved. But this time, it wasn't dreamlike at all. Everywhere his flesh touched hers, Prue tingled, and given the broad expanse of him, that was pretty well everywhere. The light fur on his chest was a delicate rasp on her nipples, his belly firm and cobbled against her softness. Muzzily, she thought she would have been happy to go on like this forever and to hell with breathing.

A dark thought broke through the surface euphoria. Perhaps it would be better.

Her vision was hazing when they broke the surface, though she wasn't entirely certain which was the greater contributing factor—the mind-numbing Magick of Erik Thorensen's mouth or the lack of air.

Idly, he tucked an errant curl behind her ear as they floated languidly together. "We should go back," he said eventually.

"Yes."

Silence save for the water lapping.

"Prue—"

"Godsdammit." Turning away, she stroked toward the dark tunnel that led back to the real world. "Don't you dare."

"I have to." He caught her easily, taking her cheeks between his palms to gaze deep into her eyes. "I hate that I hurt you. Forgive me? Please?"

Last night, he'd had her exactly where he wanted her, open and vulnerable. Then he'd discarded her, exactly as Chavis had done. Whatever it was he wanted, she hadn't been able to supply it. A great fist closed over Prue's heart and squeezed all the joy out of it, drop by drop. Such a transitory thing, happiness. Strange how heavy she felt, as though she could sink into the formless mud on the seabed and stay there, safe in the muffled, silty quiet of death. "You want an honest answer?"

After a moment, he nodded, his face drawn.

Prue picked her words with care. "I believe you're sorry, but trust's a fragile thing. Once it's gone . . ." She shrugged

"I know." His voice was so low she could barely hear it, but it rang with bitter knowledge. "Gods, I know."

"The heart remembers hurt." She blinked away the sting of tears. "Part of the human condition, I suppose."

Slowly, he released her and she swam to the ledge to retrieve her gown. Wadding it up in her hand, she said, "Let's go."

"Yes." Erik grabbed his trews. "I spoiled it, didn't I?"

"Depends on what it was you wanted. A pleasant diversion to pass your time in the city?" She shrugged in answer to her own question. "I don't need to tell you how attractive you are."

She stroked toward the entrance to the tunnel and turned in the water, waiting. "You know that and you use it. It's what you do, what you are." She tried to smile, perhaps to soften the blow, though for whose benefit, she couldn't be sure. "Not a man for the long haul."

His face grim, Erik joined her. As if she hadn't spoken, he said curtly, "On the count of three then. One, two . . . *three!*"

Together, they sank a few feet and kicked into the darkness of the tunnel.

∽

She'd stopped shivering by the time they reached the first of the small pavilions, but she hadn't said a word beyond a murmured thanks when he wrapped the towel around her shoulders. Erik glanced down at her huddled figure. Her face looked pinched, not like bright, bustling Prue at all.

Caracole was one fucking debacle after another. A slow, ugly feeling unfurled in his belly. What, in the gods' names, had he been thinking just then? Had he been thinking at all? After last night's disaster, he should have been testing each step with her, moving slowly, but he'd been thoroughly seduced by the blaze of awe and joy that suffused her whole expressive little body when the seelies bobbed up. Gods, she'd loved them! And then . . .

Make me, she'd said, her voice breaking.

Even walking through The Garden in this awkward silence, his balls tightened at the memory. One of the most perfect moments of his life, her heart beating in the delicate flesh against his tongue, his will controlling her climax, setting her free to soar. And no mistakes, well, not then. He'd been so careful, ensuring she couldn't touch more than his hair, inspecting every word before it came out of his mouth. This time, he'd held to his purpose. No Voice.

Gods, the rewards! He hadn't even been touching himself and he'd come so hard he'd almost drowned.

It was after that he'd fucked it up.

Despite the warmth of the sun, the wet trews clung cold and clammy against his skin. He shivered, and regret and fury swept over him. He'd ruined it. Her opinion was clear enough. *Not a man for the long haul*. He glared at the wet braid snaking down her back, almost hating her. How dare she offer him a glimpse of paradise and then snatch it away?

Erik's lips tightened. He didn't have time for a *long haul*, whatever that was, but he'd hold fast to what remained of his honor and make do with what she'd give him of her own free will in the brief time they had. He'd just done exactly that. In the battle for Prue McGuire, this round went to him, not the Lady. Determination firmed inside him. He'd win the next one too.

Mind you, honor didn't mean he wouldn't push Prue's boundaries as far as he possibly could—he'd already shown he couldn't resist, even if he had to walk the very edge of risk. He thought of her helpless, delicate wrists bound in jade silk and his balls tightened with mingled lust and apprehension.

His frown darkened. The physical pleasure he'd given her was nothing in comparison to the body blows he'd dealt her proud spirit. Which meant he had a responsibility to heal what he could—if he could. Erik stifled a sigh. He'd have to be careful—not only with Prue, but with himself.

Gods, he'd hurt her.

As they passed a fountain, tinkling into a grotto of pierced and fretted rocks, Prue grabbed his arm, bringing them both to an abrupt halt. A few yards ahead, a man kneeled on the path, a huge dark flower cupped tenderly in both hands. He was crooning to it, tunefully enough.

"Dai," said Prue. "What are—?"

The man held up a warning finger. Finishing the song, he patted the blossom the same way he'd pat a woman's cheek. Then he rose, dusting off the knees of his trews. All his garments were black and superbly cut, the shirt finished with fine silver buttons.

Erik recognized the beautiful face, like a wicked angel. Yesterday, he'd seen it on a barge, laughing at him. He glared, pleased to discover he was at least six inches taller.

The man slanted a twinkling glance in their direction. "I'd ask," he murmured, "but then I'd have to hear the answer."

"Dai, what are you doing? Where's Walker?"

"First things first, Mistress Prue." The man nodded at Erik, the ruby drop in his ear catching the sun like a crimson tear. "You're still all wet, my friend. What are you? Part fish?"

"What I am *not* is supper," growled Erik. "Just so we're clear."

Prue shot him a startled glance. "This is Erik Thorensen," she said to Dai. "The singer."

Dai's considering gaze traveled from Erik to Prue and back again. His lips twitched. "So I see," he said obscurely.

Prue hitched her towel more firmly around her shoulders. "If Walker catches you in his bed of dark roses, you're a dead man, Dai."

But Dai shook his head. "He sent me, said I was to keep them company for a while. I'm to take his classes as well."

"But why?"

The other man's merry face clouded. "He's back at the House of Swords, Mistress, with a fever you wouldn't believe."

"Walker? But he's never sick."

"Isn't Walker the swordsman?" asked Erik. Dai wore a long dagger at his waist, but Erik had no doubt there'd be another half dozen weapons concealed about his trim person. He looked that kind of man. Casually, Erik shifted closer to Prue, resisting the temptation to tuck her under his arm.

"Walker's many things," said Dai. "He was a shaman once. Now he's a gardener." He gestured at the flowers, their satiny petals a purple so dark it was almost black. "He bred these blooms for Mistress Rose. He's a genius with any kind of blade, not to mention purely incredible with a quarterstaff."

Shaking himself out of a moment's abstraction, Dai touched Prue's arm. "What's wrong, Mistress Prue?"

Prue raised troubled eyes to Dai's. "I was going to ask Walker to come with me. I have to go the Open Cabal today."

"Ah," said Dai. "My pleasure." He bowed.

"No need," growled Erik. "I'll be there, remember?"

"The Open Cabal is not for the fainthearted." This time, there was no heat in Dai's assessing gaze, only challenge. "You're big enough, but what use are you?"

Erik tossed the towel aside. A swift step and he had Dai in a choke hold, a brawny forearm clamped across his throat, long fingers clamped over the wrist of his dagger hand.

17

"Not bad." Standing perfectly still, Dai gave a muffled laugh. "Look down."

The blade was so small it was lost in the man's left hand. But the tip glittered wickedly, poised over the big artery between Erik's hip and thigh.

"Hmpf." Slowly, Erik released him.

Dai raised a hand and massaged his throat. "What are you best at?"

Erik showed his teeth. "Brawling. Fists."

"Blades?"

He shrugged. "A little better than average. No more."

"Hmm. Show me your sword hand."

When Erik held it out, Dai turned it palm up for an impersonal examination. "Calluses. You practice?"

"When I can." Honesty compelled him to add, "For the stage."

Dai looked him in the eye. "Tell me, singer, have you killed?"

When Erik slanted a wary glance at Prue, she spun on her heel. "Sister save me," she muttered. "I don't want to hear." She set off toward the Main Pavilion at a brisk trot.

Erik turned back to Dai. "Twice. I hated it." He shrugged.

"But there was no choice. We were attacked on the road. It's a risk the Company takes, traveling."

Dai stared into his eyes, not at all embarrassed because he had to look up a few inches to do so. His gaze was very steady, and a little grim. "All right," he said at last. "We all go to the Open Cabal. I've got your back, singer." He held out a strong, slim hand. "Agreed?"

Without hesitation, Erik took it in a firm grip. "You're no courtesan."

When Dai grinned, his eyes sparkled green gold like a cat's. "That's not quite what Walker says." He released Erik's hand. "What I am is a sword for hire, the second best in the Queendom." The grin became wry. "According to Walker."

⚭

"Grab my belt and hang on tight." Erik took one look at the crowd streaming into the Audience Hall and shoved Prue behind him. Blessing the gods for bulk and heft, he shoved a ruthless path forward, Dai placidly keeping pace one step to the left. By the time he'd secured a vantage spot near the great semicircular table at the far end of the chamber, he'd lost count of the toes he'd crushed, the curses hurled at his back.

A sour mist of excitement, fear and sweat swirled toward the coffered ceiling. His nose was stuffed with it.

A paradise for pickpockets. Suddenly, he was immensely relieved Florien was back at the theater helping with props. Lord and Lady be praised though, the lad had kept his promise and gone straight back to the boardinghouse last night. Bettsa had checked. Well, well. Progress, of a sort. A smile tugged at his mouth. What would a slum rat like Florien make of the seelies? Gods, what he'd give to see the lad's face!

Breathing hard, Erik set Prue before him, an arm tight around her waist. Only a double strand of rope separated the ordinary folk of Caracole from their betters. Not that the members of the Cabal were yet in evidence. The vast chamber was awash with noise, shouted conversations bouncing off the polished, sandy pink seastone of the walls, while in a minstrels' gallery set high on a mezzanine, a group of unhappy musicians sawed away at their instruments, adding to the unholy din.

"Now what?" he said in Prue's ear, inhaling her crisp, clean scent with gratitude.

She fished a small wooden square out of her pocket. "Once the ministers are seated, the Open Cabal begins. We wait for the number on our chit to be called."

"What number do they start with?" he asked, his heart sinking.

"One, usually," said Dai at his elbow.

Wordlessly, Prue held up the chit. Sixty-seven.

"But I have to speak to someone today. I *have* to! Who knows how long—"

Prue dug an elbow into his ribs. "Shush now, they're coming. And I have an idea."

Someone was playing a trumpet voluntary, quite well really, the long, gleaming notes insisting on the courtesy of silence. A Guard sergeant with a chestful of medals sprang to attention, holding back a heavy curtain. From behind it strolled a group of oddly assorted but richly dressed people, deep in conversation. Ignoring the neck-craning and the whispers of the crowd, they fanned out behind the heavy table on the dais and took their places. Only two of the high, brocaded chairs remained empty, the grandest one in the center, which was clearly a throne, and another on its left.

"Where's the queen?" whispered Erik.

"Only hears the most serious cases," said Dai quietly. "But see the man seated to the right of the throne?"

Erik nodded.

"Uyeda, the Queen's Right Hand. He who carries out the will of the queen."

Uyeda sat bolt upright, his hands folded in the capacious sleeves of a severely cut, formal robe. Although his hair was iron gray, the bones of his face were broad and starkly elegant. Intelligence shone in the faded blue of his eyes, only the shadows beneath betrayed the strain of his office.

Erik's gaze traveled to the empty throne and the seat beyond it. "And on the queen's left?"

A soundless chuckle from Dai. "The Queen's Left Hand, he who executes the will of the queen unseen. Her spymaster."

"Who is he?"

Prue shrugged. "No one knows, that's the point. It's all

about the separation of powers. He—or she—could be anyone. Anywhere."

Comprehension dawned. Erik fought the desire to laugh. "You mean the Right Hand doesn't know what the Left Hand is doing?

"Exactly," said Prue. "Only the monarch knows that."

The sergeant strode to the center of the floor, grounding the hilt of his halberd with a ringing impact on the stone flags. "*One!*" he intoned in a stentorian bellow, and two women stepped forward, already deep in what was clearly an ongoing argument, hands flying with the intensity of their feelings. Six pairs of eyes gazed down at them from the Queen's table with varying degrees of disapproval, boredom or interest.

"Who are the others?" asked Erik.

Rising on tiptoe, Prue explained in an undertone. If he hadn't been so tense, Erik would have enjoyed her proximity. As it was, he tightened his arm around her supple waist, bending his head to brush his cheek against her hair while he listened and watched.

The Queen's Money was the middle-aged man at the far left, frowning down at the papers in his hand. Behind him stood a harried-looking clerk with an armload of scrolls and bound ledgers. Lounging back in the next chair, the Navy shared a joke with her swarthy, hawkish neighbor, the Queen's City.

On the far side of Uyeda, the Right Hand, a small, plump man surveyed the great unwashed of Caracole with bright, bird-like interest. The Queen's Knowledge. As far as Erik could make out from Prue's hurried whispers, the office required a combination of archivist, librarian and research scholar. It seemed that the Knowledge was a learned man.

Which left the Army, with his dress uniform, his brush of grizzled hair and the scar under his eye. Erik studied the man's thick fingers drumming an impatient tattoo on the table.

In fact, apart from the Right Hand and the Knowledge, none of the Cabal appeared to be even remotely interested in the proceedings.

Lord's balls!

Erik filled his chest with a preparatory breath and Prue whirled about in his arms, slapping a small hand over his mouth. "No," she hissed, her eyes gem-bright with urgency.

"They'll throw us out if you speak out of turn. You've got to trust me, Erik. This is why I'm here."

Trust me. *Trust me.*

The echoes of his own desperate voice.

Swallowing, Erik nodded.

Absently, Prue patted his cheek. "Good."

Rummaging in her belt pouch, she produced a coin, a full cred it looked like, and a small notebook with a pencil attached. Busily, she scribbled a few lines in her neat upright script. Tearing off the page, she wrapped it around the chit and handed the whole thing, together with the money, to Dai.

Dai raised a brow. "The Queen's Money? You sure, Mistress?"

"Yes." She gave him a little push. "Go, go!"

"Ah well," said Dai. "Isn't it lucky Rhiomard owes me?" He melted into the crowd.

Fifteen minutes later, the two women having been replaced with a plump, disgruntled tavern keeper, Erik saw Dai standing behind a fluted pillar on the other side of the Hall, deep in conversation with the much-decorated sergeant. Rhiomard, presumably.

The sergeant flicked a glance in their direction, and his hard mouth tipped up at the sight of Prue. One eyelid fluttered shut in an unmistakable wink. Erik tightened his grip. "A client?" he growled.

Prue shot him a dark glance. "Yes," she said. "Of The Garden. Not that it's any business of yours." She pressed her lips together, spots of color on her cheeks.

Unobtrusively, the sergeant drew the Money's clerk aside for a low-voiced discussion in the shadows.

From behind, Dai murmured, "Any minute now. Watch."

The clerk handed a small square of paper to the Queen's Money. Erik saw the minister's brows rise, his mouth twitch. He raised his head. "Enough," said the Money, and the hum of the crowd ceased.

The tavern keeper barely paused for breath. "But, Noblelord," he babbled, "all I ask for is an extra month. No more. It's not unreasonable, not with the way business . . ."

Catching sight of the Money's face, the man trailed off. In the sudden silence, he wiped his brow with his sleeve.

"Correct me if I'm wrong." Without turning his head, the

minister held out a hand, and the clerk placed a sheet of paper in it. "You own not one, but three taverns in the Melting Pot?" He glanced at the figures.

"Yes, Noblelord." The man wiped his forehead with his sleeve.

The Queen's Money took a small silver gavel from his clerk and poised it over the dark pattern inlaid in the surface of the table, directly in front of him. A five-pointed star, a Pentacle. "You own them outright?"

The tavern keeper's face took on a greenish hue. "Yes, Noblelord, but—"

The sound of the gavel striking the Pentacle echoed through the Audience Hall, pure and vast, like the voice of the space winds. Gods, the dark material was novarine! Erik shut his mouth with a snap. Eight Pentacles around the table, each carved from the heartstuff of an exploded star. The table was worth more than the entire Hall and every person in it.

"Petition denied." The Money's eyes gleamed. "Nonetheless, my friend, I will help you."

The tavern owner did not look in the least comforted.

Turning to his clerk, the official said, "Make a note to send a tax officer to assist this citizen with his books. Every day until it is done and Her Majesty is paid the money she's owed."

Someone in the crowd snickered, another laughed. Out of the corner of his eye, Erik saw a young mother pull a bag of candied fruit from her pocket and pop a piece into the mouth of the child in her arms.

"Silence!" roared Sergeant Rhiomard. "Judgment has been made."

"For the gods' sake, man," snapped the City, leaning forward. "Get on with it. Who's next?"

Rhiomard glanced at the Money and received a barely perceptible nod in return. "Mistress Prue McGuire!"

⚭

Uproar.

The Necromancer raised his silver gavel. He hesitated. Oh no, this situation had too much delicious potential to spoil. Gently, he laid the pretty thing aside. So small to wield such power. But the merest fraction in comparison with what awaited him.

An old woman ducked under the rope, brandishing a chit. "But I'm next!" she shrieked. "Me!"

The burly fellow standing behind her exploded into action. "Be damned if you are!" Reaching over the old woman's head, he tweaked the chit out of her fingers.

The pandemonium doubled. Heads and shoulders undulated like a multicolored crop stirred by the wind. The air resounded with catcalls, whistles and hoots. A scuffle broke out. At Rhiomard's gesture, three guardsmen bore down on it, full of grim purpose.

The Necromancer barely noticed. Surely, he'd seen the woman who faced the table before? And the big fellow standing foursquare at her side? The third man, the lithe, dark one they'd left behind the rope, wasn't familiar. Interesting, this one didn't so much as glance at the table. He watched the crowd with unwinking attention.

A hired sword. Not important. The Necromancer dismissed him.

He was still puzzling over the other two when the blast of air Magick rolled over him. Startled, he pulled in a breath and the freshness, the clean power of it, seared his nostrils, made his chest tighten. When he hissed between clenched teeth, the clerk said, "Is all well, Nobelord?"

"Water," croaked the Necromancer, and a guardsman leaped to do his bidding.

Well, well. A mystery solved. The little whore from The Garden and the singer whose name he'd forgotten, if he'd ever known it. The stink of air Magick was all over them, as if they'd bathed in it. It made him want to puke.

His pulse rate slowly returning to normal, the Necromancer leaned back in his carved chair. Truly, the Dark Arts were powerful. His *will* was powerful. A smile curved his lips. There she was, his air witch, her head tilted at a proud angle as she delivered herself into his hands. So self-possessed that it seemed the threatening weight of the Cabal's authority, the restless crowd, meant nothing to her. But one hand was hidden in her skirts, gripping the paw of the brute beside her. They were lovers, that much was obvious from the way they stood, each secure in the other's space, a united front against the world. The connection between them might be a problem, but no matter, he'd contrive.

Licking his lips, the Necromancer prepared to be entertained.

❦

"Mistress McGuire," said the Queen's Money, showing a lot of teeth. "We haven't met, but I believe we have corresponded. Extensively."

Prue inclined her head, gracious as a queen. "Indeed we have, Noblelord. And I thank you for your kind offer."

Over the buzz of the crowd, Erik growled, "What offer?" He glared at the Money. Not much to look at, late fifties with a sagging jaw and hard eyes, but the man wore the aura of power and wealth the way a dandy swaggered in a fine cloak.

"Sshh," hissed Prue. Where their bodies touched, all down his side, he could feel a fine trembling. Her fingers were cold, clutching his.

The Right Hand removed his hands from his sleeves to toy with the silver gavel on the table before him. "Money," he said in mild reproof, "what are you doing?" He nodded at the sea of avid faces. "Explain."

The Money's lips went tight. Jerking his head up, he swept the Hall with a commanding glare. As the tavern keeper squirmed, the minister jabbed an accusing finger toward him. "Your accounts," he snapped, "are an unmitigated disaster." His lip curled. "By your ineptitude, you cheat Her Majesty of her rightful due."

The minister's gaze traveled unhurriedly to Prue. It warmed.

"Whereas Mistress McGuire here . . ." He smiled, and automatically, Erik drew Prue closer, looming over her as obviously as he knew how. Lord's balls, this was impossible, having Prue fight his battles for him! Words bubbled in his throat. Prue squeezed his hand so hard it hurt, but she didn't take her aquamarine gaze from the Money's face. With a supreme effort, Erik clamped his lips together.

"I want that organized brain of yours, Mistress." The minister's expression became positively wolfish. "I offer you good work. Worthwhile. Rewarding."

The Queen's Knowledge laughed, a sound perilously close to a giggle. "You're in love, Money."

The Money shot him a poisonous glance.

Prue cleared her throat. "May I speak before the Cabal, Noblelords?"

"You have the right, lass," the Navy broke in, her shrewd, weathered face faintly amused, "but it's usual to wait for the number on your chit. The queue's back there." She indicated with her chin.

Prue looked the Queen's Money in the eye. "By your leave, Noblelord?"

He leaned forward over the table. "Work for me."

Prue inclined her head. "If that is your price, Noblelord, I will consider it. May I have time to think?"

"What the hell are you doing?" Erik said in a fierce whisper.

Prue gave no sign she'd heard him.

The Queen's Knowledge gazed kindly over the shiny gold spectacles perched on the end of his nose. "Every citizen may speak before the Open Cabal. Navy's right in that." With his silver gavel, he tapped the pentacle before him. In the ringing silence, his voice carried to the back of the Hall. The acoustics were really very fine. "Go ahead, my dear." His eyes twinkled. "But introduce us to your friend first."

With her usual composure, Prue said, "This is Erik Thorensen." She raised her chin, scanning the audience. "Some of you will know he is a singer, visiting the city with the Unearthly Opera Company. Master Thorensen is from Concordia." An infinitesimal pause. "As a citizen, I present him to the Open Cabal of the Queen." Releasing Erik's hand, Prue took a half step sideways. He felt oddly bereft. Exposed. "Please, Noblelords, hear him out."

As one, the spectators exhaled, like some huge animal stirring in its sleep.

Godsdammit, he was on.

Erik squared his shoulders, conscious of the weight of hundreds of eyes. Nothing new, this was what he did for a living. All he needed was a moment alone with any one of the Cabal. He scanned their faces. Prue had said this was the business of the City. Very well.

Pasting on an easy smile, he bowed as gracefully as he knew how.

"Is this some kind of performance?" asked the Queen's Army, eyeing him with profound disfavor.

Erik pitched his voice to reach the farthest corners of the Hall. "No, my Lord." He spread his hands. "I ask only for a few moments of the City's time. In private. The matter is urgent."

The Army grunted and returned to hefting his gavel from hand to hand.

The City gave a crack of laughter. "It always is." His dark eyes were cold and flat. "By the Brother, you have a nerve, whatever your name is." He raised his gavel. "Either speak your business now or make an appointment with my office like everyone else."

The Voice rumbled in Erik's chest, fighting to be free. But fuck, he couldn't compel the man in front of hundreds of people. He swallowed the anger, along with the power. Set both aside. "Noblelord," he said, and despite himself he sounded curt. "This is not a subject appropriate for discussion in a public forum."

"Then why the hell have you brought it to one?" The City shot a malicious glance at his colleague. Silver threads gleamed in the black hair at his temples. "This is a waste of time, Money."

18

"Just a moment." The Queen's Knowledge tilted his head to one side and ran his fingers through the fringe of hair surrounding his bald dome until it stuck up in white tufts. Only the shrewdness in his expression saved him from looking comical. He smiled, slow and serious. "I confess, I am curious. What is this delicate matter?" His gaze softened as it traveled from Erik to Prue and back again. "Is it personal, perhaps?"

Erik bowed again. "No." An angry little breeze sprang up out of nowhere, ruffling his shirt, stirring the lavishly embroidered banners hanging high on the wall behind the table.

The Knowledge simply stared, the very intensity of his gaze a question.

"Git orf, ya daft bugger!" A small, squishy object hit Erik on the shoulder and burst. Soft, sweet rot. A small hand touched his sleeve and Prue's clean, warm scent drifted past his nose. He steadied.

"That will do," said a quiet, precise voice. The man seated to the right of the empty throne had been so still, Erik had nearly forgotten him. The pool of silence spread until it seemed no one moved in the Hall. Or breathed.

"Master Thorensen," said the Right Hand of the Queen. "Much may be forgiven a visitor, but this is the Open Cabal of Caracole, not a sewing circle. State your business or leave."

Erik gritted his teeth. "I have no wish to cause alarm."

An excited buzz started behind him.

The Right Hand leaned back in his chair, his pale blue eyes calm and chill. "Allow me to be the best judge of what constitutes alarm in the Queendom of the Isles."

Well, hell. "As you wish."

Erik squared his shoulders and met the man's gaze full-on. The banners flapped and billowed in the freakish wind. "The Leaf of Nobility is rotting from beneath," he said.

The Army's lips thinned with contempt. "For the Brother's sake, not another one." He turned his head. "Sergeant!"

"I saw it myself." Erik's trained baritone bounced off the polished seastone walls.

The crowd seethed, pressing against the ropes in an effort to get closer. Someone cursed, a woman called out in fear and a guardsman snapped out an order.

"Hold." The City leaned forward, his dark, hook-nosed face intent. The sergeant held up a hand and his men stopped in their tracks. "If you claim to have been under the Leaf, you lie, my friend." He looked Erik up and down, and his lip curled. "It's not possible to get that deep without Technomage apparatus. Even my trained divers wear it."

Erik set his jaw. "I had help. The stem is so soft with rot I could sink my arm in it up to the shoulder. It stinks. Can't you smell it?"

"*Smell* it?" The City stared. Then he slapped his hand on the table and threw his head back, roaring with laughter. The Knowledge giggled and even the Right Hand looked gravely amused.

A beat behind, the air erupted with jeers, catcalls and obscenities. Erik's skin crawled. Gods, if it was bad for him . . . Suddenly stricken, he glanced at the woman at his side. Prue's face was as pale as paper, but her magnificent eyes blazed with fury and her lush mouth was set in a firm line.

Lord's balls, she was extraordinary, Prue McGuire! When he took her hand, she leaned closer to his body.

"You're the best-looking lunatic I've ever seen," said the

Navy with a twinkle. "But you're still a lunatic." Her gaze shifted to Prue. "Get him to a healer, Mistress. Before he starts to drool."

"It's Sibling Full Moons," said Prue. "The tides are particularly low."

The Money looked frankly appalled. "Tell me you didn't smell it too, Mistress McGuire."

"No, Noblelord, I didn't." Prue stared the minister in the eye. "But I believe him. Absolutely."

"By the Brother, *why*?"

"No," muttered Erik under his breath. "Prue, no . . . Don't . . ."

"Because I saw the seelies," said Prue.

⌒⌒⌒

The Necromancer actually felt his jaw drop. By the time he'd snapped it closed again, the Open Cabal of the Queen resembled a riot in full cry. The noise was deafening; missiles of all kinds flew through the air. Rhiomard and his men brandished halberds, swords and even fists, to no avail. The singer shielded the air witch with his body, the back of his shirt a blotchy mess. As the Necromancer watched, he turned his head just in time to avoid the rind of a manda fruit, but a bruise already decorated one cheekbone and something horrible dripped from his hair.

The Technomage's censorious voice echoed in his head. *You've reduced the population to below a viable level.* For a man of his intellect, it wasn't a giant leap. *Such interference has unpredictable results.*

The floor seemed to shift beneath him, and for a moment, he thought he might be physically ill.

Good sense came to his rescue. What did it matter after all? The whole Leaf and every noblefamily who lived on it could go to the bottom with his blessing. It was the inconvenience that was galling. By Shaitan, he hated to be rushed, but it was unavoidable. The gods knew how much time he had—though he doubted They'd deign to inform him. He sat back, drumming his fingers on the table, watching a fat woman in the front row laugh so hard, tears streamed down her plump cheeks.

It took the Queen's Guard ten minutes to restore order, valuable thinking time.

"Did they sing, Mistress?" he asked. "The way they do in the bedtime stories?"

She didn't even flinch, the bitch. Still cradled in the arms of the singer, she raised her chin, her level gaze uncompromising. "They did, Noblelord." She really did have beautiful eyes, even if the rest of her was plain.

The Navy rose. Carefully, she placed both hands on the table and leaned forward. "This goes beyond a joke. You insult the Open Cabal and therefore Her Majesty." Her brows snapped together. "If you were on a ship of mine, I'd have you flogged, the pair of you."

Lifting her gavel, she collected nods from around the table. "Petition dismissed." Solid silver connected crisply with the novarine Pentacle.

Theatrically, the Navy waited for the echoes to die away. Enjoying herself, thought the Necromancer with an inward sneer. "Mistress McGuire?"

The air witch stopped in midstep to glance back over her shoulder. "Yes, Noblelady?"

"You are fined five hundred credits. For contempt."

He hadn't thought it possible for someone without his gifts to commit murder with their eyes. The Necromancer almost laughed aloud. But that would never do.

While the sergeant called the next chit, he watched the singer and the witch from under his lashes. As they conferred with the hired sword—the man hadn't known what they were going to say, judging by the careful immobility of his expression—the Necromancer considered his next step.

If his objective was the air witch, the singer constituted the primary obstacle. By Shaitan, look at the size of him, the fluid way he moved. His very presence fairly screamed health and virility, and he was no fool, Shaitan take him. He'd thought quickly enough, even when faced with the combined attention of the Cabal. But it was the stubborn jut of his jaw the Necromancer distrusted—no doubt, he was one of those who treasured their so-called honor. He wouldn't give up, that was clear to see. He'd persist in making a nuisance of himself until he got a fair hearing. Eventually, someone would take him seriously and they'd all be seeing godsbedamned seelies.

The Necromancer ground his teeth.

Wordlessly, the witch pulled a large handkerchief from the pocket of her skirts and handed it to the singer. Taking it with a mutter of thanks, the big man wiped his face, his mouth contorted with disgust.

He'd have to destroy the singer to reach the witch. A regrettable circumstance, because he'd give a great deal for a body like that. Fingers tightening on his gavel, the Necromancer rolled the envy and hate around his mouth with sour relish.

Every move the singer made, every glance, every touch, declared his possession of the witch, his protection of what he considered to be his. Idly, the Necromancer wondered whether he'd die for her, given the choice.

Because he was about to.

The owner of a skiff fleet was droning on about something to do with tolls and fees. The Cabal listened with only half an ear. The Necromancer didn't listen at all.

Gathering himself, he reached out with a dark tendril of power. It would be strange for a man so magnificently healthy to drop dead with no warning. If he was unlucky, there might be whispers of the Dark Arts. Necromancy was punishable by death in the Isles. He'd seen a man burned at the stake for it in Ged.

The memory made his lips thin with irritation. He'd been a fool, that apprentice, the reason the Necromancer now worked alone. If he hadn't realized in time and taken the man's tongue before he could be put to the question . . . Shaking his head, the Necromancer set it aside. The present situation was far from ideal, but the singer's death couldn't be traced to him, not even if the most skilled healer in the Enclave detected more than natural causes.

The decision made, he relaxed, a slight smile curving his lips. A little self-indulgence. He'd never been particularly good at curbing his appetites, especially when he could see no reason for self-restraint. And the temptation was so hard to resist—all six feet plus of it.

What was the harm really?

Half-closing his eyes, the Necromancer sent the black thread of his will snaking across the Hall. It brushed the arm of the fat woman who'd laughed, and she gasped, her face turning the color of putty. Those nearest caught her as she stumbled, and the stir drew the attention of the crowd. Necks craned as people fought to see.

Very good.

Now.

As he struck, the air witch stepped in front of the singer, going up on tiptoe to whisper something in his ear.

Cursing, the Necromancer jerked back. He blinked, absorbing the unexpected impact. By Shaitan, he'd been *bruised*. For all the world as if he'd collided with a solid wall.

He fumbled his water cup to his lips and sipped, aching somewhere inside he couldn't touch.

No problem. An aberration, that was all.

Setting the cup down in the center of the Pentacle—by Shaitan, he'd grown to loathe the godsbedamned things!—he reached out again, more cautiously this time.

Shit, it was still there!

Yes, like a wall. Knitting his brows, he explored. Except... it didn't seem to be aware of him. It was just . . . there, high and wide and obdurate. If he touched it, he *hurt*.

The blood beat loud in his ears, his fury made deliciously thrilling with the addition of genuine apprehension. Gods, he couldn't recall the last time he'd felt anxious. She was nothing but a witch-whore. How could she wrong-foot him this way? It wasn't possible.

But when he looked up, it was to see the broad back of the singer disappearing out the wide double doors, flanked by the witch and the hired sword. Not even a practitioner with his extraordinary skills could kill what he couldn't see. Bubbling with rage, the Necromancer beckoned the clerk.

"Noblelord?"

"Call them back," he snarled.

"Yes, Noblelord." A hesitation. "Ah, who?"

Too damn obvious. The silver handle of the gavel bent in his grip. Breathing heavily, the Necromancer released it. "Never mind."

Suddenly exhausted, he braced his spine against the chair back. Whichever came first, deification or a new body, it couldn't come soon enough. Not so long ago, he'd been able to visit victims in their sleep, when the barriers between consciousness, belief and Magick wore thin. While a sleeper dreamed, the experience was real, *lived*. In the Necromancer's hands, dreams became nightmares, screams and death. Distance had been no barrier.

He still had his dark Magick. In fact, it had never been stronger. But as for this puny physical form—by Shaitan, it let him down at every turn.

Closing his eyes, the Necromancer took another sip of water. He rearranged his thoughts, examined his priorities.

First, the singer, who was, after all, merely human. Not worth soiling his hands with really, not when his time was so valuable.

He could take it easy on himself, seek professional assistance. The Guild of Assassins, for example. That's what they were for, after all.

⁓

Out in the sun, the odor intensified, if that was possible. His skin itching, Erik resisted the temptation to dive off the Royal Bridge. The water looked so blue and clean and he smelled like a midden.

When Prue dropped his hand, he curled it into a fist. He didn't blame her. She had any number of reasons to find his touch unwelcome—public ridicule, a five-hundred-credit fine, loss of face with a powerful official. The things he'd done to her, the things he intended to do. And the Leaf of Nobility was still dying.

The gods damn it all to hell.

One of the Queen's Guard caught up with them before they stepped off the bridge. "Here," she said without preamble, shoving a folded piece of heavy paper into Erik's hand. "For you."

She grinned at Dai. "You going to the Sailor's Lay tonight?"

"Ah, Yachi, my love." The swordsman pressed a hand to his heart and winked. "Sure thing."

Yachi's bold gaze flickered over Erik from his head to his heels. "I've never had a lunatic," she said. "Let alone a good-looking one. Bring him too."

"Better bathe him first," said Prue. "You think?"

"I have a show to do," said Erik. "Perhaps after that."

"It'll be a sellout, for sure." The guard sketched a cheerful salute. "Good luck, friend. You'll need it."

As she trotted away, her boots ringing on the bridge, Erik unfolded the note and his brows rose. "The Money commands us to attend his office the day after tomorrow. Better than nothing."

"Us?"

"You and me, Prue. Gods, it might actually have been worth it." A little of the gloom lifted. Without thinking, he ran a hand through his hair, only to encounter something clumped and slimy. Swearing, he searched in vain for a clean place on his trews to wipe his fingers. "About the fine—" At the blaze of anger and guilt in her face, he broke off.

Her chin rose. "It was my mistake. I shouldn't have pushed so hard. I'll deal with it."

Not if he had anything to do with the matter. "I'm the expert on mistakes," he said. "We'll talk about it later."

"Gods, man, you reek." Dai leaned against the carved balustrade, all amusement gone. He glanced from Erik to Prue and back again. "Why the fuck didn't you tell me you've both lost your minds?"

"Why?" demanded Prue. "What would you have done differently?"

"Seelies?" Dai continued as if she hadn't spoken. "*Seelies?*" He shook his head. "She was right, the old girl. You're mad, the pair of you."

Prue's spine stiffened. "I don't care if the whole world laughs in my face, including you, Dai. I know what I saw, and I saw seelies. Two of them, dancing." Abruptly, her blue green eyes filled with tears, glittering like gems beneath a wave.

Erik reached out to draw her to his side before he remembered the filth on his person. He let his hand fall. "Can you swim, Dai?"

"Yes," said the swordsman. "I've been down the tunnels and into the hollows in the Leaves. I was young and stupid. But I never saw a seelie."

"Erik sang." Prue's voice was so husky he could barely hear it. "They came for him. It was so beautiful."

Dai fixed his green gold gaze on her face. "You saw them? Truly?"

"Yes."

"And the Leaf of Nobility is rotten?"

"If Erik says so."

The swordsman blew out a breath. "That's it then." Gracefully, he pushed away from the rail. "It'll be sunset soon," he said. "Which is closer, Erik, The Garden or wherever you're staying?"

"My clothes are at the boardinghouse," said Erik absently. "What do you mean, *that's it*?"

"It means I'm with you." Dai smiled crookedly. "Well, only because Mistress Prue is, to be honest." He glanced at her with unmistakable affection. "You're the most straightforward, sensible person I've ever met, Mistress. If you say a troupe of seelies joined hands and danced around the moons, I believe it."

Erik's mouth went dry. "Is that true? Are you with me, Prue?"

Her tip-tilted gaze met his. "Yes," she said. "In this." She looked away. "I should go."

Erik caught up with her in a single stride. "Come to the opera tonight."

Prue kept walking. "No."

"Why not? I know you enjoyed it last time."

She stopped so abruptly, he overshot and had to turn back. "They'll crucify you."

A grin tugged at his mouth. "You don't want to watch?"

She set off again, with brisk steps. "There's a water stair around the next corner."

"I'll send the boy to collect you. Prue?"

She wouldn't look at him. "What?"

"Is there a song about seelies? Something everyone knows?"

Her elbow hit him in the belly, bringing him to an abrupt halt. She tilted her head back to search his face, her eyes wide. "You wouldn't!"

"Don't bet on it." A weight lifting from his heart, Erik chuckled. "It's no use looking so prim, sweetheart. Not when there's evidence to the contrary." He raised his dirty hand to touch her dimpled cheek and let it drop. Godsdammit.

"There's the 'Seelie Song,'" said Dai thoughtfully, "but it's a nursery rhyme."

Prue gurgled, an enchanting sound deep in her throat.

"Sing it for me," demanded Erik.

Prue shook her head. "I can't sing. I really can't."

"Nonsense, everyone can sing. But I'll let it go for the moment. Dai?"

Grinning, the swordsman drew them into a doorway.

Before he'd reached the end of the first line, Erik was smiling too. "I know the tune," he said. "But on Concordia, it's about a little star that twinkles. The gods know how long children have been singing it. Centuries, I imagine. Thanks." With grim relish, he clapped Dai on the shoulder. "It's perfect."

19

Erik had been right. The "Seelie Song" *was* perfect.

In the shadows of the Royal Box, Prue sat breathing hard, listening to a storm of applause so loud the walls of the theater vibrated. Sitting inside a huge bass drum must be like this. Dai would have said Erik the Golden had balls. Her lips twitched. When he wore the demon king's breeches, there could be no question of what he had.

She'd never seen anything to beat tonight's performance for sheer, bloody-minded gall. Erik had started with a hostile, curious crowd, baying for blood. And he'd made them his. Gods, by the final curtain, he owned their souls, right down to the last rough workingman out for trouble and a night on the town.

Ever the consummate showman, he'd strode on in the breeches and tall boots, his golden head held high, ignoring the heaving clamor emanating from the stalls.

A hoarse voice yelled, "Is that a seelie in yer pocket, mate?"

And another, "Or are ye jest happy to see us?"

Gales of cruel laughter.

Prue had flinched. Merciful Sister, if she felt flayed on Erik's behalf, what was it like for him? She'd have given almost anything to be tucked up in bed with the covers drawn up to her chin. But Florien had been insistent, escorting her to the stage door, accompanying her to the box and planting himself at her side. She shot a glance to her right. The lad was perched cross-legged on the fine brocade seat, his dirty boots doing the Sister knew what damage to the queen's upholstery.

When she'd asked what he thought he was about, he'd only muttered, "I promised. Shook 'ands."

Onstage, Erik had opened his mouth and the notes had poured forth, an exquisite, airy ribbon of melody, redolent of virile power, flavored with the titillating wickedness of the demon king.

He had them in the palm of his hand long before he'd finished the first aria, Prue included. Surely she knew him better than anyone else in the city? Godsdammit, why wasn't she immune? In fact, she could swear the effect was worse tonight. As the demon king died, singing superbly right through his death throes, all she could think of was the tender lightness of Erik Thorensen's touch, the taste of his skin, his mouth sending her to the stars. Her bones melted with yearning, her blood burned slow and hot, and stupid tears brimmed in her eyes.

And then . . . Sister give her strength, she couldn't believe the nerve of the man.

He'd gazed out over the footlights, hands on hips, and announced blandly he had something special for an encore. Even now, Prue didn't know whether to laugh or cry. Gods, he'd shoved the "Seelie Song" down their throats and made them love it.

By the second repetition, he had them singing the sweet, childish words with him.

> *Seelie wash, seelie clean.*
> *Where you hide, you're never seen.*
> *Lovely fur, flash of blue.*
> *If I could swim, I'd play with you.*

After that, he let the audience carry the tune, while his magnificent baritone provided a kind of descant, swooping over and under the simple melody, decorating and embellishing, until the entire effect was almost too lovely to be borne.

> *Seelie dance, seelie joy.*
> *Beloved friend of girl and boy.*

A nursery rhyme! Sister save her!

They'd sung it a dozen times over before Erik held up his hand. "Thank you, my friends," he said into an expectant hush, his voice perfectly pitched, calm and deep. He bowed, extravagantly low. "Today, before the Open Cabal, I spoke the truth. The Leaf of Nobility is dying. Seelies exist."

No one moved. Or spoke.

"I wanted you to know that." Another bow and a level, challenging look. He stepped back and the curtains swished together in a swathe of red velvet.

Dizzy with relief and awe, Prue sagged in her seat.

The tumult broke before she could draw her next breath. Some stood on their seats and clapped. Others shouted and stamped, Erik's name on every lip.

He'd created a sensation. The entire city would be buzzing with it. Laughter bubbled up in her throat, and she pressed her lips together lest it escape.

Beside her, Florien let out a shaky breath. "Fookin' 'ell."

"Exactly." Then she recollected herself. Gods, the child had a filthy mouth. "Florien—"

Correctly interpreting her expression, he cut her off. "Don' bother." He hopped out of the chair. "Comin'?"

Prue blinked. "Where?"

"T' Erik. T' talk about t' meeting wit' t' Money man."

"Not necessary."

Rising, Prue settled the shawl across her shoulders so the embroidered seelies gamboling happily all the way to the fringed ends were clear to see. She had no idea why she'd worn it, except that, in a strange way, it seemed right, a gesture of solidarity. Besides, it was an extremely versatile garment. Abruptly, even the light touch of the silk was more warmth than she could bear. Letting the shawl slip back to her elbows, she inhaled carefully. What would it be like to feel him deep inside, to have him wrap her up, take over her senses until she was no more than a bundle of quivering sensation? To give herself over to his control, to the gentle restraint of silk?

"I'm fine," she said. "I'll take a skiff home."

Florien grabbed her sleeve. "He sed you'd say thet. An' he sed t' say . . ." His brow furrowed with concentration. "He'll give t' five 'undred he owes ye t' Rose." The dark eyes gleamed with satisfaction at a job well done.

So that was the way he intended to play it? She couldn't decide whether she was more irritated with Erik for such an obvious ploy or with herself for falling for it. By the Sister, she was going to give Master Thorensen a piece of her mind! And she wouldn't be charmed into smiling, let alone laughing. Even if it killed her.

"Lead on," she said resolutely.

Without a word, the lad trotted out of the box, taking a set of narrow back stairs down several flights to a warren of small, poky rooms. They brushed by men carrying mysterious toolboxes and a stout, harried fellow with a sheaf of papers. Everyone had a greeting for the boy, a curious glance for Prue. One of the scantily clad dancers, a lissome blonde with endless legs, reached out to ruffle Florien's hair.

"Got yourself a lady friend, sweet cheeks?"

"Fook orf, Syd." Florien ducked without breaking stride. "She'm Erik's."

Erik's. The casual assumption hit her so hard, Prue gasped aloud. She knew she ought to be outraged, and truly, she was, but she didn't have the energy to spare to deal with that right now. The world was slipping sideways faster than she could grab it and haul it back. She'd never been one for emotional ups and downs, but merciful Sister, from the moment Erik Thorensen had opened his mouth, she'd been hurtling from the pinnacles to the depths and back again. It wasn't good for her, truly it wasn't.

Unobtrusively, she hauled in a couple of steadying breaths. She'd just have to do better, that was all. Keep her wits about her.

As they turned down yet another passageway, she glanced back over her shoulder. The dancer stood stock still, staring after them. Her pretty mouth drooped.

Catching up with the boy, Prue asked, "Who was that?"

"Sydarise." Florien shot her a sly glance. "He was sweet on 'er month afore last."

The woman was tall enough to fit his large frame. From the male point of view, it all made perfect sense. Not only beautiful, but convenient.

Prue slowed. What in the seven hells was she doing? She'd always been brutally honest with herself. Here she was, trotting off to Erik's dressing room with her heart in her hands, brushing past his previous conquests on the way. She'd already decided the ephemeral pleasures of the present weren't worth the certain pain of the future.

Hadn't she?

"Wait." Prue grasped the boy's thin shoulder. She swallowed. "I need a minute. Somewhere quiet."

Florien stopped, studying her face from under his tangled fringe. Apparently satisfied, he grunted, grabbed a fistful of skirt and towed her down another passageway and into what was evidently a storeroom. The light spilling in through the doorway created a dusty twilight crowded with grotesque shapes—the gigantic haunch of some hoofed animal, a ship's tall prow, four tattered shields hanging on hooks on the wall, all askew.

Leaning against the leprous trunk of an improbable tree, Florien fished a toothpick out of his tattered trews and stuck it in his mouth.

"Alone," said Prue.

The boy's brows drew together. "Why?"

Because what I decide to do tonight will change my life. And I'm scared. "Never mind why."

"But I sed t' Erik I'd bring ye." His sharp features grew pinched with worry.

"Don't worry, I'll find him. Promise."

The child's extravagant lashes swept down, then up. He had the most beautiful eyes, dark as Concordian chocolat. "Kin we shake 'ands?"

"Shake—Yes, of course, but why?"

"'Cos then ye 'ave t' do it. On yer honor." His skinny chest expanded. "Erik tol' me."

"Oh." Prue's heart gave the strangest little skip. "Show me which is his door before you go." She extended her hand.

His pale cheeks flooding with color, Florien shook his head. "Nah," he said, whipping his right hand behind his back. Clearly holding his breath, he offered his left.

Gravely, Prue shook it, the small fingers like a bundle of thin winter twigs in her grasp. "There," she said. "My solemn promise."

"Yah." His good humor restored, Florien paused in the doorway. "Back t' way we come, left an' then third on t' right." He disappeared around the corner.

Behind the ship was a tall, freestanding swing, the upper part of its frame embellished with garlands of limp paper flowers. Slowly, Prue walked toward it, her skirts stirring up little eddies of dust.

It wasn't as if she was incapable of taking a risk. By going into partnership with Rose and purchasing The Garden, she'd gambled with Katrin's future as well as her own. Nonetheless, she'd left as little to chance as possible. By the time the decision was made, she and Rose knew everything there was to know about The Garden and how it operated.

With one hand, she set the seat swinging, testing the strength of the old timbers. Satisfied, she gathered up her skirts and sat, studying the toes of her evening slippers as she swayed gently to and fro.

What did she know of Erik Thorensen? Almost nothing—except he made her ache and burn for things she hardly understood. As clearly as if he stood before her in the gloom, she saw his delightful smile in all its incarnations, a spectrum he seemed able to range at will, from dazzling to apparently genuine, innocent to downright wicked.

Chavis had never had Erik's lightness of touch, let alone his intelligence, but his smile had been just the same—an expression of complicity, one that promised a warmth that never came. Godsdammit, what was *wrong* with her? She thought she'd learned that lesson. There must be some inherent flaw in her personality, a weakness for sunny blue eyes and guileless smiles, for a man who could make her laugh.

Prue massaged her aching temples. If her only gift was balancing the books, then that's what she'd do—assess the risks and make a rational decision.

What did she *really* want? Lifting her head, she stared blankly at the shields on the wall.

Yes, she wanted Erik—the pleasure of being encompassed, enveloped by his uncompromising masculinity. Her breath hitched. Gods, she wanted so desperately to be taken over, filled and fucked 'til she screamed aloud with the wanton joy of it. She'd never experienced that degree of abandon, but she knew, without a doubt, Erik could give it to her. And in return? In that Magickal chamber inside the Leaf of Pleasures, the taste of her most intimate flesh had brought him to climax. As he'd emerged from the water to burn her with his gaze, she'd felt the heady power of her femininity, a balm after the way he'd set her aside the night before.

Her hands clenched hard on the ropes of the swing. She was tingling all over, breathing hard. Prue's lips quirked in a wry smile. The poets had it right. Desire was definitely a kind of insanity. All right, put physical pleasure on the plus side of the ledger. What else?

She *liked* him.

Prue frowned. She hadn't expected that. He'd sneaked past her defenses with his easy undemanding company, the cunning way he ambushed her with humor. She admired his quick wits and determination as much as that fabulous voice. And there was more. Erik hadn't made hasty judgments about Prue McGuire the way most people did. In the strangest way, she felt she was safe with him.

She worried at her bottom lip.

Now that was an interesting thought. He didn't seem to care that she wasn't all fluttering eyelashes and languishing sighs. He wasn't fazed by her intelligence or efficiency, nor by her looks—or lack of them.

Mentally, Prue contrasted her own plain, neat person with that of the tall blond dancer. Her heart sank. Time to fill in the other side of the ledger.

How often did a woman reject Erik Thorensen? Her mouth twisted. Wounded vanity was a powerful incentive for seduction. She'd never meant to intrigue him, but gods, she knew enough to recognize the hunter's gleam in his eye. What did it matter that he'd made her like him? Charm, talent, acting—they were all his stock in trade. Once she'd succumbed and he'd worked off his pique on her willing body, he'd be off to the next conquest. Godsdammit, if his self-imposed mission to save the city took too much longer, he might finish up doing it right under her nose.

A *façade*—that was it. Prue struggled on. Behind the veneer of the man, there was either a wasteland or a raging storm, and she couldn't decide which prospect was the more unsettling. A chill ran down her spine and she drew the shawl closer around her shoulders. It could be that the mystery of Erik Thorensen was grubby and commonplace and he had a woman waiting for him on every world. Children.

She gave a huff of disbelief. No, it wasn't so, she'd stake her life on it. He valued his freedom too greatly. He had his own sense of honor, skewed though it might be. Once it was over with a lover, it would be over.

Oh gods. As it would be when he left her.

Merciful Sister, her head hurt! Prue brought the gentle movement of the swing to a halt, the soles of her slippers scuffing across the grit on the floor. Time was running out— and she had a promise to keep to a little boy.

Shuddering, she gazed at the imbalance on the page of her imaginary ledger. The heart wanted what it wanted, but oh, the risks! She'd had a taste of what he could offer and Sister save her, she wanted more. Her head was spinning, her stomach tight with tension.

Burying her head in her hands, she cursed softly. Suppose, just suppose for a mad instant, that she reached out for what she desired? Grabbed with both hands?

The memories might be worth the pain.

Prue sat up. She wasn't a frightened girl, abandoned by the man she'd trusted with her whole heart. Not anymore. She had maturity, resources, Rose and Katrin to love her and pick up the pieces.

Gripping the ropes in both hands, she rose, concentrating on keeping her knees steady. Outside, female chatter approached and then receded down the passageway, Florien's gruff little treble raised in response to some laughing comment. A door banged shut and the noise cut off.

Prue smiled. Such a strange child. *Erik tol' me.* She sobered. No wonder he was wary, poor little mite, with that broken finger and the marks of privation still on him. Yet the boy heroworshipped Erik, even if he didn't entirely trust him.

All the whirling thoughts within her subsided into a pool of silence. *Even damaged, even too wary to trust, the heart still wants what it wants.*

The prow of the ship looming over her shoulder, Prue stared her shrinking soul in the eye. Remaining steadfast in the face of overwhelming temptation was a grinding, exhausting business. She was heartily sick of it.

Her pulse raced. She didn't have to trust Erik to enjoy him, to take what she longed for—but on her own terms. Was it possible to be weak in one way and yet stay strong and whole in every other? Erik Thorensen might be temptation personified, but that didn't mean he was entitled to all of Prue McGuire. She snorted. Hah! The very prospect would have him running as far and as fast as possible.

Finger by finger, she released the ropes. Examining her stinging palms, she discovered the coarse fibers had rasped her flesh until it glowed.

No, thank the Sister, she wasn't a complete fool. Physical pleasure was all very well, but she'd shield the tender underside of her heart by tucking the most essential part of herself away, deep and safe. A balancing act above a bottomless fall, but hell, she'd spent all her years at The Garden keeping her nerve, walking a fine line between ruin and success. It had been . . . stimulating.

Stepping into the corridor, Prue pressed a hand over the chilly void behind her breastbone. Don't dither, *breathe*. She turned left and began counting doors. *Breathe*. One, two . . .

Squaring her shoulders, she rapped briskly on the third one along. *Breathe*.

"Come in." Erik's voice.

Her pulse leaped. *Breathe*. Head high, Prue swept in, stopping short after two steps.

Such a stark contrast to the opulence of the theater upstairs. Almost bare—a rack for costumes, a small shabby couch, Erik's chair and the makeup table. The absolute minimum, and all used and worn.

When Erik looked up, their eyes met in the mirror.

The words dried in her mouth.

Although he was seated with his back to the door, he filled the small space, his shoulders so broad and strong, the taut line of muscle in buttock and thigh shamelessly outlined by the skintight breeches. He'd removed the demon king's trim goatee, but his eyes were still rimmed with dark pencil, the lids dusted blue and highlighted beneath the brows with pale glitter.

Prue had never thought a man could be called beautiful, but the cosmetics made his eyes so brilliant she thought she might drown in the blue of them, as vivid as polished lapis lazuli from Trinitaria. The entire effect was disturbingly androgynous. Why it should emphasize his potent masculinity so compellingly she couldn't fathom.

But it did and she couldn't give him less than his due.

With quiet finality, the door snicked shut at her back.

20

"Gods," she said, "you've got an incredible nerve. That was magnificent."

He ducked his head, reaching for a sponge and a wide-mouthed jar of some kind of cream. "I did what I had to do," he muttered.

"You forced them to listen." Prue shook her head, bemused. "I'm only just beginning to understand. You never give up, do you? On anything?"

"No, Mistress Prue, I don't." Erik drew the sponge across his cheek. "I can't," he said. "Especially not now. One Leaf is bad enough. What if there are others? Think of the bridges that link them. The potential for disaster beggars the imagination."

"I saw the first purplemist tree in bloom today. It'll be storm season soon."

He didn't move a muscle. "Is that bad?"

Prue cleared her throat. "Could be. Can you still smell it . . . whatever it is?"

"Only when the wind changes." Erik got busy with the sponge. "It's getting fainter the more the tide turns."

She folded her hands together to keep them from trembling. "The whole city's talking about you now. You managed that much at least. Well done."

Twisting around, he stared at her, one side of his face clean, the other still painted. Prue resisted the temptation to squeeze her eyes shut. She'd never been at all imaginative, but she found the sight dislocating, as though he wore a diabolical half mask. Two Erik Thorensens, both brutally handsome, one hard and demonic and flashy, the other . . .

She tilted her head to one side, frowning. The naked side of his face should have looked vulnerable, exposed as it was. Instead, it was closed, revealing nothing but a control as hard as winter iron.

"What? Is there a spot on my nose?" Despite the growl, his lips twitched. Tossing the soiled sponge aside, he reached for a fresh one and turned back to his reflection. "My mind's made up about paying the fine, so don't argue."

"Likewise. And Rose does what I tell her, so the advantage is mine. You said you have brothers, didn't you?"

"Mmm. Three. But don't bet on Rose." His teeth flashed. "I can be extremely persuasive."

"I know," said Prue, with more feeling than she'd intended. She hurried on before he could reply. "How long since you've seen them? And your mother? You mentioned her."

Erik wiped the remnants of cream from his face with a small towel. Slowly, he folded it and placed it in the precise center of the dressing table. Still in silence, he rose and turned to face her. Prue pressed her spine to the door and squared her shoulders. She was having difficulty with her breath again, though a stray draft swirled through the rack of hanging costumes and toyed with the fringes on her shawl. Where had it come from? The room was snug and warm.

Completely without expression, he studied her face. "Twenty years," he said at last. He took a leisurely step forward. "I see you wore it." A triumphant curve of the lips. He flicked the jade fringe with a long finger. "Why won't you do what you're told, Prue? I've got plenty of money. I'll pay the fine."

"No. It was my mistake, my responsibility." Prue's blood thrummed with the joy of battle. Defiantly, she raised her chin, trying to decide whether it felt like flying—or coming down with a fever. "Twenty years is a long time when it's family."

"Stop trying to change the subject. You're a worthy foe, Prue McGuire." Erik's eyes lit with unmistakable heat. "All bluff and challenge. The irresistible force meets the immovable object." A second step brought them almost chest to chest. His scent washed over her, a strange mixture—a trace of cosmetics, the cleansing cream, and his own male, musky warmth. Oddly arousing.

He stared down at her. "Do you have any idea how badly I regret the way I hurt you?" Very slowly, he raised a hand to touch her face. His thumb brushed over her cheekbone.

When she didn't move, his expression lightened. "And how much you tempt me?" A slow, crooked smile bloomed on his lips.

"*Stop it.*" Her voice cracked. "For the gods' sake, just . . . stop it."

Every vestige of charm disappeared. "Stop what?"

"Flirting. Seducing." Prue blinked hard. "I know how I must seem to you."

Erik frowned down at her. "You do?"

"Ordinary," she said. "So sensible I'm a bore."

He reached out to cradle her jaw in one palm. "That's strange," he said. "So you're a mind reader now? And here I was thinking you'd been expressly designed by the gods to tempt me." His thumb stroked gently over the cheek with the dimple.

Prue stiffened her spine. "You resisted temptation perfectly well last night."

He raised the other hand to cup her face. "I made a terrible mistake and I caused you pain," he said. "I swear on my honor I won't do it again." His eyes were intensely blue, steady on hers.

She shook so hard, currents of air swirled between them, vibrating with tension. Wrapping her fingers around his thick wrists, she used the grip to anchor herself. It took all the courage Prue possessed to speak. Hurling herself off a cliff would be easy in comparison. In fact, the falling sensation was so vivid she would not have been surprised to see a vast chasm open up at her feet, in the center of the threadbare rug.

"You . . . you . . ." Gods, she couldn't do this.

"Prue, give me another chance." His thumbs continued to caress her cheekbones, but he didn't crowd her. Such an experienced hunter.

Recklessly, she pinned a smile on her lips. A shield for her heart, like the ones in the storeroom.

"If I do . . ." She plunged forward, headfirst over the vertiginous drop. ". . . you won't . . . turn away again?"

"Not unless you tell me to." His voice dropped to the velvet rumble that liquefied her bones. "Prue, love?"

Wordlessly, she nodded. Then she closed her eyes and held her breath, her heart trying to knock itself free of her rib cage. Her breasts swelled, so tight they tingled unbearably. Restlessly, she shifted her hips, the tender flesh between her thighs aching with slow, hot tears.

In the silence, she could hear the breeze pick up, the costumes flutter on their hangers.

"You're sure?"

"Yes, godsdammit!" Her eyes snapped open. "Do it before I lose my nerve!"

Erik grinned, reaching over her shoulder to bolt the door. His eyes sparkled like a summer sea under the sun's hot caress. He must have looked exactly this way as a boy, brimming with delight and mischief.

"We can't make too much noise," he said. "These walls are as thin as paper. No screaming."

"*Screaming?* What makes you think—?"

"Sshh." He laid a finger against the cushion of her lower lip. "Gods, you have a gorgeous mouth."

"I do?" she mumbled.

"Mm." Bending his head, he kissed her. Endlessly, softly, with plenty of tongue, taking his time, savoring her mouth with little flicks and wet swipes. Prue curled her fingers into the fabric of his shirt and hung on, allowing her head to fall back against the unyielding surface of the door, letting Erik take the lead. On the very periphery of her consciousness, she heard voices outside in the passage, the thud of boots, a distant door closing.

When her legs went out from under her, he caught her up in his arms, lifting her clean off the floor and placing her on the couch in a billow of skirts. He came down over her, just the way she'd imagined, his big body blanketing hers in heat, one knee pinning her gown, his hands hard on her shoulders. He was crooning, deep in his throat, a kind of purr-growl that told her he was flying. Tender nips, soothing licks, all down the sensitive spots on her neck, nibbles on her collarbones that made her want to squirm with pleasure.

But she couldn't, because she was helpless, overwhelmed by his strength, the weight of his possession.

Gods, it was good!

Small undignified sounds escaped her and she didn't care.

But Erik drew back, his eyes dancing. "Quiet," he said. A smile so brilliant she forgot to breathe. "Naughty girl."

Immediately, his golden brown brows drew together and his lips tightened as if he'd bitten back the words he was about to say. "You all right?" The strange little breeze came back from nowhere, teasing his hair so it flopped over his forehead.

If you're going to give in to temptation, the least you can do is be thorough about it, she told herself. For answer, Prue locked her arms around his neck and tugged him down again, caught between wanting to laugh and amazement at her own daring. She'd never been demanding in bed, but then she'd never had a lover like Erik Thorensen. It was beyond belief, what her body was doing to her. Such driving urgency, an absolute conviction that if she couldn't have him wedged high and hard inside her, preferably in the next few seconds, she'd die of the wanting. How was it even possible to experience this degree of desire, so acute she'd be babbling like a fool any second?

Sweet Sister, if she did beg, what would it matter? He'd take care of her. She knew he would because he'd promised. Surreptitiously, she raised her hips, the lightest press against the glorious bulge beneath the skintight breeches. It wasn't just that he was long, he was thick. She'd tried so hard not to notice. Prue licked her lips. What would he do if she took him in her mouth, suckled him right through the fabric? Would he ask her to do that? It wasn't something she'd particularly enjoyed in the past, but to give Erik pleasure . . . Her clitoris flexed, suffusing her belly with a warmth so sweet and fierce she bit back a moan.

Panting, she came up on her elbows, watching Erik's busy fingers on her laces, first the gown, then the chemise beneath. As each inch of swelling breast flesh was exposed, he bent his shining head and kissed it. Then he licked it. Then he kissed it again.

When she groaned, he looked up, his cheeks flushed with ruddy color. "You're so beautiful, Prue," he said hoarsely, and she couldn't doubt he meant it. Spreading her bodice open, he filled his hands with her breasts. They both sighed.

"Take your hair down." He paused, his chest rising and falling. Some of the color left his face. "Sorry. Will you undo your hair? Please?"

He helped her to sit up and together they untied the tapes of her gown and drew it off, leaving her clad in only brief, silky drawers and her best chemise, the one embroidered with silvery touchme blossoms. Fresh from the bath, she'd simply decided she needed to look her best and slipped it over her head with a frisson of pleasure. Now she knew why she'd chosen it.

"Ah. Pretty." Erik hooked a finger under one strap and then the other, slipping them off her shoulders. The chemise fell to her waist. "*Yes*," he rumbled, his voice very deep. "Gods." A sharp inhalation. "What would you like next, sweetheart?"

Prue pulled the last hairpin free. A sheaf of glossy brown hair slipped down over her shoulders, dark locks tumbling over the paleness of his sleeve. "What?" she said stupidly. Why ask her opinion when he was supposed to be sweeping her away?

Erik's jaw tightened. "I can't—*won't*—tell you what to do. You set the pace." But even as he spoke, he was spearing his fingers into her hair, pulling her closer. The breeze picked up, the costumes swinging to and fro on their rack.

"Off," she mumbled against his mouth, plucking at his shirt. "*Off.*"

He reared back, ripping at his laces. That accomplished, he held out a wrist. "The cuff's tight." His eyes glinted. "Help me?"

It should have been simple, but her fingers trembled so badly, the small buttons kept slipping from her grasp. Erik hummed happily, rasping her nipples with his free hand, stroking her belly through the silk, making her giggle, silly as a giddy girl.

The shirt floated, billowing in the air before it sank to the floor. She swallowed. Merciful Sister. Acres of tawny skin over slabs of hard muscle, a deliciously raspy sprinkling of hair arrowing down over a cobbled stomach. The strange talisman on its chain, the half-healed scratches. She couldn't breathe. Prue laid her palm over his heart, rubbing in a gentle circle. The small disk of his nipple peaked sharply and he hissed.

"Stop." He clapped a big hand over hers. "I can't think straight when you do that."

"Really?" She laughed out loud, fizzing with joy. "What about this?" Leaning forward, she took his nipple delicately between her lips and suckled. Then harder.

Erik bucked and swore. Sinking his fingers in her hair, he exerted a gentle, but steady pressure. With a final, regretful lick, Prue released him. "You make me greedy," he said, his voice thick. "Gods, I have to see you. Take—" He broke off, swallowed hard and started again. "Will you take off the rest?"

"Maybe." Loving this, Prue slanted him a teasing glance. "Let me go." When he did, she sank back and raised her arms over her head, arching her pelvis, gazing at his tense face from under her lashes. His stare followed every movement, as weighty as a touch, traveling up her arms to lock on her crossed wrists. It might be shameless, but gods, this was a whole new power, a game she'd never felt safe enough to play. Where his body touched hers, she could feel tremors coursing through him, bone-deep. His control was costing him dear, and it went to her head like spiced wine.

Kicking off her evening slippers, she ran a bare foot up his booted calf. "You do it," she murmured.

Long fingers sank into silk and gripped. "Are you sure?"

Prue stared, a little puzzled. "Yes."

The word had barely left her lips before Erik had ripped the garments off and tossed them over his shoulder. With a sort of formless growl, he launched himself at her body, his big warm hands everywhere, sliding up her thighs, pushing them wide, one finger sliding easily into her depths, then two.

Prue gave herself over to sensation, some small, still-rational corner of her mind astonished at her own abandon. Her body bowed up off the couch, clenching on his fingers. He grunted, setting up a rhythm of gentle thrusts, twisting his wrist, hitting the spot inside that was so sweet and wicked she sobbed with pleasure.

With his other hand, he reached over her head and gripped both her wrists, holding her with easy strength. Dipping his head, he sealed his lips over hers and stole her soul, along with her breath. His tongue was strong and deft in her mouth, his clever fingers agile, massaging her clitoris from deep inside.

She was comprehensively pinned, lost under his big body. She hadn't even realized how she'd yearned for it. No responsibility, no burdens or expectations. All she had to do was follow Erik's lead and unimaginable pleasure would be hers. It made her dizzy to think of it.

From the moment Chavis had stalked out the door of their tumbledown lodgings, she'd had no one but herself to depend on. When she and Rosarina had arrived at The Garden of Nocturnal Delights early that same bright morning, both had been desperate for work—Rose's only commodity her fierce dark beauty, Prue's her gift for numbers and the skills she'd learned in Master Ando's dusty countinghouse.

Work she'd been given—plenty of it, every day, many nights past midnight. Busy, conscientious Mistress Prue. Until she and Rose amassed sufficient funds to risk everything and buy The Garden.

All those lives—and her daughter's future—dependent on Prue's business acumen, her ability to get things done. She hadn't failed them yet, but if she allowed herself to think of it too much, too often, her belly roiled with apprehension.

But now—for this short time—she could relax into Erik's effortless mastery of her responses, give herself to him to be thoroughly and delightfully debauched. She wouldn't have to make a single decision, think a single logical thought. All that existed was the giving and receiving of physical pleasure, nothing more.

When he was gone, there'd be the knowledge that once, just once, she'd done this crazy, beautiful thing. She, sensible

Prue McGuire. Real life could wait in the wings until she was ready to pick it up again.

Prue squirmed, resisting his grip, loving the way he held her with such ease, not hurting, not crushing, just enough and no more.

Gradually, his movements slowed. He lifted his head, his hair brushing her cheek. "I'm rushing you."

"No, no." Prue squeezed her thighs on his hand, but he slid his fingers free nonetheless. Prue's jaw dropped, her arousal cooling a little.

"What do you want me to do?" he said.

"*Do?*" It came out perilously close to a squeak. "You don't know?"

Erik's jaw set in that obstinate line she already knew so well. "Tell me what you want and I'll do it. Anything. I swear." Slowly, he rose and backed away, giving her space, room to breathe, to think.

Prue's whole body resounded to the beat of her blood, as if her heart were a temple gong and he'd struck it. *Boom, boom. Boom, boom.*

"This isn't quite . . ." She squeezed her eyes shut. Then she looked at him, really looked.

He stood foursquare on the tattered rug, quivering with tension, his pupils so expanded his eyes appeared almost black with lust. A pulse ticked madly at the base of his throat and his wide chest rose and fell as if he'd been running. His hair lifted away from his shoulders, the fair, shining locks blown back by an unseen wind.

Erik Thorensen was the most erotic thing she'd seen in her life, the muscle in his long thighs beautifully framed by those absurd boots, his cock straining the demon king's breeches.

Prue wet her lips. "Fuck me," she whispered.

21

Lord's balls, *yes*! Erik had never heard anything as enticing in his life as her soft, carnal mouth shaping the wicked words, her voice, gone all husky, saying them out loud.

Fuck me.

But what he really loved was the sheer abandon of her, so far gone already she was splayed delightfully over the shabby couch, all pink-tinted, honeyed curves, topped with stiff, velvety nipples that made his mouth water. His proper Mistress McGuire, showing him everything. Erik's ravenous gaze zeroed in on the dark, springy curls between her smooth thighs, the shy, ruffled folds all pink and puffy and slick.

The taste of her from this morning, so female, earthy and tart and sweet on his tongue. Holding her eye, he lifted his fingers to his mouth and licked them clean, while his cock reared like a beast. When she gasped, her pretty eyes opening wide, the Voice bubbled in his throat, the instinct fighting to be free, to damn him forever. *Touch yourself, Prue. Show me what you like.*

He bit it back, swallowing hard. Fuck it all to hell, the strength of the temptation was incredible, ruthless, worse than ever before. Because from the moment she'd raised her lips to his, he'd known she was withholding something. A growl rumbled in his chest. Damn the perversity of his soul, because he wanted it, whatever the hell it was, with a wicked, driving need.

Command Prue and he'd have that elusive something, he'd possess her utterly. Each time, she succumbed more quickly than the time before. But if he did it, overwhelmed her with the Voice, he'd never know the difference between true and false, given and compelled. *Never* . . . Doubt—it was a poison worse than prettydeath, the favorite instrument of assassins on every known world. In the end, it'd destroy whatever it was they had together. He couldn't do it to her, to his brave, clever Prue, couldn't take the choice from her.

Even worse, she had no idea of the dark desires surging within him, battering at his resolve, making nonsense of the code he'd worked out for himself, the oaths he'd sworn. He'd be better not to speak at all, not a solitary word, because if the Voice broke through his control, he'd terrify her, straitlaced Mistress McGuire. Hell, what he needed was a gag, a way to keep them both safe. He clamped his lips together with grim resolution.

There must be a storm brewing outside, because the sound of the wind banged around inside his skull, making coherent thought impossible.

At his first fumble with the godsbedamned breeches, his cock leaped forward as if it were spring-loaded, seed thickening in his balls, seething at the root. Insisting. Erik abandoned the breeches, threw himself into the single chair and attacked the buckles on the tall boots. To a litany of breathless curses, he hauled them off, all the time conscious of a blue green gaze so intense it scorched his skin.

The talisman swung out and back, bumping his breastbone, reminding him of what he mustn't do.

Lord's balls, he had it! The perfect solution.

Ripping off the breeches, he stood before her, one hand cradling the pulling weight of his rampant shaft. "Sweetheart," he said, panting a little. "We need to slow down. I don't want to frighten you."

Her chin went up, bless her. "You don't."

Leaning forward, he ran his tongue over the soft swirl of

that fascinating dimple. Kissed it. "You've had men like me before?"

"No! I mean . . . I don't know. How could I?" Her breath was coming so hard, her breasts quivered with the force of her respiration. Inside him, the beast raged.

Softly, softly.

"Sweetheart," he said, "I'm giving you control. Come down here, lie on me." Slowly, he sank down to the rug, drawing her with him, arranging her small, supple body over his, her nipples brushing his chest, his erection prodding shamelessly into her belly. Everywhere they touched, energy sparked as if lightning lurked in the room, waiting. His head was filled with a rushing noise.

Prue's fingers dug into his shoulders. Erik stroked his palms down either side of her spine, relishing the satin of her skin, the resilience of the healthy muscle beneath. He finished by shaping his palms to the high curves of her glorious bottom, tracing the dimples there with his fingertips. Oh, the things he could do with that ass!

With a sigh, he lifted his arms over his head and wrapped his fingers around the leg of the couch. "I'm at your disposal," he rumbled. "Do whatever you like. Fuck me however you want, just fuck me."

Did she have any idea how expressive her face was?

First the flicker of shock, then the speculation as she sank her teeth into that delectable lower lip. After that . . . her eyes flared with a woman's lust. But it was the tremble of the small, strong hands braced on his shoulders that made him say, "Believe me, there's no way to get this wrong. Please yourself and you'll please me."

But he couldn't help rolling his hips up as a hint.

Slowly, she sat up, walking her hands down his chest to his stomach. When she rose and settled across his hips, his cock split the lips of her sex perfectly, dragging his burning length through her folds. Erik groaned at the blissful slipperiness lubricating his sensitive skin.

Peripherally, he was aware of the low vibration of thunder, the wind rising, so close it seemed almost in the room. But that was impossible.

"Whatever I want?" Apparently fascinated, she swirled a fingertip around his navel. But simultaneously, she shifted her hips, working herself over him again, from back to front. When his bare crown nudged her clitoris at the top of the stroke, she gasped aloud, a flush sweeping up all the way from her breasts to her cheeks.

Erik's fists clenched so hard on the leg of the couch he heard the wood creak. He should have realized it would be more than he could bear. Either he'd spurt all over himself like a green boy or he'd rise up in a storm surge of domination, bearing her down to the floor, shoving his thick, hungry cock inside, deep, deep, where his beast longed to be.

"Ah, that's good." Prue came forward, her hands braced on his chest, her hair swinging down in a swathe that brushed his ribs with a cool, tantalizing caress. Slowly at first, then more frantically, she shifted her hips, sliding their intimate flesh together, gasping at the top of every stroke.

Gods, she was sensitive! Erik squeezed his eyes shut and hung on grimly. *C'mon, c'mon*, chanted a swelling chorus in his brain. *Put it in, for the gods' sake*. A few words, that was all. A simple command. The Voice rumbled in his chest, fighting to be free.

Blessedly, Prue rose, fumbling her fingers around him, fitting him to the soft narrow opening of heaven.

Every cell in his body cried out with relief and anticipation. He loved fucking, no question of it—what man didn't?—but this was very nearly his favorite part, the first inch, the push past that initial resistance into slick, resilient walls of flesh.

Erik released his death grip on the couch to clasp Prue's curvy waist. "That better?"

Her sweet tits bobbed with the force of her breath. "Yes. Sister, you're so, so . . . Nngh." She sank down a little and his head reeled with the heat, the tight, creamy glove of her.

Reflexively, he arched up with his hips and she took another inch, gasping.

"Fuck it, Prue," he panted. "How long has it been?"

"Five, no—six—years." She shot him a glinting look. "But I haven't forgotten—*gods*—how."

It took them several agonizing, glorious minutes to work

him all the way in, an inch at a time, her sex fluttering around him in panic and arousal.

Luxuriously, Erik ran his palms over her flanks, up over her ribs, to her breasts. Without a word, he buried his fingers in her hair and pulled her down, sealing her small body all along his. His cock thumping with the strut of his blood, he opened his mouth to devour hers, sinking into the kiss.

"Now," she whispered into his mouth. "Now."

"Yes. *Fuck me.*" More than a little of the Voice had escaped that time, he knew, but it hardly mattered, because she was already rising cautiously, using the support of his big hands around her waist.

She shivered, gooseflesh breaking out on her arms, her chest, ruching her nipples to tight, velvety points of desire. "Oh, you feel so good." She slid down, releasing a small shriek. The sleek muscles in her thighs flexed. Back up, faster. Down. "I can feel you in my throat."

Erik huffed out a laugh, punching up into the escalating rhythm, meeting her with the firm slap of his thighs against her buttocks. "That's for later." Fuck, he could see it all so clearly, Prue on her knees, suckling, licking, crooning in her throat, glorying in the erotic torture she dealt him. His hands deep in her hair, her sweet tongue moving over his flesh, loving him. The mistress of his pleasure, as much as he was the master of hers.

Impossibly, he swelled, thickening. Prue cried out, her back arching in a beautiful bow, her inner walls clamping on his girth. He'd never heard music sweeter than the formless, breathy noises she made in extremis, his prim and proper Prue. He wanted more, whole choruses, rising above the clamor of the storm. She must be close. As for him—he had only seconds left, the seed boiling against the tender skin of his balls.

Ruthlessly, he tightened his grip, increasing the pace, thrusting his whole brutal length in and out, to the root. "C'mon," he panted. "Go over, love. Go over."

"Nearly . . ." Prue keened. "Can't, can't." She writhed, tears sheening her extraordinary eyes. The wind tossed her hair about in dark, silky skeins.

Erik slid one hand over the soft curve of her belly and

furrowed down into her pubic hair. He paused, choking. Godsdammit. Her choice.

"Shall I touch?"

"Yes, *yes*!" She leaned back, opening herself to him, spreading that pretty pink cleft so he could help her.

When he rubbed, as gently as he knew how, Prue stiffened. A split second later, she was bouncing so vigorously, he had to steady her with the other hand. The pad of his forefinger slid over the small prow of her clitoris, thrillingly fast.

Mistress Prue McGuire threw her head back and screamed her pleasure, loud and long. Her sex clamped down on him so hard he saw stars.

He was gone, an extended rush from his swollen scrotum, flooding the length of his rapturous cock, spurting hot jets of relief. Fuck, so good, so good. It unraveled him, this mind-numbing pleasure. The air crackled with thunder. Every muscle in his body went slack and his head rolled on the rug. Ah, the aftershocks were exquisite, a series of delicious, pointy-tongued licks deep in his loins.

Prue had subsided on top of him in a boneless bundle. Erik stroked her shoulder, trailed his fingers down to her hip. Still breathing.

Gods, he'd got through it. No mistakes. Good for him. Contentedly, he drew wobbly circles over the cheeks of her luscious ass. *Later*, he thought muzzily.

Without opening his eyes, he said, "You screamed."

A light touch traced his collarbones, soft lips nuzzled the pit of his throat. "You bellowed."

"Did not."

"Did too." A yawn.

Erik opened one eye and chuckled. "It's pretty quiet out there. We've got the place to ourselves, I think. And the wind's dropped."

No reply.

Sweat stung in the scratches on his arms and chest. The rug was rucked up under his ass in prickly ridges, the floor cold and unyielding. From where he lay, all he need do was turn his head for a clear view of the dust clumps under the couch. A sneeze tickled his nose.

But none of that was important.

Prue McGuire lay sprawled over the top of him, completely limp. Her head was snuggled under his chin, where it fit perfectly. Every so often, a ladylike snuffle escaped her.

Erik's lips curved in a tired smile. *How'd I do today on the task You gave me, Horned Lord? Great Lady? I've been such a busy boy. Swimming with creatures straight out of a fairy tale, making Prue happy, making her come, breaking her heart. Oh, let's not forget the public ridicule, that was . . . interesting. And the excellent performance of a nursery rhyme.*

But of course, They didn't answer. They never did unless it pleased Them and then only in his dreams.

He'd slipped at the end there. *Fuck me.* Luckily, it had made no difference because that's where they'd been headed anyway. Wistfully, he relived the moments she'd writhed beneath him, the feel of her slim wrists in his grip, the knowledge of her willing helplessness spearing through him. Fuck, it had been sublime, despite the fact it had only been the start of what he could teach her—if she'd trust him. His balls contracted, his cock giving a hard, hungry twitch.

Looked at dispassionately, fucking Prue McGuire had still been the best sex of his life, the very best. Why was that? She'd been hot and sweet, nowhere near as conventional as he'd expected, but she wasn't the most experienced woman he'd had, not by a long way.

How pretty she'd look, bound in silken ropes while he painted her lush tits with strokes of his tongue. His breath came a little faster. The taut, pale curves of her buttocks begged for the flat of his hand. Perhaps she'd defy him so he'd have no choice but to put her over his knee. A rueful grin quirked his lips. She'd be good at defiance, his Prue. Not too much, he'd get it just right, enough to warm, make her tingle, have her wet and pleading. He knew beyond any doubt her skin would color delightfully.

Ah, she'd love it.

Perhaps he could talk her into it—slowly, softly. She was already part of the way there, sleeping trustfully in his arms. He stroked a wayward curl with his forefinger, drawing the sweet smell of her deep into his lungs. But all she'd given him was her body. Despite the way she confronted life head-on, she was too frightened to risk more. Lord's balls, human existence was complicated. After whatever it was that bastard had done to her . . . Erik's fists clenched.

Prue murmured into his skin, her breath warm and moist. Her palm slipped over his chest, her fingers brushing over the talisman on its chain. Erik drew his fingertips along her spine, feeling the bumps of her vertebrae.

Reaching out a long arm, he snagged the shawl from where it lay on the floor in a tumble of jade silk. As always, he was acutely conscious of his breath, of the steady power of his lungs, pumping. Such a precious commodity, air. He'd nearly died for the lack of it as a boy, more than once.

One-handed, he spread the shawl over Prue's body. There. His other arm was going to sleep and the floor hadn't got any bloody softer, but what the hell—he'd pay the price, be her mattress for a while, keep her warm and safe.

She sighed in her sleep and her fingers curled loosely over the talisman.

Everything has a cost, the Horned Lord had said, all those years ago. And then He'd reached up into the vast antlers branching above His head. *Snap!*

At the brutal sound, Erik had flinched and fallen to his knees. He knew he was dead. He had to be. Lungspasm was an evil thing. No healer had the cure, not even the Technomages with all their Science. Only seventeen and his lungs had squeezed tight shut. No amount of gasping, of hideous, frantic struggling, would pry them open again. He'd been able to *feel* the life leaking out of him with the last trickle of air. Even now, he shuddered at the memory. The pain had been blinding, incredible, the terror all-encompassing.

Poor Ma. If he glanced over his shoulder, he could see her down there at the bedside, shaking his unresponsive body, weeping, crying out. "Erik! *Erik!*" His heart ached for her.

Are you listening to Me, boy? A mountain might speak like that, in a vast, subterranean rumble. When the god had called to him from down that long, bright tunnel, his soul had risen from his body and followed like an eager puppy.

Erik bowed his head. "Yes, Lord."

We have work for you to do, My Lady and I.

"Yes, Lord." He risked a sidelong glance, but it was like looking into the sun. His eyes teared.

An inquiring breeze caressed his cheek, a drift of dark, exquisite perfume. In the frozen deeps of space, the stars danced in their cold beds. Another vast presence.

So young, She murmured. *So strong. Are you strong enough, Erik?*

Oh, the feminine, velvet beauty of that voice! Erik hardened, he couldn't help it. "I—I don't know, my Lady."

Ah, the hot blood of youth. But She didn't sound displeased.

Somewhere far off, he could hear the rushing of a mighty wind. Erik licked his lips. "What . . . what would You have me do?"

An interminable pause, during which he imagined the gods exchanging glances, or speaking mind to mind—or living a hundred lifetimes. Who knew? Every cell in his body vibrated with awe and terror. His teeth chattered so hard, he had to clench them together.

At last, the Lady said, gently enough, *We cannot tell you without altering the Pattern.*

The storm drew closer, turbulence plucking at Erik's hair, pushing against his body. Pattern? What Pattern?

If you fail in this service, said the Lord, *your death will be fodder for something foul. It will be interminable.* A huge arm gestured at the shabby bedchamber. *In comparison, this end is clean and good. You are well mourned.*

Involuntarily, Erik looked for Ma, but the room had grown small and blurry, as if viewed down the wrong end of a spyglass. He squinted. His mother had thrown herself over his long frame, gut-wrenching sobs racking her body. Carl was standing by the bed, clutching his limp hand. Gods, was he *crying,* his hellion of a little brother? Where were Pieter and Lars? Oh there, with the healer, their backs pressed to the wall, their cheeks tear-stained.

We will give you your life, together with a gift, said the Horned Lord. *A weapon, a tool, a pleasure. A curse. Up to you.*

The air swirled, the pitch of the wind rising to an eldritch shriek. Ominous gray purple clouds filled the tunnel, obscuring the bedchamber. They roiled with lightning.

Quickly! urged the Lady. *Decide.*

22

"I want to live," said Erik.

Of course. The Lord chuckled, though there was little humor in it. *Everyone does. Even Death.*

Erik was still puzzling over that one when the Lord tossed him a small object. Automatically, he caught it.

A gleaming fragment of horn, intricately whorled and scored with fluting patterns. So beautiful. Erik's gaze flew to the deity. He winced, putting up a hand to shield his eyes. "My Lord!"

Look carefully, said the god dryly. *And remember that we all pay.*

Dark blood flowed freely from the horn. Glowing like liquid fire, it covered Erik's palm, dripped over his wrist. A god's blood. His mouth fell open. "But—"

The Lady's huge, star-dappled hand closed around the back of his neck and jerked him forward. Helpless, Erik hung in Her grasp, his eyes clamped shut in terror. Soft lips touched his, the caress a torment so pleasurable it burned like fire and ice. A gust of sweet breath blew down his throat—summer and sex, grass with the sap rising, flowers and the smell of rainbows.

When She dropped him, a storm picked him up and whirled him about, light as a dried leaf. It beat at his senses, punched him hard in the chest with a battering ram of air. Coughing, he opened his eyes, his mother's startled face inches from his own.

Beneath the covers, the seventeen-year-old Erik clenched his fist over the god's talisman.

In the dressing room under the Royal Theater, Erik laid his fingers over Prue's as she curled them over it.

How long would it be before he'd slip again? His track record with Prue wasn't exactly stellar. To make it worse, she was becoming temptingly susceptible to his control. Muzzling the Voice tonight had required the most severe exercise of his will. What the hell was it about Prue McGuire that clawed at his soul, slicing his self-discipline to tattered ribbons? Was it the challenge of her? Or the comfort?

If he was vigilant, censoring every word that came out of his mouth, he might manage it for months, possibly a year or so. But no spontaneity, none of the joy of loving freely and well. He'd never had that, but godsdammit, until he'd glimpsed it, he hadn't realized the loss of that bright possibility would be so piercing.

The Voice came from somewhere so deeply hooked into his masculinity, it was woven all around what it was to be a man— to be Erik Thorensen. Inevitably, it would happen, sooner or later, the end of anything real. The keener his desire, the greater the risk.

Fuck, he couldn't bear it!

Erik wrapped both arms around Prue, holding her close, aching as if he'd been in a tavern brawl. Her compact body was so warm, her soft breath a balm against his skin. He rubbed his burning eyes. Just a little longer and he'd take her home to The Garden.

⁓

As the skiff passed beneath the delicate arch of the Bridge of Amours, the Necromancer caught sight of his servant waiting at the small water stair behind The Garden, as ordered. Springing forward, Nasake offered a steadying arm as the Necromancer climbed from the small craft. His master safely delivered to the top of the stairs, he ran back down the stairs, fumbling at his belt pouch.

"Wait," said the Necromancer. He detested waste. Especially when it came to money. Catching the skiffman's eye, he smiled. "Thank you, my friend."

As he spoke, he reached into the other man's mind and smeared his memory with a spectral thumb. Unfortunately, the Necromancer didn't have time for finesse, so the skiffman would likely find he was missing an entire day. Or two.

His eyes blank, the skiffman nodded. Leaning forward, he rested his head against the pole and drifted away under the Bridge of Amours and around the bend in the canal.

The Necromancer turned to survey the pretty pavilion situated next to the water. "This it?" A narrow, shady path meandered away around the perimeter of the Leaf in the general direction of the bridge.

"Yes, Master. Clouds and Rain it's called. The farthest from the Main Pavilion."

"And you hired it for how long?"

"All morning, Master. As you instructed."

Nasake's tongue crept out to flick his lips. "Last year, there was a murder inside. The pavilion's still not popular, though they gutted it. Everything's new."

The Necromancer cocked a brow. "You felt traces?"

"Oh yes. There was . . . blood."

"Hmm." Violent death. Good. Every little bit helped. The Necromancer's lips curved with satisfaction. He could have had Nasake set up the meeting anywhere, but this little-used pavilion at the far end of The Garden? A stroke of genius. Moreover, it amused him to plot the witch-whore's destruction right under her pert little nose.

Nasake ushered him through a latticed gate and into a private courtyard.

"The assassin?"

"Five minutes."

The Necromancer's eye fell on a half-grown mongrel dog tethered to a purplemist tree that shaded the small space with an umbrella cloud of lilac. "What's this?"

At the sound of his voice, the dog squatted and peed. Its eyes rolled so far the whites showed.

Nasake's already pasty face went gray. "Master, you said a dog would do if I couldn't get a child. I . . . uh . . . There was so little . . ."

The Necromancer raised a hand and the manservant froze. "I'll deal with you later. I trust the assassin is more satisfactory?"

"Oh yes, Noblelord. She's skilled with poison. With the budget you gave me, the Guild Master said—"

"It's a woman? Oh, never mind."

A *dog*? It wasn't going to be as good, godsdammit. As he glared, the mongrel lifted a leg and scratched behind one flop ear. Disgusting creature. Full of bitemes, no doubt. With any luck, he'd be strong enough to do without it. Crossly, he stumped into the pavilion.

Nasake had everything in place, including an easy chair and a footstool. All the furnishings were elegant, gray or silver, with touches of lavender. The comforter on the bed looked as plump and soft as a cloud. A low table inlaid with light wood bore a tray piled high with sweetmeats, a tisane pot and cups, and a flask of spiced wine. The Necromancer's lip curled. By Shaitan, did the man think he was made of money?

"What's all this for?" he asked coldly.

"For her, Noblelord. Mehcredi the assassin. She likes fine food."

From outside came the sound of a heavy tread on the gravel of the path. With his usual efficiency, Nasake thrust the dog into the room and disappeared.

The Necromancer skewered the mongrel with an angry glare. "Sit." The animal collapsed, flat to the floor, as if every bone in its body had crumbled to dust.

Silently, the door swung open. The assassin would be waiting on the other side, assessing the situation. They were all trained like that. Much good would it do her.

Pulling in a breath, the Necromancer donned the cloak of his Dark Arts. "Enter," he called, his tone light and colorless.

A shadow darkened the doorway. When Mehcredi the assassin ducked her head and stepped inside, the Necromancer was hard put not to laugh aloud. The woman was broad shouldered, taller than most men. The many layers of clothing she wore exaggerated the bulky effect. She was so winter pale she had to be from the ice fields in the frozen north. A barbarian.

Her silver gaze scanned the pavilion and collided with his. The Necromancer wouldn't have thought it possible, but her ivory skin went a shade paler. Her mouth falling open, she stared into the darkness beneath his hood. "Take care, assassin," he said bitingly. "Curiosity shortens the life. Shut the door and sit. As you see, I have provided for you."

The woman blinked, taking in the pastries with their gleaming, sugared fruits, the small pies stuffed with savory meat. She swallowed.

The Necromancer waved a hand, enjoying himself. "The chairs are too flimsy. Take the bed."

As her rump made the mattress dip, Mehcredi said, "Who are you?"

"A client," said the Necromancer. "But I'm sure you're not supposed to ask that. Refreshments?"

The assassin shot a glance at the tray, but she didn't move.

"Here." He propelled the dog forward with a boot to its bony backside. "The food is safe, but you may use this if you are nervous." Although its tail was clamped between its legs, the animal's nose quivered as it raised its head. Beneath the scruffy fur, every rib showed. The Necromancer could have counted them had he been so inclined.

Mehcredi broke off a piece of noodle cake and dropped it on the floor. Inching forward on its belly, the dog stretched out its neck and snatched. It fixed hopeful eyes on the assassin's face.

Watching the dog, the woman said, "What's the job?" She lobbed another morsel in the animal's direction. A pink tongue snaked out and licked it up.

"A singer. Erik the Golden, they call him."

A startled silver gaze flew toward him and skittered away again. "The crazy one?" she said. "Everyone's talking about him. The seelie man." She bit the side of her thumb, thinking about it. Under the lacquered windowsill, the water of the canal chuckled as it lapped along the garden wall. "Might cost more." Another sidelong glance.

Soundlessly, the Necromancer laughed and watched her rub the goose bumps on her neck. "Indeed?" he said, genuinely amused. "What makes you think you're worth it? Are you a Master Assassin, perhaps?"

The woman got to her feet, selected a pastry and took a healthy bite. Her hand shook. "No," she mumbled. The dog crept forward to lick up the crumbs from around her boots.

"I see. Tell me, Mehcredi of the Assassin's Guild, how many kills have you to your credit?"

Mehcredi stared fixedly at the curl of steam wafting from the tisane pot. "Eight." She turned, her deep bosom straining her knitted tunic, and the Necromancer knew she'd lied.

He hesitated, unusually torn. Inexperience meant she wouldn't be able to command much of a fee and he was always thrifty, despite his high office. A slum childhood tended to produce that effect. Besides, he thought resentfully, housing and equipping the Technomage Primus of Sybaris had cost him a mint of money.

But, by Shaitan, time was of the essence. And a healthy dose of fear tended to encourage attention to detail.

"Two days," he said. "Ten credits."

The assassin snorted. "Don't care what the Guild Master told you. I'm not as cheap as all that. Fifty." Seating herself once more, she reached for the tisane pot. "And I'll need to know more about the man."

"Fifteen. He's an offworlder. Performing at the Royal Opera. And he hasn't wasted time finding himself a woman. Prue McGuire. She works here, at The Garden."

Mehcredi struggled to her feet. "A Garden courtesan? Are you mad? Those women have connections! The singer did a Royal Command performance. I just remembered." Her eyes narrowed with calculation. "Which means he has the favor of the queen and the Cabal. How do you expect me—?"

"Sit down!" The Necromancer's voice was sibilant, silky and utterly compelling.

The assassin fell back and the dog shot between her legs and under the bed. Claws scrabbled for purchase as it shifted until only a quivering black nose was visible behind her calves.

"You may leave the queen and Cabal to me. Twenty credits and that's my final offer." The Necromancer tossed a coin. To his irritation, it glanced off the side of the table and tinkled to the floor. But the assassin hunkered down, reaching. So he tossed her the rest, one at a time, and watched her scoop them up like a beggar child.

"All right." The task completed, Mehcredi grabbed a savory pie. Absentmindedly, she broke off a piece and dropped it near the bed. The mongrel darted forward with remarkable rapidity and snapped it up, leaving only a wet tongue print on the floor.

The Necromancer frowned, plagued by a niggling doubt. Mehcredi was a minor part of his grand plans and she was also that most useful of objects, an expendable tool. So what was it that bothered him? Watching her jaw move as she chewed, he realized.

Why wasn't she crazy with terror? When he manifested like this—a dark cloud roiling beneath a cloak, the hint of burning eyes—people frequently lost bladder control. Even a woman as intelligent and powerful as the Technomage Primus of Sybaris had been reduced to incoherence. Mehcredi was wary, true enough, but that was all. Was she completely ignorant of dark Magick? How could that be?

A lesson was in order.

The Necromancer rose—and rose—and rose. He expanded until the pretty chamber was clouded with his dark, billowing presence. Unchaining his irritation, he let it loose to run in harness with his unholy glee.

Ah, *now* she showed fear! Too late, my dear. Chuckling, he swooped, pushing insubstantial fingers through the flesh on her throat. He thrust muscle and bone aside until he could pinch her spinal cord between finger and thumb.

"Aaargh!" Mehcredi convulsed.

Delicately, the Necromancer relaxed the pressure and she surged beneath him, surprisingly well muscled, beneath the concealing garments. He increased it again and she subsided, panting, her eyes wide.

Holding her poised, he savored her soul's bouquet. Unusual, plenty of space and light. She was spotless, near as pale inside as out. Almost beautiful. Puzzled, he probed a little further.

So that was it! The assassin was extraordinary. She'd never known love—not a mother's, not a friend's. She'd never been roused by passion, never known the touch of a man. An emotional vacuum, no less. In all his long experience, he hadn't seen the like.

Moaning, Mehcredi shifted in his grip. The dear girl, she was fighting back. How fascinating.

The Necromancer was so engrossed that when the dog set up a storm of barking, he let her slip. Just a fraction, but it was enough. Mehcredi heaved like a restless leviathan on its sea-bed. The connection broke and she rolled away.

Chuckling, he chose to be amused. The assassin promised delicious entertainment. The dog, however, was another matter, standing over the woman's legs, its filthy fur on end, teeth bared. Fortunately, it wasn't a large animal. But as he stooped to it, Mehcredi grabbed it by the scruff and tossed it neatly out the window into the canal.

The howl was cut off abruptly by a splash.

The assassin lay propped on her elbows, shuddering. "Please . . . what did . . ." She licked her lips. "Sorry, I'm sorry."

Much better. The Necromancer returned to the easy chair and the woman sat up, massaging the nape of her neck. "Take your money," he said in the cold, sexless voice he used for dark Magick. "And remember the cost of failure."

Mehcredi reached for the stack of coins on the table.

"No, no," he said, and she froze.

"The fee is now fifteen credits. Two days."

Amused, he watched her swallow her fury as she thrust the money into her belt pouch. "My man is outside," he said. "Send him in to me as you leave."

Her pale cheeks flushed a delicate pink, the assassin edged around him until she reached the door. A final, wild-eyed glance, and she wrenched it open and disappeared.

Because he was busy inside the pavilion of Clouds and Rain, disciplining Nasake, the Necromancer failed to see a shivering, bedraggled bundle of fur drag itself up the water stair and collapse at the top.

Nor did he see Mehcredi the assassin glance back over her shoulder at it and pause, waiting. "Hmpf!" she snorted, fists on her hips. "So you didn't drown after all, you miserable object?"

With a shudder, she cast a wary eye toward the pavilion, rubbing her hands up and down her arms. "Gods!" Hastily, she strode away down the pretty, twisting path toward the bridge, foliage swishing with the speed of her passage.

It took the dog three attempts to stand. When it shook itself, water sprayed in all directions and it nearly fell down again. After a moment's grim concentration, it drew a breath so deep it qualified as a canine sigh and limped off in pursuit of the assassin, head down.

23

Even after all these years, Prue still hated entering the Melting Pot. Her heart beat faster, all her muscles tight, ready to run. Just there, in the dank, smelly shadows under the Bridge of Empty Pockets, that's where she'd huddled, Katrin tucked beneath her, for the first interminable night.

The market seethed with life and noise. Light wavered from behind windows of rough glass, illuminating the produce spilling off the stalls and onto the street, the raucous crowds—farmers from the Cressy Plains jostling with lordlings out for a night on the town, the occasional Trinitarian in bright silks, a curved sword at his hip, even a huge, ice-pale barbarian woman from the far north.

Sooner or later, everyone on Palimpsest drifted down the blue canals to the Melting Pot to haggle and argue and drink and whore at the tops of their voices—a cacophony intent on doing business.

Unobtrusively, Prue stepped a little closer to Erik's bulk.

A big warm hand swallowed hers. "All right?"

Prue tugged her fingers free. "Of course. Why wouldn't I be?"

In the uncertain light, Erik's teeth gleamed as he wrapped

a long arm around her shoulders and pulled her into his side. "No idea," he said, "unless you're embarrassed to be seen with me."

Prue snorted. "Too late for that. After the Open Cabal, everyone thinks we're both mad. Or on crazyspice."

She turned her head. In that dark, twisting alley, the one off to the left, leading to the vegetable market, there'd been a paunchy man with hard hands and raw liquor on his breath. Thank the Sister, he'd been drunk and not drugged. Crazyspice gave the addicted insane strength. As it was, she'd left him with a slash across the cheek that did nothing to enhance his looks.

"You're awfully serious, Mistress Prue," said Erik. He stopped and pulled her into a doorway. "Listen, we could find a skiff to take you back, but I promised Dai I'd speak to these people, and this is my only free evening."

Prue raised her brows. "I wouldn't miss it, not after the performance you gave last night."

Ah, shit! A wave of heat spread from the base of her spine to suffuse her whole body, all the deep, tender places throbbing with delighted memory. Her scarlet cheeks must be shining like beacons in the dimly lit street.

"I meant—" Giving up, she clamped her lips shut. Even now, she could hardly believe it, what she'd done, how wanton and wicked and wonderful his performance had been. Godsdammit, there was so much more to explore, to experience. She longed to crawl all over him, savor every hollow and dip with her hands, her lips—her tongue. If only she hadn't passed out like that, but she'd been so sated, so warm and safe, with his big body stretched out hard and hot beneath her.

Erik chuckled. "I know what you meant, but it was good, wasn't it?" His arm tightened around her waist, warm lips feathered over her cheek.

Prue pushed against his chest, relishing his strength, pitting herself against it. "And you're a conceited—mmpf."

The kiss took her under in a dizzying rush, the heat and the taste of him already familiar, but even more intoxicating than before, because now she knew what was possible, how far he could take her. In fact, she was beginning to suspect she might let him take her almost anywhere.

Ah, she was hopeless. *Hopeless!*

Erik had backed her into a shadowed doorway. He cupped one breast in his hand, rotating his palm against the nipple. "C'mon, Prue. Admit it." He licked a hot trail over the pulse pounding in her neck. "You enjoyed every minute, didn't you?" He blew gently on the spot, so that she gasped.

The night air pressed against her skin, a soft, caressing warmth. Prue sank her fingers into the thickness of his hair and tugged until he lifted his head. With all his experience, why did he even bother asking? Her reaction had been embarrassingly obvious.

"Yes," she said. "Stop fishing."

Some of the tension left his shoulders. "Good," he said, and swooped to press his open mouth to the cheek with the dimple. Broad palms traveled from her shoulder blades down to the upper swell of her buttocks in a long, luxurious stroke, pulling her hard into his body. His voice dropped half an octave, to that deep, rich timbre that made her tingle. "You have more dimples here, did you know?" His cock kicked against her, igniting sparks low in her belly.

Someone whistled and a rough voice called, "Me next, mate."

Erik's head jerked up. In a single smooth motion, he shoved Prue behind him and dropped a hand to the hilt of the long dagger at his waist. "Fuck off," he growled, radiating menace. "She's mine."

A stiff breeze sprang up, swirling down the alley. Debris rattled in the gutters.

When Prue attempted to step around him, he simply barred her way with a heavy arm. She might as well have tried to shift the building at her back.

The man raised a jug to his lips with one hand. With the other, he gave Erik the finger. "Pox on ye, bastard." He reeled away.

When Erik rumbled deep in his chest, all the hair rose on Prue's arms. Tygres sounded like that. Centuries ago, a Trinitarian pasha had foolishly imported a few pairs from Concordia, for sport. The animals had gone wild, thriving in the remote forests of Palimpsest. As a child, she'd seen one in a traveling circus, prowling the perimeters of its cage, yellow eyes shining with rage.

He glared down at her, his face implacable. "You stay where I put you—out of the way—understood?"

Prue blinked, refusing to show the secret thrill his possessiveness gave her. "I'm not completely helpless. I could have dealt with him. But I'm not a fool either. Thank you."

"Ah yes." He took her hand again and tucked it into the crook of his elbow, drawing her back into the narrow street. "The training with Walker. Is that it?"

"I know enough to kill a man with my bare hands," said Prue, conscious of the petty desire to shock. "But only if I have to."

"Really?" He stopped to slant a look at her, a brow raised. A heartbeat of silence. "Gods, it'd be a brave man—" He broke off, his eyes dark with mischief. "Is my life in danger, Mistress Prue?"

"Depends." She patted his arm, fighting a smile. "Annoy me and find out."

Erik's crack of laughter rang off the walls of the shabby buildings. An old woman looked up from behind an immense pile of rainbow-colored fruits and grinned, her seamed face crinkling with amusement. When Prue caught her eye, she winked, ogling Erik's perfect ass. Then she grabbed an immense, shiny green nanafruit, about a foot long, and waggled it in the air, her face full of avid inquiry.

Prue nodded, giggling. The blood sang in her veins, an exuberant rush like seelies dancing.

Merciful Sister, she was skidding down an icy slope to her doom, faster and faster, the wind whistling through her hair and whipping her cheeks. Unless her shields were absolutely perfect, there'd be a world of pain, open wounds that might never heal, but right now she couldn't bring herself to care about the risk. She'd never felt this alive, full of light, crackling with energy. Life, usually so humdrum, so serious, was suddenly full of glamour and danger. She, ordinary Prue McGuire, had an extraordinary purpose and—she shot Erik a glance from under her lashes—an extraordinary man to accomplish it with. Charming he might be, but beneath the light, beguiling manner was a core of steel, an adamantine will. He made Chavis look like a boy, and a boring one at that.

They had a job to do tonight, she and Erik the Golden, but afterward . . . Prue's breath hitched. She'd take him back to The Garden and—she exhaled slowly—indulge herself. Gorge her senses 'til she was too sated, too sore to move. The memories of pleasure were going to have to last her a long, long time, so she'd better make them good. Her lips curved in a wry smile. Funny, Chavis had offered to teach her how to juggle and she'd refused. With Erik, juggling her emotions had become a means of self-preservation. It astonished her how swiftly she was learning to hide her heart.

Directly in front of them, a boiling knot of bodies tumbled onto the street, fists and oaths flying. A small mongrel dog darted out of the way and disappeared around the corner of the building.

"What the—?" Erik came to an abrupt halt.

"We're here," said Prue demurely, taking a cautious step backward. She indicated the sign that swung over the door, a ship's figurehead with an improbable bosom. "The Sailor's Lay."

Erik only gave a disgusted grunt, but Prue laughed outright. "Don't worry," she said. "I'll protect you."

The tangle of bodies resolved itself into three men and a woman, all liberally splattered with mud. Two of the men lurched off down the alley cursing, while the remaining couple leaned against each other, shoulder to shoulder. A few deep breaths and the woman straightened. "Well, well," she said, pushing the limp hair out of her eyes with the back of her wrist, "if it isn't my pretty lunatic."

Yachi, the guard, the one who'd delivered the Money's note. Tall and muscular, she topped Prue by a good six inches.

"No," said Prue tartly. "He's *my* lunatic, though I'll grant you he's pretty."

Erik choked.

Yachi chuckled. "So I see," she said. She turned to the barrel-chested figure at her side. "Well, Rhio? What do you think? Pretty?"

Sergeant Rhiomard regarded Erik with disfavor, assessing him in a single comprehensive glance. "No," he said gruffly. "But I'm bettin' he's a fine lad in a brawl."

"To hell with all that," growled Erik. "Shall we get on with it?" Without waiting for a reply, he towed Prue in through the swinging doors.

But two steps into the fusty, low-ceilinged room he stopped

so abruptly Prue bumped her nose on his spine. Before she could recover, he'd let out a pained bellow that bounced off planked walls sticky with the residue of smoke and beer and sweat. "What the *fuck*—?"

Seated opposite Dai was a small, familiar figure, one grimy little paw poised over three battered nutshells lined up on the stained table. At his elbow was a small jug of ale and the foam on his upper lip gave him an unlikely looking moustache.

Erik strode forward, gripped Florien by the collar and lifted him clear off the seat. "You!" Although the boy snarled with outrage as Erik gave him a brisk shake, he was wise enough to hang unresisting in his grasp. "What are you doing here?"

"What's it fookin' look like?" When Erik released him, Florien landed neatly on his feet, tugging his tattered vest straight, huffy as an alley cat in a snit.

"Leave him alone," said Dai absently, his gaze fixed on the shells. "C'mon, lad, one more time and I'll get it for sure. The eye's quicker than the hand, it has to be."

Shooting Erik a glower, Florien clambered back onto the bench. "Didn't shake 'ands," he muttered. "No promises."

"My mistake," growled Erik, all grim purpose. "Who gave you beer?" He placed both hands on the table, leaning right into Dai's space. "You?"

Not shifting an inch, the swordsman met a furious blue gaze. "Boy buys his own. He's no trouble."

Caught between horror and amusement, Prue took her underlip firmly beneath her teeth. If she laughed now, three male egos would never forgive her.

Besides . . . she threw a quick glance over her shoulder . . . the place was packed with off-duty guards, mercenaries and sailors, harlots of both sexes providing splashes of color. They were gathering an interested audience. This was what he had come to do.

"Erik." She planted a sharp elbow in his side and rolled her eyes at the crowd.

A harried serving wench emerged from the kitchen, carrying two brimming tankards. "In a minute," said Erik.

When he caught the woman's eye, her face bloomed into a tired smile. Immediately, she swerved in their direction, slapping the beers down without ceremony at a rowdy table of guards. Eagerly, she bent to take Erik's order, her opulent breasts spilling out of her bodice right under his nose.

For the Sister's sake, was that the wench's navel? Prue averted her gaze, so she was surprised to hear the woman's bark of laughter. "Dunno if'n we got any of thet."

Still chuckling, she made her way back to the bar, swerving to avoid the clutching hands of a swarthy sailor with the ease of long practice.

Erik fixed the boy with a flinty stare. "Want to stay?"

Florien didn't lower his eyes. "Yah."

"On my terms. Understood?" Erik grabbed Florien's ale jug and drained the last of it in a couple of swallows. He slammed it down so hard the nutshells skittered about on the table as if inhabited by many-legged insects. "*Understood?*"

Finally, resentfully, Florien nodded.

When the serving wench slid a tall mug into the boy's eager grasp, he stared into it, then sniffed, his brow furrowed. Cautiously, he stuck his tongue out and tasted. Turning an appalled face to Erik, he said, "What t' fook *is* it?"

"Milk," said Erik firmly, passing Prue a cup of wine. He took a small, appreciative sip of his own ale. "It's good for you."

Prue chuckled, but something broke inside her, something warm and melting and foolish. Dai snorted with amusement. Florien scowled and pushed the mug away, but he said, "Ye gunna sing?"

Erik nodded and rose, rolling his shoulders and sizing up the crowd. With his usual easy grace, he hitched one hip on the cleanest corner of the table and rested a booted foot on the bench. Prue realized he'd done this many, many times before.

He didn't bother with preliminaries, simply opened his mouth and let the notes pour forth. But this was different, as far from opera as it was possible to get and still be music. Erik roughened and deepened his voice, belting out the rollicking rhythm, framing the words in a drawl so suggestive, so sensual, her jaw dropped. The beat had a wicked thrust to it, as explicit as the regular plunge of a man's strong hips and thighs. Sweet Sister, she could still feel him deep inside, cramming her full, thick and silky and fiery hot.

She shifted a little in her seat, as warm as if he'd reached out and cupped his hand between her thighs, watching the hush fan out like beer spreading from a leaky barrel, heads turning, mouths agape, one person nudging another. It reached even the shadowed booths at the back favored by those with nefarious business. Like that one, for instance, a figure so completely enveloped in a cloak it could have been male or female, fork poised over a steaming deep-dish pie. The pale face was the merest glimmer in the gloom, rapt like everyone else.

He moved on to a sea shanty next and by the end of the second verse, the sailors were roaring the chorus and banging their tankards on the table. When a skinny old man produced a penny whistle, Erik strolled over and helped him up on the table, all without missing a beat. He grinned when the serving woman wiped a grimy rag down the bar and went clean off the end, she was so enthralled. Prue's heart gave a nasty little lurch. He was so at ease with the attention, the adulation. Like all born performers, he *needed* it. Prue McGuire would never be enough for Erik the Golden.

She stiffened her shoulders. She knew that. She'd known it from the beginning.

It didn't take them long to realize who he was. Between numbers, Prue saw heads together, whispering, speculating. After "The Milkmaid's Jugs," Erik paused to wet his throat. "Hey, mate!" called a guard, a grizzled veteran. "Ye got the balls for the 'Seelie Song'?"

"You bet." Erik chuckled. "I've got more than that. Help me sing it and I'll tell you."

He sang it solo, a trio of drunken sailors stood on a table and sang it, the whole tavern sang it together, Erik and the whistle player did it as a duet. The walls of the Sailor's Lay reverberated. People streamed in from the street until the room was packed, the air so thick with excitement and sweat and heat, it swirled, making Prue's head swim. Her pulse pounded. Gods, he was amazing!

"Let's hear it then." Sergeant Rhiomard's parade-ground bellow cut easily over the applause, the stamping of feet. "About the seelies."

"Oooh, I love me a bedtime story," called a dark-skinned sailor, fluttering his lashes.

Not at all discomfited, Erik sprang onto a bench, anchored

by two husky workingmen on either side. As if he were relaxing by the fireside with a few friends, he told how he'd swum with the seelies, seen the rotten stem of the titanplant. Prue discovered she'd grown a little more accustomed to his extraordinary gift for theater, not least his innate sense of timing. But neither was she surprised to note the rolling of eyes, the suppressed chuckles, Rhiomard frowning with his arms folded.

Pushing to her feet, she worked her way through the crowd to Erik's bench. When she tapped him on the knee, his eyes widened with surprise, but he grasped the hand she offered. A single easy heave and she was standing at his side.

"Prue, what are—?"

Prue slipped her arm around his waist and faced the crowd, her heart beating double time, feeling the hard strength of him all down her side, the cage of his ribs solid beneath her palm. "I saw them too," she said.

"'Course you did, lovey," called the sailor. He leered at Erik, the lamplight striking gleams off the heavy gold loops distending his earlobes. "An' no wonder."

"Listen, idiot, I—"

The sailor scowled. He rose, a little unsteadily, supported by a couple of grumbling shipmates.

"One more time!" Erik's trained voice carried easily over Prue's. His fingers tightened bruisingly on hers.

Another hasty verse of the "Seelie Song" and the moment passed. A bow and a casual wave and he pulled Prue back to their table.

"Could've been nasty." Calmly, Dai finished his beer.

Prue bit her lip. "Sorry," she muttered. "Can't abide a fool."

Erik tipped up her chin with his fist. His sea blue eyes glowed, softer than she'd ever seen them, mesmerizing. "Thank you," he said, a deep purr that thrilled along her nerves. "Again."

Prue caught herself before she tipped forward right into his arms. "I keep my promises." Gods, she sounded prissy!

Over Erik's shoulder, she saw the serving woman bearing down on their table with a flirtatious smile, a huge tankard clutched in both hands. When a tall, cloaked figure stepped out of the shadows and into her path, she tottered, the vessel slipping from her grasp. With a muttered apology, the man steadied it, gripping her elbow with one hand, the tankard with the other. The servant brushed him off, her eager gaze still fixed on Erik.

"Here we are then." Smiling, she set it down before him and put her hands on her blowsy hips. "On the house, like."

When Erik rose and bowed his thanks, as graceful as any courtier, Prue could swear the woman simpered. But then he sat and pushed the ale aside, absently slapping at Florien's reaching hand.

"Don't you want it?" said Dai. "They serve a good brew here."

Erik shook his head. "I don't drink when I sing, or much at all really. A question of control." Something bleak flickered in his eyes. "Go ahead." His lips quirked in a wry smile. "We'll carry you home."

The swordsman's handsome, merry face creased in a grin as he raised the tankard in salute.

Erik stroked the back of Prue's hand. "Promises?" he murmured. "Sweetheart, I—"

With a dull thud, the ale jug slipped from Dai's fingers, spilling across the table in a frothy stream, splashing Prue's sleeve. Dai clutched his throat, his eyes stretched so wide, she could see the whites all around. He made a noise she had never heard before and hoped never to hear again, a wet, clotted gargle.

24

Erik lunged, grabbing his shoulder. "Dai!"

Dai's eyes rolled back in his head. Foam flecked his lips, stained a virulent, iridescent purple.

"Fook!" whispered Florien. "Fookin' prettydeath!"

The swordsman staggered, then crashed headlong to the filthy floor, body arched in agony. His bubbling screams carried clearly over the rumble of conversation.

Frozen, Prue sat staring. Erik exploded past her. He wrenched Dai's jaw open. "The milk! *Quick!*"

Florien slapped the mug into his hand and Erik poured the contents down the swordsman's gullet, planting a knee on his chest to keep him still. Dai flopped like a landed fish.

The ensuing ten minutes were hideous. Milk. Then water, pints of it, then milk again.

His eyes huge, dark pits in his ashen face, Florien inched closer until his small, trembling body touched Prue's. She put an arm around his narrow shoulders and snugged him into her side, glad of the human comfort, the grounding reality of his light, quick breaths. Despite the heat in the tavern, she was clammy and cold, her skin prickling with shock.

Eventually, the noise died away to pained whimpers, as

if Dai were trying to scream through a throat full of broken glass.

"That's enough, man." Rhiomard laid a hand on Erik's shoulder. "I've sent one of the lads for a healer." He looked down at the twitching body of the swordsman, his face grim. "You saved his life, though I doubt he'll thank you for it."

Erik wiped his forehead with his sleeve. His shirt was splattered with an unholy mix of blood and milk and the purple remnants of the poison. Even over the stale beer and sweat in the taproom, Prue could smell the evil of it, an acrid, metallic odor with a cloying undertone. Swallowing hard, she suppressed the urge to gag.

Slowly, Erik got to his feet. "Prettydeath?" he said. "But how—?" A startling sapphire blue in his pale face, his eyes met Prue's.

She wet her lips. "You," she whispered. "Sweet Sister, it was meant for you!"

The moment stretched endlessly, everything around her slowing to a crawl, as if mired in mud. That could be Erik lying there on the floor of the Sailor's Lay, his beautiful eyes glassy with pain, the magnificent voice silenced. Gone from her forever.

Sister have mercy, she wasn't ready for that, she'd never be ready.

Her heart beat, on and on, a relentless lump of muscle, keeping her alive, while her soul shriveled and died at the thought of a world without Erik. Prue couldn't seem to move, to think past it, her brain heavy and slow with the stunning impact.

No more of the charming smiles that weakened her knees, no more of the infuriating way he could make her laugh despite herself, no more of the abandon only Erik the Golden could coax from her. No more of that strange sense of safe harbor she felt in his arms. He'd blown into her placid, uneventful life like a whirlwind, his presence intensifying every sensation— colors were brighter, flowers sweeter, wine more intoxicating on her tongue. Yet with all of that, she found him so easy to be with, such good company. Perfect—with all his flaws.

The bottom dropped out of her stomach and the taproom creaked back into focus. Her fingers dug so hard into Florien's shoulder that he yelped. With a muttered apology, Prue loosened her grip. Sister save her, how could she have been so blind, so hopelessly, comprehensively stupid as to think she could keep any part of herself aside? What had happened to her supposedly cool, logical brain?

I never learn, she thought savagely. *Fool, fool, fool!*

Slowly, Prue shifted a little way away from the boy and wrapped her arms around her shivering body. Gods, she was cold!

So much for self-preservation.

There wasn't even a way to shift the blame. The responsibility was hers, and hers alone. Erik was what he was, a force of nature, dangerous in the same innately casual way as a wild animal like a tygre. She'd known all along how foolhardy it was to take the risk, but she hadn't had the strength to resist. The blood rushed in her ears, the wind of disaster whipping through her hair as she plummeted, farther and farther into the abyss. Oh gods, she'd given everything that she was—her foolish heart, her ordinary self—to a man who'd leave her tomorrow without a thought.

But no, that wasn't fair. In his own careless, charming way, Erik cared for her, she didn't doubt it. Unlike Chavis, Erik Thorensen was a man of substance, honor. Nothing would deflect him from his purpose. He'd simply set that stubborn jaw and persist in his mission to save her city from disaster.

But someone didn't want him to do that, because they were trying to kill him. And if they succeeded, she'd die too.

Because she loved him.

The only saving grace was that he didn't know. He must never know.

Utterly appalled, Prue came to her senses with a jerk.

"An assassin," the sergeant was saying thoughtfully. "Prettydeath's a Guild weapon."

And she remembered.

Prue leaped to her feet, nearly unseating Florien in the process. "I saw!"

"Who?" Erik grabbed her arm. "The assassin?"

"Yes, yes!" Frantically, she spun around, searching the room. "Tall, in a big cloak— There!" She pointed.

Half-concealed by shadow, a figure leaned against the wall near the door, watching, swathed from head to toe in a cloak like a tent. At Prue's cry, it started, the hood slipping back to reveal a glimpse of a pale face. The assassin lurched out the doors, almost colliding with a lean, broad-shouldered figure coming in.

Prue knew that hawkish profile, the thick braid of black hair trailing down the man's back.

"Walker!" she shouted. "That man—catch him!"

A split second's hesitation and Walker spun on his heel and vanished into the street. With a curse, Erik charged after him, shouldering people aside right and left, forcing a ruthless path through the crowd. The doors creaked, swinging to and fro with the speed of his passage.

The two men returned a few moments later, empty-handed. "Fuck it," growled Erik. "We missed him. Nothing out there but a mangy dog."

Walker looked up from where he knelt over Dai, his obsidian eyes bleak as death. "It was a woman," he said. "Near as tall as me, paler than a fish's belly." Gently, he touched the swordsman's wrist, but Dai made only that pathetic mewling noise.

Walker straightened, one hand going to the worn pommel of the sword at his side. "You have a healer coming?"

When Erik nodded, Walker said, "Dai works for me. Carry him to my House of Swords. I'll take care of the woman."

"Not if I find her first," said Erik grimly.

Blue eyes clashed with black.

"You won't," said Walker softly. "Because she's mine."

Prue shivered. In all the years she'd known Walker, she'd never seen him smile, though he was unfailingly patient with the courtesans he trained in The Garden's fighting salle. His reserve was so deep a pool of silence surrounded him, his step so quiet it seemed he had no footfall. She had no idea how old he was. Though silver threaded the sable of his hair, he moved with the supple grace of a man in his prime.

If she hadn't been so wild with rage and terror, she might have pitied the unknown assassin. As it was . . . Breathing hard, she watched Walker turn without another word and glide through the press of bodies to the door. People made way for him without seeming to realize they did so. He looked grim and tired and suddenly, she remembered he'd been ill.

The Sister send you strength and good hunting, the Brother

guide your blade. No doubt prayers from an unbeliever were
a waste of breath—certainly hers had always been—but there
was no harm in trying, even if the thought had been a demand
rather than a plea.

Bracing herself, she turned to meet Erik's gaze.

As he handed Prue into a skiff, Erik glanced at the Sibling
Moons in surprise. The Brother had barely risen above the
palazzo roofs, the Sister keeping pace. So it hadn't been a lifetime after all, only a few hours.

Grimacing, he plucked his wet shirt away from his skin.
His nostrils stung with the vomitus smell of evil. "Let me
change," he said, "and get the boy settled at the boardinghouse. Then I'll take you home."

For a wonder, Florien said nothing, only sat stiffly in the
shelter of Prue's arm, gazing steadfastly at a point over Erik's
shoulder, his small face pinched and old. No child should have
to witness such horrors, but he'd recognized the poison immediately. What a life, the poor little bastard.

By the time the skiff had grounded at the base of the water
stairs, the lad had nodded off, still sitting bolt upright. When
Erik bent and scooped him up in his arms, he reared back
with a panicked gasp, his eyes flying open.

"It's all right," said Erik uneasily, patting a knobby knee.
"I've got you."

Florien grunted, but he relaxed and let himself be carried
up to the street before he wriggled free.

Erik turned to Prue. "Wait for me?" It came out halfway
between an order and a question, not what he'd intended, but
she nodded, her face pale and set, her exotic eyes shadowed.
Erik blew out a long breath. He tossed the skiffman an extra
coin. "Stay here with her, all right?" He got a nod in return.

It took him no more than a few minutes to take Florien to the
dancers' room and hand him over to Sydarise. Despite the boy's
token protests, Erik saw the tension leave the wiry little body.
Refuge in a woman's soft embrace was a wonderful thing when
you were small and frightened. Hell, even for a grown man—

He paused with his shirt half unbuttoned, his skin peb-
bling with goose bumps. Another night, a little more of the

comfort and the pleasure. It wasn't much to ask, surely? Shit, if it wasn't for Prue, he thought with a kind of weary savagery, he'd book the Company on the first starship back to Concordia and get the hell out. Let the whole fucking city go to the bottom. That could have been him writhing in agony on the taproom floor, his throat a bloody ruin. Fuck, what if he'd offered Prue a sip—or the boy? Blindsided by the enormity of the thought, he grabbed the door frame in a white-knuckled grip, panting.

He could hardly bear to think of it. The desire to race down to the skiff and snatch her up against his heart was so strong, he was down the stairs and out the door before he knew it, his breath still choppy.

Prue hadn't moved a muscle. She didn't speak or acknowledge him in any way, though when he settled beside her, she turned her cheek into his shoulder. Wordlessly, Erik put his arm around her, and the skiffman poled slowly away down the canal.

The air felt heavy and still, almost suffocating. A fitful, salt-laden breeze blew in off the sea, still carrying with it the reek of corruption. Erik rubbed his nose. Far away, thunder rumbled. A chill slid down his spine. "Is that—?"

Prue straightened, pulling away from him. "The first storm of summer." A trio of Technomage flitters buzzed toward the mainland, racing before the wind.

As their eyes met, the sky out to sea split from top to bottom with a great fork of lightning. Simultaneously, a fat drop of water plopped onto Erik's sleeve and the world echoed with a long, rolling boom. With a curse, the skiffman bent his back, digging in with the pole. The small craft leaped forward.

At The Garden, Erik shoved the fare into the skiffman's fist. "Keep the change." Subduing the impulse to pick Prue up and sling her over his shoulder, he grabbed her hand and together they dashed toward the lights, trying to dodge the thickening drops. Almost helplessly, she began to giggle. Erik frowned. It had an edge of hysteria to it he didn't care for, not for level-headed Prue.

With a tug, she drew him away down a side path and under some sort of shelter. "Here," she panted. "In here."

"Where are we?" Before him loomed the vaguely familiar

bulk of one of the smaller pavilions, the graceful soaring lines of the roof silhouetted against the racing clouds, the thick, velvety scent of Walker's dark roses hanging heavy in the damp air.

Prue gave a sharp bark of laughter. "If I'm going to lose my mind, I may as well do it properly." She withdrew a key from her belt pouch and fumbled with a door he could barely make out. It swung open soundlessly. "Welcome to the Bruised Orchid." She vanished and light flared, flashing across his retinas.

Erik's jaw dropped. He thought he'd seen decadence—after all, he'd performed at the Oligarch's palace on Green IV—but never had he seen anything to equal the hedonism of this. To call it a bathroom was an insult. His startled gaze traveled from the deep, square tub of black marble to gold spigots, glitter-veined onyx tiles on the wall and a crimson and cream rug on the floor. In the mirrored wall, he could see Prue's back, ramrod straight, her hair straggling down her back in a wet mass, her damp trews molded to the pert curve of her bottom. She looked very small, completely common-place in the opulent room.

"This is the top of the line," she said. Her face was very pale, save for two spots of color burning on her cheekbones. No trace of humor remained in her expression. "Do you like it?"

"Well, yes, but—"

"The bedchamber's through there." She indicated a connecting door with her chin.

Erik's heart began a slow, slamming beat. Turning, he found a serviceable bolt on the exterior door and slid it home. "And no one knows we're here," he said slowly. "We're safe, for tonight at least."

Outside, branches creaked in the rising wind, the rain spattering harder on the roof of the pavilion, but the room itself was warm, lit by a uniform golden glow. Wonderingly, Erik reached up to touch a light globe in its wall sconce. "These are Technomage devices," he said. He flipped on one of the elaborate gold spigots and steaming water gushed into the tub. "Even the plumbing. Gods, Prue, how did you afford it?"

"Went into debt." Prue's jaw firmed. "We took a calculated risk and it paid off. Sometimes they do." Her eyes went bleak and flat. With a shrug, she turned away and bent to adjust the flow of water, the fine fabric of her trews outlining the peach of her bottom, clinging to the shadowed cleft between the taut curves of her buttocks. His eye was drawn immediately to the plump purse of her sex, pushing against the material.

The punch of arousal had him hardening so fast, he felt light-headed. As Prue straightened, he took a step forward, reaching. The heavens boomed, a long, rolling reverberation, and the room was illuminated by a flash of sheet lightning as bright as a summer's noon. Prue jumped, a stifled noise escaping her. The light blanched her face, highlighting the bones beneath the skin, the shadows beneath her eyes. She looked like some small startled animal, poised for flight.

Long before the thunder had faded, Erik had her hard against him, one palm cradling the back of her head, settling her against his shoulder. Foolishly, he rocked her back and forth, crooning nonsense, patting her back. "It's all right, love. It's all right."

Prue set the heels of her hands against his chest and pushed, looking up into his face. "No," she said, "it's not." When her lips trembled, she pressed them together for a moment. "The prettydeath was meant for you. If it wasn't for poor Dai, you would have . . . have . . ." She turned her head away.

Behind her, water tumbled into the bath and steam rose, curling toward the coffered ceiling. Rain drummed on the roof, splashed from the gutters.

"But I didn't." When he cupped her cheek, her skin was chilled velvet against his palm. "Look at me, Prue. It wasn't just luck." He frowned, thinking how best to put it, how much to reveal of the secrets he'd never told a living soul. "The Lord and the Lady have a plan for me. Call them the Sister and the Brother if you like, but the gods have a purpose for me, something I have to do." Slowly, he began to rub her arms, not caring for her pallor, the shivers running through her small frame.

She nodded. "You have to save the city, yes, I know."

Erik raised a brow. "And you, Mistress McGuire? What about you?"

"The gods mean nothing to me."

"They don't?"

She stiffened in his grasp. "Why should they? They weren't

there when I needed them. No one was." Her lashes fell, veiling those aquamarine eyes. "You can't save me either, Erik. I'm none of your business."

He gave her a little shake, the hot lick of temper taking him by surprise, as shocking as the thunder and lightning outside. "Like hell you're not! Look at you, you're wet through, freezing."

Her chin went up. "So are you."

Erik ignored that one and slipped the first fastening on her collar. "Do you like these clothes?"

She glanced down. "I did, but they're ruined now."

"Good." The storm seemed to have entered his head, rattling around inside his skull. Erik gripped Prue's tunic in both fists and ripped it straight down the middle.

"Erik!" Her cry echoed off the marble as he dealt likewise with the chemise beneath.

Her breasts tumbled into his eager hands, the nipples tightly furled, the flesh firm and very cool. Too cool.

He went to his knees, taking her hand and planting it on his shoulder. "Lift your foot." When she hesitated, he growled, "Do it. Or I swear to all the gods I'll put you over my knee."

Only the Horned Lord knew what she saw in his face, but she gasped and a pretty flush of pink brightened her honeyed skin, all the way from breast to cheek. After a pause, she complied, one foot at a time. With grim amusement, Erik recognized the feeling coursing through him as disappointment. He pulled her boots off.

"You," she said, her nails digging into his shoulder. "You're cold too."

"In a minute." Hooking his fingers into her waistband, he peeled off her trews and the drawers beneath. "Step out." Unable to resist, he spread his palm over the creamy globe of one buttock and squeezed gently. Shit, even her ass was cold! Tremors were running through her whole body, bone-deep.

Blinking hard, Prue stared at something past his left ear, wrapping one arm across her breasts. The other hand stole toward the dark thatch between her thighs.

"No." Gently, Erik took her wrists and drew her arms away from her body. "It's way too late to hide." She was all creamy curves, voluptuous flesh underpinned by excellent muscle tone.

Prue McGuire could never be described as slim or lissome. She was a pocketsize goddess—a divinity so hot and lush a man could sink into her and lose himself—cock, soul and heart.

Her smooth flank was right next to his face. Before he knew he meant to do it, Erik had turned his head and taken a tiny nip, high on her hip.

Prue hissed and he gave her a grin that bared his teeth, wondering how badly his hunger showed.

Leaning over, he swished a hand through the bathwater. Perfect.

He licked the spot he'd bitten, conscious of an insane desire to sink his teeth into the tender undercurve of her gorgeous backside. "Get in." Even over the steady drumming of the rain, his growl was loud enough to threaten like the thunder.

Though she was still shaking, she stood her ground, glaring at him, the little fool. "When I'm ready," she said. "You have something horrible in your hair. Did you know that?"

25

Erik's precarious control evaporated. He rose to loom over Prue, taking ruthless advantage of his height and weight. "My hair can bloody well wait, you can't! Why the fuck won't you let me take care of you?"

Her eyes widened to enormous blue green pools. Just as swiftly, she lowered her gaze to his boots, apparently struck dumb. Godsdammit, a fucking miracle.

Erik grasped her hand. "Get in or I'll put you in." He steadied her as she climbed into the bath. The thing was so deep, it had a set of steps. The sides were carved with shelves and hollows, varying the depth of the water and providing spaces for lounging, edges for holding on to. There was even a kind of hose arrangement, attached to the spigots, worked by flipping a separate lever. Lord's balls, the erotic possibilities were endless!

She spoke so softly, so much to herself that it was only because he'd just turned off the taps that he heard her at all. "I don't know how to do that, let someone . . ." Her voice trailed away. Her back was to him, her thick hair curling outrageously with damp, the clean line of her shoulder hunched a little, as though she nursed some tender spot over her heart. When he glanced into the mirror, she looked weary to the bone, utterly defeated, not like the fierce little Prue he knew at all.

Erik stood rooted to the spot, besieged by temptation. Why not set her free to soar with pleasure, take control and give her the peace that came with complete abandon? It would require absolute trust, but all he need do was speak with the Voice. He bit his lip hard enough to hurt.

Clearing his throat, he said, "Towels?"

"In the cupboard." Now she sounded almost normal, moving her hands under the water, splashing languidly. To his relief, there was more color in her face. Beneath the surface, her skin glimmered, her nipples a serene pink, plumped by the warmth. The indentation of her navel winked at him, the pale curve of her belly drawing his gaze to the shadow between rounded thighs.

His tongue felt too big for his mouth, his arousal pressing painfully against the lacing of his trews. Gods! If he let himself go, he could no longer tell whether he'd devour Prue or fuck her. Fucking her would be a simple matter, blessedly straightforward compared with this overwhelming desire to possess absolutely, to keep her safe and make her his.

He'd lost his battle with the Dark Lady, but he didn't give a fuck. The challenge was no longer relevant. It simply didn't matter.

His chest heaving, he wrenched open the carved doors of the cupboard. There were stacks of fluffy towels, black and crimson and cream, row after row of vials and bottles and ointment pots from a high-class apothecary, all neatly labeled. Grabbing a couple that looked useful, he placed them on the low bench near the tub together with a washcloth. That was better. He had his breathing regulated now.

Conscious of an unwinking tip-tilted gaze, he sat to tug off his boots, strip off his shirt and set aside the talisman on its chain. When Prue's lips curved, he felt heat rise in his face. Ridiculous. Especially after last night. Was he a performer, or was he not?

Unobtrusively, Erik sucked in his stomach, squared his shoulders. He paused in the act of unlacing his trews and arched a teasing brow. "Like what you see?"

A little pink tongue crept out to moisten Prue's pouty

lower lip and a hard shiver of anticipation whispered over his balls. The skin there was so sensitive. "You're fishing again," said Prue calmly, but beneath the water, he saw her grip her hands together, her shoulders rigid with tension. She shot him a glinting half smile, all woman, all challenge and hard-won courage. "It's rather . . . sweet."

That did it.

Rumbling with pretended outrage, Erik dropped the trews and kicked them away. Ignoring the weighty demand of his rampant erection, he surged into the bath, so focused on Prue he barely noticed the delicious heat lapping his thighs. When he reached her, he seized her shoulders and jerked her up into his arms.

"You," he said, fighting against the insistent press of the Voice in his chest, his breath lost in the struggle against instinct. "You . . ."

He spread a big hand over her cheek, his fingers aligned along the fine bone of her jaw, holding her steady. "Do you have any idea what you do to me?"

Her hand came up to cover his. "No." Her lips framed the word, but no sound emerged, her eyes huge, cynicism fighting with the temptation to let go and believe. "I'm not . . ." She cleared her throat. "Not the type to . . . stir strong passions."

She'd gone rigid again, her body like smooth, warmed marble under his hands. Prue didn't know the first thing about subterfuge, she was honesty to the backbone. The tragedy was that she took self-assessment from beyond clear-eyed to brutal. How could she not see her own worth? His eyes stinging, Erik gentled his grip. "Do you believe I want you?"

"Oh yes." By way of emphasis, she pressed harder into his embrace, nudging his hardness with her belly. But her smile went awry even as she did it.

All he could do was show her he wanted more than her body. Much more. "I can wait," he said. Sliding his palm down her arm, he entwined their fingers. "Come here." Gods, that had come out perilously low, commanding. Settling his back into the concave shape at one end of the tub, Erik tugged Prue down so she was nestled between his spread legs, her spine pressed against his chest. He reached for the hose, frowning over the lever arrangement.

"But what—?"

Ah. Warm water gushed out in a fine spray. "Close your eyes and hold still."

Carefully, he wet her hair, smoothing it over and over with one hand, watching it darken and soften with the weight of the water, like sodden silk.

"Erik, what do you think—?" She tried to look over her shoulder, but he cupped the small, precious shape of her skull in his palm, preventing her.

"Sshh," he said, dismayed by the thread of desperation in his voice, but helpless to prevent it. "Let me do this for you. Please."

A pause. "Will it make you feel better?"

He didn't answer. Instead, he opened the bottle labeled as a hair cleanser and poured a good dollop onto the crown of her head. It smelled of something green and fresh, with a hint of astringency beneath, rather like Prue herself. He found he liked it.

Gently, Erik worked the sudsy stuff through her hair, using the tips of his fingers, first one hand, then both. Once all the tangles were gone, he massaged her scalp, starting cautiously, his touch light and soothing.

"Oh," said Prue. "Oh, gods." Her head tipped back and her eyes fell shut, the wet lashes lying on her cheek like lace fans beaded with water. Her mouth was no longer pale, but a satiny pink, the upper lip so prettily carved, the lower so carnal, he could feed on it for hours.

Some of the knots inside him slithered loose and he relaxed into the water and the warmth. She was right. He did feel better. Methodically, he worked his way over her scalp, and when she purred her pleasure, he smiled, pleased to his bones.

The stuff in the second bottle was thicker, smelling of roses. Erik slathered some on the washcloth and stroked it over Prue's shoulders, her collarbones, down her arms. She stiffened, but he ignored it. He was very thorough, picking up her hands to rub the cloth between her fingers, gliding it over her ribs, taking exquisite care of her sweet breasts.

With a sigh, Prue melted back against his shoulder, turning her head into his neck. "I'm not a child," she complained, but her voice was very soft, almost drugged with pleasure.

Erik grinned. "I know." Deliberately, he passed the cloth over her nipples, watching them ruche into velvety buds under the caress. Prue quivered and his mouth watered. Letting the cloth float away, he used his hands, stroking over the smooth satin of her stomach, learning the hard contours of her hip bones. Nerves jumped under the skin and her breath hitched. He transferred his attentions to the luxuriant curves of her bottom, closing his eyes so he could concentrate on the feel of the resilient flesh, the dimples either side of her spine and the tempting cleft between her buttocks.

Lord's balls, she felt good, a beautiful, confiding weight against him, letting him give her what she needed, what they both needed.

Without speaking, he shifted her so that she lay across his lap, her head in the crook of his arm. When she opened her mouth, he bent his head to hers. "Sshh." He skated his lips across hers, enjoying the tingle, the promise of it. Her mouth parted, inviting him in, her tongue like hot velvet, shy and desperate against his. She tasted intoxicating, a blend of tenderness and passion that made his breath come short and his arousal expand painfully against her hip.

He'd just escaped an agonizing disfigurement, possibly death. In some long-forgotten rational part of his brain, Erik knew the beast was driving him to reaffirm life, to plant his seed, but he couldn't care, because his body was vibrating with the force of his desire, a dark whirlwind of need that threatened to tear him loose from his moorings. Outside, the storm howled and thrashed. Or was that inside?

With a gasp, Erik wrenched his mouth free. He estimated he had seconds left before either he spurted against her hip or fucked her then and there. He might even drown them both in the process, but gods, it would be worth it!

Prue's eyes fluttered open, still hazed with passion. If a man wasn't careful, he'd fall into those blue green pools and be gladly lost forever.

Breathing hard, Erik forced a smile and stroked her cheek. "Better now?" Shit, his hand trembled! Quickly, he pulled it away.

One small hand crept up, the pads of her fingers brushing the corner of his mouth, a fleeting caress. "Yes. You?"

"I will be soon." A subterranean rumble, full of feral promise. Prue blinked.

Gently, Erik set her aside and stretched out an arm to snag the hose. "In a bed." Even to his own ears, he sounded hoarse. He swallowed hard. "I'm getting us clean and dry, and then I'm going to spread you out in a big, comfortable bed." He began to rinse the suds from her hair.

To hell with it. He wiped the water away from her eyes and stared deep. "Under me. Your legs over my shoulders."

Ruthlessly, he directed the spray back over her head. Prue made a muffled noise. He couldn't tell what it meant.

"You'll be helpless, Prue. Do you hear me? Helpless with pleasure."

"Stop, stop." She grabbed his wrist. Wriggling away from him, she pushed the wet hair out of her eyes.

Those aquamarine eyes blazed. "I'm done," she said. "Get your hair wet. I'll wash it for you."

⌒∾⌒

Prue was hard put not to laugh aloud. For an endless second, Erik's handsome face went slack with surprise. A ruddy tide swept up over his neck and cheeks, making his eyes glitter like molten sapphires. Seizing her by the shoulders he planted a hasty, bruising kiss on her lips. Then he sank beneath the water, reappearing in a flurry right in front of her.

He scooped up a bottle from the bench next to the tub. "Hurry," he said, slapping it into her hand. Dipping his head, he nibbled a tingling path across her collarbone, while his broad palms slid around her waist and wandered up and down her spine. "Get on with it."

Prue filled one palm with the green stuff and buried her hands in his thick hair. The nerve-memory of his clever fingers throbbed all over her skin. In the short time she'd known him, Erik Thorensen had given her the most intense sexual experiences of her life. For the Sister's sake, he'd pleasured her better than she could do for herself.

She wanted more, as much as he could give her while it lasted.

Her fingers slowed, massaging his scalp, the hard curve of

bone unyielding beneath her fingertips, his hair sliding over her knuckles like heavy, waterlogged silk, cool and slippery.

Helpless.

He'd said it, his deep, beautiful voice thrumming along her nerves. The word, the delicious, wanton promise of it, still echoed in her mind. Would he hold her down? He'd done it that way in his dressing room, and though it had been for only a few minutes, she'd felt soft and small and oh so feminine. Empty—yearning for the thick girth of his cock furrowing into the hot core of her, his magnificent length nudging her womb. She'd wanted, *needed*, so badly, she hadn't been a rational being, just an instinctive bundle of sensation and hunger. For once in her life, she'd felt truly desired. By a man who was everything she'd ever wanted—and feared.

She might be insane, but gods, it was a beautiful madness.

Erik hummed against her skin, alternately kissing and sipping, chasing droplets with his tongue. Without once removing his hands from contact with her body, he skimmed his fingertips over her ribs and cupped both her breasts in his palms, hefting their weight.

Every thought in Prue's head stuttered to a halt. She froze.

Erik licked over the inner swell of her breast, leaving a trail of hot tingles in his wake. Prue gasped, her nipples contracting so fast they ached. Gods, she hadn't thought that was possible! "Rinse," he growled into her cleavage.

When she managed to direct a wobbly spray at the back of his head, his lips curved against her skin. Transfixed, she watched clumps of suds slide over his broad shoulders and slither down the indentations on either side of his strong spine. Such a smooth golden expanse. She was about to trace the foam with a wondering finger when Erik shifted slightly, just enough to seal his hot mouth over her nipple.

She jerked, the spray arcing across the room to wet the wall. Erik pulled her nipple taut with careful relish. "Fuck, I want you." When he spoke, his breath puffed across the wet skin and she stifled a yelp. "Finish it. *Quick.*"

He licked a heated path around her areola, then engulfed her distended flesh, compressing it against his tongue and the roof of his mouth, humming while he did so. Her whole body fizzed and sparkled with the luscious vibration. Using the same rhythm, he rasped the nipple of her other breast with his thumb.

"Erik, I—" Gasping, Prue broke off. Gods, had she whimpered? She was having to fight to keep her eyes open against the pleasure.

Barely missing a beat, Erik changed sides, but he raked her flesh gently with his teeth. A sensual reminder. Clumsily, she jammed the spray right against his skull, moving it about until the water ran clear.

"Done," she panted.

He administered a final deep suckle that made her toes curl. "Thank the gods." Flipping the spigots off, he pulled her against his chest with one brawny arm and surged to his feet, creating a wave that threatened to swamp the room. In some hidden recess of her once-practical mind, Prue remembered the shocking expense of the fittings, especially the elegant, deep-pile rug, but all she could think now was that when she pulled him down, the silk would be soft against her back as he shoved that thick, heavy cock into her until she screamed. Over and over while she wrapped her legs around his waist and pulled him deeper and deeper and—

Erik set her on her feet and wrapped a crimson towel around her shoulders. Before she had a chance to take in the whole of his glorious nudity, he'd flung another over her head, spoiling the view. "Dry your hair," he ordered.

Strong hands patted her shoulders dry, moved the towel down her back.

Swearing, Prue fought her way free. "What about you?"

"You first." He was behind her now, rubbing the towel over the globes of her bottom in a decidedly sensuous way. She twisted around to glare over her shoulder and lost her breath.

Clothed, Erik Thorensen was a big man, but stripped he was even bigger, the depth of his chest fully revealed, the latent power of the muscle in his trim belly, his solid thighs, obvious to see. He was all hard planes and angles, the density of big bones and resilient male flesh, covered with smooth, tawny skin and dusted with golden hair that glinted in the warm light. Dripping as he was, his hair plastered to his skull, his masculine beauty was brutally apparent. Frowning with concentration, he went to his knees to dry the backs of her thighs, his buttocks flexing, the sides delightfully hollowed with the fluid shift of muscle.

Prue's fists clenched. Her mouth watered. Clearing her throat, she said, "What about my front?" Despite her best intentions, her voice came out strained and husky.

Erik's head jerked up and his wet hair brushed the back of her knee. Goose bumps skittering up her spine, Prue turned slowly to face him. His eyes blazed with a hot blue flame, like the secret heart of a furnace. Towel held loosely in his hands, he rose, towering over her. Her blood singing, she raised her chin to meet his gaze. "Then it's your turn," she said.

"Godsdammit, woman." Erik appeared to be breathing hard through his nose. "Do you have a death wish? Do you know how close—?" He broke off.

Deliberately, Prue lowered her gaze. His cock arched up toward his navel, so engorged the satiny skin looked stretched, except for the soft, wrinkled collar beneath the head. Like the rest of his body, his shaft still glistened with bathwater. As she watched, a fat droplet rolled from the smooth, rosy glans to course his length, tracing the path of a throbbing vein, disappearing into a sandy tuft of curls, drawing her eye to where his testicles were drawn up between his thighs, plump and tense.

With a dark bolt of lust that nearly took her to the floor, she realized the liquid wasn't water at all.

Erik lifted her chin with two fingers. "You want to play games with me, pretty Prue?" Though his jaw was set hard, his eyes danced with wicked delight.

"You took care of me. I should return the favor." Exhilaration pumped through her blood. No man had ever challenged her the way Erik did—on every level. Letting her tongue creep out to whisk over her lower lip, she raised limpid eyes to his, trying to look innocent, aware she was failing. "You'll, ah, catch your death."

Erik rumbled with amusement. "There's a price to be paid for games, sweetheart."

26

Her belly fluttering with mingled excitement and apprehension, Prue placed the pad of her forefinger on the center of his chest. Slowly, slowly, she drew it down, following that intriguing arrow of hair, watching his nipples go small and tight, gooseflesh rising on his skin. The muscles of his stomach jerked under her touch. A hairsbreadth above the bobbing head of his cock, Erik caught her wrist in a hard grip.

Her gaze flashed up to his and something deep in her belly flip-flopped with relief and joy. Gods, he looked wild, his cheeks deeply flushed, the tendons in his neck standing taut. The fingers grasping her wrist felt like an iron band. Sweet Sister!

Fascinated, she followed the movement of his throat as he swallowed. "Prue, I can't—" He broke off.

In a single movement, he scooped her right off the floor and into his arms, high against his wet chest. Turning, he kicked open the door to the bedchamber and strode through, muttering under his breath, the words so broken, she caught only a few. "Don't . . . worry . . . swear I'll—Fuck!"

Erik stopped so abruptly Prue banged her cheek on his collarbone. His arms loosened, then tightened, catching her before she slipped to the floor. "What the fuck *is* this?"

"I told you, the Bruised Orchid."

Still staring over her head, Erik let her slide down the front of his body until she was steady on her feet. A ruddy flush swept up over his neck and cheeks, his eyes blazing. "Lord's balls!"

What, in the Sister's name—? Frowning in puzzlement, she turned to follow his gaze. Everything shone with luxury and good housekeeping, from the dark wood of the four-poster bed, to the tall, burnished doors that hung open on the far wall, revealing serried rows of whips, paddles and cuffs. The plugs and strange, erotic devices Rose had purchased from the Technomages at enormous expense sat in neat rows on shallow shelves, scrupulously clean and ready for use. The wooden whipping cross had been specially crafted of polished cedderwood, the weight of it heavy enough to withstand the struggles of even the strongest man.

And if he was restrained facing out, his wrists stretched above his head in the fur-lined manacles, he'd be able to watch each stripe bloom on his body, observe every gasp and wince, because the opposite wall was mirrored.

"Don't you like it?" she said. "It was the only pavilion free." Lightly, she patted Erik's chest, just above his pounding heart. "I didn't mean for us to use the . . . um . . . equipment. But this is the top of the line. The bed's huge."

He'd stopped breathing, every muscle rigid against her. Erik wet his lips, studying the bed, the items on the shelves. His big body jerked against her, just once. Prue glanced over her shoulder. What was he staring at? It could only be the sturdy canopy of latticed wood above the bed, with its attachments of plaited silken ropes, light chains and cuffs.

"Not fair play, my Lady," he muttered, so low she could barely distinguish the words. "Ah, hell."

"Erik?" Her belly fluttered. "I don't understand."

He nuzzled her temple. "It's all right, love. I'll manage."

When she glanced the length of his body, if anything, he was stiffer, larger than before, the head of his cock flushed a deep urgent pink. *Manage?*

The room swung dizzily as Erik picked her up and virtually tossed her into the middle of the bed, coming down over her like a great bird of prey. Before she had a chance to open her mouth, he had covered her body with his, stealing the breath from her lungs, addling her wits. Grasping her thighs in his strong hands, he splayed her wide, surging into her, a single thrust taking him halfway home.

Prue shrieked into his mouth in shock and pleasure. In the last few moments of confusion, she'd lost the high edge of her arousal so he stretched her almost unbearably, her satiny, internal walls fluttering around his girth in mingled terror and delight. But, oh Sister save her, he felt sumptuously good!

More slowly, he withdrew, only to shove in again with a grunt of masculine satisfaction, a little farther this time. His fingers dug into her buttocks. Prue tilted her hips, wrapping her legs around his waist, and he slid all the way to the root, his testicles pressing warm and insistent against her folds. The wonderful breadth of those massive shoulders more than encompassed hers, his weight pressing her deep into the mattress. He was sealed against her, wrapping her up, all unyielding muscle, breast to breast, belly to belly, hot and damp. Water dripped from his hair onto her face and neck. Her fingers slipped on his wet skin and she gripped hard.

"Gods, I want you," he mumbled between drugging kisses. "Good . . . ah, *fuck* . . . it's good."

"Yes," she panted, twining her tongue around his. "Yes!"

Erik grabbed one of Prue's wrists and then the other, arranging her arms over her head, curling her fingers into the elaborate fretwork of the headboard. With a final lick and a soft swipe of the tongue, he freed his mouth. Panting, he stared down into her eyes, his own a brilliant, blinding blue. His expression was so focused, so compelling, she couldn't have looked away to save her life.

When she opened her mouth, he said only, "Sshh."

His hands slid from her buttocks to her thighs to her calves. Quickly, he lifted her legs over his shoulders and leaned right into her, tilting her backward, supporting his body on powerful arms. It put her in the most vulnerable position imaginable, spread out beneath him, crammed full of the hard bulk of his cock, completely at his mercy.

Helpless.

The instant the thought entered Prue's head, every muscle in her lower body convulsed with lust, clamping down so hard she could swear she felt every vein and contour of that magnificent shaft. Erik groaned as if she'd reached out and torn the heart from his chest, still beating.

His hips flexed as he drew back. An instant's pause, hanging on the edge, and then he was thundering into her, the bed shaking. Because of his size and the acute angle, it was an extraordinary sensation, on the borderline between pleasure and pain. Prue gripped the headboard with manic strength, thin whimpering noises escaping her with each gasping breath. Jabs of lightning hit her clitoris with every jolting stroke. Within seconds, the high, tight friction had built to a pleasure point so fiery it felt agonizing.

She tried to writhe, to reduce the awful, wonderful pressure, but he was everywhere. She couldn't move. Her arousal lifted another excruciating notch. "It's too much!" Her head thrashed on the pillow. "I can't take it."

"Yes, you can." He drove into her powerfully, deep, then deeper still. "Not long." A shuddering breath. "Stay with me, love."

Amazingly, she found she could. Because there was nothing left to do but to trust, to follow where he led. Higher and higher he took her, until she was keening her pleasure aloud, flying, soaring on a burning wind to a high, airy place, where she rode the lightning in truth.

The spiraling intensity of it quivered on the very cusp of culmination, a summer storm heavy with the potential for utter destruction. Prue forced her eyes open. Erik hung above her, his face fierce with passion, his shoulders and chest sheened with sweat and water. "I have to—" she gasped. "Gods, *please!*"

"Yes. Ah, Prue, you're . . . perfect."

A final twist of the hips, a long, hard stroke, and she was gone, the swell of sensation shattering, a hot, rushing wind that flashed up and down her spine, digging deep into her pelvis, her ass. She shrieked.

"Fuck!" Abruptly, Erik grasped her calves and let her legs slip to his waist. He dropped to his elbows, gripping her head between his hands, and she heard his long groan as he jammed himself high and hard inside her, his buttocks clenching with the force of his orgasm. The deep, formless sound morphed into words, rumbling out of his chest, echoing around the chamber like thunder in the mountains, strong and imperative, a masculine command.

"*Love me, Prue. Gods, love me!*"

The Necromancer sat propped up in bed, a bank of pillows at his back, listening to the rain. Scowling, he reached forward to rub his knee, and his back twinged. He'd done his best to control his temper, but he had to admit he'd failed. He let out a breath, gusty with irritation. The Technomage Primus should have known better than to provoke him.

For a start, she'd panicked all over him, and he couldn't abide that. Flapping and wailing—faugh! She hadn't even had the courtesy to say thank you. He'd relayed the singer's story about the seelies out of the goodness of his heart, because he thought she'd be interested. All the more information for her Scientific mind. What did she call it? Data.

But oh no—she'd gone pale, swaying where she stood. Then she'd begun to babble like a lunatic, spewing statistics and calculations like one of her own machines gone mad, darting from one end of the room to the other, gathering up sheets of transplas, putting them down again. Shouting at him, by Shaitan!

He had to close the palazzo immediately. *Right now!* Her equipment, her records, her *data*. How could they be moved safely? The Technomage Tower would know, she said. They'd told Nasake—

She'd bitten the words off, her face going a ghastly shade of gray, but it was too late.

The Necromancer had smiled, inhaling the sour-sweat stink of fear. "My dear Dotty," he said, "I *own* Nasake, soul and body, in this life and the next. Whatever made you think you could bribe him to run your silly messages?"

The Technomage had braced herself, one hand on the back of her chair. "How do you expect me to work in isolation?" she demanded. "They don't have to know about you." Her eyes blazed with the intensity of her feelings. "But they could help, with the seelies, with the Magick reservoir. With everything."

"No."

"For Science's sake!" She thumped the chair with her fist. "Why won't you listen? I was right about the seelies, wasn't I? I told you so!"

Not the wisest thing to say to any man, particularly a tired, aching Necromancer at the end of his tether.

He'd very nearly killed her, there and then. As it was, he wasn't entirely sure she'd be in her right mind when she came around.

Poor, foolish Dotty. She'd meant well.

The Necromancer tipped his head back and closed his eyes. How old had he been the day the original Dotty brought the healer for his mam? Seven, eight?

Slowly, his hand closed and the thick silk of the coverlet bunched under his fingers. Much good it had done, she'd died anyway—because neither of them could read the healer's instructions on the drug vial. Between them, they'd dosed her to death. The smell of poverty and damp assaulted his nose. And he was there again, lost down the dark tunnel of the years, mired in memory, his life divided into before and after.

He gritted his teeth. As always, he was grateful for the reminder of what ignorance truly was, what it meant—fiercely, bitterly grateful. Without it, without that pivotal moment, he would never have become what he was—a usurper whose very existence threatened the gods. His smile grew grim.

"I cain't let you stay here, lad," Shima had said, all those years ago. "Not less'n you earn your keep."

When at last he'd raised his gaze from his mother's limp body to meet the innkeeper's eye, Shima took a step back, sucking in his breath. In his thin treble, the boy had said, "Teach me to read an' I'll do whatever you want."

But Shima had shaken his head. "I ain't good enough. Anyways, I ain't got the time. You need a man who knows his letters. Lemme think." His face cleared. "Tolaf'd do it. He's a drunken sot, but he's clever." He hesitated, but only for an instant. "You know what he's like. He'll want you fer his bum-boy."

The child shrugged. It would hurt, he knew, but nothing came free in the slums.

The Necromancer shuddered, and a silken pillow slipped out from under his arm and flopped to the floor. He sank deeper into the soft embrace of the mattress.

Casting a final look at the still shape on the ramshackle bed, he'd trotted out of the room, hugging his treasure box to his chest. Knowledge was the key. The cost didn't matter.

Once he knew everything, everything there was to know, there would be no more mistakes.

Inside the box was a pretty pebble, the skull of a cat and a live scuttleroach. It was quite a big one, blue brown and shiny. The day before, he'd touched it, cold and smooth and wriggly, and snapped off one of its legs to see what it would do. As it blundered around the box, careering off the walls, he'd come to the conclusion that scuttleroaches were not very bright.

By Shaitan, he could still hear it!

The Necromancer shot bolt upright, his heart thumping.

Someone was tapping at the door. "Master? Master, you said you wanted a report."

"Come in, Nasake," said the Necromancer grimly. He had a bad feeling.

⁓⁂⁓

Frozen with horror, his balls still pulsing with the last spurts of pleasure, Erik stared down into Prue's vivid eyes. The richness of her soul was laid out before him, clear to the depths, like the clean, crystal beauty of a tropical sea.

Shit, *what had he done*? His chest tightened in the way that used to presage an attack of lungspasm, leaving him breathless and dizzy.

Prue's dark lashes swept down, once, slowly. "Yes," she said with an almost eerie calm. "I do." Her hand shaking, she reached up to brush a lock of wet hair out of his eyes. "I do love you." Her mouth twisted. "More fool me."

Oh, gods.

Numb with shock, Erik let her touch him, let her trace his mouth with gentle fingertips. The dark laughter of the gods reverberated in his head, the voice of the Horned Lord. *Everything has a cost*. In the duel of wills, the Dark Lady had triumphed.

"Erik, are you all right? Speak to me." The warm clasp of Prue's thighs slipped away from his body and at once, he felt bereft.

He shook his head, everything inside him bruised, scraped bloody.

It was all accomplished, Their vengeance. No, not vengeance, the Lord and Lady would call it justice—and They'd be right. Dropping his head, he buried his face in the damp, sweet-smelling mass of Prue's hair.

All his adult years, he'd fought a vicious guerilla campaign against memory, shoving the dreadful images aside, covering them over, ignoring them. *Don't think of it. Don't think of her.* With the practice, he'd become quick and deft, his gifts as much about willful forgetting as they were about music. There were some days when Inga's name didn't enter his head at all.

But what else could he do? If he crippled himself with guilt, he'd go slowly, but surely mad. The gods wouldn't want him doing Their work. Erik's guts clenched.

Would They?

Because tonight he'd come full circle. The symmetry of his two crimes had an awful, dispassionate perfection, like the precision of the intricate locking mechanism on a cruel choke collar. First Inga, now Prue. He rubbed his fingertips over his throat.

All those years ago, the pockets of Inga's winter coat had been lumpy with rocks. Staring, he'd reached out a trembling hand to touch the hard, bulky shapes under the soaked fabric, appalled with the first glimmerings of a terrible knowledge.

A soul for a soul. His anguish as atonement for Inga's.

Tonight, the Voice had been Their instrument as much as his. He'd never come so hard in his life, a rush of intense physical sensation, unbearably amplified by the beauty of Prue's surrender. It had swept him up, blown away every rational faculty, leaving only instinct. The Voice had roared out of his throat, as much a part of that incredible orgasm as his seed. He hadn't even realized he'd spoken until it was too late, the damning words ringing loose around the chamber, like a great peal of baritone bells.

Love me.

The words had welled up from the deepest part of his subconscious, chosen intuitively and with devastating, pinpoint skill. Shaking, he pressed his cheek into the sweet curve where Prue's neck met her shoulder. Murmuring something unintelligible, she stroked his back.

At seventeen, he'd confused lust with love, but not now.

Love me, Prue. Gods, love me!

Oh gods, he loved Prue McGuire more than life itself. Everything he was—heart, soul, body and mind—yearned to know she loved him back.

Yes, the required response had come out of her mouth, but the mess he'd made of his life wasn't some hearts and flowers tale with a happy ending. He couldn't afford to believe her—he couldn't *let* himself believe and still retain his sanity. Because even if, by some amazing twist of fate, she'd told him true, he'd never know for sure.

Command what you so deeply desire, the Horned Lord had said, *and by its very nature, you can never be sure you have it. Neither trust, nor love.*

Trembling, Erik pressed a kiss to Prue's forehead. Then to her eyes, one after the other, and lastly, her soft, sweet mouth. When she sighed in response, he thought he might cry, the small sound had such a wealth of weary acceptance in it.

Ducking his head so he didn't have to meet her eyes, he withdrew from her body as gently as possible, unable to prevent the shudder of pleasure as he slid out of her warm creaminess. Rolling over, he drew her into his arms, stroking wobbly circles across her shoulder blades with his fingertips. When she snuggled, throwing a leg over his, he caught his breath.

He'd thought he'd discovered what anguish was. Guilt and bitter regret and shame. He'd been wrong.

As if she'd read his mind, Prue took a brisk nip of the skin beneath his ear. "It's all right," she said. "Relax. I don't expect you to say it back." Her voice was tightly controlled, quiet and steady.

27

Propping himself up on one elbow, Erik gazed at her face, drinking her in as if he'd never seen her before—the straight, silky brows, that cushiony lower lip coupled with a determined chin. Exactly as the Horned Lord had said, he was finely caught indeed. Fucked to the seven hells and back.

"Ah, Prue." He forced a smile. "That's the most beautiful compliment anyone ever paid me. But it isn't true, you know. You don't really love me, not deep down."

Prue sat up so rapidly he couldn't help but watch her gorgeous tits quiver as her spine straightened with a snap. "How the hell would you know what I feel?" Spots of color burned on her cheeks.

Erik flinched. It was such a secret part of him, the curse of the Voice, a burden he'd carried alone from the beginning. No one need know how he'd fouled the gods' gift—especially Prue, with her clear-eyed honesty and courage. How would he bear it when her eyes darkened with judgment and she turned away, sickened by his crime? She might not intend to condemn, but she would. Gods, anyone would. No, he'd rather die.

But he owed her some part of the truth.

Drawing a fortifying breath, he grabbed her hands in both

of his. "Shut up and listen to me. This is important. I *commanded* you to love me, Prue."

She sent him a level, steady look. "Yes, I heard you."

He struggled. "No, no. You don't understand."

"Of course, I do. For the Sister's sake, Erik, I know what you are." This time, when she tugged her hands free, he allowed it. "I know you'll go, sooner rather than later."

Erik wrapped his big hands around her shoulders and held on tight. "When I was a boy, I nearly died of the lungspasm."

Her eyes went wide and soft. "Sister, that's awful." She pressed a quick kiss to the inside of his arm. "I'm sorry, but I don't understand what—"

Erik pulled her forward until they were nose to nose. "The Lord and the Lady gave me a gift. Do you understand? A special Voice."

Her brow creased. "I love your voice," she said. "It's beautiful."

"Prue." He forced himself to speak slowly. "The Voice gives me the power to command anyone to do anything."

Prue chuckled, though her amusement was threaded with uneasiness. "Don't be silly. You know that can't be true."

"You didn't want to try the shawl on, but I commanded you. Remember?"

She shrugged. "I changed my mind."

"I compelled you!"

Prue made a noise suspiciously like a snort. "No one *makes* me do anything, Erik." Her chin lifted. "Especially you."

Assailed by a creeping sense of unreality, Erik ran a hand through his damp hair. "I made Florien take a bath," he said desperately.

Prue gave a short laugh. "Oh, well done. You frightened him half to death, I imagine. Sweet Sister, he's a little boy. You could break him over your knee. What did you expect?"

Her eyes narrowed and she tilted her head. "If you have this amazing power, why aren't you lord of the universe?"

"Because I have rules!"

"Rules?" Her brows rose. "Right."

Erik sprang off the bed, breathing hard. "Do you think I'm mad?" he demanded.

"A little, perhaps," she said calmly enough, but he had the

sense she was picking her words with care. "You've been acting the demon king too long, I think." She sighed. "But the way you sing, I don't doubt your voice is a gods-given gift. Almost like Magick."

"You told me you didn't believe in Magick until you saw the seelies."

"I still don't." She shrugged again. "The seelies are real. Flesh and blood and fur." Her expression became thoughtful. "It's funny though, Purist Bartelm said Magick believes in me even if I don't believe in it."

Erik stared at her as she sat bolt upright on the bed, framed by sumptuous, bloodred hangings. Her hair was beginning to curl wildly as it dried, a dark cloud around her piquant face.

"You're the only person who's ever resisted, even for a moment. I wasn't ready for that," he said slowly, thinking it through. "You don't believe in much, do you, Prue? Not even the gods?"

"I believe in hard work. The gods help those who help themselves, my da used to say." A fleeting expression of pain crossed her face. "When I was little, I loved the idea of the Sister watching over me, so wise and lovely in the sky. I had a Sisterbook, all blue and silver and gilt, a gift on my birth from my grandmother. Mam used to . . ." She traced a pattern on the quilt with one finger.

"And then?"

She looked up, her eyes gem-bright with the tears she refused to shed. "I met Chavis. Came to the big city and grew up in a hurry. When I finally went back—" Her breath caught. "They were both . . . gone, my parents. The winter ague was bad that year, and they were old. Sad with missing me."

"Sweetheart." Erik came to stand beside her, tucking a curl behind her ear. He let his hand linger on the softness of her hair.

"Don't pity me. I have all I need."

"What's that?"

"A place in life. People I love, who love me in return. Katrin, Rose." Her voice shook. "Work to d-do." Prue sniffed, blinking furiously. Slowly, so slowly, tears welled up, sparkling on her lashes.

It was the small, defiant sniff that broke him.

"I love you, you know," he said.

Prue's face went stiff. She stared fixedly at the end of the bed. The words hung in the air, flat and dull.

Reaching out, Erik wrapped his fingers around a bedpost, anchoring himself. "Sorry, I only realized a minute ago."

"That's nice." Prue grabbed for a pillow and hugged it into her body, concealing her sweet curves, hiding from him. "But I told you. You're not obliged. I might be a fool, Erik Thorensen, but I'm not that stupid." Her sweet lips took on an ugly line. "You've got what you wanted. You don't have to say it again."

Swinging her legs around, she rose. "There should be clean robes in the cupboard."

"Fuck it!" He ran a hand through his hair, took a turn about the room. "All right, all right. The seelies were real enough, weren't they? Suppose I could prove it's all true—the power of the Voice, how much I love you?"

"Erik," she said, her brow creasing. "This command thing, it's a delusion. Impossible."

"Godsdammit! *Get back on the bed!*"

For the space of a single heartbeat, Prue wavered.

"*Do it!*" The bed hangings billowed in an unseen breeze.

Her eyes wide, she scrambled back and knelt in the middle of the bed. Then she pulled in a steadying breath and looked him dead in the eye. "So much for sheer volume. Now what?"

"Do you trust me, Prue?"

The silence dragged on and on. Eventually, she said, "Physically I'm sure I'm safe enough, but that's not really what you mean, is it?"

"No," he said heavily. "It's not." He took both her hands in his. "Prue, I could command you to do things, feel things, you've never dreamed of." He paused, his heart thundering. "In bed."

"Nonsense," she said sturdily.

"I wouldn't hurt you, I swear. You'd love it." But he made a production out of glancing around the chamber, letting his gaze lift to the ropes curled around the latticed canopy of the bed, and then linger on the strange, erotic devices lying quietly on the wooden shelves.

When he heard Prue's sudden intake of breath, he turned.

"I think you know what I'd want. It happened the moment I saw you." Lifting one of her hands, he raised it to his lips, licked the palm. "Give your pleasure over to me, Prue, body and soul. Let me control it, control you." He nipped the ball of her thumb.

Prue went still. When her pink tongue crept out to moisten her lips, his cock throbbed, hard and heavy.

He kept his voice low, seductive. "I've seen you tremble at the thought, love. Deep down, there's a part of you that yearns to give the reins to someone else—to me." Her wrist turned in his grasp, fingers curling over his jaw. She didn't even know she'd done it. "You fear the freedom as much as you crave it, don't you?"

Her wide-eyed gaze skittered away from his. She gave the faintest shake of the head, her hair falling forward in a curtain so he couldn't see her face. Gently, Erik reached out and brushed it aside. "Because it means surrender, absolute trust."

"I-I can't," she whispered.

"I know, but you see, I could make you—with the Voice." His heart aching, Erik sat on the bed and gathered her into his arms. When she sighed and nestled, he began to rock them both back and forth, in an instinctive rhythm. Prue ran her hand over his shoulder, rubbed the swell of his biceps, again and again.

Eventually, she spoke into his chest. "Assuming you're not completely insane, what . . . what would you do?"

"Worship, adore—take complete control. Strip your soul as bare as your gorgeous little body. You'd come only at my command, be bound if I wish, as I wish. I want to hear you sob with pleasure, beg me for release." He stopped, his breath coming short. "Nothing to do, nothing to think, nothing to worry about—except obedience."

⁓

Erik's heartbeat reverberated under Prue's ear, heavy and a little fast. Her mind was a mishmash of competing desires and terrors, and she couldn't seem to think straight. She'd never met a man so compelling, that was true. And he could sing the birds from the trees, that was true also, but this . . . this delusion! It went beyond confusing to crazy. She should be concerned, she knew, but she felt so safe, curled up in his arms.

She raised her head a little. "Obedience?" Her snort of disbelief stirred the hairs on his chest. "Gods, typical male thinking! What is this supposed to prove?"

Erik's chuckle had a strange sound, deep, but hollow. "What greater proof of the Voice could there be? I command a stubborn, independent woman to give herself into my control, to deliver everything she is to a man she doesn't truly trust. And you, Prue McGuire—you obey."

He grasped her chin in his hand and stared deep into her eyes, his own sheened a brilliant blue. "I'm damned, love. By my own bloody weakness. You're the trap the gods laid for me, the ambush I walked straight into. I tried so hard not to—" He swallowed. "This isn't the first time I've slipped, used the Voice on you. Remember when I nearly—up against the wall? It just about killed me to stop. I'm so sorry I hurt you like that.

"If I was even half a man, I'd walk out of here right now." His lip curled. "But it's too late, the damage is done."

Setting her a little way away from him, he skimmed his fingers over her shoulders, curving under the swell of her breast, drifting over a furled nipple. His gaze followed his touch, a perceptible brush against her skin. "Gods, I want you more than my next breath."

When he traced figures of eight from Prue's sternum to her navel and back, nerves deep in her pelvis fluttered with delighted apprehension. Her sex tingled and glowed, softening. Against her thigh, his cock stirred like a warm, sleepy animal.

"I can't make it right, what I've done," he said, the velvet voice strained and curt. "So instead I'm going to make it worse. And I can hardly wait. Ah, fuck it!" He turned his head away, but he'd forgotten about the mirrored wall.

The expression that crossed his face was so utterly desolate, it was beyond the benison of tears. She didn't think she'd ever seen such a purity of anguish. Prue found herself patting his shoulder, murmuring nonsense, the way she'd done when Katrin was little.

"Erik," she said at last. "You realize this is too bizarre to be credible? I don't—I can't—believe you."

He pinched the bridge of his nose. "You will."

Surreptitiously, Prue inhaled the scent of his skin. It made her blood sing, a bittersweet melody. Connection between two hearts, even between two bodies, was such a transient thing, so fragile and precious. "Look, we've got tonight." *I've got tonight.* "Just hold me."

She took a cautious nibble of his neck. When he jerked and his grip tightened, she licked a leisurely trail over the pulse pounding in his throat. "Make love to me."

"Can I tie your hands?" His mouth curved in a tender smile, but his eyes blazed.

Immediately, her sex tightened, a hot arrow of sensation streaking through her lower belly. *Helpless.* "N-no," she whispered.

Because when he'd held her down on the shabby couch in his dressing room, his long fingers wrapped around her wrists, the real Prue, the sensible Prue, the woman she knew, had disappeared—leaving her to drift, an empty, yearning vessel with only his hands, his voice, his body, to fill and anchor her in a world of overwhelming sensation.

She should forget how satisfying it had been, on some level so visceral, so deeply buried, she still couldn't quite grasp its true significance, or even understand where it had come from.

"There are clasps over there," said a soft, dark voice in her ear. Lightly, Erik tugged her nipple, startling a gasp out of her. "Jeweled ones. I could dress up these sweet tits, make them tingle."

Prue bit her lip. "No, they'd look better on you," she managed. Turning her head, she nipped his pectoral muscle, then suckled one brown disk deep and hard.

Erik swore and bucked against her, but he laughed. "Gods, Prue, you're perfect. I won't mention the dildos then." He paused, then whispered, "Some of them are bumpy, ridged. Did you know that?"

He tasted salty, dark and fascinating. Prue licked her lips, her sex pulsing with heat and moisture, wetting her thighs. *Ridged?* "All I want is you," she said.

Their eyes met. Erik's smile faded as his gaze searched hers. "Ah, Prue."

Without further speech, he slipped his hand under her hair, cradling the nape of her neck, the touch firm and comforting. Willingly, Prue lifted her face and he kissed her. His lips were soft and smooth, the kiss satiny, excruciatingly tender and never-ending. She sighed into his mouth, her whole body inclining forward into his, melting. He kept it light, almost chaste, his other hand brushing her cheek, stroking her hair, but the heat of his muscled body, the smell of his skin, was so enticing that by the end, he was leaning back among the pillows, Prue sprawled across his lap, clinging to his shoulders.

When he freed his lips, she murmured a protest without opening her eyes.

"Sshh," he said. "Give me a minute. I want to remember you exactly like this." Tucking her head under his chin, he skimmed his fingertips over her shoulders, her back, her ribs, the tender side of her breast. He stroked her cheek, traced her ear with a delicate touch, feathered her curls. All the time, he was crooning, something melodious, but nothing she recognized. It was strangely soothing.

Prue smiled into the curve of his strong throat. "What are you doing? Memorizing me by feel?" She glanced up.

"Yes," he said seriously, smiling as if she were already a dear memory, part of a distant past. "We'll never be the same again, love. Not after tonight."

28

"Master," wheezed Nasake. *"Master!"*

"Bah!" The Necromancer released his spectral grip and the man slid down the wall of the bedchamber, his face an interesting shade of gray green. Ignoring him, the Necromancer reached for the glass of bracing elixir he kept by his bed and took a healthy swig.

The liquor burned down his throat, and his galloping heart settled back to a regular dull thud. By Shaitan, was he surrounded by incompetents? It was true enough, what Tolaf used to say: If you want something done properly, do it yourself. Excellent advice, and the Necromancer had followed it to the letter when he'd made his first kill. The old sodomite had lasted a satisfyingly long time.

He pulled at his lower lip, brooding. His Magickal abilities had never been stronger, more magnificent, but the physical envelope betrayed him at every turn. Wistfully, he remembered the way he'd swooped on the Technomage Primus in her dreams, right across the vacuum of space. In his prime, he could have plucked the air witch right out of a nightmare and devoured her whole.

Now . . . he grimaced . . . the only stimulus that helped at all was the death energy of a seelie.

From behind, Nasake rasped something, a distorted echo of his thought.

"What?" The Necromancer turned.

"A seelie, Master." The manservant shook with coughing. "I found another in the trap."

"Help me dress. Hurry, fool!"

It was a mature male, so big it barely had room to turn in the tank. Strong. Still puffing from his dash down the stairs, the Necromancer surveyed it with enormous satisfaction. He didn't spare the crumpled, white-coated heap in the corner a glance.

An hour later, he allowed the limp form of the seelie to slip to the floor. His blood seethed with power, every nerve tingling with eager purpose. With the ease of long practice, he tallied the sum of his Dark Arts. Ah yes.

The Necromancer strode from the lab, so pleased he even patted the Doorkeeper on its horned head, adroitly avoiding the clashing fangs.

But his smile faded soon enough. Settled deep in his favorite armchair in the study, he unfurled a tendril of his dark power and sent it questing across the sleeping city toward the soft, clean glow that was the air witch.

Shit! He recoiled.

She was awake. Not only conscious, but with the singer. The Necromancer ground his teeth in frustration. No guesses as to what they were doing, not at this advanced hour. He could feel the swirl of erotic energy they generated, the passionate caring, the *love*. Filthy, undisciplined—

For a moment, he panicked. The seelie's death energy was a finite resource. More of it bled out of him with every second that passed. What should he—?

Of course!

The signature of the assassin's peculiarly empty soul was so distinctive, he located her immediately. Smiling, he settled back in his chair and sent his will winging to a shabby inn on the fringe of the Melting Pot.

∞

Erik held her so tightly she could barely breathe. Opening one eye, Prue caught sight of their entwined bodies in the mirror, posed like an erotic painting. He was hunched right over her, wrapping her up in his arms, his cheek against her hair, eyes closed. As she watched, a single fat tear leaked from the corner of his eye, rolled over his cheek and lost itself in her hair.

A foul gust of chilly air swirled around the bedchamber, like a sly questing presence. It brought with it the faintest reek of rotting garbage. Erik shivered and the odor disappeared as if it had never been.

Her heart contracting, Prue burrowed even closer. He felt so broad and warm, so strong and unyielding, but where they were sealed together, his pain seeped into her skin, her bones. Gods, she couldn't stand it! "Sshh," she found herself saying, pressing closer still, patting and soothing. "It's all right, love. I'm here."

How could she have forgotten the way a loved one's suffering peeled off the emotional layers? It burned away the selfish and the petty, so that everything took on a merciless clarity.

She pressed her lips to Erik's collarbone, breathing in the scent of his skin, the fresh, green smell of hair wash underlain with a dark male spice, full of virility. It spoke to the primeval female within her, promising both passion and protection—safety forever—though her rational mind knew full well he was the greatest threat she'd ever faced.

Did he truly love her, or had he lied? Her breath hitched. Perhaps he had delusions about that as well. The truth of it mattered, of course it did. Her entire future turned on his honesty. But nothing—*nothing*—was going to change the fact that she loved him with a totality that encompassed every fiber of her being, in all ways possible. His brush with death had skimmed off the layers of self-deception. All the foundations had been knocked away from beneath her, leaving her floundering.

Erik sighed into her hair, his breath warm against her scalp. Stroking his open palm the length of her spine, he shaped the curve of her bottom and pressed her closer still.

Oh, that felt good. Prue tried to relax, her entire body strung so tight her nerves thrummed, her thoughts running on.

Loving Erik had become part of the very weft and warp of her soul, one of the ways she defined herself. A business owner, a bookkeeper, Katrin's mother, Rose's friend, she lived all those roles, but now there was another to add—the woman who loved Erik Thorensen.

Hopelessly, deeply. Forever.

Prue shivered violently.

"Are you cold?" murmured a deep voice.

Lost for words, she shook her head, sliding her hand down over his chest until she could feel the tiny bump of his nipple against her palm. The pulse of his life beat there, cupped in her hand, strong, vulnerable and infinitely precious.

She loved him.

Whether he saved the city or Caracole sank to the bottom of the sea, she loved him.

Sooner or later, he'd be gone among the stars, off on a Technomage starship, the gossamer-thin slingshot sails spread to catch the winds of space. She couldn't count the number of times she'd gazed up into the night sky, wondering. She'd been no more than ten when she'd first seen a starship take off, rising on a plume of flame into the heavens, a spear hurled at the heavens by a warrior god. Traveling with Mam and Da to the city. Such an adventure for a little girl. Her lips curved in a sad smile.

Erik would sing his way from world to world, that superlative voice enthralling his audiences, other women flocking to his bed—and still, she'd love him.

He believed he had some gods-given power over others. The memory of a seelie's anxious, blue-furred face popped into her mind. *Hoot! Burble!* He'd been right after all—myth had turned out to be real. Perhaps . . .

No, Erik was just a particularly strong-willed man, dominating and persuasive. Her heart sped up as she remembered him pounding into her, no mercy, sending them both soaring to a shattering climax. Oh yes, she could acknowledge the power of his will. But to *compel* with his voice? A fantasy. Such things weren't possible, but so what? She loved him, she'd deal with it.

I'm damned, he'd said and his voice had been thick with self-hatred.

How could he think like that? How *dare* he?

Godsdammit, he'd done nothing so very dreadful, or even dishonorable. He'd seduced a full-grown woman who—she had to admit it—had been more than willing almost from the very beginning. It wasn't as though she was a foolish virgin.

She knew what he was, she'd always known. In every other way, he'd acted with honor. Comparing him with Chavis was an insult, and she was a fool to have done it. For the Sister's sake, she thought ruefully, the more she learned of him, the deeper she fell.

And it seemed he was more perceptive than she. *You fear it as much as you crave it.*

Her stomach pitched—with terror and excitement and longing.

The final step. She'd be his irrevocably. Because she couldn't conceive of such complete surrender unless she threw her heart and soul into the mix.

If she reached out and took what he offered, willingly, joy-fully, he'd see how he'd deceived himself.

Prue nearly laughed out loud—but she wasn't able to catch her breath.

Because it *was* funny. Who was she fooling? *You're no sacrifice, Prue McGuire,* she told herself. *You're going to do this for yourself as much as for him.*

Merciful Sister, why not? How he'd done it she had no idea, but Erik had brought forth another Prue—a woman so alive with passion, with life and love—that she hardly recognized her. Gods, had she always been so dull?

Turning her head, she took a tiny nip out of his firm shoulder, then soothed the spot with her tongue. His arms tightened around her, and his cock kicked against her thigh. She drew a shaky breath, heat and moisture plumping the lips of her sex.

He wouldn't hurt her—unless she asked him to. Gods! Her vision hazed for a moment.

Her heart beating right up into her throat, she trailed her fingers across his chest, stroking the light mat of hair between his nipples. She followed the intriguing line of it down over his sternum, his muscled stomach.

Erik hissed and his cock swelled, stretching toward her touch. The foreskin pulled back to form a soft collar, reveal-ing the rosy dome of the head with its slit already weeping for her. "Don't stop there." He picked up her hand and jammed her palm against his length.

Automatically, Prue flexed her fingers, and he grunted, his hips punching up into her grip. His life throbbed in her grasp, urgent, hard and hot, velvet over steel. Gently, she squeezed, and the satiny skin moved under her fingers, sliding over the engorged core. Erik shuddered, his breath stirring her hair, but he didn't speak.

She should tell him. Prue glanced at his face and froze. His eyes burned into hers, his cheeks flushed and sweat standing on his brow. "Harder," he rumbled. "I won't break."

Fascinated, she traced a throbbing vein with her thumb. "Prue . . ." he growled, and she smiled and tightened her grip. Up and down, up and down. Erik purred and arched.

What was the etiquette? What did one say? *Take me any way you want. I changed my mind. I'm yours.* She had no idea how to begin the conversation.

Prue began to fist him, hand over hand, pausing occasionally to swipe over the head, smearing it with its own moisture. Under the pad of her thumb, his glans felt dense and velvety, mouthwateringly smooth and searingly hot.

Prue's lips twitched, her heart soaring. Actions spoke louder than words, she'd always believed. He wasn't likely to be interested in a chat at the moment. It might be better to show him.

Bending forward, she extended her tongue and took a cautious lick, all around the head. She'd never much enjoyed doing this, but with Erik . . . She dotted a row of small, sipping kitten kisses wherever she pleased, at random. Oh, soft and firm, all at once. Musky and strong and sweet, all at once.

Erik's hips jerked. "Sweetheart . . . stop now."

Ignoring him, murmuring her pleasure, Prue licked her lips and went back for more.

Strong fingers threaded through her hair. Despite her preoccupation, she heard his preparatory intake of breath. "*Stop, Prue. Sit up and look at me.*"

⌒∞⌒

The assassin was a long heap covered by a light blanket. Soft snuffling snores stirred the lock of pale, silky hair lying across her pillow. The Necromancer's lip curled. Ah well, a tool was a tool.

Bracing himself, he slipped seamlessly into her dreams.

There was a man there—a man with a dark, relentless hunter's face. Mehcredi was running down an endless alley, her lungs laboring, but every time she turned a corner, the man waited there, his pitiless eyes black as pitch, watching, implacable. She'd whirl and run in a different direction, the breath rasping in her throat.

Over and over.

Without compunction, the Necromancer interposed himself between them. "Assassin," he hissed.

She pressed her back to a wall, her silvery eyes darting everywhere. "I'm sorry! Don't hurt me!"

"You failed me."

A pause and she regained her equilibrium, gulping for breath. Locating him by the sound of his voice, she turned her head, staring into the impenetrable shadow beneath his hood. "Oh," she said, and her shoulders sagged with what looked oddly like relief. "It's you. Sorry, what did you say?"

The Necromancer shut his mouth with an irritated snap. Shaitan, this one was remarkable! More than a little piqued, he repeated himself, something he rarely did. "*You failed me, assassin.*"

Mehcredi shrugged. "Not my fault."

"You were seen, weren't you?" That produced an interesting reaction.

The assassin knuckled her eyes like a frightened child. "He looked into my eyes, he'll find me." Her voice cracked. "Kill me."

"That's your problem. And here's another, assassin." The Necromancer paused for effect. "You owe me a death." Another pause. "Don't you?"

Long fingers clenched on her thigh. "I did everything I was supposed to."

"Excuses do not interest me. I contracted with you for the murder of the singer. You failed to deliver. What are you going to do about it?"

The assassin's lower lip jutted. "You can have your godsbedamned money back." Panting, she wrenched her belt pouch open. Credits tinkled on the cobbles as she flung them away. "Here, go hire yourself an army."

"My dear, I think you've forgotten what I can do." Almost affectionately, the Necromancer reached out with dark, insubstantial fingertips and brushed the skin behind her ear.

Mehcredi gave a hideous, choking gargle as all the strength leaked out of one side of her body. Listing, she slid down the wall and collapsed.

Impatiently, the Necromancer waited, counting off the precious seconds of the seelie's energy.

Eventually, the assassin rolled over, retching. "I'm d-dreaming," she said. "I'll wake up in a minute."

"True enough," agreed the Necromancer. "But you can feel pain in a dream. You can *die* in a dream. For the last time, *what are you going to do*?" He watched her mind racing, vastly entertained.

Sitting up, she massaged the side of her neck, rubbed her limp arm. "Try again?"

"No," he said immediately. "Not *try*. This time, you'll succeed."

Mehcredi shot him a sideways glance. "I'll get help." One-handed, she began to gather up coins.

"One more thing." The Necromancer allowed the smile to appear in his voice. "The fee's dropped. Ten credits. You can deliver the change along with the singer's body."

The assassin's face darkened. "But that's not fair!"

"That's life." The Necromancer shrugged, his shadowy presence now so vast, it blanketed the night sky of Mehcredi's dream. "Allow me to remind you." Eager to taste the astonishing purity of her soul once more, he swooped.

But as the assassin shrank back, her eyes widening until they were as round and silvery as the Sister at full, he became aware of foreign sounds, scrabbling, scratching. The woman's body wavered, then steadied again. The noises escalated. Growls and yips, a fusillade of hysterical barks, a small body hurling itself against the door. Again and again.

"That's . . ." Mehcredi wet her lips and her presence faded in and out. She was waking. ". . . dog. Have to . . ."

Abruptly, she vanished.

29

The Voice echoed around the chamber and Prue froze, Erik's cock cradled against the heated velvet of her tongue. It nearly killed him, but he tugged gently at her hair and she came up easily enough, though she resisted long enough to administer a final suckle that made his balls clench. She was delightfully flushed, her breasts quivering with the force of her breath, nipples tight and rosy. It suited her, he thought wistfully.

"Ready?" he asked.

Prue chuckled. She trailed a fingertip along the crease between his hip and his thigh and his cock jerked in helpless reflex. "I'd say so." She shot him a challenging look from under her lashes. "What exactly did you have in mind?"

"Proof," he said heavily. "Remember? Proof of the gift the gods gave me. My blessing and my curse."

"Oh," she said. "That."

"Yes, that." Erik caught her chin in one hand and gazed deep into her eyes. "I just used the Voice on you, compelled you to stop."

Her lips quirked. "Yes, with your hand in my hair."

His brain felt foggy, slow-moving and stupid, stunned by the unaccustomed storm of emotions. They flashed by so quickly, in such gut-churning combinations, he had difficulty snagging one long enough to face it, let alone deal with its import. He could discern love and lust, that was easy enough. He'd lost the high edge of his erection, but his cock was still half-hard, the stupid thing, what with the lingering effect of Prue's oral ministrations and the press of her silken skin all down his side. His nostrils were full of the luscious, mind-numbing scent of feminine arousal.

The curse of the Voice and the pain it brought with it were lifelong, intimate acquaintances, but not this bittersweet, aching tenderness. With every second that passed, it threatened to shatter his precarious composure. Hell, he was on the point of tears, no better than a little girl.

Erik gazed down at the woman in his arms. Such a valiant heart, braver than he'd ever be. What would she do if their positions were reversed?

She'd do what was right and honorable, what was best for him.

A spiky lump of ice formed in his guts. His chest tightened. She'd walk away.

Prue sighed and stirred, pressing closer to his body heat. "Erik, we have to do something about this, ah, problem of yours."

"I know." Time—that was what he needed—a few more minutes to summon up the resolution. Her fingers skated over his inner thigh, perilously high. Every muscle tensed. He sat up a little straighter, removed his arm from around her shoulders.

Prue drew away slightly, a crease between her brows. "Old Purist Nori attended the reception on your opening night, remember? She was wise, sensible." Prue shot him a wary glance from under her lashes. "I can't imagine there's anything she hasn't seen. Why don't we go talk to her tomorrow?"

Erik counted his breaths. One. Two. Shit! Three. Four. "Prue," he said as steadily as he could. "I'm in my right mind, truly. The Voice is real."

"It is or it isn't." She looked him in the eye. "You said . . ." A long pause. ". . . you loved me. Why did you do that?"

"Because it's true." He swung his legs off the bed and rose, achingly aware of the frozen silence behind him. He'd reached the door to the bathroom when she spoke, her voice soft but steadier than he'd expected.

"A strange way to show it. *Leaving me flat*. Again."

"This is the best thing I can do for you, the only thing." He didn't hear the pad of her bare soles on the thick pile of the silk carpet, but suddenly, the air was full of Prue, of the fresh, sweet smell he'd come to associate with her. Her dark hair swirled madly around her face, her fingers dug into his forearms. Erik had to set his feet not to be knocked sideways.

"C'mon," she said, her face vivid with the intensity of her purpose. "Let's get this fantasy of yours out of the way. We'll sort out the rest later." Stepping back, she set her hands on her hips and tilted her head to one side, a smile trembling on her lips, both tender and mocking. "Like you said, this is the best thing I can do for you. Command me, Erik."

He squeezed his eyes shut. "No."

Prue's brilliant aquamarine gaze burned into his. "Prove you love me," she whispered. She went up on her tiptoes, her lips brushing his. "I dare you."

"Gods, Prue!" All his thoughts fragmented, blown apart by a great rushing tempest of feeling, the force of the Voice unstoppable, overwhelming, blasting his good intentions to smithereens. It felt as if it came from the soles of his feet, the back of his skull, the base of his spine. His heart.

"*Give your trust to me, Prue, everything you are. Be mine.*" With his last scrap of sanity, he added, "*For tonight, just tonight.*" The words hung in the air, almost tangible.

She swayed and he caught her to him. "Prue!"

Her dazed eyes fluttered open and she gave a shaky smile. "See? That wasn't so hard, was it? What do you want me to do?"

Erik swung her up into his arms. "Whatever I tell you," he growled.

⁂

Erik lowered Prue to the center of the bed. Dipping his head, he placed a sweet, serious kiss on her lips. "Kneel up, sweetheart, and give me your hands."

Her stomach fluttering, she did so.

Big warm hands closed over hers. He pressed a kiss to her palms, one after the other. "I'll take good care of you, I swear," he murmured, his voice husky.

Prue held his eye. "I know."

"Sshh." He pressed the cushion of her lower lip with a gentle thumb. "You've never played like this before, have you?"

She shook her head. "What about you?"

"A little, but it meant nothing." His brows snapped together. "Which is hardly to my credit." When his thumb drifted back and forth across her mouth, she teased it with her tongue. Erik hissed. "You're all that matters, Prue."

He gazed intently into her face, as if he was imprinting her on his mind, feature by feature. She'd never seen him look so stern—or so beautiful, pared back to an elemental purpose. "Here's the first rule."

Prue choked. "Rule?"

His mouth kicked up at the corners. "Of course. For tonight, your pleasure belongs to me, not to you. Do you understand?"

Watching him from under her lashes, she nipped at his thumb. "Not really."

"You'll learn," he said cryptically. "Don't take your eyes off me either."

"What if I can't do that?"

His face hardened and a hot chill ran down Prue's spine. "I'll punish you."

"Punish?" It came out perilously close to a squeak. "How?"

Erik's expression grew positively devilish. "In a way I'll enjoy and you . . . might." His eyes danced. "Put your hands behind your back, love."

Trembling with nerves and a strange, dark excitement, Prue did so. Erik placed his forefinger in the hollow of her throat. In a leisurely fashion, he drew it down her torso, between her breasts, over her solar plexus, his eyes following the gooseflesh that rose on her skin. He circled her navel and then tracked back up again.

"This is the most important rule. Are you listening?"

She wouldn't have been surprised to see a silver trail of sensation follow his touch. Gods, it tingled! Prue had to clear her throat before she could answer. "Yes."

"You can beg all you like and it won't make any difference. In fact, I'll enjoy it."

When she stiffened, his eyes gleamed with pleasure. "If you're in real pain, disgusted, truly terrified, then I'll stop, but only then."

Prue wet her lips. "But how, how will—?"

He considered for a moment "Sing the 'Seelie Song.'"

"I told you I can't sing."

Erik smiled grimly. "You'll manage if you need to. Just the first line. Got it?" When she didn't reply, his voice lowered to a bass baritone growl. "*Answer me, Prue.*"

"Godsdammit, yes!" She tossed her head. "I've got it."

He gripped her chin in hard fingers. "You looked away then. Don't do it again. You're mine, all of you." His eyes were almost black, his cheeks flushed. "Starting with this gorgeous mouth. Bring it here. And don't move your hands. I won't let you fall."

Her pulse thundering in her ears, Prue rose on her knees. Because she had to stretch up to fit her mouth to his, she wobbled on the yielding surface of mattress. Erik slid his fingers deep into her hair and cradled her skull, the single point of contact enough to keep her steady. With a deep murmur of satisfaction, he took possession of her mouth. She couldn't think of any other word for it. *Possession.* He luxuriated, indulging himself with nibbles and licks, sinking deeper by slow degrees, overwhelming her with his passion.

Prue twined her fingers together behind her back and gripped hard so she wouldn't forget herself and wind her arms around his neck, press herself close to the furnace heat radiating from his skin.

Somehow, he seemed to know. He lifted his head a fraction. "I've got you."

That was all. But it was enough. Prue sighed into his mouth, relaxing. Her head fell back in surrender. He'd never kissed her like this before, as if her mouth were a pleasure garden created solely for his delectation.

Her head reeled with the power of it. She need do nothing beyond the giving of herself. Her only responsibility was to please him. It was impossible to get it wrong because he would tell her, show her.

Prue whimpered against the hot, sleek velvet of his plundering tongue. How extraordinary, she thought dizzily. She felt so light, if it wasn't for the anchoring grip of his fingers, she'd float to the ceiling like a feather lifted on a spring breeze. Yet her body was heavy, suffused with hot blood, soft and slick and ready to be taken. A trickle of moisture ran down the inside of her thigh. Her breasts were so engorged the creamy flesh was taut, her nipples distended.

Deliberately, she arched, hissing into Erik's mouth when the sensitive crests brushed over the light mat of hair on his hard chest. She was about to go back for more when he wrapped his hands around her shoulders and freed his mouth. She groaned with frustration.

"Wanton baggage." But he smiled, his eyes brilliant with pleasure. He curled a lock of her hair around one finger and it clung, still a little damp. "Your hair needs brushing out."

"No, no, it's fine. Leave it."

Erik arched a brow and turned away, leaving her bereft. In complete silence, he padded over to the shallow shelves that held the erotic devices. Prue's chest went tight with shock. She wasn't naïve, she knew what some of them were for and she could have told him to the last cred what they cost, but some of the objects . . . Well, she preferred to remain in ignorance.

He stood there for an endless time, reaching out to touch first one, then another. Watching him, Prue had no problems with obedience—she couldn't drag her eyes away from the eloquent line of his shoulders, the way his thighs tensed and his buttocks went taut. When a drop of water coursed out of the dark gold of his hair and over his bent neck, so strong and yet so vulnerable, she quivered with the desire to press up against him and lick it off, to kiss and comfort and love.

When he picked something up, she tensed, but his body obscured her view. Both his hands disappeared and Prue craned forward. What in the gods' names was he doing? With a pained grunt, he dropped his head, his shoulders heaving. A long pause and he went back to pondering his choice.

By the time he made his final selection, Prue's thought processes had degenerated to a gibbering soup. *Gods, gods, oh gods, what is he going to—?*

All he held was a hairbrush and a scrap of fabric crushed in his hand.

Prue's breath whistled out from between her teeth. But when her gaze dropped to his magnificent erection, jutting proudly from a nest of sandy curls, she forgot to breathe entirely.

A smooth, tight ring surrounded the root of his cock, glinting gold against the flushed skin, the constriction continuing under his scrotum. No wonder he hadn't been able to muffle his discomfort.

Before she knew it, she'd licked her lips.

When Erik chuckled, she itched to hit him, but of course, she couldn't, could she? Her hands were clasped behind her back. Words tumbled out of her mouth. "That's not fair!"

"Do I care?" Grinning, he tossed the brush and the fabric onto the bed behind her. "Thank the gods I already took the edge off." He leaned forward to drop a kiss on the tip of her nose. "Waiting's going to be pure torture, but fuck, it'll be worth it, every second."

Prue curled her lip and shot him a killing glare, but all he said was, "Sit on your heels, sweetheart, and get comfortable."

The mattress dipped as he settled himself behind her, her hips bracketed by his knees. Automatically, she flexed her fingers, encountering his flat belly, the drift of the rough hair intriguing beneath her fingertips. When the heel of her hand brushed something velvety soft and very hot, he swore and jerked away. Prue grinned to herself.

Erik leaned forward to nip her earlobe, a tiny, reproving sting. "Put your hands on my knees and don't forget I can see you in the mirror."

30

Startled, Prue glanced up and saw his attention narrow to
focus on her hair, the brush in his big hand. Carefully, he drew
the bristles through the first lock. He was clearly unpracticed,
even a little awkward, but his concentration was absolute, the
touch of his hands light and soothing. Muscle by muscle, she
relaxed, the high edge of her arousal fading to a banked glow.
Her eyelids drooped with the soporific pleasure of it, but she
wasn't quite brave enough to defy him and close them. Erik
hummed as he worked, a deep croon so formless she couldn't
recognize any melody in particular. She had the sense he'd let
himself go, that he didn't often sing like this, without a purpose, and she liked it—very much.

The brush skimmed from her hair to the skin of her upper
back, leaving a pleasant tingle in its wake. Then again. And
again. A little harder, a little farther each time.

Erik dragged the bristles the length of her spine, raising
bumps on her skin. Looking up, he caught her startled gaze
in the mirror and smiled. "Your skin colors beautifully." The
brush traveled across the curve of her buttocks, back up to
her waist. Every nerve quivered, every inch achingly alive and
excruciatingly aware. "Do you like it?"

"It's . . ." Prue wet her lips. "It's very intense." She shifted on her heels, swaying away from the long, insistent strokes.

"This better?"

Something beautifully soft caressed her shoulder blade, moved down over her ribs. "Oh. Oh, yes." After the uncompromising drag of the brush, it was exquisitely soothing, gliding over her sensitized flesh. Velvet perhaps? Or fur?

"Good." One muscular arm wrapped around her hips, an immovable restraint. "Hold tight, love." The brush slid over her shoulder and down between her breasts all the way to her navel, a trail of panicky flutters following it the whole way.

Prue stiffened. "I don't think . . ."

Ignoring her, Erik repeated the stroke, slightly harder, humming under his breath. The bristles tingled over her ribs, the underside of one breast, up one swelling curve, down the other, skirting her nipples. They tightened in such a rush, Prue let out a huff of surprise.

She'd never felt so vulnerable in her life, her breasts soft and tender, her sensitive nipples exposed to the firm attentions of the brush. Except that he hadn't touched them. The sensation hovered on the verge of discomfort. She couldn't decide if she wanted more of it or less.

"Stop," she gasped. "Gods, stop!"

Erik brushed across her belly and every nerve trembled with delight and terror. "In a minute," he said inexorably. But he paused long enough to tilt her chin with strong fingers. "Look how beautiful you are."

Prue stared at her reflection, astonished. She knelt bolt upright between Erik's brawny thighs, her hair gleaming around her shoulders, her eyes huge aquamarine pools, the shy, pink folds of her sex gleaming with moisture between her pale thighs. She was still plump, still Prue McGuire, but she *glowed*. She couldn't think of another word for it. Yes, the heated trails left by the brush were plain to see on her skin, but it was more than that, so much more.

This other Prue vibrated with pent-up passion, yet she was utterly relaxed in a way she'd never been before, his big body surrounding her smaller one with heat and strength. This Prue had found a place where her soul could rejoice, a sanctuary of trust and love and sheer excitement. It was extraordinary.

Erik pressed his lips to the pulse drumming in her neck, kissed the skin. "You see?" Lingeringly, he smoothed the velvet over her tingling breasts. Prue had to bite her lip to stifle the cry of pleasure. When her head fell back against his shoulder, he gave a dark chuckle.

That was all the warning she got before he started with the brush again, harder than before, still avoiding her aching nipples. It was hell and heaven together, waiting for the rasp of the bristles on her most exquisitely sensitive flesh. The anticipation was almost literally painful, her nipples standing so proud and rosy she wanted to take them between her own fingers and pull and twist to relieve the erotic pressure. Prue arched and shook until she couldn't stand it another second. "Please. Erik . . ." Her nails dug into his leg.

His breath stirred her hair. "Gods, yes."

The brush clattered to the floor and Prue's world swung. "I've got you," he said. And he had, sprawled across his lap, her head in the crook of his arm. Without a word, he bent his head and engulfed a nipple in the hot, wet cavern of his mouth, suckling strongly, no mercy.

Prue shrieked, but the sound stuttered in her throat when he reached between her legs and pressed the flat of his thumb directly over her quivering clit.

Her world disappeared in a luscious, all-encompassing explosion of soft red sensation. There was no room left inside her for breath, or thought, or awareness of anything save the whirlwind of heat that roared up and down her spine, pooling low in her belly, in her sex. A hurricane of release tore through her, winds that blew her conscious self away, leaving only Erik's big hands and deep voice to tether her to earth.

It took forever and it took no time at all.

The aftershocks were still washing through her when she cranked her eyelids open. Oh Sister, she'd forgotten she wasn't supposed to close them!

But it seemed to have slipped Erik's mind. His palm moved in warm, gentle circles on her stomach. "That was, was . . ." He shook his head, his eyes wide and very blue. "I had no idea. This is actually working, isn't it?"

Prue smiled, tears stinging her eyes. "Oh yes." On impulse,

she locked her arms around his neck, dragged his head down and nuzzled his stubbled jaw. "What about you?"

"It's . . . like flying. Knowing I have you, that for tonight you're mine and only mine. You make such gorgeous little noises, Prue, like music. I . . . Ah well." He blinked, shrugging.

Prue slid a hand down over his chest, toward his stomach. "Doesn't it hurt, that thing?"

Erik caught her fingers in a hard grip. His cheek moved against hers as he smiled, but there was little humor in his voice. "I'll survive." Gently, he drew back. "Roll over on your front, sweetheart, and stretch out."

With a deep sigh, Prue did so, every muscle, nerve and tendon languid with the release of tension. When he returned to the shelf holding the devices, she was so lost in studying the hard, high curve of his ass, she forgot to worry. The light picked up the golden glow of skin and body hair, a downy fuzz like that on some delectable fruit. Her mouth watered. On the way back, she was so focused on the astonishing rigidity and girth of his bound cock, she barely noticed what he had in his hands. A small bottle and something else.

Didn't matter, she trusted him. She was wet and soft and open, she'd be able to accommodate him, whatever he wanted. It would be her pleasure. Or she could take him in her mouth, taste him, lick and suck and drive him wild. Now that would be something. Her lips curved in a sated smile, but Erik looked stern, even forbidding.

He sat at her hip. "Hold on to the headboard."

When she did so, he untangled two of the silken ropes draped over the latticed canopy above the bed. "Prue, do you remember the things I said to you earlier?" As he spoke, he looped a rope over her wrist and tied it to the fretwork of the headboard.

The knot was a token effort, so simple she'd be able to release herself with ease. Prue smiled. "Which one? You said an awful lot, you know."

"I have a point to prove." Erik secured the other wrist. "I said I could make you do things, feel things, you've never wanted before."

A chill slithered on little cat feet down her spine. Prue moistened her lips. "Like what? It's only a different angle. Fine, I've done it this way before."

"Lift up." Erik grabbed the other pillow and shoved it beneath her hips, cupping the generous curves of her bottom in his palms. It must be her imagination, but she could have sworn his hands shook. "Lord's balls, I'm going to fuck you into the mattress."

She must be presented to him like a meal on a plate and it seemed he was hungry. Prue purred. "Good."

"But first . . ."

Picking up the bottle, he uncorked it and dribbled a trail of something cold and wet over her tailbone and into the cleft between her buttocks.

"What the—?" Prue tried to rear up, only to have Erik press her down with a firm hand in the small of her back.

"Sshh. It's a lubricant." He pushed her legs farther apart, following the liquid with a thick forefinger, swirling around the shrinking pucker of her anus.

Prue could barely speak. "You w-wouldn't!"

"You have a truly fabulous ass, sweetheart. Don't move." He smacked her bottom, enough to sting but not to really hurt. As he leaned forward to whisper in her ear, one fingertip penetrated, very gently. "No more than you can take, I promise. You're doing wonderfully. Here, look."

He placed an object on the table beside the bed. Prue stared. It was made of a dark gray, flexible substance, reminiscent of Technomage transplas, in a series of graduated bulges, fine at the tip, thickest near the base, where there was a broader, flatter piece.

Erik's finger sank in to the first joint and swirled. His other hand drifted up and down her spine, petting and soothing. Prue gurgled, her brain reeling. Gods, she'd never imagined anything so naughty in her life, but neither had she known the nerves there were so sensitive.

Erik said something and she missed it. He swatted her other cheek. "I asked you a question, Prue."

"W-what?" Every square inch he'd brushed tingled, prickling and burning, as if that single sharp smack had set off a chain reaction all over her body. But it was no hotter than the dark, fiery sensations in her ass. When his finger advanced another inch, Prue shuddered, unable to process the competing sensations, the strangeness of it all.

"Do you know what this is?" He laid a finger on the very tip of the object. "What it's for?"

Prue groaned into the pillow. "I can guess."

"Is it thicker than me?"

Merciful Sister, was that a *second* finger inside her? "N-no."

"Longer?"

"No!" He was stretching her now, gentle, but implacable. She didn't *not* like it, in fact—Godsdammit, this was insane, *wrong.* "Stop, Erik, I can't—"

A big hand came into her field of vision and scooped up the plug. "You can take it, love. I know you can."

Prue pulled back as far as her bonds would allow. "No, don't." Her voice came out deeper than she'd intended, husky. "I don't want—*Gods!*"

He'd cupped her sex, pressing the slick, cool surface of the plug the length of her slit. "You're not just wet, Prue. You're dripping." He slid the first third of it inside her sheath, setting off a series of clutching spasms she was helpless to prevent. "You see?" He gave the plug a twirl, leaving her aching for something thicker, longer. *Harder.*

Erik's voice dropped a full octave as he withdrew the plug and trailed the flexible tip back over her perineum, making her quiver. "I'm dying for you, Prue. So tight around my cock. Like a soft, hot fist gripping, sliding—" She heard his breath hitch. A momentary pause and the cool, silky weight of his hair swept across her thigh. Strong teeth worried delicately at the slope where buttock curved into thigh.

He replaced the fingers in her ass with the plug and began to work it in, using plenty of the lubricant. He did it one bump at a time, ignoring her incoherent protests. Prue's thoughts whirled about like small birds tossed in an updraft. She could stop him in an instant, she knew she could, knew what she had to do. But he wanted it so very badly, and she loved him so much—and besides, she'd always said she couldn't sing.

The plug wasn't especially thick, even at the base, so it

didn't hurt, but it stretched her enough to be a fiery presence in her rear, invading and filling in a way it was impossible to ignore.

"There." Erik gave the diabolical thing a final twist, seating it firmly and setting off a complicated tangle of fireworks that had Prue clenching her hands around the headboard until her knuckles shone. The carved surface bit into her palms, but she had no attention to spare because Erik had grasped her hips and lifted her to her knees. The front of his thighs pressed against the back of hers.

"Fuck, Prue," he muttered. "You're killing me."

Searingly hot and hammer hard, he worked the first inch into her body. His long, low groan and Prue's shocked gasp echoed off the walls together. His fingers bit into her hips as he slid back a little, only to thrust back in. She could hear the harsh rasp of his breath, feel the rock-hard tension in his thighs.

"Feel it?" He had to be speaking through clenched teeth because she could barely make out the words, but oh, gods, yes, she could feel every twitch of his cock, every curve of the device inside her!

The difference was indescribable. The bulk of the plug narrowed her sheath, so that Erik had to move unbearably slowly, finessing and furrowing his way through slick, delicate tissues. When he was finally crammed all the way in, planted balls deep, he froze, waiting for the Sister knew what.

Prue dropped her head, whimpering. All the blood and every nerve she possessed had migrated to her pelvis. Gradually, she became aware of his heartbeat, transmitted through the girth that spread her so wide. Her own marched together with his, an insistent rhythm in her sex, her ass, her belly, her heart, her head. Ah, gods, she was on fire—lost, so lost in him, consumed utterly. Owned.

Had he spoken? It took so much of her willpower to prevent her shaky knees from collapsing she must have missed it.

"Prue." Erik tapped the plug, which sent hot sparks streaking through her ass to pool behind her clit. Prue gritted her teeth and hung on.

"I know how strong you are, how stubborn," he said. "I want you to fight it. You're not to come until I tell you." A light smack that nearly destroyed her. "Do you understand?"

"Yes, damn you! I—*nngh*—get it!"

Erik placed his lips between her shoulder blades and made a noise against her skin that went beyond words, a sort of purring growl, redolent of dark anticipation and masculine satisfaction. Sliding his hands down the fronts of her thighs, he gripped her knees and pulled her legs back straight, lowering her flat to the surface of the bed, her hips still slightly elevated by the pillow.

Startled, Prue tried to turn her head, but he slid his arms up under her to curl strong fingers back over her shoulders. The heated width of his chest lowered slowly to rest all along her spine, his body sealed to hers so that she was pinned, utterly helpless. Erik nuzzled her neck, licking a long, sizzling line up her pulse.

"Now," he growled in his dark velvet voice, "now I'm going to fuck you, Prue, like you've never been fucked before."

Prue had gone beyond speech, but gods, it was the oddest position. It would never work, it—

Erik began to move, setting up a long, deliberate stroke, and she realized at once how little she'd understood. Each withdrawal was a dark, fiery drag past the unyielding curves of the plug, each thrust back in a thick, luscious invasion. The angle was shallow, but perfect, his cock long as well as wide, so that as he picked up the pace, he hit her clit from behind with each thrust. When his flesh smacked into hers, his weight jarred the plug, jostling it. Erik was everywhere—in her sex, her ass, his huge body blanketing hers with power, his hoarse breath hot and moist against her throat.

She'd thought she'd had some idea of what it meant to submit, to give control to another, but even her most vivid imaginings had been nothing like this. The pleasure was so dark, so overwhelming, her vision began to haze. Panicked, she thrashed beneath him, tugging against the ropes.

Erik slowed, though he didn't entirely stop. "I've got you, love." He pressed a kiss to her shoulder. "You're safe."

The darkness receded somewhat. Beyond pride, stripped bare, Prue slipped one hand free of the bonds and reached back to bury it in his hair. She turned her head to meet his eyes. "Promise?"

"On my honor." The smile that curved his lips was

suffused with a bittersweet tenderness. "You're strong and beautiful, and I love you." He kissed the inside of her forearm. "Ready for more?" His hips moved in an instinctive shimmy he seemed unable to prevent.

Prue hissed at the lightning whips of sensation. "I feel like I might pass out."

"No, you won't. I'll catch you." Another heart-wrenching smile. "I'll never let you fall."

Prue wriggled her hips, clenching on his hardness. "Please."

His eyes darkened. "Wait, let me . . ." She felt his knuckles brush her buttocks, a snap and a small noise as he threw the cock ring aside. "Oh, fuck—" A tide of red ran up from his throat to his cheeks. "Remember," he rasped. "Not 'til I say."

With that, he was surging into her, deep, hard strokes with his full, fat length, giving her no quarter.

Not that she wanted any, because she was flying on the relentless physical stimulation, as high as if she rode a gathering storm front of purple-dark clouds. The fierce pressure in her ass and her sex merged into an imperative she could no longer deny, swelling behind her quivering clit. The pleasure had become so acute, it approached exquisite agony.

Inexorably, the storm swept closer, no matter how she struggled to hold it back.

Her head thrashed on the pillow. "Erik!"

The rhythm paused for a second, then resumed. "Ten seconds," he growled. "Count with me. Ten, nine, eight—"

In sheer desperation, Prue grabbed his hand and sucked an index finger deep into her mouth, lashing at it with her tongue.

Erik made a guttural noise, a cross between a sob, a groan and a laugh. "Fuck it! Now, love. *Now!*"

The snap and recoil of the releasing tension made her buck and writhe. Keening around the hard finger in her mouth, Prue let herself tumble toward the dark. Flashing sparks of light darted across the inside of her eyelids, stars and comets and haloes of lightning. She was dissolving, spinning, losing her grip on consciousness. Gods, this degree of intensity wasn't possible, she'd never, never—

Erik caught her, as he'd promised he would, his cheek pressed to hers, his deep voice calling her name, pulling her back into his heat, his solidity and strength. Prue gasped and shook with reaction, tears streaking her cheeks.

He stiffened, his hips jerking as he poured his life, his essence, into her body. "Love you," he groaned into her neck. "Love, love you."

She pressed back against him, clenching her internal muscles, making it as good for him as she could. For endless, precious seconds, he froze, buried deep, his pulse marching with hers. At last, he relaxed with a shuddering sigh. "Ah, Prue."

In the silence, she could hear their breaths rasping together. After a moment, he braced himself on his elbows. "You all right?"

Prue swallowed. "Not sure."

Gently, Erik withdrew and rolled aside. He gazed deep into her eyes, his own shining a deep and vivid blue. Whatever he saw, he seemed to be reassured, because he leaned forward to press his lips against hers. "Back in a minute." He loosed the last of the silken ropes. "Close your eyes. Rest."

Prue did as she was bid, rousing only to murmur a sleepy protest when he removed the plug and made her comfortable with a warm, wet cloth. She sensed movement, water running in the bath chamber. Returning, he patted her dry, then settled beside her, arranging her body to his satisfaction, her head tucked into his shoulder, her palm resting over his heart.

He curled a lock of her hair around one finger. "You're a wicked woman, Prue McGuire."

"Mmm?"

"You tipped me over before I was ready. I should beat you."

Prue dragged the scent of his skin into her lungs, nuzzling her nose into the pit of his throat. "Not now. In the morning."

His fingertips skated over her hip in slow, wobbly circles. "I proved my point," he said at last, not sounding any too pleased.

Prue yawned. "Uh-huh."

"You did something for me you've never done before. Because of the Voice."

But she hadn't. She'd done it because she was a grown woman who knew her own mind. Her decision had already been made when he'd spoken to her in that extraordinary way. Merciful Sister, she had to admit it had been everything she'd dreamed of—a life-altering experience. She hadn't had the slightest desire to resist, Voice or no Voice, though she could have, she was sure. She should let him know that, stop him taking it all so seriously.

Prue opened her mouth to tell him, but exhaustion tugged at her in great dark waves, so that all she could manage was, "N-nonsense."

The last thing she heard was Erik's sigh as he stroked her hair.

31

A light breeze drifted in through the open window, bringing with it the scent of a world newly washed and the singing class working its way through a series of arpeggios. How lovely, thought Prue, settling her cheek on the pile of papers on her desk. Ah, that was better. Her body felt like well-worked putty, every muscle humming and utterly content. She purred, wriggling a little in the chair, relishing the frisson that ran down her spine to spread over the cheeks of her bottom. Sweet Sister, she still couldn't quite credit what she'd done—what she'd allowed, trusted Erik to do to her. There was nothing left of Prue McGuire that wasn't his.

How had he known? Just enough and no more. Even the tenderness deep within was welcome, her internal tissues still tingling with the memory of ecstasy.

Erik's voice rose on the air, his deep bell tones flirting with the silvery timbre of the flute. Prue's yawn finished with a smile. A love song, and it felt as if he sang it for her alone. It sounded ancient, the words exquisitely simple, describing the singer's first sight of his beloved's face. He'd thought the sun rose in her eyes. A tear trickled down and plopped onto a column of figures. Hastily, she sat up to deal with the blot.

With the movement, a tendril of unease unfurled in the pit of her stomach. Prue banished it, but it sneaked back, bringing a host of whispering brethren. A chill spread over her, until even her fingertips were cold.

Someone wished him ill. Behind her eyelids, she saw Dai's lithe body bent up like a bow in his agony. Oh gods, *prettydeath*! Her skin crawled with the presentiment of evil. Erik was a singer, a *performer*, for the Sister's sake. Yes, there was power in that tall, athletic physique, but what would he know of violence? Her fingers went white on the ink brush.

Last night, or rather early this morning, she'd collapsed, asleep the moment he settled beside her. Dimly, she'd been aware of the big body spooned around hers, the heavy arm he threw around her waist. Murmuring her content, she'd snuggled. It seemed only a moment before he was nuzzling her cheek, stroking her breasts, her belly, her buttocks.

"Sweetheart," he'd whispered. "It's dawn. I have to get something from the boardinghouse and be back before singing class. Kiss me."

Without opening her eyes, she rolled over and offered her mouth. He'd taken it as if he owned it. Long, languorous kisses, her hands smoothing over his beautiful shoulders and strong spine, then clinging hard, fingers gripping.

Panting, he'd forced himself away and she blinked up at him, standing naked and magnificently aroused by the bed. "Fuck, woman, don't look at me like that."

"Like what?" she asked drowsily. "Mmm." She raised her arms over her head and stretched, luxuriating in her power. "Where are you going? Come back here."

Erik gave a hoarse chuckle. "Godsdammit, if I do I'll never leave." He spun on his heel and headed for the bathroom, swearing under his breath.

Prue turned her face into the pillow, his scent surrounding her. She dozed off.

When his lips ghosted over her cheek, she murmured her pleasure. "I'll come for you after singing class," he murmured, nibbling a trail down the side of her neck. "For our appointment with the Queen's Money."

Not even that could disturb her. "Mmm." When she reached for him, Erik was gone. It was only later that she realized she'd forgotten to warn him to watch his back.

She'd gone down to the kitchens for a late breakfast, needing to ground her shaky emotions, wanting the calm of Katrin's presence, but her daughter had taken one glance and her brow had furrowed. "I heard about the Open Cabal." Deftly, she removed a tray of rolls from the oven, setting it down on the bench next to a row of others. "Bloody hell, Mam, five hundred credits!"

"Don't swear." It came out automatically.

"Well, it's a lot." Katrin was unrepentant. "It's not good for your reputation either. Here." She placed a steaming cup in front of her mother, tipped a couple of rolls onto a pretty plate and opened a bottle of conserve. "Eat something."

"Erik said he'd pay. We'll still arguing about it. And I did see the seelies," she mumbled through a warm, sweet mouthful.

"Sister, how wonderful!" Katrin's face lit up, reminding Prue of the little girl who'd loved fairy tales. "So he was telling the truth, after all?"

"About that, yes."

"People are saying you're as mad as he is," came Rose's voice from the door. She sauntered in, perfectly groomed and ready for the day. "Katrin, Cook's down at the water stairs in hysterics. Something to do with moldy taters and a cheeky delivery boy." She waved an elegant hand. "Would you mind?"

Katrin rolled her eyes. "I'm gone," she said, whisking out the door.

Rose found another cup and seated herself opposite Prue. "You're late for breakfast this morning," she observed mildly.

Prue made a noncommittal noise, cursing the heat in her cheeks.

"Ah," said Rose. "Thought so." The shadow of a saucy grin. "How are you this beautiful morning, my dear?"

"None of your business." Prue shifted slightly on the seat, the memories astonishingly vivid.

Rose chuckled. "That good, huh?" After a short silence, she reached across the table to take Prue's hands in hers. "What's wrong, love? I heard about the seelie thing."

Prue shook her head. "It's not that, or at least, that's not all." Carefully, she put her cup down. "Someone tried to poison Erik last night."

"*What?*"

It took her half an hour to tell the whole tale and another half hour to persuade Rose that going straight to Dai's bedside would be no help at all.

"Sister save us, this is awful. Poor Dai. All because I accepted Erik's invitation to the queen's reception." Drying her eyes, Rose shot Prue a shrewd glance. "How serious *is* it between you?"

Prue hunched her shoulders. "Don't want to talk about it."

"Not good enough. You're my friend and I love you. But Erik Thorensen?" Rose shrugged. "I like him well enough. No question that he's handsome. But obviously, I don't I know him at all." She leaned forward, all amusement gone. "Do you?"

How could she answer? On one level, Prue was sure she'd known Erik forever, soul cleaving to soul. On another, he was a mystery, and her bafflement hurt. He seemed so open, but it was all part of the façade he presented to the world—and to her.

"Is he worth all this . . . mess?" persisted Rose. "Does he make you happy?"

Helplessly, Prue shrugged. "I don't know the answer to either of those questions."

But she did. He *could* be worth it. He *could* make her happy. That was the problem.

◯∞◯

Prue shook herself out of her daze. He was here now, safe, his voice rising like a gift woven of air and supple gold. She'd see him soon. Her heart beating uncomfortably hard, she rubbed the sleep from her eyes, took her underlip firmly between her teeth and applied herself to the Unearthly Opera's accounts.

Half an hour later, she heard the thud of boots on the stairs, two at a time. Carefully, she laid the ink brush on the block and clasped her hands together in her lap to stop the trembling.

Just for tonight, he'd said in that strange, compelling voice, but she wanted so much more! Clearing her throat, she arranged her features in an expression of friendly welcome.

A single brisk rap, the door banged back and Erik surged into the room like a whirlwind. "Prue!" Without hesitation, he strode around the desk, plucked her out of the chair and into his arms. Growling happily, he kissed her, taking his time, soft and wet and luxurious.

Prue tangled her fingers in his hair, pressing close. When he raised his head, he said, "Did you like the song?"

"I—"

She got no further, because he picked her up and carried her over to the couch in the sitting room, where he kissed her until they were both breathless. "I sang it for you. Because that's how it was, the first time I saw you."

Prue smacked his shoulder, but lightly. "You're insatiable." Ah hell, now she was blushing. "I mean for compliments."

His eyes danced. "Of course I am," he said. "On all counts." Then he sobered, staring down at her in silence.

Prue dropped her gaze to the wedge of golden, hair-dusted skin in the collar of his shirt. "What?"

Erik cleared his throat, his cheeks pink. "You all right? I wasn't too rough?"

Unable to think of a response that didn't betray her utterly, Prue shook her head.

Erik drew a black velvet bag out of his belt pouch. "I know I said just the night." He thrust it into her hands. "But—" He broke off to run a hand through his hair, a blond lock flopping back over his forehead. Impatiently, he brushed it out of his eyes. "I wanted you to have a remembrance."

"I already have the shawl. Erik, you mustn't—"

"Yes, I must." His jaw set. "I *will*. Open it, Prue. I don't want to compel you."

As if he could. Prue snorted. The tygre at the table. The issue neither of them had broached from the moment he'd laid her down on the bed in the Bruised Orchid and reached for the hairbrush.

She untied the bag's drawstring and upended it. Two bands of gleaming silver tumbled into her lap. Each bracelet was about an inch wide, light, yet sturdy, and chased with a delicate design of touchme flowers interlaced with lover vines.

"Oh," she said. "*Oh*."

"Here," murmured Erik. "Let me." Taking her hand, he slid

a bracelet onto her wrist with careful fingers. In fact, it was more like an elegant cuff, because there was no clasp, but set into it at either end were two large, brilliant cut aquamarines.

He ran his thumb over her knuckles. "The stones are first grade, the same color as your eyes." His beautiful voice sounded husky. "Give me your other hand."

Cuffs.

Prue snapped out of her daze. "Erik, I can't accept—"

"Don't you like them?"

"They're exquisite." Sadly, Prue caressed the curling lines of a vine with a fingertip.

Erik rose and took two jerky steps to the window. "Last night," he said, apparently speaking to the bushes in the garden, "was the most amazing night of my life. It may not have come freely, but nonetheless, you gave me a gift I will always treasure."

He turned to face her, his expression carefully neutral, his hands clasped behind his back. "The bracelets are cuffs, to symbolize what we shared, though only you and I will know that. I won't force you to wear them, Prue, but I'd like it very much if you would."

Prue met his eyes and made a discovery. "Erik Thorensen," she said severely, "you're playing on my sympathy. Don't you have any principles at all?"

"When it comes to you?" His smile went awry. "No, none."

His face in the mirror. Despair and pain and an odd sort of resignation, as if it wasn't a question of whether life would kick him in the teeth, but when. Prue's heart contracted.

Slowly, she slid on the second bracelet and extended both hands to study the effect. The metal was light against her skin, the merest hint of restraint. Her breath quickened and a pulse pattered between her legs. Why she should feel simultaneously stimulated and comforted, she couldn't fathom, but the sensation was so unsettling, she spoke before she thought. "You don't own me, Erik."

A brow rose. "No," he agreed, equably enough, but a small, satisfied smile graced his lips.

∽

"Walk with me." Prue tugged at Erik's arm. Under her fingers, the muscles were so rigid, they felt like sun-warmed iron.

Reluctantly, he allowed her to lead him away from the offices of the Queen's Money and into a broad avenue lined with mature purplemist trees. "Useless," he growled. "Fucking useless." He stopped to glare back at the building, his face dark with fury. "All he wanted was you, the cunning old bastard."

Prue sighed. "I should have expected it. The Money's been trying to lure me away from Rose for years."

"Why were there so many clerks?" asked Erik, pursuing some thought of his own. "Gods, they were in and out the whole time with their ears flapping. Sign this, check that." His lips twisted. "I couldn't use the Voice, and without it, he didn't hear two words of what I had to say."

"Voice or no Voice, he wasn't interested, Erik." She came to a stop, looking up into his face. "No one in authority is."

"The Leaf of Nobility is going to drown. Maybe the whole fucking city." Erik's jaw knotted. "I'll go elsewhere." He strode off so rapidly, she had to trot to catch up with him.

"Where?"

He cast her a narrow glance. "The people. I'll work the taverns and the markets." His teeth flashed in a savage grin. "A riot, a rabble. I don't care. Get enough people in the streets and I'll have the Cabal's attention."

"The City Guard's too, I imagine."

"Don't give a shit. This is too important." His steps slowed as he took in their surroundings. "Where *are* we?"

Prue smiled. "The Sibling Gardens. Come and sit in the shade."

Erik stared at the sculpted landscape shimmering before them in the sun, green, peaceful and so elegantly spare that he blinked. Lord's balls, Caracole was an amazing place! They stood beneath a tall, arched gate constructed of wooden beams lacquered a deep shiny red. At his elbow, Prue had turned her head to gaze at a narrow, graceful bridge spanning a pond, the dark water a mirror for the trees and clouds above. Her lips were curved with pleasure and some of the trouble had left her eyes. Good.

Erik slipped an arm about her waist and they walked on, planning, past families picnicking on the grass, lovers twined together under the trees.

"Wait," said Prue. "I should take notes." From her belt

pouch, she withdrew her notebook and pencil and sat down on a wooden bench. She indicated the formal glade around them, mercifully empty, though he could hear the squeals of happy children from nearby. "This is one of my favorite places."

A waterfall sparkled cheerfully through a maze of rocks and into a narrow stream bordered with weeping plants and reedy grasses. The skeins of water arched like thin bridges made of glass, their splashing voices singing a melody he could almost discern. Framed by the brushing fronds of a couple of bending widow's hair trees, a huge, rectangular block of seastone baked in the sun.

There was something familiar about the juxtaposition of rocks and water, the dense grove of touchme bushes tinkling as they swayed in the light breeze off the sea. Erik turned to Prue. "Who—?"

She smiled. "Walker. We need to show him the seelies." Briskly, she scribbled his name. "Who else?"

"Sergeant Rhiomard, I suppose. Yachi the guard. Rose, of course." He shrugged. "You work it out. I don't know many people here. Prue . . ." He hesitated. "I doubt the seelies will appear on command. They're wild creatures, not pets. It might backfire, though I guess we can try. Make a list of taverns as well, all the places I can sing." He hummed the first bar of the "Seelie Song."

Someone hummed it back to him, very softly.

"Who was that?"

"Hmm?" enquired Prue, her pencil moving rapidly down the page.

"Listen." He did it again and got the same response. There had to be someone behind the block of seastone. It was certainly coming from over there.

"Oh, that's the flow sculpture," she said without looking up. She waved the pencil in a preoccupied sort of way. "Read the plaque over there. You have to provoke it."

"*Provoke* it?"

Prue set the notebook and pencil aside, the aquamarines in her cuffs distracting him as they glittered, though they were no brighter than her dancing eyes. Primitive satisfaction moved through him. *Mine*.

"Blow on it," she said.

"*Blow*—? All right." Pulling himself together, Erik moved closer, pursed his lips and blew.

The surface of the flow sculpture slithered and spun in a kaleidoscope of gentle color. It formed a tiny mouth that puffed out a scented breeze.

Erik reared back. "Lord's balls!"

Prue laughed outright. "Wonderful, isn't it? It responds to different stimuli." Rising, she came to slip a hand into his. She did it unthinking, so naturally that his heart lurched in his chest. "Sing again, Erik."

Cautiously, he began the "Seelie Song." After a few seconds, little ripples stirred, flexing in time with the music, combining and recombining in complex patterns. The stone changed color, until it was every possible shade of blue and green, cobalt to emerald, with infinite variations.

Prue pointed. "Look, there's a seelie. And another."

There were. Tiny seelies gamboling among the feathery fronds of water weeds. The air smelled briny and fresh.

A work of genius.

Erik switched to the "Lullaby for Stormy Eyes."

Without missing a beat, the flow sculpture reassembled. Broad swathes of amethyst and lavender swept back and forth. Slow drops of water trickled down like tears squeezed from a diamond. It wasn't until threads of gold and silver wove themselves into the pattern that he realized the sculpture was singing harmony in an impossibly high key, clear and pure.

The last note lingered and died, leaving silence save for the tinkling voice of the waterfall.

Someone clapped.

Erik whirled around. They had an audience of about a dozen strangers, some wearing formal, light-colored robes, others obviously families out for the day. A couple of guards stood with their arms folded, watching impassively. Laughing, he grasped Prue's hand and pulled her down with him into a bow.

"Mistress McGuire." A short, tubby figure stepped forward, beaming. "And Master . . . um . . . ?" He cocked his head to one side like a curious bird.

Erik remembered that gesture. The Queen's Knowledge.

"Thorensen," he said shortly. "The singer."

"Of course, of course." The Knowledge rubbed his hands together, the long sleeves of his robe swinging. "That was quite delightful. Come, walk with me. I'm on my way back to the Library. After a session with the Cabal, I find such beauty—ahem—soothing." He twinkled.

When the Knowledge turned onto the path, the ordinary folk melted away, leaving the minister surrounded by his subordinates, with the two guards taking up flank positions, hands on their sword hilts.

Praise to the Lord and the Lady, another chance! A single swift stride and Erik was at the man's elbow. "May I speak freely, my Lord?"

"In Caracole, the correct form of address is Noblelord," the Knowledge said mildly. He shot Erik a shrewd glance from over the rims of his spectacles. "Speak about what? This seelie nonsense?"

The older man kept their progress down to a dignified amble, whereas Erik had the sense he would have preferred to trot down the path, bouncing on his toes. The Knowledge seemed to have a lot of energy.

Gritting his teeth, Erik bowed. One minute. Hell, give him thirty seconds and one sentence. The minister would be his to command, the city safe. "For your ears only, Noblelord."

The Queen's Knowledge chuckled. "Can't be private with anyone, lad." He gestured toward the guard on the left. "The captain here would kill me himself." He plucked a flower from a lover vine as they passed, raised it to his nose and sniffed. "Speak or don't speak." He flung the blossom away. "Up to you."

Erik could have strangled him quite cheerfully.

"Very well." Wearily, he went through the whole improbable tale again, and by the time the small party had entered the echoing cool of the Library colonnade, the back of his neck was hot, embarrassment warring with fury. The minister's entourage of clerks maintained complete silence, as was proper, but Erik didn't miss the nudges, the smirks and side-long glances. Perfectly pleasant, unfailingly courteous, the Knowledge had asked penetrating, logical questions, some of which Erik knew he'd fumbled.

Coming to a halt, the minister raised a hand. "Enough, Master Thorensen. I am a scholar. Wild speculation is of no interest to me. You see this?" He moved aside, revealing a small niche in the wall.

"Sweet Sister!" Prue gasped. "What is it?"

The colonnade had been lined with statuary, all of it extraordinarily fine, though Erik had barely noticed. But this object was breathtaking, a sinuous-waisted shape, no more than a foot tall, made up of colors so vibrant they glimmered with sumptuous life. Amber, russet, terracotta, apricot, ochre and cream, all the colors of the living earth, and, if you turned your head just right, spiced with a gleam of green bronze.

Irresistibly drawn, Prue lifted a hand to touch, only to meet a glass barrier. "Are those *feathers*?" she said, staring.

The Queen's Knowledge folded his hands in his sleeves and nodded, smiling. "Indeed they are. We call it a feather vase. Aetherian work." He paused. "Well, supposedly."

"Supposedly?" asked Erik. He had a bad feeling he knew where this was going.

"For centuries, we've heard rumors from beyond the Horsehead sector about a race of . . . ah . . . altered humans. Winged and tailed and exquisitely beautiful." He shrugged his plump shoulders, well into lecture mode. "Most creatures of myth are, of course. But not so long ago, a Technomage starship patrolling the farthest frontiers discovered a derelict pirate floating alone in the vacuum of space. When they salvaged it, they discovered a number of unusual artifacts, including this one." He rapped the glass with a knuckle. "Let me tell you, the negotiations with the Technomage Tower were protracted and difficult. If it hadn't been for my—"

"What happened to the crew?" asked Prue.

"Don't interrupt, my dear. They'd been dead many years." The Knowledge flipped a dismissive hand. "In any case, they were pirates. The point is that the vase could be the first evidence of a civilization as yet undiscovered. Or"—he caught Erik's eye, his gaze steady and chill—"it could be an elaborate fake. We at the Royal Library are attempting to establish provenance and the Technomages have taken two feathers to test with Science." His pink lips curved with satisfaction. "Thus we have the best of both worlds."

Erik lost what little patience he possessed. "You want *proof*, is that it?"

As one, the clerks froze, staring fixedly at their feet. The two guards stepped forward. Prue's hand stole into Erik's. Shit, no man reached high office without a certain degree of bastardry in his makeup.

The Queen's Knowledge pursed his lips. "I see you comprehend." He inclined his head. "Finally. Good day to you, Master Thorensen, Mistress McGuire." Turning, he swept away in a dignified swirl of silken robes. The clerks scuttled after him, heads down.

Fuck, his last chance. Desperately, Erik seized it. "*Wait!*" The Voice boomed off the seastone walls of the building.

32

They froze midstep—two guards, half a dozen clerks and one member of the Queen's Cabal.

Slowly, the Knowledge turned. "I believe our conversation is concluded, Master Thorensen," he said, his tone arctic. "Why are we still standing here?"

Erik opened his mouth and shut it again. Godsdammit, the command bubbling in his throat was only applicable to one man—the one who had the power to implement it. The others would go mad trying.

All right then, a blanket compulsion for the lot of them. *Do what I tell you.* That might work. No, no, they'd be a set of puppets. Gods, what if they wouldn't eat or drink without his direct command?

"Erik!" hissed Prue. "You're hurting me."

"Sorry." He released her hand.

"*What is it?*" said the Knowledge, pink with irritation.

Erik bowed. "Thank you for your time, Noblelord. I was wondering, do you have maps of Caracole in the Library? Oh, and a list of taverns?"

"Do we—?" The Knowledge swelled with indignation until Erik thought he might pop. "What, you think I'm a clerk? You"—he snapped at a tall, thin woman with gray hair—"assist him."

Spinning on his heel, he vanished into the cool depths of the building, leaving Erik and Prue alone with the trembling clerk.

∞

"Lord's balls, that was good," said Erik. Wrapping his arms around Prue, he rolled over in her bed. She finished up stretched out on top of him, breast to breast, belly to belly, the hair on his chest a delightful rasp against her nipples. The warm, furry bundle of his genitals pressed against her thigh, slack and satisfied. Pleasure still thrumming between her legs, she buried her nose in the curve where his neck met his shoulder, breathing him in.

"You're going to be the death of me." With a tired chuckle, he sifted a lock of her hair through his fingers.

Prue's stomach lurched. *Death.* Two days and nights of watching him work the taverns, visiting them after the last curtain at the Royal Theater and staying into the early hours of the morning. Two days and nights of torture. Walker had sent men to watch Erik's back—men with hard eyes and sword hilts worn with use. Dai still lived, which she supposed was a good thing, but the pale assassin continued to evade capture. The swordsmaster's silent fury had become such a terrifying, palpable force Prue couldn't bear to be in the same room with him.

Everywhere they went, her spine prickled with atavistic terror. Danger could come from anywhere. Godsdammit, it could be anyone, anything. She found herself watching people's eyes, their hands, quivering at every unexpected movement.

A soft snore rumbled out of the man beneath her. Prue propped herself up on one elbow. Sister save him, he was exhausted. There were dark shadows beneath his eyes, stubble roughened his chin. He looked worn to the bone, hard and dangerous. Surely there had to be an opera about a pirate king, because he could step out of her bed and straight onto the stage.

By unspoken mutual consent, they hadn't returned to the Bruised Orchid. Instead, they'd snatched a few hours here and there to make love in Prue's rooms, very much like normal people—in bed, aching and sweet; over the desk, hard and fast; on the couch, breathless and laughing. Once on the rug, though Erik complained his knees would never be the same. Prue had opened her mouth to tell him his knees were perfect, then shut it again. Dizzy as an adolescent and twice as foolish, she thought ruefully.

She glanced over at the silver cuffs, gleaming on the dresser next to her hairbrush. The aquamarines called to her, sparkling in the afternoon sun like chips of seawater imprisoned in a lantern. She hadn't worn them since the day they'd spoken with the Queen's Knowledge and perversely, she longed to. Her body was more in tune with Erik's than ever, but she ached for more, the power of helplessness, the intense erotic charge of complete surrender.

Listening to him breathe, she worried away at it, the longing throbbing like a sore tooth. Why did she want Erik's mastery again? It made her vulnerable, exposed her to emotional devastation, swept up all that she was and gave it into his keeping. Squeezing her eyes closed, Prue made a deliberate effort to recall the physical sensations—her fingers twisting in the ropes, the pressure of his heavy shaft invading, impaling, his low voice growling in her ear, the expression on his face when she'd turned her head to meet his eyes—

Her breath stopped, stuttering in her lungs, her heart tumbling in her chest. No wonder he hadn't asked her again!

It cost him as much as it cost her. Why hadn't she seen it before? The vulnerability was right there in his eyes. To enter her soul so completely, he had to allow her into his. One surrender required another, a never-ending circuit. He'd asked her to trust him, he'd even thought he had to order her to do it, the silly man. But trust was a double-edged sword and they'd both been wounded to the heart.

He'd said he loved her and—merciful Sister!—it was possible he did. Erik had given *her* the precious gift of his trust.

Hope sprang up, twining around her heart, bright and vigorous as a rampant lover vine. A little bemused, she gazed down at his strong face, remembering the hunger in his eyes, so swiftly concealed she'd thought she imagined it at first.

Everything fell into place. She could tick the items off, as easily as she tallied The Garden's accounts.

She loved Erik Thorensen. Even thinking of the assassin made nausea bubble in her throat and a cold sweat prickle all down her spine. Prue shifted her hand until it lay over his heart, the regular beat reassuring under her palm.

He was a man worth the loving, with his own ironclad code of honor. Thinking about it, she couldn't recall that he'd lied to her, ever.

It might be insane, but in his arms she found a safe harbor, a refuge.

She craved his body with an intensity she found alarming; she loved listening to him sing, speak, laugh, grumble. She didn't care what delusions he had about his voice. In fact, it was downright astonishing how little she cared. Godsdammit, she'd deal with it when the time came. In all else, he was eminently sane, the sanest man she'd ever known.

But lastly, lastly . . . Soon, he would go, leave Caracole, leave *her*.

Prue took four deep, calming breaths, one after the other. *The irresistible force meets the immovable object*, he'd said, laughing. Well then, she'd convince him to stay. And if he wouldn't . . .

Tears threatened, her thoughts circling like corpsebirds. Katrin had found her love, her Arkady. He was a fine young man, serious and steady. Soon they'd have a family of their own. A salty drop landed on Erik's bicep, and when she bent to lick it off the smooth, tawny skin, he sighed in his sleep. Prue's lips twisted. Her daughter was a grown woman, she might understand if her mother abandoned her to follow her foolish heart, but she wouldn't forgive—not until she came to trust Erik for herself.

How had life become so complicated? Prue sniffed. One step at a time, the way she did everything. The first order of business was to save Caracole of the Leaves. Her private life would have to wait.

Hating to do it, she shook his shoulder. "Erik, wake up."

"Go 'way."

"No." She nibbled his earlobe, tugged his hair. "You promised Florien, remember?"

A grunt.

"He'll be in the kitchen with Katrin, eating us into bankruptcy."

"Florien?" He levered open a bleary blue eye.

"Yes. And then you have an opera to sing and after that—"

"Yeah, I know." Erik sat up, rubbing his chest and yawning. "Another tavern." With a sigh that seemed to come from the soles of his feet, he rose, pulled her into his arms and kissed the top of her head. Then he stood, stretching the kinks out of his back.

∽

Prue sat on The Garden's water stairs, watching the sun sink toward the horizon, a long, golden shimmer already flung across the pewter waters of the canal. She raised her head, enjoying the quiet and the solitude of late afternoon, a breathing space in the chaos her life had become. Ah, there was the Sister, a waning crescent peeping over the shoulder of an orange pink cloud.

She ran an admiring finger over the lover vine on one of the silver cuffs she wore. Erik had noticed of course, the way he seemed to notice everything about her. Over the boy's head, he'd stared from the bracelets to her face, his intensity so tangible she could taste it on her tongue. When his eyes flared a dark, dangerous blue, she realized she'd licked her lips. After what seemed an eon, he'd relaxed, muscle by muscle, but she'd been achingly conscious of his attention ever since.

At this late stage of the afternoon, everything was hushed, no one about. All self-respecting courtesans were primping for the evening ahead. Katrin would be toiling in the kitchen, helping prepare an exquisite supper.

As for Erik . . . She frowned, watching the ripples lap at the base of the stairs. He'd taken the boy down once already. When their heads had broken the surface, Florien's face had told her all she needed to know. "They came, then," she said, laughing.

"Yah." The boy was transfigured, his eyes wide and soft and shining, his lips trembling on a smile.

"Did they dance for you?"

"Yah."

Erik stroked toward the steps, the lad's skinny arms wrapped around his shoulders. "Four of them," he said, grinning. "Go on, tell her."

Florien wriggled with joy, the first uninhibited expression Prue thought she'd seen from him. "I touched one."

"It brushed past his fingers," said Erik.

"So fookin' soft," breathed Florien, his hair plastered flat to his small skull. "So blue, ya know?"

"Yes," said Prue gently, rising to offer a towel. "I know."

"Kin we go back down?" The boy patted Erik's face, his eyes beseeching. "Just fer a minute?" He swallowed. "Please, *please*? I ain't skeered no more."

Erik wavered. Then he said, "If we do, there'll be more handshakes in your future."

A pause. "Yah. All right."

Erik sent Prue a wicked wink over Florien's head. His gaze dropped to the silver cuffs and darkened, as explicit as if he'd reached out to cup the throbbing flesh between her thighs. "Won't be long, love." They'd disappeared back under the stairs, the boy's excited chatter floating across the water.

Smiling, Prue unfolded the towel and draped it across her lap. Then she closed her eyes and turned her face up to the fading warmth of the sun. Basking wasn't something she did often.

"You Mistress McGuire?" The dark silhouette of a man appeared at the top of the stairs.

Reluctantly, Prue turned. "Yes. What is it?"

The man waved a sheet of paper. "You hafta sign."

What now? Prue rose and climbed toward him. "Sign?"

"Laundry bill."

The man was middle-aged, with a weary, pleasant face, clad in a workingman's trews and shirt. Sitting behind him on the path was a large, rectangular basket with two sturdy leather handles. Prue saw ones like it every day. A younger man, similarly dressed, perched on top of it, nibbling a thumbnail.

"Invoices go to my office," she said absently, reaching for the bill. "Why did you bring it out here?"

A scruffy little dog trotted out of the bushes and stopped to cock its leg on a purplemist tree. The first man ducked his head, smiling. "Wanted to meet that seelie fella. You know, the singer? They said he was with you?"

"Well, he's not," said Prue shortly. "Wait a minute, this isn't a—"

They were on her before she could complete the thought. The younger man dug his fingers into her hair from behind and twisted, the other held a knife to her throat. His pleasant expression didn't change. "Where is he, Mistress?"

Every muscle in Prue's body locked with terror, her eyes teared with pain. "Who?" she managed.

He increased the pressure of the blade. The first sensation was an icy burn, the second a slicing pain. Blood dripped down her neck, warm and tickling. "The singer."

"No idea. *Sister have mercy, keep them down there with the seelies, don't—*

From behind, she heard bushes rustle, then a heavy footfall, the whisper of fabric. The dog wagged its tail, its whole rump in motion.

The man's eyes shifted to look at someone over her shoulder. "Want me to get it out of her?"

"No time." The voice was deep and husky, but strangely androgynous. "I don't know . . . maybe we should . . ."

"Make up your bloody mind, woman."

The assassin!

Prue flung herself backward, dropping to her knees as she did so. The point of the knife dug into her cheek, but she was so busy it didn't register. She sliced upward between the older man's legs, hearing his howl as the side of her hand connected with the softness of his testicles. The younger man had lost his grip in her hair. She could hear him cursing, the dog barking. Using the power of her thighs and pelvis, she surged upward, catching him as he bent over her. Her skull collided with the point of his chin and she saw stars. But he fell away, hitting the path with a satisfactory thud.

Thank the Sister for Walker's lessons! Now for that bitch of an assassin. Where was—?

Something soft and heavy fell over her face. It smelled sweet and rank, the stench of it clogging her nostrils. Prue raised her hands to rake it away, but her muscles refused to obey.

Her fingers caught in the folds of a voluminous garment like a cloak. A strong arm wrapped around her. She was lifted off her feet and dragged toward the laundry basket.

"What the . . . fuck are you doing?" gasped a male voice, one she hadn't heard before.

That had to be . . . who? Her brain spun. Oh . . . the younger man.

The assassin's arm around Prue tightened until her ribs creaked. "We'll take this one instead." A pause for breath. "Not going back empty-handed."

Prue struggled. Was this what lungspasm was like? A sticky, mind-sucking fog that stole the will and the wits and the strength? In a sudden upwelling of terror, she flailed and twisted like a fish on the hook.

The dark rose over her in a crushing tide and took her under.

⌒∞⌒

A towel lay on the water stairs, but there was no sign of Prue.

"Here." Erik set the boy down, scooped up the towel and wrapped him up from head to heels. "Get out of those wet clothes before you catch your death."

"Wot? 'Ere?" Florien looked so scandalized, Erik chuckled.

"Your lips are blue," he said. "Don't want anything to freeze and drop off."

The boy cast him a suspicious glance, but he peeked under the towel when he thought Erik wasn't looking.

Odd, she must have gone in. Or she'd been called away. A thread of uneasiness wormed through his gut.

"Erik." The note in the boy's voice was so strange, Erik was at his side in a single stride. "Look." A skinny little finger pointed. It trembled.

A black, low-heeled slipper lay on its side near the side of the path.

Just the one.

33

The world turned inside out, Erik's only anchor the icy little paw that crept into his and clutched.

Shaking, he bent down and picked up the slipper. Dirt from Walker's garden beds had been kicked over the path; deep footprints indented the soil behind a purplemist tree and a touchme bush whimpered, high and soft, its broken branches drooping.

Marring a silvery flower was a streak of red, already drying to a rusty brown.

Erik's lungs squeezed to the point of pain. Not now, not now. With a whoop, he gulped in air. A vicious breeze sprang up out of nowhere, swirling around them, raising goose bumps on Florien's skin and chilling Erik to the bone. The touchme bush thrashed and moaned with the force of its passage.

Grabbing the boy, Erik lifted the slight body high in his arms and took off for the Main Pavilion at a dead run, the wind at his back.

Her dreams were strange, peopled with looming, distorted figures, all of them fish-belly pale. Moaning, Prue rolled over in bed, but the covers were so tight they held her down. Frustrated, she lashed out an arm and straps bit painfully into her wrists.

Her eyes flew open. Seated opposite in a high-backed chair was a neat middle-aged woman all in white. Her blue gray eyes were bright with interest. "Welcome back," she said. "How do you feel?"

Prue ran her tongue over her teeth. Her mouth was so dry she could barely speak. "R-revolting."

When she looked down, nausea rose in a horrible greasy wave, roiling in her stomach. Sister save her, she sat in a large chair made of some kind of smooth gray substance she hadn't seen before. Both her ankles and her wrists were restrained with wide leather straps, wound about with black and silver wires. Her head pounded and a place on her neck throbbed. Already the muscles in her back were protesting. How long had she been there?

Where was Erik?

Most horrifying of all, she was naked beneath some kind of soft linen garment done up with ties down each side. Her body was completely accessible—and she was helpless. "Get me out of here," she choked. "Please."

The woman smiled. "All in good time." Rising, she moved out of Prue's line of sight and returned with a cup and a straw. "Here, it's water." She held the straw to Prue's lips, waiting patiently while Prue decided whether to drink. In the end, she drained the cup and the woman set it aside.

Without warning, she leaned down to lift first Prue's left eyelid with her thumb, then the right. "Aargh!" Prue's instinctive flinch was brought up short by the back of the chair. Her spine crawled.

"Hmm," murmured the other woman, peering from a distance of inches. There was gray in the part of her soft brown hair. Producing a small oval shape from her pocket, she passed it over Prue's forehead, pausing at her temples. "No activity." She straightened, her lips curving in a small smile. "Excellent. The dampers in the restraints are working as they should. You're safe enough, for the short term at least."

Prue's jaw sagged, but the woman continued without pause, as if she were talking to herself. "I should give you a shot of something," she said, her brow creasing, "but I'm not sure what that idiot woman used." She tapped a fretful finger against her lower lip. "I can't have rogue variables affecting my data. We'll have to wait."

So many questions jostled in Prue's brain they got tangled on her tongue. "W-who are you?" she managed. "What woman? What are you talking about?"

Through the ache in her head, she fumbled for the memories. Two men with a—a *laundry basket*? Gods, it must have been for her. No wait, they'd asked for Erik. It was for him, his *body*. And they'd taken her instead. Shit, she was going to vomit! Desperately, she sucked in one breath after the other, until the urge subsided. That hesitant contralto, the feel of the body behind her, its solid curves, full of flesh, nothing like a man's.

"It was her, wasn't it? The assassin?"

As if she hadn't spoken, the other woman hitched up her white trousers and sank back into her chair, her legs decorously crossed at the ankle. "I," she said, with the air of someone making an announcement, "am the Technomage Primus of Sybaris."

Prue shook her head to clear it, but that only increased the woolly sensations so she gave up. "*Who?*"

The woman stiffened. "The Technomage Primus of Sybaris," she said, articulating every word as if to the mentally deficient.

"Primus?" Prue forced herself to concentrate. "That means first, doesn't it?"

"Yes, and it is also the correct form of address. Well done." The Technomage smiled, smoothing a fingertip over the numeral one embroidered on the collar of her shirt.

Prue stared. "What are you doing here? Let me go!" She writhed against the straps, which shifted not at all.

"Stop that, you'll damage yourself." The other woman stood beside her, cool fingers on Prue's wrist. "Tell me, how much do you remember?"

"Two men from the laundry. Except they weren't." She wrinkled her forehead. "A knife. They had a funny little dog. A cloth over my face, couldn't breathe . . ." Her throat closed.

"Ah, so that's how she administered it." The Technomage

bent over her desk to scribble a note on a sheet of gray filmy stuff with a stylus. *Transplas*. Prue had seen it when she'd paid The Garden's plumbing bills at the Technomage Tower. "Hmm, primitive, but effective nonetheless. I'm afraid I don't know the woman's name or anything about her." An elegant shrug. "We have many subordinates."

"We?"

The Technomage frowned down at the transplas on the desk, fiddling with her stylus. "I have a . . . partner," she said finally. "Nasake is taking him a message." She sighed, moving behind Prue's chair. A series of clicks ensued, followed by a barely audible humming noise. "There. It shouldn't take long to warm up."

Prue strove to turn her head, but the back of the chair was too high, her bonds too tight. "What won't?"

The other woman crossed the floor to a long bench, her heels tapping on the flagged floor. The room looked like a basement, the walls supported by brick arches, the ceiling beamed. "Hmm?" She spoke over her shoulder, meanwhile donning a pair of white gloves made of some thin, flexible fabric. "The reservoir machine."

Prue forced the panic down, clamping a lid over the bubbling screams. Godsdammit, what was going on? "I don't know what that is."

"Of course, you don't." Turning, the Scientist leaned back against the bench, gloved hands folded over her stomach. "Let me explain." Her eyes shone, her expression animated.

"Strictly speaking," she said, "it's a conduit attached to a reservoir. There's also a three-tier filtration system." She shook her head with a rueful twinkle. "I had the most extraordinary trouble with the design for the metabolic mesh until it occurred to me that . . ."

Prue heard about one word in ten, enough to retain the general gist. The Technomage Primus had a penchant for convoluted paragraphs and long words, but she did like to repeat herself.

Prue began to wonder . . . Seizing her chance, she inserted her question when the other woman paused for breath. "Where are your staff, the other Technomages?"

Two beats of silence and the Primus said stiffly, "This project is utterly secret."

"I see." Prue arranged her face in an expression of sympathy. "So you haven't seen much of the Caracole? What a pity. It's a beautiful city."

The Technomage turned away, blinking rapidly. "I've been working."

"Hardly seems fair," murmured Prue. "When does your, ah, partner return?"

The other woman began assembling objects on a tray, her motions clipped and angry. "Soon." She carried it over to the desk. "I need something to show him." Her voice trembled, then firmed. "Your Magick, in the first instance."

Prue was so surprised she laughed. "Don't be silly," she said. "I've got about as much Magick as you have."

The Technomage Primus sent her a thin smile. "As much as I *will* have in a few moments. In my reservoir."

Prue blinked. "You're serious."

"Absolutely." Carefully, she lifted a gray wire from the tray. Attached to the end of it was a small, circular pad. "I let the fire witch slip through my fingers. I won't make the same mistake with you."

"*Witch?*" The word emerged as a croak. "I'm not a witch."

"Yes, you are." The Technomage pressed the pad to the side of Prue's neck, where it stuck. It felt cold, and a little greasy. "An air witch. The metabolic comparisons between air and fire should be fascinating." A second patch went in the hollow of her throat.

"Will it hurt?" Prue cursed herself for the quaver in her voice, for asking in the first place, but she had to know.

Gloved fingers brushed her hair aside, almost gently, and attached a pad to her temple. "Not much," said the other woman, frowning in concentration.

And Prue knew she'd lied. "Please," she whispered, despising herself. "I'm not a witch. I don't even believe in—"

A latch clicked and the Scientist's head jerked up, her eyes going wide. The air grew chill, and a huge dark shadow slid over the ceiling, the wall.

"Nasake was excited but a trifle confused," said a sibilant, sexless voice. "What do we have here?"

The sound of it slithered down Prue's spine like a fistful of slime. She trembled.

The Technomage gripped her gloved hands together. "Your assassin fumbled the kill, but she's redeemed herself. Look what she brought us. This is the air witch herself." A pause. "Are you pleased?"

"Ah. I'll tell you in a moment." A cloaked figure glided into view, its outline strangely distorted, both filmy and impenetrable. Prue had the sense that its boundaries shrank and expanded at will.

Oh gods, if it touched her, she'd throw up. What could have been a sleeve reached toward her and Prue pressed herself back into the chair, every joint locked with terror.

"Shaitan!" With a hiss, the figure jerked away, the hood of the cloak turning toward the Technomage. Did it even have eyes? "There's a barrier I can feel from here." A short pause. "Her shields are naïve, but quite excellent."

Shields?

Prue wet her lips. "W-who are you? *What* are you?"

Like a portal opening to the depths of hell, the dark stain swelled and grew against the wall. The toneless voice boomed off the walls of the chamber. "I am the Necromancer." It lowered to a hiss. "I am Death!"

Somewhere in the back of Prue's mind, a small voice snorted, "Overdoing it." But the Technomage Primus was cowering in a corner and she couldn't hang on to the thought.

"Hold still, my dear." The Necromancer chuckled. He flowed toward her. "All I need is a chink. *Aargh!*"

The dark shape recoiled, and for a second, Prue thought she glimpsed the swish of an embroidered sleeve, deep in the shadows.

"Bitch! By Shaitan, you'll pay for that!" The Necromancer's featureless head turned toward the Technomage. "Turn up the dampers, you fool!"

Obediently, the other woman flipped a lever, fiddled with a dial.

The Necromancer hissed his satisfaction.

Prue followed his gaze to where the wires wrapped around her leather cuffs sparkled with pretty lights. She didn't feel any different, but the Necromancer no longer hesitated, swooping over her like a foul cloud.

"Now where was I? Ah, there . . . slowly now."

Prue slammed her eyes shut, but it was no use. A sliver of ice slid down her spine, wrapped itself around her heart and invaded her lungs. "Ah," said that whispery voice.

"Hurts."

"Of course. Let me see . . ."

Sly, ghostly fingers probed her most private emotions, tweaking with malicious glee, stroking over her soul with a leisurely intimacy that was tantamount to rape.

"Gods, no," she gasped. "*No!*" She heaved in the chair, fighting the straps, fighting the invader.

After an age, the Necromancer withdrew and Prue sagged, whimpering. He regarded the Technomage. "You have failed," he said, completely without inflection. "This is no witch."

"T-told you," said Prue, shuddering all the way to her bones.

"Sorry." The Technomage lifted a shaking hand to her lips. "N-not my fault. The assassin—"

The Necromancer rode over her. "This one is something else. Find out what it is." His attention swung back to Prue. "Where is the air witch?"

"Listen to me." Prue tried to hold the burning gaze lurking within the hood and failed. "I don't know anything about Magick or witches. Nothing, I swear it."

"Nonsense!" The Necromancer loomed over her. "The stink of air Magick is all over you, you and the—" He broke off, his substance condensing.

"The singer," whispered the Technomage. "It's him, has to be."

The silence was so profound, Prue thought she could hear the lapping of the water in the canal, the creak of the enormous Leaf beneath the foundations of the building. *Erik?*

"*Yess!*" The Necromancer's boundaries blurred, expanding as if he'd gorged himself on something ripe and swollen. She caught a gut-churning whiff of old blood, thick and clotted. "By Shaitan, it's perfect!"

"What is?" whispered Prue, struggling to comprehend. If the situation had been different, she would have been helpless with laughter. Erik and Magick?

The Necromancer continued as if she hadn't spoken. "You, my dear," he said, his focus all on her, "you are the honeyed bait that will bring me everything, not only the power, but the flesh to house it. You are the fated instrument of my destiny. Who'd have thought?" A soundless chuckle. "A plain little thing like you."

In a parody of affection, his touch ghosted over her hair, brushed across her lips. Suddenly, urgently, Prue needed to spit. She could have sworn her mouth filled with something foul and sweet.

A final lingering pat and the featureless head swiveled toward to the Technomage Primus. "Pace yourself," he ordered. "Complete the tests. I want to know where that shield comes from. But remember, I need her alive and reasonably whole for"—he calculated—"another two days."

The Technomage's mouth tightened. "No vivisection. Very well, I understand." She stared into the darkness under the hood, her gaze both intent and wary. "What are your plans now?" Unobtrusively, she braced herself against the desk. "If you don't mind me asking."

Vivisection? Prue's vision hazed and a scream bubbled in her throat. Ruthlessly, she clamped her lips shut, forcing herself to listen.

"I have a trap to set and a message to send." The satisfaction streaming off him made the air glutinous. "Ah, death is full of simple pleasures." He drifted away from Prue's vision. Distantly, a latch clicked and she thought she heard teeth snapping, a low feral growl abruptly chopped off.

The Technomage let out a long breath. "We'd better get on, I suppose." She picked up her tray and approached the chair. "The most likely hypothesis is that you broadcast some kind of nullifying field."

Prue met her eye. "You're as much a prisoner here as I am, aren't you?"

"We're partners. An alliance between Science and Magick. Building bridges."

Prue snorted. "So you're free to leave this room any time you want?"

Silence. "There's a . . . guardian on the door." The Technomage pulled a high stool close to Prue's chair and perched on it. "Besides, this is important work. Exciting." Her eyes glowed and her white-jacketed chest expanded. "I'm a pioneer in the field." A shadow crossed her face. "In fact, I'm the only one."

"Is scientific curiosity worth sacrificing your freedom? Your life?" Prue stared straight into the blue gray eyes. "He's going to kill you."

"I have my resources. He can try." The other woman shrugged, though her gaze slid away from Prue's. "Every endeavor has its risks.

"Caracole of the Leaves is a beautiful city," said Prue. "Let me tell you what you're missing."

The Technomage's heels hit the floor with a sharp clack. "It's been months since I spoke with anyone . . . normal. Or anyone at all." She took a pace away, then spun around. "Clever of you." Her smile looked pared to the bone. "What a pity you weren't born a Technomage. I could have done something with a mind like yours."

She reached for the machine behind the chair. Something clicked, the hum increased in volume. The gray pads on Prue's skin began to tingle, not unpleasantly.

"We'll establish our benchmarks first," said the Technomage Primus. "Take a deep breath and let it out slowly. Controlled respiration makes the sensations easier to bear."

34

Quiet!" roared Erik.

The agitated babble ceased. Around the big table in the cavernous kitchen of The Garden, six startled faces turned to face him. That had been perilously close to the Voice, but he didn't give a fuck. Night had fallen and they hadn't resolved anything. Prue could be . . . She could be . . .

He swallowed, then steadied. "We need to plan. Florien, run up to Prue's study. There should be a map of the city on the desk. Bring it."

"Yah." The boy hopped off his chair and trotted away, still chewing.

After the first shock had worn off, Katrin had stalked over to the big ovens and retrieved one dish after another, moving with automatic efficiency, but blindly, as if in a dream. Now she sat next to a slender, serious young man wearing spectacles, her hand tucked into his. Arkady.

Across the table, Erik met Walker's flat black gaze. "I'll find the assassin tonight," said the swordsmaster. "I guarantee."

"Haven't done too well so far."

Walker's jaw set like a granite cliff. "Three times now I've entered a building minutes after she's left. As if she knows I'm coming."

"The assassin's the obvious lead." Rosarina sat with an arm around Tansy, who still shook with the occasional sob. Rose's eyes were dry, her lovely mouth thin with resolve. "But whoever's paying is the one we really want."

Erik's lips drew back from his teeth. "Oh yes." He took the map from Florien and swept aside the tisane cups to spread it on the table. He anchored one corner with the empty pot, another with his bowl of reheated stew. It had been hot and savory, and he knew he needed the fuel, but he hadn't been able to choke down more than a few mouthfuls.

Hell, Prue, *Prue*! Even now, she might be lying at the bottom of a canal or abandoned on a midden. Or she might be at the mercy of cruel men with rough hands and hard bodies, men who'd violate and break her. Her flesh was so soft, her breasts so tender and sweet. Oh gods.

Thoughts rattled around in his skull, buffeting him as brutally as a gale. The very air he breathed seemed to set his chest on fire.

"Control it, Erik." Strong brown fingers wrapped around his upper arm and squeezed hard. "Now think," said Walker. "This started when you went public with the seelies, the death of the Leaf." He leaned back, releasing his grip. "Didn't it?"

"Yes." Erik filled his lungs, reaching for his singer's discipline. Breathe in the power, breathe it out again. For a moment, he thought he saw the air streaming before him, tinged an angry red. "You believe me?"

Walker blinked, an extraordinary show of emotion for a man with his degree of reserve. "I was a shaman among my people once," he said, as though the words were yanked out of him on barbed hooks. "There is a . . . wrongness in Caracole. It made me ill."

Katrin slapped her palm down on the table. A bread roll tumbled off the edge. "How does this help find Mam? Anyway"—she turned a tear-stained face to Walker—"you look fine to me."

"I dealt with it," said the swordsmaster curtly. "Once I understood what it was."

"Katrin, you and Arkady go to the City Guard and report your mother missing," said Erik, making a heroic effort not to shout. "Talk to Rhiomard if you can. But every minute counts, we can't afford to wait for them to get organized." He tapped a finger on the map. "Walker, you and your men cover the Melting Pot. The assassin's probably gone to ground there anyway."

"Maybe." The swordsmaster set down his empty bowl with a decisive click and rose. "You'll take the Leaf of Nobility?"

Their eyes met. "Yes." Something powerful roiled in Erik's chest, fighting to get free, to blow the world to bloody smithereens. Panting, he harnessed the gathering storm. *Later, later,* he promised it. In response, it roared so loud he was sure the others must be able to hear the eldritch howling of the winds.

Rose patted Tansy's shoulder. "Go get the others," she said. "All of them. Tell them to come armed and to wear something practical. Dark colors."

Small, hard fingers tugged his sleeve. "Fook, what 'bout me? I kin help."

Before Erik could answer, someone shrieked outside in the garden, a cry full of shock and fear. With a crash, the shutters splintered and a heavy bird blundered into the room, wings laboring as it circled above their heads. Even in the spacious kitchen, it was huge, with a wingspan greater than a man's outstretched arms. It squawked continuously, a low, harsh bray.

Heads ducked as the bird floundered, its flailing wings knocking crockery from shelves. Cauldrons and pans clanged together in the wind of its passage.

With a final strangled honk, the bird folded its wings and fell out of the air like a stone, landing on the map with a meaty thud. Delicate cups jumped and shattered. A shudder and the creature lay still, its body and scaly legs covering most of the table.

In the echoing silence, Arkady covered his nose. "Faugh! What a stink!" He slipped an arm around Katrin's waist. Her face had gone gray with horror. Tansy wavered on her feet, clutching at Rose.

"Siblings save us, it's a corpsebird!" Rose stretched out a hand and snatched it back. "What's it doing here?"

Erik stared at the vicious, curved beak, the hooked talons. A carrion eater. The internal tempest surged, roaring like the hungry breath of a forest fire. His head spun and wind swirled around the chamber. All along one wing, the tips of the dusty black feathers ruffled.

"The bastard . . ." He dragged in a breath. "It's a messenger."

Forcing himself, he reached for the pouch hanging round the naked, scrawny neck. A stream of bitemes and other parasites crept from under the feathers, but he ignored them, ripping open the ties and pulling out a slip of paper.

The script was a clerk's. Innocuous, anonymous.

Singer, come alone. Midnight, tomorrow night, two water stairs to the east of the Processional Bridge. Speak and she dies—slowly.

Katrin snatched it from his fingers, and as she scanned the lines, her features took on an expression he hoped he'd never see again. What was she? Nineteen? But this was how she would look as an old, old woman, lying on her deathbed. She lifted those almond eyes, so like Prue's and yet so unlike, to his face. "This is all your fault, Erik. We were fine before—" She choked. "Gods, what have you got her into?"

Frozen, Erik shook his head. Inga's slack features, her bright hair wreathed in weeds. Was this how the man who'd loved her had suffered? The way he felt now, swallowing the prettydeath would have been preferable.

A vicious gust rattled every pot and pan. Dishcloths flew around the room, a curtain ripped from bottom to top. Dimly, Erik heard Walker mutter, "Careful." And then, "Rose, is Purist Bartelm here, by any chance?"

"I'll find her," Erik croaked. "I swear." *I'll take him apart, piece by bloody screaming piece. Horned Lord, I swear it.*

When he used his fists to brace himself on the table, a biteme skittered onto his knuckle and nipped him. Cursing, Erik crushed it, leaving a small bloody smear on his skin. He lifted his head in time to see Tansy slip out the door, to hear her light steps recede down the passage, breaking from a trot into a run.

Calmly, Walker plucked the paper from Katrin's hand. "This is excellent," he said. "It indicates she's alive and it narrows the search area."

Erik upended the pouch. With a quiet tinkle, two silver cuffs bounced across the table and came to rest against the corpsebird's bare, leathery neck. Aquamarines winked at him, a sly blue green.

Prue!

He threw his head back and roared his rage and pain from the depths of his soul. It hurt the whole way out, a burn he relished, dark pleasure and relief and bloody murder in an unholy mixture. It was the Voice he used, but it emerged without words, a full-throated, formless bellow that rattled the walls. Something shattered with a sharp crack and a tinkle. A woman shrieked, a man swore.

Erik opened his eyes.

Every loose item in the kitchen was whirling in the air above his head, including the corpsebird. Bowls, kettles, dishcloths, trays, shards of glass from a broken window. The massive table floated two feet off the floor, revolving majestically. Out of the corner of his eye, he saw Rose shove Florien into the pantry.

That was strange enough, but what was even stranger was that he was standing with his legs spread, his arms raised, and he could *see* the glinting streams of air supporting all the various objects. Every cell in his body fizzed with power, he shuddered with it, vibrating right down to his bones. Gods, he couldn't contain it. He was going to disintegrate, explode like a star going nova!

The Voice strangled in his throat and the objects slowed. A heartbeat later and everything fell to the floor with an earsplitting clatter, the table thudding down an inch from his foot, the corpsebird sprawling across Katrin's spotless workbench.

Erik staggered where he stood, his jaw sagging.

"For an adult, your lack of discipline is appalling," said an acid voice from the doorway. "And you're noisy."

The old man wore one of The Garden's familiar robes, belted tightly around his spare waist. He was dark-skinned, with a high-nosed, imperious face and a gray beard, neatly groomed.

"Who the hell are you?" Erik tried to say it, but no sound came out. Instead, he stared, feeling oddly empty, scoured out.

"Purist! Thank the Sister Tansy found you." Rose reappeared from behind a cupboard, shook her skirts into place and took the old man's hand in both of hers. "I'm sorry to interrupt your massage, but we need you."

His dignity unimpaired by his state of undress, the wizard patted her arm. "Happens all the time, my dear. My poor old bones can wait." He exchanged a cool nod with Walker. Katrin, Arkady and Florien, he simply ignored.

"I am Purist Bartelm," he said to Erik. "And you're a disgrace to your Enclave. Which is it?"

Erik wet his lips. "Enclave?" He dropped into a chair. "I don't—I'm not—" He pulled himself together. "I don't have time for this." Pushing to his feet, he said, "I have to go. Prue—"

"Young Tansy told me." The wizard's dark eyes narrowed, bright with interest. "Is it possible?" He stroked his beard. "You don't know, do you?" he said at last. "Unbelievable."

"Know what?"

"Have you done that before? Moved objects in the air?"

"No!" Erik took a step toward the old man, subduing the urge to pick him up and break him over his knee. "What is it that I don't know?"

"I have been a Purist for more than sixty years. I thought I'd seen every form of Magick the gods permit." Bartelm's lips quirked. Erik stopped dead, his spine prickling with apprehension. "But I've not seen anything like yours."

Erik gave a harsh bark of laughter. "That's ridiculous. For the last time, get out of my way. Rose, we'll start at the Processional Bridge. I'll meet you there."

But Rose shook her head. "This could help. Erik, you have to listen."

The power surged again, a clear, clean blast of it, blowing through his body, feeding his impatience. Erik growled, heading for the door, and the old Purist stepped aside. "A gift from the gods," he murmured.

The huge voice of the Horned Lord. *We will give you your life, together with a gift—a weapon, a tool, a pleasure, a curse.*

Erik turned. *A weapon?* Everything within him leaped.

He searched the wizard's face in silence.

"How long do we have?" said Bartelm softly.

Erik pulled the note from his pocket and handed it over without a word. The old man scanned it, frowning. Then he closed his eyes and passed his fingertips over the characters. His wince was barely perceptible, but it was there nonetheless. "It stinks of the Dark Arts," he said. His gaze lingered on the corpsebird and his lips grew tight. "Necromancy."

Sighing, he pulled out a chair and lowered himself gingerly into it. "Rose, my dear," he said, "send someone to the Enclave for Purist Nori. I'll give you a note for her. She won't want to come."

Could it get any worse? A brisk wind plastered Erik's shirt to his chest, lifted the hair on his forehead. "Lord's balls, how bloody long is it going to take? Whatever this thing is I'm supposed to have, godsdammit, I don't care. Just show me how to make it do what I want."

Bartelm chuckled with genuine amusement, his eyelids crinkling like plum-colored parchment. "Magick's not a blunt instrument, though I can see why a man like you might think so."

Erik ground his teeth. "Necromancy's death Magick, isn't it?" At Bartelm's nod, he thumped a fist on the table, making shards jump like bitemes on a hot griddle. "I don't have time for finesse. A blunt instrument will do." He skewered the old man with his glare. "*Teach me!*"

~∞~

"Well done," said the Technomage, frowning down at her transplas tablet. She made an annotation.

Prue gurgled.

"Here, I'll take that." The other woman removed the thick leather strap from between Prue's teeth. "Would you like some water?"

Her jaw aching, her mouth too parched to form words, Prue made a noise of assent.

Establishing the benchmarks hadn't been as bad as she'd feared, but the first battery of real tests had ratcheted up her discomfort by inexorable degrees—building from subtle hurt to bright pain to bone-melting agony. The worst part was that even if her hands had been free, there was nothing to stroke or soothe on the outside. Every cell, every organ and vessel deep inside her body ached with the abuse.

The straw made an obscene slurping noise in the bottom of the cup.

The brutal labor she'd endured to birth Katrin was nothing in comparison. For the Sister's sake, after this she'd be able to pump out one babe after another and laugh while she did it. With cruel clarity, her imagination painted a picture of Erik's face as she laid his child in his arms, Katrin's fond smile as she stroked the baby's plump cheek. Prue hadn't shed a single tear, but suddenly, her face was wet. Gods, she was a fool! Happiness had been within her grasp, and she hadn't had the guts to reach for it. *Gone, all gone.* She swallowed a hiccupping sob. She'd never see either of them again.

"Finished?" The Technomage removed the cup. "Sleep now while I tabulate the data." She bent to work some mechanism under the chair. With a creak, the back tilted and the foot rose until Prue lay flat. The relief was exquisite.

"Sleep?" she croaked. "You must be . . . joking."

"No." The Technomage looked up from her transplas notes. "You need to rest. The initial readings seem to confirm my hypothesis. You generate some kind of field. The question is whether it's reflective, absorbing or simply a barrier. I need to do a triangulation."

Prue's eyelids slid down. She levered them open again. "You mean . . . three . . . more times? *Three?*"

The Technomage Primus patted her on the knee. "No, only two. The first is complete."

"Won't . . . live . . ." Her tongue banged around in her mouth, numb and clumsy. ". . . through another, let . . . alone . . ." With a heroic effort, Prue peered through her lashes. The beamed ceiling blurred and swung. "Water . . . what was . . . ?"

"Nothing sinister. Just a sedative."

"Oh," mumbled Prue. "That's all right then." A black cottony wave swept over her, drowning the sound of her hollow laughter.

35

(decorative flourish)

"Again," said Bartelm. "And cut the volume. Barge in bellowing like that and you won't need a doorbell."

Erik clenched his fists, concentrating fiercely. Gathering the Voice, he opened his mouth to—

"Clear your mind first," said a creaky old voice from a cocoon of blankets huddled in a big chair. "You're trying too hard." Calmly, Purist Nori sipped the last of the tisane from the cup cradled in her gnarled fingers.

"I have to try," Erik snapped. "If I don't, Prue will die. Fuck, for all I know she's—"

With surprising strength, the old woman flung the cup at his head.

Between one breath and the next, Erik's hand flashed up and the cup stalled in midair as if it had been glued there. He was so astonished, his mouth fell open and the cup lurched toward the floor.

"Keep it there!" snapped Nori.

Instinctively, Erik did . . . *something* . . . and the cup steadied, hovering three feet above the flagstones.

He heard Bartelm's gusty sigh, but he didn't dare take his eye from the cup.

"For once, Nori, could we do something the orthodox way?" asked the wizard plaintively. "It usually works, that's why it's *orthodox*."

"The boy's right," said Nori absently. "No time." She raised her voice. "Tell me what you see, Erik."

"A cup." Sweat gathered on his brow, dripped into his eyes.

"Unfocus your eyes. Squint if you have to."

"Can't . . . too much." The cup dropped, shattering with a delicate tinkle. Erik stared at it, fumbling his way to a chair. He sat with a thump. Gods, he ached as if he'd hoisted a full-grown milkbeast over his head.

"Ah well." Nori shrugged her bony shoulders. "Surprise only works once."

"I saw . . ." Erik wet his lips. "I thought I saw . . . lines, a shimmer. Like the time before. I don't know." He tugged at his hair. "Something."

The two old Purists exchanged a glance. "Orthodoxy, hmm?" said Nori with a twinkle.

Bartelm cleared his throat. "We think your medium is the air, Erik. After all, it's what you do every time you sing—shape the air to produce music."

"But there are other ways, not so loud." Nori leaned forward, her rheumy eyes glittering in their nest of wrinkles. "Especially if you can *see* the flows. Here." With a small huff of effort she bent to scoop up a small piece of china from the floor near her feet. "Try this."

Automatically, Erik caught it one-handed and placed it on the table. He regarded it dubiously.

Half an hour later, he was still glaring at the fucking thing, urgency crawling under his skin, an itch he couldn't scratch. He'd moved the shard a whole quarter of an inch sideways. His head pounded. "Give me a minute." He strode out the door into the welcome cool of night, seething.

The dark air was a soft caress on his skin, light spilling from the kitchen windows and across the path. The graceful rooflines of The Garden's pavilions were silhouetted against the racing clouds, the Sibling Moons shining high in the sky. It had to be past three in the morning. Despite himself, Erik yawned. Rose and a couple of the boys had insisted on going to scout out the Leaf of Nobility, but they'd returned empty-handed and crestfallen. He'd sent them to bed, and sensibly, they'd gone.

Gods, where was Prue? Was she waiting for him even now, every minute that passed without rescue sapping her confidence, her will to survive? *Lord and Lady, don't punish her for my sins. I can pay all by myself.* He bit his lip until he drew blood.

Walker though . . . There was still Walker and the assassin. A sweet wind swirled by, bearing the heavy purple scent of dark roses. Erik's nostrils flared in appreciation.

He blinked. *Purple?* Well, hell.

Eddies of air, limned in a deep burgundy violet, drifted by, flirting with the moonlight. Deliberately, Erik blurred his vision, the way the Purists had taught him. The color intensified, marking the passage of the light breeze.

Right.

With infinite caution, he raised his arm and pointed at a leaf that lay on the path, uneasily conscious he must look like a complete idiot. *You*, he thought fiercely. *Now.*

The leaf quivered. Then it rose, floating upward in a gentle spiral, the way leaves did. Erik squinted through his lashes. *Ah.*

The faintest of glimmers supported the leaf, so nearly transparent that if he moved his head, even slightly, it disappeared.

Experimentally, he made a tugging motion with his fingers. The leaf jerked toward him as if on an invisible string. Erik smiled with grim satisfaction. Well, a string that was visible to *him*, a tether made of air.

Fine. He could do this, he could do anything—for Prue. Narrowing his gaze, he concentrated on focusing his will.

The leaf lurched and fluttered down to the path. Shit!

Shuffling footsteps, the slow tap-tap of a cane. "You can't force it, son," said Purist Nori from behind him. "Magick is the gods' gift. It comes from the heart, not the intellect."

Erik turned to stare down into her face. "You mean it's instinctive?"

The old woman folded her knotted hands on the head of her cane and shrugged.

"In essence." Purist Bartelm came to stand at her shoulder.

"Mind you, that's not permission to throw discipline out the window. Nor scholarship."

A heavy wooden table revolving in the air, a miscellany of objects circling above his head like crazed planets. The single silver cuff coming to rest against the corpsebird's neck, touching that horrible scrawny skin . . . Remembering it, the hair stood up on the back of his neck. For a few moments there, he hadn't been completely sane, the power of his emotions reducing him to a bundle of knee-jerk reactions, all of the most primitive sort. He'd no longer been a man, but a creature made of Magick.

Abruptly, he couldn't wait to be gone, to be *doing*. "Then I'm as ready as I'll ever be," he said. "If I'm angry enough, it . . . the power . . . will come." It felt so patently ridiculous, he couldn't say the word out loud. *Magick*.

"That's not quite what we meant," said Bartelm immediately, but Nori just shrugged again.

From out of the darkness, a soft, deep voice said, "I have the assassin."

Three heads jerked around.

Soundlessly, Walker stepped from the shadows into the light. There'd been no footfall, no sense of movement, nothing to indicate his presence. Gods, the man was uncanny. His slashing cheekbones were flushed, his clean-cut mouth curved in a cruel smile. "It took some doing, but Mehcredi's safe in my House of Swords."

Nori cackled. Walker said nothing.

Erik took a pace forward. "She talked?"

"Yes." Again that hunter's smile. But then his dark brows drew together. "She didn't know much. She was contacted by a man wearing the livery of an upper-class servant and directed to come here to The Garden."

"Here?" Bartelm's eyes widened.

"To Clouds and Rain. Where she met with her employer. She thinks it was a man, but he manifested as a black cloud."

"Dark Arts," murmured Bartelm.

Walker ignored him. "He gave no reason, but he wanted Erik dead. The fee was twenty credits, reduced to fifteen after the fuckup with Dai. The man came to Mehcredi a second time in a dream. At both meetings he hurt her in order to ensure her obedience." An infinitesimal pause. "Also for the pleasure of her pain."

Fuck! Erik's pulse boomed in his ears like a mighty, rushing wind. What would such a man do to Prue, with her bright-eyed courage and her sharp tongue? He clenched his fists so hard his nails dug into his palms. Shit, what was the bastard doing to her *right now*?

"Why—?" He had to stop to moisten his lips. "Why did she take Prue? And *how*?"

"Mehcredi hired two thugs, but you weren't there and they couldn't find you, not in time. When Prue wouldn't tell them where you were, the assassin panicked. She decided Prue was better than nothing." A flash in his dark eyes. "She fought the way I'd taught her, but the assassin used a stupefying drug."

Erik's eyes stung. She'd refused to give him up? She'd tried to protect *him*? Ah, gods!

"You have the woman secure? Under guard?" asked Bartelm.

"Yes." Walker bared his teeth. "She's mine to do with as I will. Don't worry, she'll pay for what she did to Dai."

The old man took Nori's arm to usher her back into the building. "Come," he said over his shoulder. "We need all the details."

The moment they'd taken the first few steps, Erik strode away toward the water stairs, breaking first into a trot and then a run. Walker's skiff bobbed gently in the water, a pale, slender shape, double shadowed. The canal lay deserted, silent and mysterious, the water a black, shifting expanse, relieved only by the shivering glint of wavelets caressed by the moonslight. It smelled cool and briny, the sea breeze playing with Erik's hair.

Stepping into the little craft, he unhitched the tie rope and shoved off. The skiff rocked alarmingly when he picked up the pole, but he managed the first couple of strokes without tipping himself into the water. As the current carried him around the bend, he thought he saw Walker's lithe figure, standing, hands on hips at the top of the water stairs. His body was outlined against the martial glow of the Brother, flaring red as it dipped toward the horizon.

All Erik had to do was follow his nose. Gods, he'd been so

preoccupied with his terror for Prue, he'd almost forgotten the corpse-marsh stink of rotting vegetation surrounding the Leaf of Nobility. As he grew closer, his nasal passages burned with it. Inga's face, glimmering beneath the water, her eyes open wide, unseeing . . . Erik set his teeth, swallowing the bile that rose in his throat.

He didn't have a clue what he was going to do, but the heart of it was here, he was convinced of it. The corruption still lurked beneath this Leaf, as it had for the gods knew how long. But nothing had happened until he'd revealed it in public and then capped off the performance with a clear demonstration of just how stubborn he could be.

With a gentle bump, the skiff grounded under the Processional Bridge. Very well, two stairs to the east. He had to start somewhere. Poling silently on, Erik tried not to inhale. The first water stair was obviously a private mooring, with some kind of pleasure barge tied to a large bollard. He snugged the little skiff in next to it, flung the rope over the overhanging branch of a widow's hair tree and secured it.

The tall gate of iron bars at the top of the stair was locked, but it presented no obstacle to an athletic man filled to the bursting with fear and rage and the first intimations of a power beyond his wildest dreams. Erik stretched and jumped. He hung for an instant, then tightened his grip and hauled himself over with a quiet grunt. Dropping to a crouch on the other side, he took stock.

Nothing moved, only the barge creaking at the other end of its cable, the occasional flower trembling at the end of a branch.

Even in the cool half-light of the approaching dawn, he could see this noblefamily's garden had been sculpted to within an inch of its life. Every plant, no matter how insignificant, had been clipped, forced or constrained. The lawn was a velvet swathe, paths intersected at right angles, even the pond was a perfect circle.

Cautiously, he sniffed. Faugh! Yes, that way.

Beyond the pond, a small gate gave out onto the narrow alley he remembered. Erik latched it carefully behind him and headed east, his long legs eating up the distance. Drawing on his early walk-on roles as servants of various types, he projected the air of a man busy about his master's business, with every right to walk where he pleased.

Three minutes and two sprawling palazzos later, he stared without surprise at a familiar wooden gate, his head swimming with the intensity of the odor. He rested a hand on the cool wood and turned to stare at the luxurious dwelling behind him. A light flickered high up in a room under the roof, so someone was awake, but all the other windows gazed back at him with dark, blank eyes. Erik's lip curled. How did they stand the stink?

This garden was lovely, nothing like the other, all flowing curves that intrigued and delighted the eye, vaguely reminiscent of the Sibling Gardens surrounding the Library. If he survived this, he'd have to ask Walker if he'd had a hand in the design.

Opening the gate, he gritted his teeth and walked down the steps toward the lapping water, now the color of pewter. He'd always known it would come to this, hadn't he? It was horrible, but fitting.

Where were the seelies? They were the only lead he had, his sole advantage in this cruel game of bluff.

Very softly, he began to sing, no more than a sweet, deep croon. A traditional ballad of unrequited love, one of his mother's favorites. But this time, he watched out of the corner of his eye, pretending nonchalance on the off-chance he might convince himself. At first, all he saw was a glassy shimmer above the water, but when he hit and held a note in a melancholy minor key, the flow of air firmed, a narrow brush of transparent color laid out before him. Note after note, bar after bar, the streams multiplied, drifting and dancing in spirals, weaving together and splitting off.

For a few precious moments, the stinking miasma of *wrongness* lifted.

"Hoot?"

Still humming, Erik glanced down. Bobbing in the water, a row of bug-eyed, whiskery faces stared up at the flows, entranced. There must have been at least a dozen of them. He gave a harsh bark of satisfaction, surprising himself with a gusty blast that sparkled with motes of strong orange.

"Prue," he said to his furry audience. "I have to find Prue."

Blue bodies flashed through the water. "Hoot? Burble?"

Erik crouched and leaned toward them, holding out his hands. "You've got to help me. Where is she? Prue? Remember Prue?" With every particle of mental strength he possessed, he projected an image of her—her vivid little face, animated with curiosity and brisk intelligence, the honey-cream of her skin, those wonderful tip-tilted eyes, brighter even than the aquamarines she wore on her slim wrists, the fall of her shiny brown hair, gleaming with gold high—

"*Hoot!*" A furry body arced out of the water and hit him in the small of the back with unexpected force.

Before he could regain his balance, Erik tumbled forward, arms flying. The chill of the canal closed over his head as he sank, his clothes pulling him down. Fuck!

Seething, he clawed his way back to the surface. "You stupid little shits!" he hissed as soon as his head was clear. "Why didn't you wait? I was going to—Ah, fuck!"

"Burble?"

The seelies withdrew to a safe distance, large eyes watching him reproachfully as he floated on his back to haul off his boots and toss them onto the lowest step, followed by his jacket. He checked the long dagger sheathed at his waist. Still there. Good.

Erik rolled his eyes at the circle of anxious, bewhiskered faces, the quivering snouts. "All right," he said, treading water. "I'm sorry I yelled. *Prue?* Can you take me to Prue?"

As one, they surged toward him. "Stop!" Erik held up his hand, provoking a positive chorus of hoots and burbles. "I'm a land animal, remember? I need to breathe."

Relentlessly, he pumped his lungs full of hair, his chest expanding to what should have been bursting point—but wasn't. As he inhaled a little more and then more yet, the air fizzed and sparkled in his blood, his body effervescent with power.

Erik extended his arms to the sides. "Now," he gasped, "Take me now." Immediately, two of the biggest seelies barreled into his ribs, and he wrapped his arms around them, his fingers sinking into cool, silky fur.

36

Prue stared at the ceiling, dry-eyed. Dully, she wondered how many hours had passed. The room was dark, save for the dim light of a single glowglobe, but she had the sense she'd slept for several hours at least. Thanks be to the Sister, the Technomage had removed the straps from her ankles so she could twist and stretch her lower body. The return of sensation to unused muscles had been agonizing, but she'd been ruthless, cursing under her breath as she contorted her body, testing the wrist restraints to their limits. Her life might depend on whether she could stand unaided—and run.

Katrin must be frantic by now. Rose would be beside herself. As for Erik . . . She clamped her eyes shut and breathed through the pain. *If I live through this, I'll . . .*

What? What would she do? Clenching her fists, Prue whispered, "I will reach for what I want and hold it fast. I will not doubt him. And I will not doubt myself. By all the gods, I swear it." She needed to hear the words to make them real.

It . . . it . . . it, the walls murmured back to her. The machine looming behind her hummed in counterpoint.

If she strained her ears, she could hear the faintest ladylike snuffle coming from behind a plain, unpainted door off to the right. Her guess had been correct, the Technomage slept and lived down here. Prue shivered.

No matter. Erik and the others would be searching for her, she had to be ready.

Once again, she began the painful process of stretching, tense and release—left foot, right foot, left leg . . .

~~~

By the time they surfaced again, the sun had risen, the day beginning to heat up. Erik scraped the hair out of his eyes, struggling to hold on to his temper. "Look," he said to the ring of intent, blue, furry faces, "I've seen it before. You don't have to show me again. I *know* what the fucking problem is, all right? I'm trying to fix it, but first I have to find Prue. *Prue?* Get it?"

One of the smaller seelies made a pathetic bleating noise and disappeared, leaving only a ripple behind. A number of the others wavered, their snouts whiffling in distress. He honestly would not have been surprised to see them burst into tears.

The little creatures had taken him back under the titan-plant, straight to the rotting stem. He wasn't sure how long they'd kept him down there, the water so full of suspended flakes of slime it was a filthy gray, but he knew it had to be more than five minutes. His lungs had shrunk to the size of manda fruits, and he'd lost buoyancy. Without the support of the seelies, he would have slid unresisting all the way to the seafloor. Lord's balls, if it hadn't been for the air Magick . . .

"You danced for her," he said desperately. "Don't you remember? She loved it, she laughed, she—" He choked, her image vivid in his mind, her face transfigured with delight, her eyes shining. His pretty Prue.

"Hoot, burble, burble?" said one of the seelies, so sleek and sinuous Erik was sure it was female. She slipped through the water until she floated nose to nose with the biggest of them all. "Hoot, burble, *burble*!" she insisted.

"Honk!" said the big one emphatically and Erik stared. *Honk?*

The two creatures conferred a moment longer, before spinning around to float on their backs, searching his face.

"Prue?" said Erik again, his brain racing with strategies, possibilities. He'd do the palazzos. Hell, he should have tried them first. Every noble house had a discreet entrance for the hired help. With the Voice, it shouldn't take him long to extract the truth from any servant, even the most loyal. Conscience be damned, it was the only way left.

Almost hesitantly, the two seelies approached. The female nudged his biceps with her nose. "Burble?" When Erik lifted his arm, she snuggled beneath, pressed tight against his ribs.

Within seconds, the pack surrounded him with a wall of blue-furred muscle. There was only time for a snatched breath before they pulled him under.

Fortunately, the trip was rushed, but short. About thirty feet farther along the canal, the seelies back-paddled, slowing their forward momentum to a crawl. Abruptly, they backed off, leaving Erik to drift to the surface. Puzzled, he gazed around. The female shot past him, circled and returned. "Hoot!" Then she did it again. And again.

Erik squinted. Fuck, there was a rope! The strangest rope he'd ever seen, almost transparent. It hung from a garden wall, entered the water and disappeared. He looked back over his shoulder. The property was huge, the garden extensive, but it was definitely the same palazzo, the one with the water stair—the center of the corruption.

The blood turned to ice in Erik's veins. What was at the other end of the rope, fathoms deep? Ruthlessly, he pumped his lungs full of air, feeling the Magick suffuse every cell in his body.

Heart hammering, he jackknifed into the depths, bubbles streaming back over his body. Exerting all his considerable strength, he hauled himself hand over hand down the rope, deeper and deeper. It felt slick in his palms, invisible in the filthy water. If he hadn't been holding on to it, he wouldn't have known it was there.

He lost track of how deep he went, accompanied by only the sleek female. She darted about his head, brushing back and forth, distracting him. Cursing, he tried to bat her aside, his guts twisting with sick horror. A hopeless litany pounded in his head. *My Lord, Great Lady, please, no. I can't bear it. I'll pay, I promise. Just let it not be her. Please, please.*

In the gray murk, he made out a small patch of blue. Small, very small. Too small for a human body. Relief streamed out of him in a plume of bubbles. But it was only when the female went crazy, circling at a dizzying speed, nudging him with her snout, that he began to understand.

The blue was the fur of another seelie, a kit no more than a foot long, with huge eyes and a small round face.

When it saw the female, it went mad, turning and twisting in a circumscribed circle. Its little snout whiffled pathetically, although he couldn't hear it bleating through the water.

Erik frowned, feeling the burn beginning in his lungs. Shit, even with the air Magick, he might still drown. What use would he be to Prue then?

The female scrabbled at his shirt with her web-claws, recapturing his attention. That was odd. Why didn't the kit make straight for its mother? With the last of his breath, he reached for the little creature, only to encounter a rigid structure. He fumbled his way around it. Corners, struts, bars— virtually invisible, like the rope.

Shit, a trap! And he was out of breath, spots dancing before his eyes.

Releasing the rope, Erik shot back toward the surface. The female went berserk, clawing at his head and shoulders, ramming into him with her sinuous, muscular body. He did his best to fend her off, to shield himself without hurting her. Scratches stung on his back and arms, his shirt tore and his ribs ached.

Trust me, he tried to say to her. *You can trust me.*

But of course, it didn't work. Wasn't that fucking ironic? Exactly like another female he knew, the seelie wanted proof.

Breaking into the open air, Erik inhaled in huge gasps. Then he grasped the rope again and tugged hard. It didn't shift. To a chorus of protesting hoots, he hauled himself up the rope and over the garden wall, landing dripping wet behind a small shed, almost exactly like the one he'd seen in the palazzo down the alley. Panting, he scrambled to his feet. All was quiet.

When he tilted his head just right, he could see the early morning sunlight sparkle on the rope. The wooden door of the shed was slightly ajar and the rope snaked through it and disappeared.

Godsdammit, a clue, a lead he could work with. Someone was hunting seelies. Someone else knew they existed and was prepared to have him killed to shut his mouth. It all added up—the same son of a bitch who'd taken his Prue.

It seemed the bastard liked to lay traps.

Erik's lips peeled back from his teeth in a soundless snarl. A vicious wind blew up out of nowhere, rattling the doors and windows of the shed. He took a step toward it, then stopped and pinched the bridge of his nose.

"Fuck," he said under his breath.

Spinning on his heel, he walked back to the garden wall and leaned over it. "I said you could trust me," he said to the seelies still circling in the water. Then he set his feet, grabbed the rope and hauled, hand over hand.

The closer the trap drew to the surface, the louder the seelies hooted and burbled, churning the water in their excitement.

Erik glanced over his shoulder at the quiet of the velvety lawns, the windows of the tall palazzo. His skin crawled. "Godsdammit, will you shut up?" The noise abated somewhat.

The trap emerged into the sunlight, the seelie kit looking both astonished and alarmed. Out of the water, the cage was easier to see, a cunning and complex construction of interlocking struts with a flexible one-way chute that closed behind the prey, blocking the opening. Inside, along with the kit, was a juicy-looking bunch of water weeds. Delicious, if you liked that kind of thing.

Something about the trap reminded Erik of the Technomage starships he'd traveled in so many times, though he couldn't imagine why that might be so. In any case, it was the work of moments to hold the chute open with one hand and grab the squirming kit with the other. For his pains, he got a cry halfway between a shriek and a hoot and a deep scratch across the back of one hand.

"Shit!" Erik leaned over the wall and let the kit plop into the water. Immediately, the mother curled her body around it, nosing at it with her snout, emitting a continuous stream of low humming noises he hadn't heard before.

From farther down the canal came the regular splashing of poles, grunts of effort. The first skiffs of the morning. Caracole was waking up.

The seelies froze. A series of swirls and they were gone as if they had never been. Erik turned away. It had to be his imagination, but he could swear the female had shot him a final glance over her shoulder. Was it possible for a seelie to look embarrassed?

Dabbing at his bleeding hand with the tail of his wet shirt, Erik smiled as he padded toward the garden shed.

He sobered. Now for the bastard. And Prue.

The inside of the shed smelled fresh and green, not musty as he'd expected. Various garden implements hung from pegs on the walls, all shining bright with good care. The rest was the organized detritus of a gardener who loved his work, but Erik hardly noticed. His entire focus was on the rope and where it led.

A few quick strides and he fell to his knees to rummage in the far corner. His heart thundering with excitement, he yanked aside three bags of what must be well-rotted compost, to judge by the loamy odor.

Yes!

Lady love the seelies, the rope disappeared through a neat hole drilled into the top of a sturdy wooden trapdoor made of narrow planks and set flush into the floor.

As Erik considered it, his brain racing, two empty flower pots and a garden fork floated gently off the floor and began a placid gavotte at shoulder level. They were joined by a stately, thick-waisted watering can.

"Stop that," he said, barely glancing at them. "I have to think."

The fork fell out of the air with a tinny clatter, followed by the flower pots. Lunging, Erik grabbed the watering can just in time. His heart climbing out of his throat, he reeled to the door and peered out.

Nothing. Just the cultivated wilderness of the garden basking in the sun, and the morning traffic on the canal—a barge laden with vegetables for market and half a dozen skiffs, their owners yelling cheerful insults across the water. Ambient noise. Thank the Horned Lord.

With extreme care, Erik pulled the door closed and returned to his contemplation of the trapdoor. It was closely fitted to the floor, no gaps, only a large ring in the center. Locked or bolted on the inside, he'd bet his life on it. In fact, that was exactly what he was doing—gambling with his life and Prue's. Experimentally, he tugged. It didn't budge.

Setting his jaw, he braced his feet, wrapped both hands around the ring and hauled until his shoulders cracked. The hinges protested, but nothing more.

No surprise, but . . . shit.

All right, all right. Forget brute force, what about the air Magick? Erik glared at the trapdoor, and the fork shifted along the floor, the tines scraping in a suggestive kind of way. In the kitchen at The Garden, he'd lifted a heavy table, surely he could blast the damned door out of existence? He was certainly angry enough. A few stray leaves spun in the dusty air, slowly at first, then faster. The flower pots rattled.

Erik flexed strong fingers. For all he knew, he'd blow the roof right off the shed trying. His control was so poor, he couldn't risk it. Gods, it would be so much simpler to knock boldly on the back door of the palazzo and overpower the servant who answered. But every instinct he had was screaming at him that he needed to be on the other side of that fucking trapdoor—now!

Coincidence be damned. Everything was clicking into place like the pieces of a giant puzzle. He no longer doubted his destiny. Somehow, the gods had set this whole debacle pinwheeling, and it was up to him to retrieve Caracole, the seelies—and Prue—from disaster. Him, and him alone. Erik inhaled, feeling the Magick fizz in his lungs.

Drawing his blade, he grabbed the rope and pulled. Whatever anchored it was solid. Not giving himself time for second thoughts, Erik sawed through the rope. The severed end slithered away and disappeared underground.

Feeling like a fool, he dropped to his knees, put his eye to the hole and peered through. There was a set of brick steps illuminated by a faint, greenish glow. His nostrils flared. Something unfamiliar, acrid and vicious, the slightest hint of it. The sense of wrongness was so palpable that he jerked back, cursing.

That settled it.

Erik seized the fork, but the planks of the trapdoor were so closely and skillfully fitted, there was no gap in which to set the tines. Godsdammit, *how*? His eyes narrowed as he studied the disk of pale green light that was the hole in the trapdoor. If he could control the air seething in his lungs, *focus* it . . . Very quietly, he began to hum, a soft vibration deep in his chest. It took him five minutes of sweaty, straining effort before he could see the flow of air, a sinuous ribbon washed with steely gray, the color of his furious determination.

Ignoring the thump, thump, thump of his heart, he sent it snaking through the hole. Where was the godsbedamned bolt? Kneeling on the dusty floor, he squeezed his eyes shut, sent the narrow current questing along the underside of the trapdoor. Ah, there!

Now to grasp, and pull . . .

The air flow slipped past the bolt as if it were greased.

All right. He'd push instead.

Every muscle in his body tense and shaking with the effort, he gathered up the air Magick and *pushed*. But he couldn't control the power of the flow and direct it at the same time. Cursing, he dropped forward, the wood warm and dry, vibrating under his palms. His head bowed, Erik froze.

The Magick was dispersing, spreading out under the wooden boards, pressing up from underneath, making them creak and tremble. Concentrating fiercely, Erik hummed harder. Fuck, he mustn't overdo it or the whole thing would explode right through the ceiling. And that would be that as far as stealth was concerned.

Wood groaned, a plank bowed up and a nail popped. Then another. And another. Erik's heart leaped. By the Horned Lord, *yes*! Sweat beading his forehead, he increased the pressure until the timbers of the trapdoor were singing their own creaky chorus.

Enough, enough. Panting, he released the Magick. Nails stood proud all along one edge of the trapdoor where the air flow had been strongest. Well, hell, it would have to do. Half of them were so loose he was able to wiggle them out with his fingers. He levered the others free with the tines of the fork.

Then he worked the fork under the loose board and leaned

on it with all his considerable weight. The wood twanged and fought, but slowly, slowly, it rose, revealing a hand's width of that strange green twilight below. Reaching out, Erik grabbed a sturdy-looking flower pot and jammed it into the opening. His chest heaved as if he'd run full pelt across every Leaf in Caracole, from one side to the other.

Dropping flat, he shoved his arm into the gap, clear up to the elbow. A couple of fumbles and he got a firm grip on the handle of the bolt. It came easily, as if it had been oiled. And when he raised the whole door, it was whisper quiet.

Erik touched his fingers to the talisman on its gold chain. *Thank you, Horned Lord, Great Lady. Tell her I'm coming.* Lowering himself into the opening, he discovered the passage was no more than five feet high, the rope secured to a large metal hook with a complicated knot. Bent low, he started down the brick steps, toward the faint green glow.

He estimated he was under the garden two-thirds of the way to the palazzo when the snarling whispers began. A wave of shivers rolled down Erik's spine, raising every hair on his body. "Thmell," something lisped. "Thweet flesh. Thmell it."

The passage flattened out. By the time he reached the last curve, Erik was walking so lightly he would have been on tiptoe if the height of the ceiling had permitted it.

"Ah," sighed the voice. It made a revolting lip-smacking noise. "Thuck on bones."

Erik came to an abrupt halt. A few paces before him, a short flight of steps led up into a pool of sickly light. It *pulsed.* The sweet, gut-churning reek of old blood rolled down the steps, and he clapped a hand over his nose and mouth. It was every nightmare he'd had as a child, every monster that hid under the bed or in the shadows behind the door.

But he wasn't a child, and Prue was up there somewhere, he was certain of it.

One hand on the hilt of his blade and his back pressed to the wall, Erik took the steps one at a time, the foul litany growing louder as he approached. With the utmost care, he crouched on the final step, well below sword height, and hitched an eye around the corner.

The passage widened into a small chamber, a cul-de-sac. A dark curtain made of some heavy, dense material hung on one wall from ceiling to floor. Opposite was a plain wooden door, the strange light streaming off it making his eyes ache and his head swim.

"Thweet meat," said the door in that sly, glutinous voice. "Thoft, hot blood."

Erik tilted his head and unfocused his eyes as the Purists had taught him. Under the grain of the wood floated a face straight from a madman's vision of hell and everlasting torment. It was a caricature—a wide, lipless mouth with protruding fangs, slit-pupilled eyes. One set of curved, twisting horns grew from its forehead, another from the corners of its jaw.

The large eyes swiveled toward him, vertical pupils expanding with bloodlust. "Come close, thweet one." The horrible light grew eager, pulsing green and vicious. "Tho big. Ah . . ." Again, the lip-smacking, but this time he could see the obscenity of its long tongue, shockingly pink and slick with spittle.

Erik didn't move. "Who—what are you?"

The creature blinked. "Doorkeeper." It swirled restlessly beneath the wood. "Trapped," it added mournfully. "Hungry."

"But you're a demon," said Erik, widening his eyes and looking suitably impressed. "How can one so powerful be trapped?"

With shocking suddenness, the Doorkeeper surged out of the wood, its snarling visage becoming three-dimensional. "*Him!* Cruel thpells. Hurts me." Its fangs clashed and green-tinged saliva flew, hissing where it hit the floor.

"Who?"

The Doorkeeper appeared to shudder. "*Him*," it said with finality.

Erik advanced a cautious half pace. "What's behind the door?"

The demon leered, waggling its tongue. "Girl flesh. Thoft . . . Mmm . . ."

The stench intensified, catching in Erik's throat. Struggling not to gag, he said, "What . . . what does she look like?"

"The newest? Thoft, plump. Thweet tits." The long tongue curled around one fang. "Oh, yeth . . ."

Erik advanced on the demon, his fists clenched. His heart banged against his rib cage. "Does she have brown hair?"

The Doorkeeper shot him a sly glance. "Hair?" it murmured.

Quick as a striking snake, long wiry arms shot toward him, huge taloned paws open to grab.

37

Barely in time, Erik swayed back. One long claw snagged his shirt, slicing it open from shoulder to waist as neatly as a razor. A gob of green spittle hit the hand he flung up, searing his skin. Swearing, he jumped back, wiping the mess off on his sleeve. But it had already risen in a puffy, yellow blister that hurt like hell.

Shit! Warily, he eyed the Doorkeeper, seething with frustration. Disregarding the reek, he inhaled deeply, preparing himself for the Voice. But godsdammit, would it work on something without a soul?

By his estimation, the creature's grasp didn't extend to the other side of the chamber. His back to the wall, Erik sidled over to the curtain and peered beneath while the Doorkeeper snapped its fangs and drooled in frustration. His brows rose. Books, row after row of beautiful, leather-bound books. When he put his hand to the shelf, it moved soundlessly, sliding open a crack to reveal a luxuriously appointed study, full of dark, gleaming wood and plushy rugs in jewel tones. Thankfully, it was completely empty, but it had the hushed sense of expectancy of an often-used retreat, as if the owner were beyond the far door, about to set his hand to the latch.

"Don't go."

Erik turned. "Lonely?"

The creature snorted and spittle flew. "Thirsty." Its large eyes fixed hungrily on his jugular, where the pulse pounded just beneath the skin. Its face grew crafty. "Thtay or I yell. Loud."

Erik shrugged. "If you shout, I'll run away, or be captured. Either way, you won't get to feed—though I suppose your master might throw you a bone."

The Doorkeeper growled, fangs clacking, and Erik turned away to examine the study, pretending nonchalance. Under his breath, he hummed a snatch of the "Seelie Song."

"Theelies? Oooh, thweet, *thweetest*."

Erik looked over his shoulder. "You like seelies?" He gripped the bookcase so the creature wouldn't see his hands tremble with eagerness, with the desire to rend and tear, to crush and destroy . . .

"Yeth, *yeth*!" The demon extruded its tongue, right down over its chin. "Thing more theelies."

Commanding his guts to behave, Erik closed the bookcase door and sang the "Seelie Song" half a dozen times over, threading the Voice through the tune as subtly as he could. By the end, the demon was nodding its hideous head in time. It even tried to sing along, in a thin falsetto so appalling Erik didn't know whether to laugh or throw up.

He tried "The Milkmaid's Jugs," thinking the creature might like the raunchy lyrics. It did, but so much so, it bounced with prurient glee, making the door rattle and bang. Hastily, Erik switched to a solemn elegy and then to a funeral hymn. The Doorkeeper calmed.

Racking his brains, Erik the Golden gave the strangest and most important performance of his life, pulling out everything in his repertoire that was slow, sad and achingly beautiful. It wasn't easy to maintain the flowing, legato lines without increasing the volume, but he managed it somehow.

The demon's third eyelid had slid partly across from the inside of its eye. It gazed vacantly at him.

The music makes you sleepy," said Erik softly.

"Doesn't." Disconcertingly, the Doorkeeper blinked with both sets of eyelids at once. "Does not."

Hating to soil the beauty of it, Erik sang the first verse of the "Lullaby for Stormy Eyes."

The demon snorted and sniffled. Green mucus trickled from its nostrils. But its eyelids drooped and it sank back into the wood like a tired traveler in a featherbed.

Over and over, Erik sang the lullaby, knowing he'd never be able to stomach it again after this. After ten minutes, he began weaving suggestions through the words.

> *Storm clouds gather, love,*
> —Sleep deep, do not wake—
> *In your eyes, in your pretty eyes.*
> —Let me pass unharmed—

Twenty precious minutes later, he let the notes die away. The Doorkeeper's head lay on its shoulder at an inhuman, broken-necked angle, its thick tongue protruding from its mouth. The whole door vibrated with its guttural snores.

Erik glanced at the acid green shine on the timbers. Then he shrugged off his shirt and wrapped it around one hand. With the other, he drew his blade. Treading as softly as possible, he approached the door and reached for the knob.

The demon snuffled in its sleep and he froze, his guts cramping and the pulse thundering in his ears. A fraction at a time, he turned the handle, until he could ease the door open and poke his head through. Another passage, brick paved like the first, leading away around a gentle curve. A more even, natural light, like that of a glowglobe. Quiet, save for a background hum like wires thrumming.

Grimly, Erik studied the slumbering Doorkeeper. It was very likely he'd have to return this way, and he doubted there'd be time to lull an angry demon back to sleep. Where the fabric of his shirt touched the door, it was green and sticky. As he watched in disgust, the stains turned a dirty brown. They sizzled, very slightly.

A pity his boots were back at the water stair.

Using the tip of his blade, Erik prevented the door from closing while he wedged the bundle of his shirt between the door and the wall. With a savage grin, he stepped away to pull a couple of hefty tomes from the bookcase, low down, where they might not be missed. He shoved them in behind the shirt.

There.

Barefoot and silent, he eased through the space and padded down the steps, blade at the ready.

∞

"Morning," said the Technomage cheerfully. "How are we?"

"How do you damn well think?" Prue rolled her head to glare. "I hurt all over and I need to pee."

Fascinated, she watched a delicate flush stain the other woman's cheeks.

"Oh. Yes. Of course. Well, um . . ." The Technomage steadied. "A moment."

She moved away and a drawer opened and shut. "This is a powerful paralytic drug in the form of a spray." She held up a red tube about six inches long where Prue could see it, her thumb resting over a depression near the top. "The slightest suspicious move and you'll be helpless faster than you can blink. Do you understand?"

"Helpless. Fine, I've got it. Can we do this now? I'm going to wet myself."

Again the blush. "Very well." The Technomage cranked the chair until Prue sat upright once more. Then she stepped behind and placed the cold tube against Prue's pulse. Two clicks, and whatever attached the wrist restraints to the arms of the chair released.

Almost sobbing with the rush of blood to numbed muscles, Prue lifted her arms, stretching.

"Stop that!" The pressure of the tube increased, a thread of panic in the Scientist's voice. "Place your wrists together in front of you." She jabbed with the tube. "Now!"

Reluctantly, Prue complied and the cuffs clicked together, held by some force much stronger than she was. By all the gods, she was going to enjoy causing this woman pain, killing her if she had to. First, to relieve her aching bladder, all obedient and cowed, then . . . Her lips peeled back from her teeth. She couldn't take another night like the last. As for the prospect of vivisection . . . shiny, silver edges of razor-sharp metal, bright blood welling, never-ending screams. The bile rose sour in her throat, vile and choking.

She would either die or she would win. There was no other course and no other chance.

"Stand up, slowly."

Clumsily, Prue swung her legs to the floor and rose, swaying. Her limbs felt as if she'd borrowed them from an old crone with a terminal illness.

"Turn right and walk."

The Technomage's gusty breath stirred the fine hairs on her neck, the woman's thighs brushing the back of hers in lockstep. The red tube didn't waver.

One-handed, the Scientist opened a plain white door to reveal a cramped bathing chamber containing a low white stool, a sink and a square-tiled space with some kind of spray nozzle projecting from the wall.

"Go on." The Technomage gave her a nudge.

Prue glanced over her shoulder. "With you here?"

The other woman colored to the roots of her hair.

Prue pressed her advantage. "Don't you have any concept of human dignity?" It wasn't difficult to fake the sob in her voice. She jerked her head to indicate the Spartan room. "There's nothing in here to use as a weapon anyway," she said forlornly.

The Technomage hesitated for an endless second. Finally, she said, "Very well. But I'll be right on the other side of the door, ready for anything. Don't try me." Smiling thinly, she withdrew. The door closed softly behind her.

For a luxurious moment, Prue allowed herself to sag, her bound hands braced on the sink. Then she hastened to relieve herself. Gods, that was better. She wiggled her toes and fingers. Thank the Sister, sensation was returning to her extremities.

Concentrating fiercely, she turned a full circle. Well, shit. She'd spoken more truly than she knew when she'd said there were no weapons. No faucets, only push buttons. The spray nozzle was higher than her head, she'd never be able to reach it. Even the strange privy was a single molded piece.

Splashing her face with water as best she could, Prue quelled the incipient panic. Now was not the time. She could go to pieces later, safe in Erik's arms, holding Katrin close. Tears welled. Ruthlessly, she scrubbed them away.

"Come on," called the Technomage through the door. "Out with you."

Prue raised her voice. "Nearly finished, I promise. Just a moment."

The door opened outward. She'd noticed that.

There was nothing for it but a shoulder charge. If she could hit the other woman at knee level, smash her with the door . . . The Technomage obviously wasn't getting much exercise, locked up down here, and she was at least twenty years older. Briskly, Prue jiggled her arms and legs. Not too bad.

Merciful Sister, she prayed to the deity she only half believed in, *watch over those I love, You know who they are. Erik, my darling, live long and be happy, but please, don't forget me. Katrin, my baby girl.* She swallowed the burn of tears. *Katrin, sweet, name the first little one after me.* Her lips curved in a bittersweet smile. *Even if it's a boy.*

Drawing in a huge breath, she crouched low and flexed her thighs like a runner.

Now!

∽

The Necromancer yawned and blinked up at the silken canopy over his bed, conscious of a delicious sense of anticipation. He must contrive to bump into the singer today, savor his fear and frustration, taste his Magick. Such a treat, like a fine aperitif before a gourmet meal.

Not an air witch, but an air *wizard*. Ah, how the fates conspired to smooth his path! Lustfully, he dwelled on the man's magnificent body. To be frank, he was beginning to think he was going to enjoy his new dwelling as much as the Magick it housed. He'd almost forgotten the pleasures of the flesh, it had been so long. Idly, he wondered about the size of the singer's cock, while his own lay shriveled between his thighs. To have women look at him with admiration . . . Men too. He had a vague recollection of boys, their smooth, hard flesh, the boundless energy of youth, rutting . . .

As an added fillip, he had the woman, the little whore. If he extended his dark senses, he could feel her even now, a small blank spot in his universe. His tame Scientist would discover what it was she did and how she did it. If it was useful, he might keep her, but if not . . . No matter.

Perhaps he should drink her down while the singer watched. Hmm . . .

His brow wrinkled. That was odd. He checked again.

The Doorkeeper was asleep. But it never slept. He didn't permit it.

The Necromancer sent out a mental blast. *Nasake!*

∽

Erik could hear the murmur of an unfamiliar feminine voice. As he rounded the last curve, a woman said, "Come on. Out with you."

He blinked, taking in the chamber and its contents in a single comprehensive glance. The big empty chair resembled those used by starship captains and navigators. In fact, the entire room was very like the bridge of a Technomage starship, the walls lined with a bewildering array of machinery and consoles.

Even more puzzling, the woman standing with her back to him was dressed all in white like a Technomage. As he watched, she leaned forward to put her ear to the door and another voice replied from the other side. He'd know the timbre of it anywhere, every inflection, every cadence.

Prue.

The wave of relief almost took him to the floor, and he put out a hand to brace himself against the wall, breathing hard.

A gods-almighty crash jerked his head up. Prue came charging out of the door, her head down like a little battering ram. The impact of the door slammed the Technomage back against the wall. Blood sprayed from her nose. When Prue drove into the woman's soft midsection with a determined shoulder, the breath punched out of the Technomage with a painful whoop. The two of them fell to the floor in a tangle of thrashing arms and legs.

With a roar, Erik leaped forward. He plucked the white-coated woman off Prue as if she were a biteme, lifted her clean off her feet and wrapped a brawny forearm around her throat.

Prue looked up and her eyes widened. "Erik!"

The Technomage drummed her heels against Erik's shins, something red clutched in one waving fist. Emitting a horrible strangled noise, she tried to brush it against his arm.

With a scream of pure fury, Prue surged up from the floor and sank her teeth into the woman's wrist.

Erik's eyes widened. The red tube fell to the floor with a clatter and rolled away.

"Drug," gasped Prue and collapsed as if her legs would no longer support her.

⁓

She didn't think she'd ever seen anything as beautiful as Erik Thorensen, dripping wet, half naked and in a towering rage. His damp hair streamed back from his face, blown by an unseen wind. The shadows under his eyes showed as clear as bruises, but energy crackled off him, the horn talisman on his chest glowing like a hot coal.

"Prue," he said in a hoarse rasp. "Gods, Prue, are you—?" He choked.

She smiled, unable to stop the trembling of her lips. "Don't worry. I'm"—she swallowed—"all right."

His eyes burned into hers, darkly blue. "Truly?"

"Truly."

Erik's gaze dropped to Prue's hands, still shackled in front of her. His face darkened, and he pulled the Technomage hard into his chest. Almost lovingly, he whispered in her ear, "*What did you do to her, bitch? Tell me.*" The words hung in the air, a soft, menacing echo. Utterly compelling.

Prue's jaw dropped. The Voice. Oh gods, sweet Sister!

Blood suffusing her cheeks, the Technomage Primus of Sybaris answered like an obedient child. "Benchmark measurements first. Then one full battery of tests. A light sedative after to make her sleep. That's all."

"*What was next?*"

The air in the chamber began to swirl. Instruments clattered on the benches, sheets of transplas fluttered like large-winged insects. Prue shivered.

The Technomage wrapped her hands around Erik's forearm and dug her nails in.

"*And next?*" he repeated, tightening his grip a fraction.

The woman's eyes bulged. "Another two batteries of tests, to triangulate. Then—" She choked, clamping her lips shut.

"*After that? Tell me.*"

Merciful Sister, the instant he heard, he'd kill her. And afterward, he'd never forgive himself. Frantically, Prue turned her head, looking for the red tube. Shit, where—? Ah, there, near the door. She scrabbled it up in both hands.

"V-vivisection," said the Technomage at last, as hoarsely as if Erik had reached a big fist down her throat and ripped the word straight out of her shrinking soul. Well, in a sense, he had. Because this was the Voice, exactly as he'd described it to her. Gods, it was true.

All of it.

A heartbeat of awful, frozen silence.

A tygre growl rose from deep in Erik's chest. The muscles in his forearm flexed and the Technomage's face went purple. As he gripped her chin with his other hand, his lips pulled back in a snarl, and everything that wasn't tied down in the room went flying up to the ceiling.

38

Prue lurched to her feet and shoved the end of the red tube against the other woman's wrist, right over the semicircular imprint she'd made with her teeth. She gripped the tube hard and squeezed. Something hissed, and abruptly, the Technomage's eyes rolled back in her head. She went limp in Erik's arms.

Prue touched his shoulder. "Let her go, love." She smiled shakily. "I have to touch you, hold— *Please.*"

The fury died in his eyes. "Gods, yes," he said, in a voice like gravel. Objects wavered uncertainly in the air, but when he looked up and frowned, they descended in a decorous fashion, floating toward the floor.

Without a moment's hesitation, Erik opened his arms and the Technomage fell to the floor with a meaty thud. Her skull bounced.

Erik stepped over her body and caught Prue up in an embrace so fierce her ribs felt bruised. Gods, it was wonderful. He was saying her name over and over, as if it were the only word he knew. She buried her face in his warm, bare shoulder and breathed him in with great gulps.

"Sweetheart." He stroked her hair and set her back a little. "We have to get out of here. Show me your hands."

When she did so, he grunted. "Leather," he said. "And what are these wires for? I've never seen any— Ow!" He snatched his fingers back and blew on them. "They burned me!"

"She said they were dampers." Prue shot him a glance from under her lashes. "For my air Magick."

He was frowning down at her shackles. "But you don't have any Magick."

"That's what I told them," said Prue, as gently as she could. "But you do. Which is why the wires caused you pain."

Erik drew the knife at his waist. It had a long, wicked blade with an edge that glittered in the light. "Yes, I know," he said absently. "Hold out your hands, sweetheart, and keep very still."

Prue obeyed, fixing her eyes on his face. If she looked down, she'd imagine the vivisection, the first slice, the first scream. "Why didn't you tell me?" She had no right to feel hurt. She'd refused pointblank to believe in the Voice. What would make him think she'd believe this?

"I only found out the full extent of it—*don't move, I said*!—a few hours ago. There."

The leather bindings fell away. Prue stripped the wires off and tossed them to the bench, already feeling better on a number of levels.

When she turned back, Erik was weighing the blade in his hand and staring thoughtfully at the Technomage, lying sprawled at their feet. "How did you get those cuts?"

"What?"

He touched her cheek, her neck, with his gentle fingertips. "Here. Someone slashed you."

"Oh, that." Sweet Sister, she had to think for a minute. "That was the laundry men." When he raised a brow, she added, "The kidnappers."

"Hmm," said Erik, returning his attention to the limp form of the Technomage. "They'll keep. What was in that tube? Will it kill her?"

Prue rubbed her wrists, considering. "I don't think so. She said it caused paralysis." Every muscle protesting, she knelt next to the woman and peeled back an eyelid. *See how you like it, bitch*, she thought, enjoying every second without shame.

"Well, well." Prue sat back on her heels. "She's awake in

there and she's terrified." She let Erik pull her up, back into his arms. "Let's go."

"Yes." Swiftly, he pressed a kiss to her lips, fierce and hot and full of promise. "I love you, Prue. Don't you dare forget it." A pause while he stared intently into her face, as if cataloging her features. "From here on, don't speak unless I tell you. Complete silence, all right?"

She barely had time to nod before he slung an arm around her waist and half lifted, half carried her into the passage at a rapid jog trot. The door at the farther end was wedged open with a pile of thick books. It looked ordinary enough, but something in the immediate vicinity reeked like an abattoir. Erik went through first. A few seconds later, he beckoned. Gripping his hand, Prue pinched her nose shut with her fingers and slid through the gap.

Holding a finger to his lips, he drew her over to a dark curtain and pulled it aside to reveal a set of bookcases. With the utmost caution, he tugged until the shelves moved noiselessly aside. A rich man's study, it looked like, though all she could see was the merest slice of it.

Apparently satisfied, Erik drew his blade, widened the space and stepped through, Prue right on his heels. The room smelled pleasantly of furniture polish, ink and flowers, undercut by the stale blood stink from the secret passageway. When Prue pushed the bookcase with a careful finger, it slid into place without a sound. Erik nodded his approval and reached for her hand.

He pointed to tall, arched windows that framed the garden vista. Early morning sunlight streamed through the glass, illuminating the jewel tones in the carpets and gleaming on the patina of well-cared-for wood. Their bare feet made no noise on the plushy rugs, but glancing over her shoulder, Prue noticed they'd left impressions in the deep pile as if they'd tracked through damp grass.

On the wide desk were three trays, all containing papers, an ink block carved from what she suspected was the finest grade of marly jade from Trinitaria and a matching brush. Everything was aligned with finicky precision.

Intrigued, Prue tiptoed closer, but Erik tugged her back to the windows, his eyes bright. When Prue followed his gaze, she sagged with relief. Windows were a vulnerable point in any wealthy household. Naturally, they were locked—but from the inside. How very thoughtful.

The click of the key turning sounded very loud in the quiet room, almost as if it had an echo.

Prue turned her head, meeting the flat black gaze of the man who stood in the doorway.

She gasped. Smoothly, but with astonishing rapidity, the man's hand rose, holding a sleek metal object with a bulbous nose and a handle that fit snugly in the palm.

"Down!" roared Erik, and what felt like a mountain hit her in the small of the back, bearing her down behind the desk.

A sizzling beam of light crackled through the space they'd just vacated.

Immediately, Erik rolled away. With one hand, he seized the tray of papers nearest the edge of the desk and flung it across the room.

More crackling shots and the tiny *whuff* of papers disintegrating. Then a strange smell—a combination of scorched rug and something Prue couldn't identify, acrid and somehow metallic, as if the air itself was burning. Out of the corner of her eye, she saw Erik grab the ink block.

"Come out," said the man, his voice soft and even. "The master will wish to see you."

"Fuck you," growled Erik, rising silently to a crouch.

From under the desk, Prue could see the man's boots, scuffed at the toes. He'd been dressed in unremarkable livery, a serviceable black. The master? Her spine crawled.

The boots moved two steps closer and stopped. "This is a lasegun," said the servant, still in that oddly emotionless voice. "It is set to heavy stun, not to kill. Come out and I won't hurt you. But there is no escape."

"There are two of us and only one of you." Watching Erik inch toward the far side of the desk, Prue projected her voice to cover any noise. "And we are not so fussy."

She had the impression the man was smiling, even though she couldn't see his face. "I do not fear death," he said simply. "Why should I fear you?" He came another pace closer.

Erik rose from behind the desk like an avenging god and

hurled the heavy ink block, straight at the man's head. He followed it up by lunging across the room in a long, flat dive.

The block missed, striking their enemy's shoulder, so that his arm flew up and back. The lasegun discharged into the wall, scoring a long black line across what was undoubtedly a priceless tapestry.

But Erik didn't miss. He cannoned into the man in a driving tackle, sweeping his legs out from under him. They hit the floor with a jarring crash, Erik's more than two hundred pounds of fury, muscle and bone on top.

Her mouth open, Prue saw his arm draw back and his big fist connect with the point of the servant's chin, every ounce of pent-up rage and terror behind it.

A sickening crack and the man's head lolled to the side, his hands falling limp, flopping on the rug like pale, upturned flowers.

Shakily, Prue rose to lay a hand on Erik's heaving shoulder. "Is he dead?"

"Shit!" Erik fumbled under the man's collar. He let out a whistling breath. "No, but I think I broke his jaw." Slowly, he got to his feet, rubbing his knuckles. "Let's get out of here before he comes 'round."

"Gods, yes." Prue darted to the window and pushed it open. As she threw a leg over the low sill, she said, "You don't want to meet the 'master.'"

Still shuddering, she stood blinking on a flagged path, her face lifted to the clear pale blue of the sky. How strange. She'd thought she'd never see it again. "What time is it?" she asked, as Erik took her hand and set off, striding out so rapidly she had to trot to keep up. "And where are we?"

"A couple of hours after dawn, I'd say. And we're on the Leaf of Nobility. Can you go faster, sweetheart? I have a bad feeling."

At any other time, Prue would have enjoyed the beauty of the palazzo's garden, but now the curved, jinking paths were no more than irritating obstacles. Plunging indiscriminately across lawns and flower beds, they left wholesale destruction in their wake.

"You didn't use the Voice," said Prue.

"Didn't think of it until I was almost on top of him." Erik slanted a bright blue gaze her way. "And then it was too late." He inspected his bruised knuckles. "Anyway, I enjoyed the hell out of hitting him, the slimy little bastard. Though I may have overdone it."

He unlatched the wooden gate at the bottom of the garden and they stepped into an alley, a narrow back track for servants. "Who's *them*?" he asked suddenly. "You said you told *them* you had no Magick. Was he one? The servant?"

"No." Prue glanced back over her shoulder. More lights shone in the windows of the palazzo, but every now and then, one of them was obscured by a shadow, as if something impenetrably black had passed before it. It was descending from floor to floor. Soon it would reach the study.

Prue broke into a jerky trot, envying Erik his long legs. "He said he's . . . the Necromancer," she panted. "He's not a man. Like a dark cloud . . . of evil. Darkness."

She slanted a sideways glance at him, her breath rasping in her throat. "I'm not mad."

Erik's answering smile was grim. "After what I've just seen?" He huffed out a laugh without a trace of humor in it. "Fuck, after what I've done? I made a table dance in the air, right under the ceiling. I sang a demon to sleep. This"—he glanced back over his shoulder—"this is the task the gods gave me. I'd believe in anything now, up to and including death Magick."

They passed one palazzo, then another. A stout woman carrying a basket walked by, ostentatiously averting her eyes from Prue's precariously fastened garment. But although she sniffed and tossed her head, she took a lingering look at Erik's chest from under her lashes. A man pushing a delivery cart grinned, whistling softly from between his teeth.

"In here." Erik unlatched a spotlessly white gate.

Breathing heavily, Prue stared into the fanatical neatness of the garden beyond. Surely she knew this place? "Where are we going?"

"I've got a skiff moored at the water stairs here."

Prue clamped her lips shut on a giggle. If she started she wouldn't stop. "Do you know whose palazzo this is?"

"No," said Erik. "And I don't bloody care."

"The Queen's Money lives here and I doubt he'll like—"
Over Erik's shoulder she watched a dark cloud rise to drift
over the tall roofs and obscure the sun. It floated and spun, as
if it were looking, searching . . .

"*Holy Sister!*" She clutched Erik's arm. "Look! He's coming! The Necromancer!"

Erik whirled to follow her gaze. "Fuck!" Without ceremony, he shoved her bodily through the gate. "Get down to
the water stairs. Can you pole a skiff?"

"No, no!" Prue set her feet. "It's not me he wants, it's *you!*"

Erik stared. "Me?"

From farther down the alley came a thin scream, abruptly
cut off, followed by a soundless vibration, like the silent
laughter of a thunder demon. Gods, the stout woman! The
bright morning grew dark. At Prue's elbow, a touchme bush
whimpered and died in a burst of brown rot.

Prue grabbed Erik's arms and shook, not that he moved so
much as an inch. She fairly danced with impatience. "He said
I was the bait. For you, Erik. For your air Magick! Oh gods, I
can *smell* him!"

Erik had gone pale to the lips, but he glared at the shadow
racing over the rooftops, its edges spread like the wings of a
gigantic corpsebird. "All right. If it's me he wants, I'll keep
him busy. You run, Prue. *You run.*"

The Voice compelled her feet to move. Prue covered her
ears with both hands. She dug her bare toes into the grass,
concentrating on the cool blades brushing her soles. "Forget
it," she gritted.

Erik growled, picked her up and hustled her into a thick
stand of ticklewhisker bushes.

"Very sweet," said an odiously familiar voice. The Necromancer glided toward them across the green velvet of the
lawn, leaving a trail of scorched brown grass in his wake.
"So . . ." The cowled head tilted to the side, the gesture nag-
gingly familiar. "You are the air wizard. Perfect."

Erik folded his arms. An angry wind played with the foliage of the garden, tossing it about. "Perfect for what?"

"For my private use."

The Necromancer hurtled forward, but not toward Erik.
Prue squeaked. The dark arms elongated, reaching for her.

With a roar, Erik flung out a hand and a small tornado erupted in front of the ticklewhisker bushes. Clods of earth, twigs and leaves whirled in a mad dance.

With a dark chuckle, the Necromancer fell back. It had been a feint. "You know nothing," he said, contempt thick in the toneless voice. "Less than nothing. You are a child."

Erik bared his teeth and the tornado subsided. "The young have strength, energy." His lip curled, and his voice dropped. "But you're old, aren't you? Old and tired."

"With age comes experience. Knowledge." The Necromancer swelled, his substance remaining dense and dark. "I am strong now, well fed." He executed a mocking travesty of a bow. "My apologies. That is why I was late."

Prue stared, horror turning her blood to ice.

"I only took the merest sip," murmured the Necromancer, greasy as an illicit fondle, "but you wouldn't believe how the Technomage screamed. Of course, that was only on the inside. Because, thanks to you, my dears, she couldn't move a muscle."

Gods, she was going to vomit. Here and now. Prue clapped a hand over her mouth.

The Necromancer sighed. "A remarkably irritating woman, the Primus. It's a pity she's so useful. I had to leave, ah, a portion." He brightened. "But the taste was worth the wait. I promised myself that particular indulgence a long, long time ago, and I simply couldn't rush it. Sorry."

Prue swallowed hard. "And your servant? He said he didn't fear death."

"Nasake?" Another good-humored chuckle. "He does now." The Necromancer made a repulsive sound, as though he'd licked his lips.

"Don't tell me," said Erik. "You included the Doorkeeper."

"A cultivated taste, demons. They're a trifle, ah, thorny."

Erik's fists clenched. "Well, you're not having Prue. Over my dead body."

"Oh, it won't be *dead*," drawled the Necromancer, and Prue saw Erik's eyes widen in appalled comprehension. Beads of sweat popped on his brow.

She thrust the bushes aside and stepped forward. "It's not a problem," she said. "Because he can't touch me without those damper things." Trying desperately to hold her nerve, she stared deep into the fathomless darkness of the hood. *"Can you?"*

The Necromancer waved a dismissive hand. "Only Shaitan knows what you really are. Some mongrel aberration, I imagine. Fortunately, you're not worth soiling my hands."

Without any preamble, he rose and dropped over Erik like a filthy blanket woven of purest evil.

39

The pain of the Necromancer's touch was indescribable. The *wrongness* of it seared like fiery claws, raking and gouging at the core of what formed the essential Erik, a unique and beloved creation of the gods.

His guts heaved, his entire body rebelled, and a blast of air Magick burst from him with a sound like a thunderclap. The concussion made his ears ring, but it flung the Necromancer back into a bed of bright summer blooms. They crisped and died.

Slowly, Erik got to his feet, never taking his eye from the threat. "Prue?"

"Y-yes?" Her voice came from behind him.

"Get clear. Quick, love."

"All right." A shuddering breath. The rustle of bushes as she retreated a short distance.

Erik flexed his shoulders. Magick was instinctive, or so Purist Nori had said. It seemed he did best if he worked from his emotions, the more primitive the better. Well then . . .

"So much for finesse." The Necromancer floated a few feet above the ruined garden bed, his outline contracting and expanding as if he breathed. "You're an amateur, boy."

Erik brought the image of Prue as he'd found her to the forefront of his mind. The expression on her face when she first looked up from the floor, the flash of incredulous hope, her wounded soul shining out of her eyes. So cruelly used, so small—so indomitable. Gods, a woman in a million!

Growling, he let the rage boil over him, submerged himself in it, relished it, bathed in it. The Voice erupted from his chest, louder than thunder. The air cracked from top to bottom with invisible lightning, winds howled, trees moaned and creaked, their branches thrashing. Erik tracked the movement of the manic silvery flows all about him, sustaining the note as they grew darker and darker, until each was edged with the nimbus-purple of storm.

By the Horned Lord, *yes!*

But the Necromancer laughed, folding his arms. Flickers of a familiar acid green sparkled over his shadowy form, and the flows parted around him, leaving him untouched.

Cursing, Erik flung out a hand. A furious purple cable of air arced across the garden and coiled itself around a stone sundial set in the center of a parterre bed. With a sucking groan, the sundial came free of the soil and shot across the garden with blinding speed.

The Necromancer skipped aside at the last moment, but the stone edge caught him across one hip before thudding to the ground, half buried in the lawn.

Crouching behind a cedderwood tree, Prue was almost certain she heard the crunch of bone, their adversary's sudden intake of breath. The Necromancer's outline wavered and a garden bench came hurtling from the opposite direction, striking him squarely across the small of the back with a sickening crack. Emitting a strangled scream, he spun head over heels in the air.

Cautiously, Prue came to her feet. Erik stood, panting, sweat matting the hair on his chest, the talisman gleaming like pale ivory.

When she would have moved forward, he held out an arm, barring her progress. "Not yet."

"Siblings preserve us!"

Prue whirled around. Behind her stood three servants, their faces white as paper. A weather-beaten man with a spade over his shoulder and two girls carrying stout wicker baskets. Probably on their way to the kitchen garden.

The man took a pace forward. "What are ye doin' here? What the hell *is* that thing?"

"*Shit*!" said Erik.

Her stomach curdling with dread, Prue turned. The Necromancer was regrouping, steadying, his shadow spreading like a foul stain over the garden. "I am a god." The sexless voice was bell-clear. "What makes you think you can kill *me*, boy?"

Erik clenched his fists. "Someone has to."

One of the girls gave a stifled shriek. "Sister, it's a demon!"

Without moving her head, Prue said, "Run! If you value your life, run! Get help."

An empty basket bounced past her feet. The spade hit the path with a clang. Three sets of feet beat a hasty tattoo up the path.

The Necromancer swelled horribly, pulsing. "I am Death," he hissed, and this time, it sounded like simple truth rather than melodrama. "I am made of its emptiness, as near dead as makes no difference." He swooped closer and Erik inhaled deeply, setting his feet and raising his hands again. The winds rose, shrieking. Then they reversed, creating a howling vortex.

The Necromancer's sibilant chuckle raised all the hairs on Prue's body. "Forget it, wizard. You cannot pull the air from my lungs. There is none."

Prue wrapped her arms around the cedderwood and hung on with all her strength.

The darkness drifted forward, inexorable as the slow advance of black ice down a mountain. Erik's hands moved and a cloud of dirt and twigs and crushed flowers whirled all around him.

Chuckling, the Necromancer surged straight through it. "At last," he hissed. "All is accomplished. You are mine—*mine*!" Her eyes stretched wide with horror, Prue watched him inflate, expanding until he was twice Erik's height and width.

He swooped. Erik stumbled backward and fell.

The Necromancer cried out, a high eldritch shriek of triumph and greed, but Erik roared.

She'd never heard anyone make a noise remotely like it

before—a dreadful, full-throated bellow of utter revulsion, terror and pain. The sound catapulted her into action. Before she knew it, Prue had seized the gardener's abandoned spade and darted forward.

She was too focused to waste her breath on a shout. With a grunt of effort, she set her feet and swung the spade like a scythe, straight down at the writhing form of the Necromancer. The edge of the implement sliced into his dark substance and connected with something both fleshy-soft and solid. *Thunk!*

The Necromancer gave a choking cry. Prue growled her satisfaction and stepped forward for another swing. As she did so, her bare foot came into contact with the trailing edge of the Necromancer's shadow.

Completely without warning, Erik was wrestling on the grass with a plump little man with a fringe of white hair, his spectacles all askew.

Prue's jaw dropped. Time slowed, and stopped.

The man turned his head, his faded blue eyes boring into her, burning with hatred. "Should have killed you, bitch."

Erik recovered almost immediately. Wrapping his big hands around the man's throat, he got to his feet, hauling the small, limp figure with him. "Fuck!" he grunted, staring, "I know you."

His brow furrowed, he set the other man on his feet, looming over him, all muscle and power, his broad chest still heaving with exertion. "You're, you're . . ."

The Queen's Knowledge bared his teeth. "Death," he said, snatching Erik's blade from the scabbard at his waist. In a single swift motion, he shoved it hard under Erik's ribs and wrenched it out with a cruel twist of the wrist.

"No," whispered Prue, light-headed with terror. "No."

The Knowledge laughed, high-pitched and breathy.

Erik's eyes went wide, then blank. He tried to speak, but blood bubbled on his lips. With an enormous effort, he turned his head toward Prue and half raised a hand.

"Erik," she said, but no sound came out.

He swayed, steadied, then fell full length on the torn-up lawn.

The Knowledge pounced, his elbow drawn back for another thrust.

"*No-ooo!*" The spade struck him in the back of the head with a hideous, bone-cracking clang. "No!" shrieked Prue, advancing, berserk with rage and grief and terror.

The Knowledge reeled back and scrambled to his feet. When he touched the back of his head, his fingers came away bloody.

Another step. "No!" *Clang!*

Holding his arms over his head, the Knowledge scrambled backward toward the low wall at the end of the garden. His mouth worked as if he were about to spit, but Prue was exalted by her fury. She gave him no respite.

"Kill . . ." she panted. *Clang!* "Kill you!" *Clang!*

His back to the wall, the queen's minister made a last desperate grab for the shaft of the spade. One eye was purple, half-closed, and his glasses had disappeared. They glared at each other, nose to nose.

The Necromancer's gaze shifted to something over Prue's shoulder. "Look, dear, he's dying." When he spat out a tooth, his bloody spittle sprayed Prue's cheek.

Her guts iced over. Oh gods, no, no, no . . .

With shocking suddenness, the Necromancer strained against her. He was an old man, but he was a man nonetheless, ruthless and utterly desperate. He ripped the spade from her grasp, but before he could swing it, Prue struck upward, hitting him over the heart with the heel of her hand, bending her knees and putting the strength of hip, thigh and shoulder into the blow, the way Walker had taught her. The impact rang bright bells of pain all through her body, but the Knowledge staggered backward, his arms flying. The low wall caught him behind the knees and he wavered for an instant, before disappearing with a splash.

Out of the corner of her eye, Prue thought she glimpsed blue forms cutting through the water, but she couldn't care because she was sprinting across the grass, back to Erik.

She reached him in a stumbling rush, falling to her knees at his side. "Erik, *Erik!*"

Vaguely, she was aware of voices, the rapid thud of many feet approaching, but Erik's pale face filled her whole world. He was blue to the lips, his eyes half-lidded and glassy with pain. "P-Prue." It was no more than a whisper.

Instead of wasting words, Prue lifted the bloodstained hand he'd clamped against his side and pressed the heels of both her hands against the wound.

Someone crouched beside her. "Here." Holding a bundled-up shirt, calloused hands joined hers, applying steady pressure.

"Can't . . . breathe," rasped Erik.

"Sshh," said Prue. "Don't talk."

The man at her side said, "A healer's coming, Mistress. Hold on."

"N-no air," said Erik. The ghost of a smile curved his lips and his bloody fingers fumbled for her wrist. ". . . funny." His touch on her skin felt like ice.

Prue leaned down until her breath stirred the matted blond lock that fell over his forehead. "You listen to me, Erik Thorensen. You will not die. Do you hear me? I. Will. Not. Permit. It."

"B-bossy."

"I will follow you to the depths of hell and drag you back. Got it?"

Erik lay quietly, and she had the sense he was gathering himself for some final effort. She wanted to scream her rage and frustration into his face. *No, no—a thousand times no!* But she didn't. Instead, she set her jaw and pressed the reddening shirt harder against his side.

His eyes opened, intently blue on hers. "It's not . . . so bad." An otherworldly smile that chilled her blood. "Done . . . it . . . before." He hissed, trembling under her hands. "Shit, it hurts."

Prue laid her cheek against his. "Shut up," she whispered. "You're making it worse."

"Promised I'd . . . p-pay . . . my debt." Slowly, so slowly, he lifted his fingertips to brush her jaw. "P-pretty Prue. So . . . s-sorry. Love . . . you."

His eyes glazed, then cleared, but his attention had shifted to someone behind her. "I'm here, Lord," he said clearly.

His eyelids fluttered, then fell shut. Something rattled in his throat. Relaxing beneath her, he went still, his hand falling to the grass at his side.

"Mistress?" said the man.

Prue ignored him.

"Mistress, I'm sorry. He's gone."

❦

Gods, she was a terrier, his Prue. Snapping orders, having him carried into the palazzo of the Queen's Money. All the time, she kept her small, strong hands shoved hard against him, staunching the wound.

Refusing to let him go.

You did well, said a huge voice in his ear. *She loves you truly.*

How bittersweet, how appropriate, to be so intensely conscious of the transience of life now, in its very last moments. "Yes," said Erik sadly, "she does. I was lucky." He squared his shoulders, even though he couldn't bear to look into the bright nimbus that was the Horned Lord. "But in all else, I failed You."

The sense of another presence. Star-dappled fingers stroked his filthy hair. *How so*? asked the Lady.

Watching a flood of tears wash Prue's aquamarine eyes with brilliance, Erik flinched. The room below was a huge kitchen. The household staff had laid him out on the scrubbed wooden table like a corpse.

"I didn't save the city," he said. "And I was so blind and stupid I didn't see the entirety of your gift until the air Magick slapped me in the face. As for Inga . . ." He choked. "I tried so hard not to think of what I did, not to dwell . . . But in my heart, I've always known what You would require of me." He couldn't bear to look at Prue, to acknowledge her grief or his own. He wanted to throw his head back and howl. "My death is the price of atonement, and I will pay it."

Bah! said the Lady, and Her dark velvet voice rolled like thunder. *A fine opinion you have of divine love, let alone divine justice.*

So fucking what? he thought savagely. *What does it matter to You what I think?*

Screwing up his eyes, he caught Her gaze deliberately, falling into an infinity of cold, starry space. "Great Lady, You gave me the Voice," he said, every word falling diamond hard into a tingling silence. "A power no living being should have over another, a burden only a god is strong enough to carry.

The rest of the Magick, I could learn to handle, but that . . . Hell, I'm"—he caught himself—"*was*—only human."

Clenching his fists, he waited for the final obliteration, his gaze filled with Prue. His last sight as a living man. She was bedraggled and bloodstained, her eyes puffy and her nose red, the tied-on garment hiked up over one smooth thigh. A dark-robed healer was busy at the site of the wound, which left Prue free to clutch the horn talisman in one small fist. With her other hand, she grasped Erik's chin. "Hold on," she was muttering, over and over, her voice low and urgent, "hold on to me. I'm here. I won't let you go."

Erik has You there, My love. Unexpectedly, the Horned Lord laughed. In the sound was the bubbling of a mountain brook, the whisper of green grass in the wind, the screeching cry of a bird of prey. *Though I grant You, his songs were well worth the hearing.*

The Dark Lady growled Her displeasure, and despite himself, Erik's bones turned to water, dropping him hard to his knees.

But in all else, Erik, you are mistaken, the Lord went on. *Look.*

Erik stared down the long, bright tunnel as the kitchen door banged back and a new crowd of people surged in to join the dozen or so already there. Foremost among them was the Queen's Money, clad in a brocade dressing gown, his face stiff with outrage. Erik strained to hear, but sounds were growing muffled, far away. When Prue spoke a few crisp sentences, the Money's expression changed, at first blank with shock, then intent and worried. Gripping his gnarled hands together, the gardener nodded in emphatic agreement to whatever Prue had said.

The Queen's Money turned to a couple of hard-eyed men wearing short swords. Erik caught only a couple of words. "Fetch Rhiomard and his guards . . . Search . . . palazzo . . . Careful . . . basement."

The evidence is there, murmured the Horned Lord. *They will find it. The Money is nothing if not efficient. The City is less so, but nonetheless, he will organize divers. Caracole will be saved, the Leaf of Nobility healed in time.*

The Lady's breath blew over Erik in a sweet gust. Her hand

closed over the nape of his neck. *The kit you freed will grow to be a patriarch of seelies. His progeny will be legion.*

"I knew You'd like them," he murmured, his brain gone all muzzy with the comfort of Her touch. Death wasn't so bad. Smiling, he closed his eyes, feeling his soul begin to drift, the moorings loosen . . .

No, that wasn't right . . . was it?

Something small and persistent tugged at him, relentless as a biteme. Mumbling his irritation, he tried to brush it away, but it refused to be dismissed. "I am here," it said, hanging on grimly. "I won't let you go."

Erik forced his eyes open. His view of the kitchen had shrunk, no more than a keyhole through which he saw Prue pick up his limp hand, wrap his fingers around the Lord's horn and hold them closed with her own.

Very gently, the Lady said, *You have paid your debt for Inga, Erik, paid it in years of buried, festering guilt. You are free. All that is left is to beg Prue's forgiveness. Only then will you heal.*

Erik's head rolled. "No, that can't be right. What I did—"

Is forgiven, rumbled the Horned Lord. *Do not presume to question.*

"Why not?" said Erik, with a tired grin. "It's not as though You're going to kill me—again."

The Lord's chuckle reverberated around the inside of his skull, rattling Erik's brains as though they were dice. *Incorrigible,* said the god, shaking His great horned head. *Stubborn and brave. Which is why you must choose once more. There is work still for you to do, Erik Thorensen—if you wish it.*

Choose? Fuck, he was so weary. Why wouldn't They leave him be?

"Stay with me, Erik." Prue's biteme voice, right in his ear. "I've got you. Darling, darling—" She broke off on a gulping sob like a child's.

Erik stirred. "Not without her."

Of course. Was the Lady laughing at him? *There is a place in the Pattern even for a skeptic like a null witch.*

A null—? Never mind, he'd worry about it later.

His heart banged painfully behind his ribs. "And the Magick?"

That was Our gift, said the Lord. *As was the Voice. They are yours.*

A slow tide of compressed agony washed over the left side of Erik's chest, bringing with it a deathly chill. "T-tell me what You want me to do," he said, his teeth chattering.

No, said the Lady softly. *If We touch the Pattern directly, We alter it.*

The Lord's horn was a glowing ember under his fingers, Prue's frantic grip cold in comparison. With a supreme effort, Erik rallied his forces. "I have a price," he said between his teeth.

You dare to bargain with the gods? The Lord's voice dropped so deep it went beyond the threshold of hearing. Erik felt it only as a vibration in his bones, his skull.

"Take the Voice from me."

Silence.

"I beg You. Take it."

At last, the Lady said, *The curse and the blessing are one, Erik. No more music. Are you sure?*

Erik's chuckle turned to a rasping cough. "Great Lord, long ago, You told me . . . everything has a . . . cost." He fought for breath. "I cannot afford . . . the Voice."

Another silence. Constellations wheeled past while the gods considered, stars lived and died, planets settled in their orbits.

Done, said the Lord, like a great bell.

Close your eyes, little one, whispered the Dark Lady. Huge, slender fingers stroked over his eyelids, his nose, his lips. Something hot and wet plopped onto his temple and rolled into his hair. Erik's breath stopped. A tear?

An enormous force collided with his chest, hammering him into the kitchen table like a body slam from an angry mountain. The agony was all-encompassing, red-hot fists squeezing his lungs until he couldn't find the breath to scream. Shit, shit, shit.

He fought. "Nngh."

"Erik?"

Levering one eye half-open, he grunted.

Prue's shriek of joy was so loud he would have winced if the fists of pain buried deep in his chest had permitted it. As it was, he dared not move a muscle, but he pressed her fingers with his own. Small though the action was, the effort left him exhausted.

"Told you!" she said, turning her head.

Purist Bartelm came into view, accompanied by another Purist, a middle-aged woman. "So you did," he said, but he smiled at Prue. "Now you need to move well away and let me work, Mistress."

Shaking water from his hands, the old wizard dried them on the spotless cloth the woman handed him. "Roll him onto his side," he said to someone out of Erik's line of sight. "And stretch that arm over his head."

His features tightened. "This is going to hurt." He picked up a small, flexible tube and a slim, shiny knife from a metal tray. "Your lung's collapsed and your chest cavity is full of air you don't want."

"Nngh," said Erik. He didn't see how anything could be more painful than what he was enduring now.

Unfortunately, he was wrong.

40

Several centuries and a world of pain later, Erik surfaced, fighting his way out of the murk by slow degrees. His recollections were confused—being stuck with that godsbedamned tube, the astonishing hiss of the air escaping, Prue kissing his cheek, prizing his fingers away from the talisman so she could wash his chest with warm water, a long black period of terrible cold that had him moaning and shuddering, though he clenched his teeth against it.

But none of his memories included the tall, slim woman with the swathes of blazing red hair at her temples who sat placidly by his bed, reading.

It took him three attempts to get her name out. *"Cenda?"*

Her head jerked up, joy turning her eyes to gold. "You're awake! Oh, my dear." Shyly, she bent to brush his cheek with warm lips.

When he tried to speak again, she hushed him, supporting his head so he could sip water from the cup she held for him.

Reading the questions in his eyes, she smiled, and suddenly, she was breathtakingly beautiful. "Yes," she said. "Gray is here too." The smile became wry. "We came with Deiter."

She whisked herself to the door. "Prue's exhausted. She's taking a nap. I'll go wake her."

"D-don't." Gods, was that his voice, so rusty and unused?

Cenda's eyes danced. "She's a terror, your Prue." The fire witch gave a theatrical shudder. "Five-it, she made me promise—the minute you opened your eyes." A final twinkle, and he heard her light footsteps running up a flight of stairs.

No more than three minutes later, Prue hurtled through the door like a small tornado, her hair flying in a great tangle of glossy brown. She wore only a night shift, her arms and legs bare. "Erik!" She skidded to a stop beside the bed, stretched out a hand and let it drop. "You . . . you're . . ."

"Come here," he managed, no more than a husky rasp. "Let me . . . hold you."

Prue stared, and all the breath left her in a shuddering sigh. Her face crumpling, she fell to her knees and laid her head next to his on the pillow. Sobs tore out of her, shaking her whole body, dampening his shoulder.

Erik could do little except stroke her arm with the tips of his fingers and make soothing noises, but something warm and comforting settled inside him, the caress of it like sweet balm soaking into a bruise. Vaguely astonished, he puzzled over it, considering the sensation from every angle. All he could compare it with were the golden memories of childhood—cuddled up with Ma in the big bed while she told stories so outlandish he and his brothers forgot to wriggle and fight, their mouths falling open in wonder. Rolling over and over down a hill covered with warm summer grass, arriving at the bottom in a tangle of sweaty arms and legs, smelling the sweet crush of green and hearing Carl explode with laughter. A dim memory of toddlerhood, his father carrying him home after dark, big arms holding him safe.

Good times. When everything was *right*, completely as it should be, as it was meant to be.

But not in his adult life. Not until now.

Very slowly because of the pain, Erik lifted his hand to rest on Prue's bowed head. "Sshh," he murmured.

One side of his chest still hurt like a bitch. More aches and pains shrieked at him from every limb. He was thirsty again, and now that he came to think of it, hungry.

But none of it mattered. Because this was what peace really was, sweet and easy as a perfumed bath. No fanfare, no fireworks.

It wouldn't last.

The black tendril of apprehension was thin, but persistent, wriggling its way into his consciousness, a suckworm invading his paradise. *Enjoy this while you can*, it hissed. *Because if you want her in your future, she's going to have to know about Inga. And what you did.*

Every muscle in Erik's body tensed. All his various hurts combined in a ghastly chorus, sung fortissimo.

The Lady's voice, echoing in his head like the music of a star. *All that is left is to beg Prue's forgiveness. Only then will you heal.* Fuck, he didn't have the guts. He'd been better off dead, at least the gods had forgiven him.

But then Prue raised a tear-stained face and sniffed. "Erik?" She stroked his jaw. "Love?"

No, the peace of death paled in comparison, not when he could have this. Even if it only lasted 'til she walked out the door, this joy was worth any struggle, any pain. Good, ah, gods, it was good. Blinking drowsily, he tried to smile.

Prue brushed her lips over his stubbled cheek. Drawing back with a shaky smile, she said, "I should leave you to sleep. Purist Bartelm's been very worried."

"Mm. Me too."

"You should have been better almost immediately. If it had been an ordinary man who stabbed you . . ." Her brows snapped together. "But it wasn't, it was *him*." Her lips trembled. "Just as well you're so strong."

"How long have—?"

"Two days and more. It's not far off midnight. Here, take these." She dosed him with four pellets of concentrated healall, washed down with more water.

After swallowing obediently, he asked, "Where—?"

"You're at The Garden, in the Main Pavilion." She gestured at the room. "This is—or was—the Spring Green Parlor on the ground floor." Her straight, dark brows drew together, and for the first time, he noticed the shadows under her eyes, the pallor of her skin. She went on, "I had them bring a bed in here rather than try to get you up the stairs."

It was a big bed, he noted with approval, plenty of room for two. "You," he said, wrapping his fingers around her wrist, "sleep here." He didn't intend to waste a moment of this precious, fragile peace.

Prue shook her head. "I'll jostle you."

"No," insisted Erik, tightening his grip. "Not without you."

He frowned, thinking. The words had a familiar ring, important somehow.

"Please?" he said.

Prue capitulated, as he'd known she would, settling carefully at his side, linking their fingers together.

After a few minutes, her breath deepened. She murmured something unintelligible into his neck and fell asleep. Erik lay a little longer, watching the double shadows move on the ceiling, listening to the lap of the dark water in the canal. The pain receded a little. Good stuff that healall.

Eventually, he too dozed off, his brow furrowed.

A day later—or was it two?—he was lying propped up on a pile of pillows, one hand drumming a tattoo on the sheet, frowning. Prue had brought him lunch, then pecked his cheek and departed at a brisk trot, admonishing him to sleep. But hell, he couldn't. The livelihood of an entire company of players depended on him.

The Voice was gone, as if it had never been, an aching absence like a phantom toothache. Deep in his bones, he knew it, though he'd only had the strength to hum a few bars. With a grunt, he squared his shoulders. Not so long ago, he would have been crushed, his life over, but now, although the loss grieved him, he couldn't regret it. Vaguely, he wondered if it would hurt more as his wound healed.

Very likely, but he'd deal with it then. He still had perfect pitch, though he wasn't at all certain it wouldn't drive him to distraction without the Voice to go with it.

But nonetheless, he hadn't realized what an intolerable burden he'd carried until it was taken from him. More a curse than a blessing. He felt . . . lighter . . . cleaner.

With his usual calm, Gray had stepped into a hastily rearranged program and houses had been reasonable, but they couldn't bank on the curiosity factor forever. In any case, Gray's husky tenor was a crowd-pleaser, but not enough to carry an entire production. A grin curved Erik's lips. It had been beyond good to see the other man. Someone whose self-contained good sense and loyalty he could count on. The spurt of humor fled.

Godsdammit, Magick was a chancy thing—fuck, he should know—and now it seemed Gray was mired in it hip-deep as well. A man with a sentient *shadow*? Erik shook his head in disbelief, stopping with a curse when his wound pulled.

He'd had a little time to become accustomed to Cenda before the Unearthly Opera left Concordia, and he'd approved. Not only was she a sweetheart, she was good for his friend. So what if rills of flame sparked from her palms and fiery salamanders danced in her hair? Gray and his fire witch were *mated* in such a way that having seen them together, he couldn't imagine them apart.

But a few hours ago, Gray had strolled into the Spring Green Parlor, followed by a dark replica of himself, and introduced his shadow to Erik, his eyes glinting silver with amusement. Damn him. Erik's skin had pebbled, all the fine hairs rising on the back of his neck.

"Uh," he'd said stupidly, "pleased to meet you."

Shad—gods, it even had a name!—had nodded pleasantly enough, and Erik had been embarrassingly relieved the shadow hadn't offered its hand.

By the Horned Lord, he hoped to hell Gray knew what he was doing. But when he'd asked why they'd come, his friend would not be drawn, merely raising those slanted brows and saying it had been Deiter's idea. Erik rubbed his nose, brooding. The old reprobate never did anything without a reason—unless there was alcohol involved. And gods, the man was a Purist. The irony of it was incredible. Grimly amused, Erik snorted.

The latch clicked and a figure in a shabby robe slipped through the door. Well, well, speak of a demon and he appears.

"Purist Deiter," said Erik. "I've been looking forward to speaking with you."

"Shut up," said the old wizard. Cautiously, he cracked the door and peered out. "You're supposed to be asleep." He closed the door. "All clear. Gods, bossy women make me want to spit."

Framed by a neat gray beard tied off in three plaits, his mouth contorted as if he were about to do just that.

Erik raised a cool brow. "You're talking about my Prue?"

"Her and that daughter of hers and that Rose woman. Not to mention Bartelm. Bah!" The drinker's paunch wobbled beneath the robe.

Erik fought the desire to smile. "Your eyes must be going if you think Bartelm's a female."

"Bartelm's as much an old woman as Nori."

"He saved my life. And Nori showed me how to use my—" Erik broke off. It still felt so strange to say it out loud. "Magick."

"Hmpf." Sinking into a chair by the bed, Deiter scowled. "Yes, well. You don't get to the rank of Purist by being a complete fool." He settled back. "About the Magick—"

"Get me out of here and we'll talk." Erik threw back the sheet and swung his legs to the floor, letting the breath whistle out from between his teeth. That wasn't too bad.

Deiter's brows rose. "Don't you think you'd better dress? You're a lot of interesting colors, man, but you're still, ah, *interesting*." His rheumy gaze roamed the length of Erik's torso in nostalgic appreciation. "Shit, getting old makes the Dark Arts look tempting."

"There's a robe behind the door. Tansy brought it for me."

"She the tasty little morsel with the big eyes and sweet tits?" Deiter tossed the garment over.

Erik grunted an affirmative, concentrating on working his bad arm into a wide sleeve.

The old wizard grinned, watching him struggle. "I think she fancies me, that one."

Fuck, it still hurt to twist his upper body. "Sure, same way she fancies her granda." With a vicious jerk, he sashed the robe around his waist.

"I'm an old man," said Deiter mildly. "You just said so yourself." He rose to hold the door open. "I'll yell for help if you fall. Where are you going, by the way?"

Erik gripped the dresser, testing his legs. He didn't need nursing, he was feeling stronger by the minute. Casting the patiently waiting wizard a dark glance, he said, "Where I belong. To Prue." She'd be pissed with him, but too bad.

The Main Pavilion drowsed in the afternoon sun, silent

and apparently deserted. Erik negotiated the stairs, one determined step at a time, Deiter babbling all sorts of nonsense in his ear—fire Magick, his less than flattering opinion of the gods, pentacles, life and death on a cosmic scale, the future of civilization as he knew it. Erik let it all float past, and with a huff of exasperation, the old man fell silent.

"Fookin' 'ell," whispered a voice from below.

A second's pause, the pattering rush of feet and a small, wiry body cannoned into him, skinny arms wrapping around his waist as far as they'd go.

"Ow! Shit!" Pain lanced into Erik's side and spread in a gleeful red-hot tide. Careful," he grunted. "That hurts."

To his surprise, hard little hands patted his chest, dark eyes studied his face from under impossibly long lashes. "They sed ye was better," said Florien accusingly.

"I am." Lord's balls, the boy cared.

The child snorted. "Ye look like shit."

Unexpectedly touched, Erik grinned and ruffled the dark hair. When the lad glared, smoothing it flat, he felt strangely reassured. His brother Lars had been like that, all swagger and bluff and cheek. His vision blurred for an instant.

Deiter chuckled. "Out of the mouths of babes . . ."

Florien shot the old man a killing glare. "Ain't no fookin' bebbe."

The shifting, transitory world of the theater had been his family for so long, but these feelings were different—warmer, closer, more demanding and exacting. Prue and Florien, even Katrin and Rose. Shit, he was collecting people!

Unperturbed, Deiter stroked his beard. "Lad has promise."

"Don' move, yah? I'll git 'elp."

"There's no need, don't—" But the boy had already darted away toward the kitchen.

Erik growled under his breath. Slowly, he climbed another couple of steps. Gods, he used to take them two at a time. But that was in another life.

He heard Florien's chatter approaching, a feminine voice responding. A moment of shocked silence and Katrin arrived beside him in a flurry of skirts. Wedging a strong young shoulder under his arm, she muttered, "For the Sister's sake, Erik, what are you doing? Mam will kill you."

Erik grinned. "You think?" He liked it when Prue fussed.

"I know," said Prue's daughter, with a rueful twinkle. "Me too probably. All right, lean on me. Where are we going?"

Erik held her blue gray gaze. "Where do you think?" There was a smudge of flour on her cheek. She'd been baking.

"Oh." The faintest tinge of pink crept into her cheeks. "Florien," she said, "see if you can find Mam."

"Yah." The boy trotted purposefully away.

Stiffly, Erik disengaged himself from Katrin. "I'm fine."

"But—"

"*I said I'm fine.*"

Katrin's spine straightened with an almost perceptible snap. "Right," she said coolly. "I'll go ahead. I've got a key."

Erik smiled wryly. Well, hell, he hadn't thought of that, had he? A real fool he would have looked, beating his head on the wrong side of Prue's door. Deiter ambled along beside him, mercifully silent as they negotiated the last few steps, the passage and the entry to her suite.

Her expression studiously blank, Katrin appeared in the doorway of Prue's bedchamber. "I've turned the bed down," she said.

"And very nice too," said Deiter approvingly, peering around her. He prowled into the sitting room and gazed out the window. "Lovely view of the—Lord's balls, the boy's found her." Backing toward the door, he favored Erik with a thin smile. "I'll be off then."

He disappeared.

"Erik?"

"Yes." He sank onto the couch with a grateful sigh.

Katrin clasped her hands over the front of her apron. "Thank you."

He opened an eye. "What for?"

Shyly, she reached out to touch his shoulder. "You saved her."

Erik opened both eyes. "If it wasn't for me," he said grimly, "your mother wouldn't have needed saving in the first place. Anyway, she saved me too."

Katrin's eyes misted. "Did she?" She drew up a chair. "I'm not surprised. How?"

Erik hesitated. "She was . . . there, that's all. When I

needed her." She'd refused to let him go, holding his fading soul captive with the power of sheer, bloody-minded love. The irresistible force and the immovable object.

"Oh." Katrin wiped away a tear. "Do you love her?" she said abruptly.

"You've asked me that before."

Her jaw firmed. "I'm asking it again. There were a few hours . . . Bartelm thought we might lose you after all." She fiddled with the edge of her apron. "I saw her face."

Erik leaned forward to lay his hand over hers. "Yes," he said simply. "I love her and I always will."

All the breath left Katrin in a gusty sigh. Her soft blue eyes went wide and starry. "Thank the Sister."

Something clenched in his chest, and it had nothing to do with his wound. "Don't be grateful too soon," he said.

"I know." Another tear trickled over her cheek. "You'll take her away with you." She sprang to her feet and took a couple of restless steps, skirts rustling. "But if she's happy . . ." Katrin swallowed hard. "That's all that matters."

Erik opened his mouth and closed it again. Reassurance would be a lie when he had no idea of what lay ahead. The little boy in him hoped desperately for forgiveness, absolution, but the man was certain it was too much to ask. Far too much.

The door opened.

"What do you think you're doing, Erik Thorensen?" Prue skewered him with a blue green glare.

Erik lifted his chin, fighting not to lapse into a besotted smile. "I came for my clothes," he said coolly. His eye fell on the hands Prue had placed on her hips and everything within him went hunter-still. Silver and aquamarine circled each wrist.

He raised his gaze to Prue's. "On second thoughts . . ." he growled. The air thickened, he could see the sparkle of it. Experimentally, he sent a flow swirling toward her to flirt with her hair, brush her cheek.

Katrin gave a funny little gasp. "I'll be off then," she said, making for the door, pausing only to drop a kiss on her mother's cheek. "Be happy," he heard her murmur. The door closed softly, the lock clicking home.

Prue cleared her throat. "You should be in bed."

Erik bared his teeth. "Not without you." Pleased to the

marrow of his bones with his new skill, he wafted his little breeze over her shoulder and down over her breast, darkly delighted when her nipples beaded up. He nodded at the silver cuffs. "You're wearing them."

"Yes, I—" Prue broke off, wetting her lips.

"Come here, sweetheart."

"You're in no condition—"

"I'll be the judge of that." Weaving the ribbons of air into a thicker band, he wrapped it around her waist and tugged her close. "Kiss me."

"You're mad," she grumbled, but she bent to give him her smiling lips.

Ah, so sweet. One kiss at a time, Erik lured her in, until he had her down on the couch beside him, sprawled over his lap, that tender, carnal mouth all his to plunder and adore.

When he finally let her up for air, she looked dazed, her hair mussed and her lips swollen. Gods, he loved that expression, innocence debauched. "No," she whispered. Then more firmly, sitting up. "No."

Erik pressed a kiss to her palm. "Don't say no to me, Prue, not while you're wearing my cuffs."

"But Erik, you've only just—"

"See what you did." He gestured at his lap, where his cock reared, fighting to be free of the concealing robe.

Prue licked her lips and the robe twitched. "Oh dear," she murmured. "That looks . . . uncomfortable." She slanted him a sparkling glance, the mischief still underpinned with a touch of anxiety. The dimple quivered and his heart squeezed hard with love and lust.

"It is," he said, trying not to pant. And waited.

Prue frowned. Then she folded her arms and stuck out that stubborn chin. "I refuse to hurt you," she said.

Every physical sensation was magnified unbearably by emotion—the dull ache of the wound, the sly caress of soft fabric across the sensitive head of his shaft. Godsdammit, he couldn't think straight, helpless as a leaf at the mercy of capricious winds. Overwhelming tenderness buffeted him one way, guilt and apprehension another. For a disconcerting second, he thought he might cry.

Well, hell.

How much more would he have of her? How many more opportunities to create the memories he'd have to live on for the rest of his life? To see love and joy illuminating her sweet face instead of disgust and condemnation?

Clearing his throat, he leaned back, spreading his knees. "I don't want you to hurt me either," he said. "But I'm sure you can think of something."

41

"Mm." Erik licked his glistening fingers, curling his tongue around each digit like a great cat. "You smell so female. And gods, I love the way you taste."

A reminiscent tingle streaked through Prue's belly. She'd loved the way he tasted her. She was still quivering with the silvery force of it when an enormous yawn caught her unawares.

"Go to sleep," he murmured, the dark velvet rumble as intimate as what they'd just shared.

Her hair tangled with his on the pillow, gold and brown, all mixed together. Placing a big warm palm on her stomach, he rubbed, very gently. "Close your eyes now, sweetheart. You need the rest."

So she did.

The dreams tumbled past as fragments—that awful chair, the Technomage, razor-sharp implements in her gloved hands, the Necromancer's toneless voice, evil incarnate. Worst of all, the dreadful noise Erik had made in the back of his throat, the blue of his lips, the big body she loved no more than an empty husk.

But when she jerked and trembled, her eyes flashing open

on a choked cry, he was right there, his muscled warmth spooned around her, his deep voice murmuring reassurance in her ear. Prue pressed her lips to the smooth swell of Erik's biceps and drifted off with a sigh of relief.

This time, her dreams were different, so vivid they were glimpses of an erotic scene in stained glass, bright chips showing what she'd done to him. Like the sun shining through pure color, a warm glow of triumph suffused her soul.

Her pulse thudding in her ears, she'd gone to her knees before him and parted the robe. Sister save her, but he was beautiful, velvet soft and steel hard, roped with a delicate tracery of blue veins.

When she'd run a considering finger from root to tip, his cock had jerked against his belly. "Don't tease," he'd grated.

Her heart singing, she'd raised a cool brow. "Is that an order, Your High and Mightiness?"

Erik almost laughed, she saw his lips twitch. He painted on a scowl, color flying high on his cheeks. "Your mouth," he rumbled. "Give me your mouth." But the fingers in her hair were gentle.

Oh gods. Permission to play.

Prue smiled in her sleep, her breath growing choppy.

Every part of his genitals fascinated her—the dense, velvety head of his shaft, all rosy red and salty sweet with desire; the contrast of the satin smooth skin over a solid, engorged core. The beat of his life throbbed under her tongue, deliciously hot and oh so vulnerable. Cupped in her palm, the furry bundle of his testicles was drawn up tight, his thighs rock hard with tension against her shoulder. Experimentally, Prue slid a finger up and over the seam of his balls and then back over his perineum.

Erik caught his breath. When she added a leisurely lick all around his glans, he hissed and his hips arched.

Sweet Sister, the power of it! Who'd have thought? Prue suppressed the wriggle of delight and set herself to drive him out of his mind, lick by lick, nibble by nibble.

Strong fingers tunneled into her hair, but she refused to be rushed. He tasted like sherbet infused with strong musk, making her tingle, the flavor all male, strangely compelling. Moaning, she pressed her thighs together, compressing the soft, slippery flesh of her nether lips. All she need do was strip off her trews, straddle him and impale herself. He was too far gone to resist.

No, she might hurt him. In any case, she couldn't give up the intoxicating joy of control, not quite yet. The soft, wrinkled collar of his foreskin deserved a specially gentle nip, the heart-shaped head a spiral trail of kitten licks. And there was a sweet spot, beneath, just there . . . When she flicked it with her tongue, he—

Groaned.

As if the heart were being torn from his chest, while his hands urged her into a rhythm and his buttocks tightened with the desire to thrust. In all the time she'd known Erik the Golden, she didn't think she'd heard him make any music as beautiful as that helpless, yearning noise.

Prue bent her head, fisted him from the root and swallowed as much hard flesh as she could manage. The groan dropped an octave, though she wouldn't have thought it possible. Her eyes closed with pleasure, she began to suckle, softly at first, then more firmly. Moisture trickled down her thighs, dampening the trews.

Erik froze beneath her, no longer breathing, every muscle locked.

Prue chuckled, deep in her throat, which made him curse. Then she slowed down, lightening the pressure.

He tugged at her hair. "Godsdammit, woman! Finish me!"

Taking her time, Prue released him. "Ah," she murmured, blowing a thoughtful stream of warm air over his crown, watching the muscles in his stomach contract. "Is that an order too?"

"Nngh!" His teeth clicked together. Vividly blue, his eyes blazed down into hers. "Fuck it, you need a spanking."

Prue's clit tightened into a burning knot, the tiny spasm nearly enough to tip her over, there and then. Gods, she'd never . . .

She swallowed hard, then turned her head to press a breathless kiss to the inside of his wrist. Holding his gaze, she allowed herself a wicked grin, knowing the dimple was quivering in her cheek. "Do you promise, Oh Master?"

A bead of sweat rolled down the strong column of Erik's

neck and lost itself in the golden fur on his chest. His nipples were hard disks, tightly peaked. "Over my knee," he said, his voice gone to gravel. He raised a big hand. "Fingers buried deep inside for your pleasure, while I smack your gorgeous ass 'til it's red. Until you can't help but scream because it's so fucking good."

Prue gurgled.

One more word and she'd explode, right here, kneeling on the rug. Gods! He was still talking, painting wicked, decadent pictures in her head. Slipping a dildo into her ass, clamping her nipples . . .

With more haste than grace, she engulfed him again, ramping up the pressure, applying strong pulling suction, her head bobbing.

"Shit!" Erik's body bowed right up off the couch. "Move, love. If you don't . . . want . . . Ah, gods! Fuck!"

His length rippled against her hard palate, but at the last second, he clamped her head between his hands and jerked her away, ignoring her muffled cry of protest. Ropes of warm, creamy fluid hit her cheek, her neck, splattering her tunic. Prue licked her lips, savoring. Salty as tears, harsh as grief, pungent with masculine passion. The essence of the man, inexpressibly precious because she loved him.

When she looked up, tears stood in Erik's eyes. "Gods, Prue, you're perfect." Fleetingly, she wondered why his smile had a bittersweet edge, but the expression illuminated his face with such pure male beauty that she felt dizzy, her body still thrumming with desire. Taking her hands in his, he came to his feet, and she rose to tuck herself against his side. "Bed."

Still favoring his side, he'd chivvied her into bed. With ruthless dispatch, they stripped the tunic and trews from her together, grinning like idiots. Erik descended on her like a storm, sending the lightning whipping through her with fingers, lips and tongue. Again and again, until she lay limp and sweaty among the tumbled sheets, pleading for mercy.

Gods, it had been incredible. So good, so damn good.

And then . . .

She couldn't believe what he'd done next.

With a gasp, Prue shot bolt upright, her heart pounding. The dream fragmented as she returned to reality. Erik lay beside her, fathoms deep, his hair all mussed, falling over his eyes. He mumbled in an irritated sort of way, reaching out to pat the warm place where she'd been, searching. The bandage over his ribs shone pale against his tawny skin. Grim lines bracketed his mouth where there'd been none before.

"Sshh. I'm here." Prue stroked the back of his hand, avoiding the scabbed knuckles. She shivered, remembering the horrible crack of bone on bone when he'd hit the Necromancer's servant.

Golden brown lashes fluttered. Erik grunted, threw a heavy arm over her thighs and fell back into slumber.

It was evening. They'd slept right through. A single lamp cast a pool of light, the hair-dusted skin of his arms gleaming as if he'd been sprinkled with gold. He must have lit it before he dozed off.

She stared at him. A big, beautiful man, his long limbs sprawled across her bed. More than she'd ever thought she'd have, that was true enough.

But more than just a man.

Erik Thorensen was some principle of nature made manifest. He was destined for a huge cosmic purpose. If Prue McGuire loved him more than life . . . Well, that was completely immaterial.

On some instinctive level, she must have always known it, she thought, her heart aching, but until he'd made love to her with his Magick, she hadn't realized how it would affect *her*.

"One more time," he'd said, shooting her a devilish grin. Rising, he went to lean against the dresser, casually, splendidly naked. "And look, no hands."

Prue had frowned in puzzlement.

Still smiling, Erik exhaled slowly, his fingers moving fluidly as if he were shaping—

"Ooh!" An inquiring breeze wafted over Prue's right breast and her nipple tingled. Another, a little more insistent, curled around her left breast, pushing and tugging, circling her areola as if he were breathing on her delicate flesh, all warm and moist.

"Erik, what are you . . . *doing*?" The last word emerged as a squeak. Invisible currents of air swirled all over her body, stroking, tickling, pleasuring, relentless as the man himself.

His grin became blinding. "What does it feel like?"

Gasping, Prue shot him a glare. "You know very well what— Oh, gods!" She flopped back onto the pillows, boneless. A gentle, inexorable force was pushing her thighs open, fingering her slick folds excruciatingly lightly, nudging her clit.

"Fuck, you're gorgeous." His voice dropped to a purr-growl. "Show me, sweetheart. *Show me.*"

The pressure increased, swirling, pressing, urging her higher and higher. She'd never felt so exposed, so wanton in her life. Nor so desired. His passion was a tangible force, in every possible sense. Prue didn't know whether to laugh, cry or scream. In the end, a thunderous climax pulled all three sounds from her throat.

But now, as she watched him sleep, tears prickled her eyes. Because she knew going with him was inevitable—she just hoped Katrin would forgive her. But she'd never known what it was to love like this, with everything she was and everything she ever could be, with her whole heart and mind and body. She'd always thought it a fairy tale of hope, told to make humdrum lives more bearable.

Easing herself away from under Erik's arm, she padded over to the dresser and picked up her hairbrush, watching him in the mirror.

Yes, she'd be with him when he left Palimpsest—because to live without him would break her. Oh, not at once, but little by little, one tight, bitter shard at a time. Better to wrench herself away from Katrin, knowing her daughter had a bright future with Arkady, filled with family and love and good work, an adult life.

Prue tugged the brush through her hair. She'd never been in a starship, never even seen the Technomage spaceport. To travel to other worlds—Sister, that was an adventure she'd never thought to have.

When Katrin had her first babe—The brush caught on a knot. Erik's reflection blurred into a fuzzy, golden outline. She'd come back. Yes, she would. In the meantime, Rose would be here, Rose who was Katrin's second mother, Prue's best friend, closer than any sister . . .

Very gently, Prue laid the brush down and began to braid

her hair into thick, sensible plaits, as she did every night. She was Prue McGuire. She'd survive this.

Even if it ripped her heart to pieces.

Florien knocked on Prue's door midmorning. "Yer t' come down t' t' kitchen, both o' ye," he said the moment she opened it. His dark eyes flicked from the robe she'd flung on, to Erik, lounging bare chested on the couch behind her. A knowing smirk curled his lips. "Now," he added.

Prue stiffened. "Who told you that?"

"T' old one. Wit' t' three beards."

Prue frowned, nonplussed. Erik gave a great crack of laughter, followed immediately by a curse. When she turned, he had a palm pressed to his side, his brows drawn together. "Deiter," he said, the ghost of a smile still curving his lips. "He means Deiter."

"Was there a 'please' attached anywhere?" Prue asked the boy.

Florien thought about it. "Nah," he said at last.

Prue stiffened. "Well, you go back and tell him—"

Erik's hand landed on her shoulder. "We'll be there. Fifteen minutes." He leaned past her to shut the door in the lad's face.

Prue spun around. "Who does Deiter think he is?" She narrowed her gaze. "More to the point," she said more slowly, "who do *you* think he is?"

With a sigh, Erik patted her bottom. "He's the most powerful Purist I know, for all that he drinks too much." Crossing to the couch, he sat and bent gingerly to pull on his boots. "I don't think he possesses such a thing as a heart, but he doesn't lack for guts." He gave a wry chuckle. "Or gall, for that matter. But Gray and Cenda trust him."

Prue loosed her plait and unraveled it. "Gray's your friend, isn't he?"

"I suppose so." Erik shrugged. "Or the nearest thing to it." His face closed. "I haven't let anyone close since I was a lad." He glanced up. "Only you."

Prue stared, shocked into speechlessness. A couple of words and she was overwhelmed. She'd never thought of herself as special—but to Erik, she was. Who'd have thought it? Before she could gather her scattered wits, he went on, "I doubt there's anyone who knows more about Magick than Deiter, not even Bartelm and Nori put together. If anyone can make sense of"—he paused to clear his throat—"the Necromancer and the seelies, the whole fucking debacle, he can."

"I'll get dressed then."

Erik's eyes brightened. "I'll watch."

Which meant it was thirty minutes, not fifteen, before they entered the kitchen, and Prue still felt flushed, her skin tingling.

Cenda, Gray and Deiter sat at the big table, Katrin pouring cups of a steaming tisane from a large pot. Setting it down, she crossed the room and bent to peck Prue on the cheek. "You all right?" she whispered.

Prue gazed up into her daughter's face, her heart aching. "I'm fine."

"Come and sit." Katrin smiled. "Are you hungry? Let me get you something."

"*Not there!*"

Prue froze, her hand on the back of the chair next to the old wizard's. Deiter's mouth worked. Fumbling in his robes, he produced a small jug, removed the cork with his teeth and took a healthy swig.

"Why not?" Erik had gone completely still at her back, his voice arctic with offense.

Shuddering, the Purist wiped his mouth with the back of his hand. "Because it hurts, that's why."

"Hurts?" said Prue, bewildered. "What hurts?"

"Your godsbedamned Magick," snarled Deiter, tilting the jug once more. "Lord's balls, woman, get away from me, will you?"

Erik's hand closed over hers, warm and comforting. "Over here, love." He drew an unresisting Prue to a seat at the far end of the table.

"M-Magick?" She recovered enough to glare. "Don't be ridiculous. I'm about as Magickal as . . . as this table." She slapped her hand down hard on the wooden surface, making the cups jiggle.

"That's just it, Prue," Cenda said gently. When she wrapped

slender fingers around her cup, steam rose from it in little puffs, one after the other. "Your Magick is that you have none."

"I don't know what you mean."

Cenda wore a beautiful golden ornament in her hair, fashioned like a tiny lizard. To Prue's amazement, it opened sapphire eyes and blinked, then it sat up on its haunches, miniscule claws clutching at the red swathes of hair over the fire witch's temples. Prue was so bemused, she almost missed Cenda's next words. "I can feel it too, and I'm nowhere near as old in Magick as the Purist."

Prue's brain creaked back into gear. Over the past few days, she'd grown to like the fire witch, to enjoy the quiet humor and bright intelligence Cenda hid behind an unassuming manner. But now she came to think of it, she and Cenda had never been physically closer than about three feet. The other woman hadn't been obvious about it, but she'd managed to keep her distance.

A cup of fragrant tisane appeared before her, Katrin's hand touching her shoulder in reassurance. Prue cleared her throat. "The Technomage said . . . she said I broadcast a field, whatever that is. She wanted to know how. She was going to . . . to . . ."

Cenda muttered something under her breath and rills of flame sparked from her fingertips, wreathing up her arms. Under Prue's astonished gaze, Gray reached over, his shadow following, and placed a hand over hers. The flames subsided.

Deeply shaken, Prue lifted her cup and took a sip.

"Ah yes, the tame Technomage." Scowling, Deiter rummaged through the battered leather satchel that hung over the back of his chair. Coming up with a thick bundle of papers, he plunked it down on the table and undid the string tying it together. "There's something here." Pages rustled.

After a moment, he looked up. "Well, don't just sit there, woman, go on, tell us the rest. But for the gods' sake, start at the beginning." He waved a dismissive hand at Katrin. "You can go, lass."

"No." Prue held his eye down the length of the table. "Katrin is my daughter. I trust her and I want her to understand." *Because then she might forgive me when I go.*

With a rustle of skirts, Katrin settled herself beside Prue.

Deiter shrugged. "It's on your head." He aimed a gnarled

finger at the young woman. "Your life is of no consequence, girlie, do you understand? Speak of the business of gods and Magick and I'll obliterate you."

Before she knew it, Prue was on her feet, her chair toppling with a clatter. "Not if I get to you first." Blood boiling, she advanced on the old wizard. "Does it hurt yet?" she snarled.

Deiter's face went a pasty shade of gray green. Prue took another step. He clutched his chest. "Cenda!" he gasped. "Fireball, quick!"

As if from a distance, Prue heard the fire witch say quietly, "I'd do the same. You're on your own, Purist."

Erik growled. The tisane pot rose a foot off the table and poised itself to pour, right over the old man's lap. Gray laughed aloud.

42

❧

"Mam!" Katrin's shocked voice cut over the confusion. "Whatever you're doing, stop it! You'll kill him." She tugged at Prue's arm.

Shivering, Prue unclenched her fists. Her head reeled, stupid with confusion and the sickening remnants of murderous rage. "For a minute there, you looked just like Purist Nori," she told the old man. "I thought she was going to die too."

"Nori?" With trembling fingers, Deiter pushed the tisane pot aside, breathing a sigh of relief when it subsided gently to the table. Erik snorted.

"The first time I met her, at the theater. It was me that made her ill, wasn't it? Something about me?" Horror washed over her in an icy, numbing wave. "The Necromancer knew. Oh gods, he wanted it, he wanted *me*." Despite herself, her voice rose. "*What am I?*"

"Sshh, love." Erik's arm slid around her waist, guiding her back to her chair.

Deiter's color had improved. "I'm not sure." He sighed. "Nori and I are so old, Magick is all that holds us together. It's painful to come undone, so to speak." He shot her a keen glance from under shaggy brows. "Do you believe in Magick, Mistress McGuire?"

Prue rubbed her aching temples. "That's what Purist Bartelm asked at the time."

"And the answer?"

Five pairs of eyes regarded her with unwinking interest. "No, I don't." She gave a harsh laugh. "Or rather, I didn't."

Erik laid his hand over hers. "What about the gods?"

"I've told you before." She looked into his face, seeing the concern there, the love. "If they exist, they haven't done much for me."

"I wasn't going to say this." Erik stroked her cheek. "Sweetheart, don't be distressed, but I really did die."

"You've got a strange way of showing it," said Gray dryly. Cenda clutched his arm, her amber eyes bright with concentration.

Erik ignored him. "I thought I . . . I saw the gods, the Lord and the Lady." He flushed. "I know it sounds mad, but I did." He lifted his gaze to meet Deiter's intent regard. "The Lady said there was a place even for a skeptic like a null witch."

The old wizard stroked his tripartite beard. "A null witch." When he snapped his fingers, Prue jumped. "That's it! Wait, wait." Sheets of paper fluttered across the table as he scrabbled. "There's an eyewitness account of the way you killed the Necromancer. It's here somewhere."

Erik's bellow shook the rafters. "You *what*?" The windows rattled and pots clanged together.

Prue shook her head. "But I didn't. Or I don't think so. He went into the water."

Erik had gone pale to the lips, his eyes blazing cobalt blue. "You *fought* with him?"

"What do you think she did?" asked Deiter, amused. "You weren't much use to her at the time."

Erik shot him a poisonous glance. "I thought he must have run. There were so many people by the end."

"Prue." Cenda leaned forward, her golden brown eyes intent. "Just tell us in your own words, every action, every thought. It's important."

Except for Katrin, who sat in stunned silence, they all had

questions, so it took longer than Prue expected. Every now and then, a wave of red would sweep over Erik's golden skin and the table would rise an inch or so off the floor or all the papers would whirl around the room and have to be collected again.

But in the end, they established the salient points. Prue's presence nullified Magick within a certain radius of her person, and the more frail the physical health of the witch or wizard, the more it hurt. When she'd touched the Necromancer, the shield of his Dark Arts had simply evaporated, exposing his true self.

Deiter had never heard of anything like it, which appeared to cause him considerable annoyance. But null witch was as good a term as any.

"I don't know how you stood it," said Cenda, her pretty mouth contorted with disgust. "I touched him once, when Deiter was teaching me to scry. It was . . . foul." She shuddered and the salamander in her hair opened its tiny mouth wide and hissed.

"What about me?" asked Erik suddenly. He clasped the nape of Prue's neck with warm, strong fingers. "I don't understand. Why doesn't she affect me?"

Deiter tugged at his beard in frustration. "You're right. It's an anomaly."

"No, it's not." Gray rose, all lean, lithe grace, his shadow climbing the wall behind him. "Prue's power comes from belief—either its presence or its absence. She has complete faith in Erik's . . . ah, regard. So at some level, probably unconscious, she accepts his Magick too, because she believes unconditionally in *him*."

When he smiled, Prue caught her breath. He'd been so quiet, she hadn't really noticed him. Merciful Sister, he was a handsome man!

"It's a soul connection, I think." He glanced down at Cenda, his face alight with an expression so intimate and tender Prue felt she should avert her eyes. "Cenda and Shad and I complement each other. Together, we make a whole. I suspect Erik and Prue are the same. And that the gods intend it."

Prue's brows drew together, her logical mind tussling with the foolish part of her that wanted to dissolve into a happy puddle. "Sounds good," she argued, "but what do you know of Magick, Gray? It's Cenda who's the fire witch."

"I know enough," said Gray softly, his eyes gleaming.

Her brain snagged on something else. "And who's Shad?"

Gray grinned. "Allow me to introduce you." He pushed his chair back and sauntered around the table, his shadow wavering behind him.

"Gray . . ." Erik's growl held a warning. His hand closed hard over Prue's.

Gray stopped and looked Erik in the eye. "We're in this together," he said. "Every single one of us, with whatever gifts we can bring. Deiter's made that clear enough. She'll have to know sometime." He shrugged. "Might as well be now."

His attention swung back to Prue, his head turning, but his shadow was strangely immobile, as if it searched Gray's face still. "Shad is the name I give to my shadow, Prue." He glanced at the man-shaped piece of darkness standing at his side. "Shad," he said gravely, "this is Mistress Prue McGuire. Behave yourself."

Under Prue's astonished gaze, Gray's shadow swept a deep bow, as elegant as any courtier. Prue's jaw dropped. Katrin choked on her tisane, Deiter thumping her on the back in a helpful kind of way.

"Please, Prue." Cenda came to stand between Gray and his shadow. She laid a slim hand on each shoulder and their arms crept around her waist. "Don't be frightened. Shad would never hurt you. He's dear and sweet and funny." Shad's head tilted, and Prue got the distinct impression he was laughing.

"You forgot to mention modest," Gray said dryly, but his lips twitched.

Shad leaned in to nuzzle Cenda's cheek, and Prue could no longer restrain herself. "But *how*—? I don't understand."

Gray shrugged, and his shadow turned to look at him. A second later, Shad shrugged too. It was uncanny. "Shad and I have been together for as long as I can remember. I've never known a time without him."

"You're a sorcerer of shadows," said Deiter. "Face it, man. Once and for all."

Again, that elegant movement of the shoulders. "To me, this is how it's always been. Nothing unusual, nothing Magickal." Gray's smoky gaze shifted to where Shad was stroking Cenda's cheek with long, dark fingers. "If I were a real sorcerer," he said with some asperity, "you'd think I'd have better control over my . . . minions. Shad!"

Shad snuggled a grinning Cenda into his shoulder. Behind her back, he raised one finger in an unmistakable gesture.

At Prue's side, Erik chuckled and the tension in the room relaxed. Then he said, "Shad smells different, sort of cool and dark, not like you at all, Gray."

Gray and Shad appeared to exchange a glance, but before anyone could speak, Katrin said, "You're not like the Purists at all, are you?"

Every head turned to stare. A scarlet flush soared up out the neckline of her gown to stain her cheeks. "S-sorry. I mean . . . I only meant Mam doesn't bother Gray. Not the way—"

Deiter reached out to clamp a hand on her shoulder. "Shut up, girlie. Let me think."

Gray arched a dark, flyaway brow, but he said nothing.

At last, Deiter stirred. "Well," he said, "if I've learned one thing in a long and misspent life, it's that the gods exist. But also—" Obviously relishing the drama of the moment, he took a sip from his tisane cup, only to set it aside with a grimace. "Also that They are fallible. Whatever you call Them—the Lord and the Lady, the Brother and Sister, whether you believe in one or a plethora—They don't know everything.

"In the Enclaves," he went on, "the Purists teach that Magick is a gift of the gods. It's conventional wisdom. True enough, I'm sure, but no one believes They literally hand it over." Among the whiskers, his lip curled. "Like a prize in some ridiculous contest of virtue. Except . . ." His piercing gaze traveled from Erik to Cenda and back again. "They did with you two." Planting both hands on the table, he leaned forward. "*Didn't They?*"

Cenda flushed a fiery red. Erik's mouth snapped shut. His fingers tightened on Prue's so hard she winced.

"Look here." With an impatient grunt, Deiter bent to extract a leather tube from his satchel. "Clear a space, lass," he said to Katrin, and she hastened to obey. Using an unusual degree of care, the wizard eased out a thick parchment and unrolled it on the table.

Next to Prue, Erik inhaled sharply. On the thick, creamy surface was a Pentacle, magnificently rendered in colored inks and gilt—all except for one side, so lightly drawn as to be barely there. "Gods, it's beautiful," she said. "Where did you get it?"

Deiter shot her a narrow glance. "I made it." A pause. "In a vision. I've been having them for about a year now."

"But what does it *mean*? Why isn't it complete?"

"Hasty piece, aren't you?" He beckoned to the fire witch with an ink-stained finger. "Show her, Cenda."

Slowly, Cenda came forward. With a muttered prayer, she touched her forefinger to the Pentacle. Immediately, it burst into flame, tongues of fire running greedily around the pattern.

"No!" Prue leaped for a dishcloth to smother the flames, but Gray's arm barred her way."

The fire subsided with a contented crackle. Sweet Sister, the parchment was untouched, save for one side of the Pentacle, but there . . . Prue resisted the urge to rub her eyes. Tiny salamanders, each one a perfect miniature of the one in the fire witch's hair, danced back and forth, the essence of fiery joy.

"Now you, Gray," ordered Deiter.

Gray shot him a glance. "You sure?"

"Bloody well get on with it, man!"

"Fine." With a shrug, Gray placed a fingertip on the line that wasn't there.

The diminutive salamanders turned as one and hissed their defiance, but beyond that, nothing happened.

"Right as usual," said Deiter with satisfaction. "Whatever Magick you have, it comes from within, not from the gods." Raising pouchy eyes, he smiled thinly. "Moment of truth, Erik."

Erik's jaw bunched. Without a word, he strode forward and slammed a big palm down on the parchment. "This what you want, old man?"

But Deiter wasn't even looking at him, his eyes were fixed on the Pentacle. "Oh yes," he breathed.

"Fuck!" Erik snatched his hand away, but the parchment was already rippling.

Prue squinted, staring. Was that—? Merciful Sister, it was! Dust motes danced in a gentle turbulence above the five-sided shape. A current of air made its chuckling, merry way around the Pentacle, again and again, faster and faster. It was perfectly visible because it was forming tiny, sparkling clouds that whirled with rainbow iridescence. Surely it was her imagination, but the air in the kitchen vibrated as if everything innocent and sacred had been distilled into pure joy—the gurgle of a baby's belly laugh, a soaring hymn of adoration, true love's whispered promise, the liquid trill of a night bird.

A blazing smile lit up Cenda's face. The tiny salamanders capered about with delight. "That's it, that's what I felt. Oh, thank the Lady." She touched Erik's arm. "It *is* you."

Erik stared down at her, his brow knotted. "What the hell are you talking about?" When Prue laid a cautious hand against his back, every muscle was rigid beneath her palm.

"Don't give me that, Erik. You know. Deep inside, you've probably always known. You're the second Side. Air." Deiter studied the parchment, brooding. "Cenda's Fire." He tugged at his beard. "So where the fuck is Water?"

"Hold on, you've lost me." Erik pinched the bridge of his nose. "What's a *Pentacle* got to do with anything? And in case you hadn't noticed, it has five sides, not three."

The old wizard snorted. "Give me credit." He took a hasty gulp from his wine jug, his wrinkled throat working.

"The elements," said Prue slowly. "But aren't there four? Fire, air, water—and earth? And what about the blank Side, the one that's missing?"

"Only the gods know who or what the fifth Side is." Deiter's mouth took on a sour twist. "Of course, They haven't seen fit to enlighten me, for all that I'm supposed to fight Their damn battles for Them."

The wine jug rose six inches off the table and dropped abruptly. Deiter's hand shot out with astonishing speed to break its fall. "Godsdammit, what's wrong with you?" He skewered Erik with a furious glare.

Erik stared right back, his jaw set. "I don't have the faintest idea what any of this is about. It's all fucking riddles."

Deep offense flitted across the old man's features. "I told you yesterday." He folded his arms.

"When?"

"On the way upstairs."

"I wasn't listening."

"Too bad."

"It's all right, Purist. I'll do it." Cenda stepped forward. "It's simple enough—on the surface," she said to Erik. "The gods have sent Deiter a . . . prophecy, I guess you'd call it. Or a warning. In the shape of a Pentacle." She slipped her hand into Gray's. "There's a great evil out there, growing in strength, a spreading darkness." The salamander in her hair stirred restlessly.

"There is always evil, wrongdoing," said Erik. "It's a part of life."

"True enough." Deiter shrugged. "But this . . ." Suddenly, he looked not only old, but frail. "It's the very antithesis of all life, good and bad." He struggled. "A great . . . emptiness, sucking everything down into the dark."

Cenda said, "Deiter believes, and I do too, that we are pieces of a great Pattern, a game if you like, played between the gods. The Lady and the Lord at one end of the board, and . . . Their adversaries on the other." She turned to Prue. "It's not just the Sides of the Pentacle either. Gray and Shad saved my life." She lifted their clasped hands to her cheek. "You've already played a significant part, Prue." She grinned. "Thanks to you the Necromancer is gone."

The old wizard grunted. "That's too bloody easy." Every head in the room swung toward him. "I can still feel him, the bastard. Like the smallest fleck of shit on the cheek of the Lady."

Cenda paled. "Five-it, don't talk like that. It's . . . blasphemous."

"So's evil," said Deiter. "And it gets worse."

"Worse?" demanded Erik. "How can it be worse?"

"Bartelm sent me a note." Deiter dug in his satchel and produced a crumpled piece of paper. "He was talking to a guard called Rhio something—"

"Rhiomard," said Erik and Prue together.

"Yes. Ah, here we are." He squinted at the note. "They never found the body of the Technomage. And in an interesting coincidence, there was break-in at the Queen's Library night before last. The office of the Knowledge was ransacked. Including a false drawer hidden in a filing cupboard.

Rhiomard interviewed all the staff. None of them knew the drawer was there, or so they claim."

In the appalled silence, the slosh of wine in Deiter's jug seemed very loud. Something scuffled beneath the window.

As silent as his own shadow, Gray took a few quick strides, leaned over and pounced.

43

"Fook! Lemme go!"

Florien wriggled and swore as Gray hauled him over the sill. Then he kicked, catching the man on the shins. "Shit!" Gray dropped him.

"Weren't doin' nuthin'." The boy glared at Gray as he edged closer to Cenda.

"Don't come to me for sympathy," she said, looking more imposing than Prue had thought possible. Flames flickered from her fingertips. "I've told you repeatedly not to eavesdrop. How much did you hear?"

"Nuthin'."

"*Florien*," said Cenda warningly.

The boy's lower lip jutted. "Everythin'."

Deiter's gnarled fingers closed hard on a bony shoulder. "More to the point, how much did you understand?"

The dark eyes flashed. "Ain't stoopid."

Deiter raised his hands, sketching a complicated shape in the air, murmuring under his breath.

Erik reached out, grabbed the boy and thrust the small body behind his. "Hell, no!"

"He's a risk we can't afford."

Prue stepped in front of both of them. Finding her voice, she snapped, "Killing a child does the Necromancer's work. You want that?"

Slowly, Deiter lowered his hands. He cleared his throat. "Was only going to shut him up."

With an irritated grunt, Erik picked Prue up and set her aside. Florien peered around his hip, the whites of his eyes showing. "Won' say nuthin'. I swear."

"You most certainly won't." Erik squatted to hold the boy's gaze. "Because you're going to make a solemn promise and shake the hand of every person in this room." He held out his left hand. "Agreed?"

"Yah." Slowly, Florien placed his small hand in Erik's big one. His shoulders stiffened. "I kin do thet."

Bemused, Prue watched him move composedly from one adult to the next, his head held high. He had his own funny little dignity—and amazing courage. Sister, he was going to be an extraordinary man. A reluctant smile curved her lips as she gravely shook a small paw. If he lived that long.

Florien's skinny frame trembled as he approached the old wizard, but he managed the handshake creditably enough, skittering immediately to Cenda's side. He barely flinched when she bent to drop a peck on his cheek, screwing up his face in a way Prue found dangerously endearing.

She wondered if the lad had a part to play, because it seemed as if she did, and Gray. Oh, and Shad. Fire and Air, with Water and Earth still unknown. Her thoughts hitched. That was odd. "Purist?"

Deiter grunted.

"You didn't mention Earth."

"No," said Erik. "That's right, you didn't. Well?" He arched a brow.

Deiter flapped a hand. "Oh, I know where to find Earth."

An instant's silence, and everyone spoke together, Erik's practiced bellow rising above the hubbub. "*Who? Where?*"

The old wizard pinched the bridge of his nose. "That's not for me to say. He's proving . . . recalcitrant." He pulled out a chair and flopped into it without grace.

"*Recalcitrant?* But we need him!" Cenda's voice rose to a

near shriek. Florien jumped back as the salamander tripled in size, skittered to her shoulder and reared back on its haunches, spitting. "Have you told him what's at stake?"

"Leave Earth to me, girlie. There's no such thing as coincidence, not in the Pattern of the gods. Water's close. You concentrate on finding him—or her." He cast her a stern look from under shaggy brows. "And on doing better Magick. You have to be fast and deadly, and you're nothing near it." He turned. "You too, Erik."

"The world's ending and that's what I'm supposed to do?" Erik's growl rattled the windows. "*Practice?*"

Deiter's lips went thin amid the wine-stained whiskers. "What did you have in mind? Heroics on a universal scale, Magick among the stars?"

Erik shook his head, the shadows she'd noticed before darkening his eyes. At last, he said slowly, "I have no fucking idea." He sank into a chair. "About anything." He stared blankly at his hands clasped before him on the table. "The Voice is gone. I don't even know how I'm going to make a living."

A cold lump of ice formed in Prue's stomach. Gray said sharply, "What do you mean? Aren't you well?"

Erik's chuckle was very dry. "Apart from being knifed by a Necromancer? No, I'm fine. I just can't sing anymore, or not the same way." His eyes met Prue's, and though they were troubled, his gaze was steady. "My blessing and my curse, both gone together." He laid a hand over hers where it rested on his shoulder, and with a deep shock, she realized what he was trying to tell her. "I'm glad."

"Man, are you *sure*?" Gray was aghast. "I don't believe it. Music was your life."

Erik gave a weary smile and Prue's heart ached for him. All that beauty, gone as if it had never been. "A small price to pay for peace."

"I don't understand. What about the Unearthly Opera?"

"We'll meet with Ranald and decide what's best. They go can home to Concordia, where they'll be safe. They're due for an extended period of leave anyway. I don't care if I lose money on the contract."

Prue sat down beside him and rested her head against his arm, blinking back tears of relief. *He wasn't leaving.* Oh gods, oh gods! Suddenly, she was exhausted, her head about to explode with conflicting emotions. She was fiercely glad the Voice had gone, never mind how, but she could only imagine the piercing loss of that sublime musical gift. How it must hurt!

Her gaze traveled around the familiar, mundane space of the kitchen. How many times had she sat at this very table, leading her most ordinary of ordinary lives? Yet here were people talking calmly of death Magick, of gifts spilled from the very fingers of the gods. A woman who could weave fire and not be burned, a lean handsome man with a shadow that *lived*. All the hair on the back of her neck lifted. Next to her sat the man she loved more than life itself, *a wizard who'd made love to her with Magick*. Feeling chilled, she pressed closer to Erik's heat.

Out of the corner of her eye, she saw Katrin tug Florien's hair and slip him a pastry. Something sweet. Such a comfort for a child.

And she was a thing called a null witch, an aberration, a negative. An *absence*.

Wearily, she wondered if Katrin had more pastries. She could use a little comfort too.

⁓

A fortnight later, Prue was at her wits' end. In her own calm, logical way, she'd worked her way through the readings Purist Deiter gave her, listened to Cenda talk about life in a Purist Enclave, helped Erik with his Magick practice. She even came to terms with Shad, though his silent presence could still make her jump. When Erik and Gray sorted out the sale of the Unearthly Opera to Ranald and the group of backers he'd found, she offered financial advice and drew up the deeds of sale.

Erik displayed quite astonishing business acumen, but it wasn't until she'd commented on it for the third time that he explained what he'd done to the Opera's accounts. No one had ever said Erik the Golden was a fool. He waited until he'd loved her into a purring, satiated bundle. By the next morning, it was too late to be angry.

Yes, she thought she'd reached some sort of understanding of the Magickal situation and the part a null witch might play. To her dismay, it was only Erik who baffled her.

By tacit agreement, he'd moved his things from the boardinghouse and into her suite. Florien came unasked, part of the baggage, taking up residence in a small room on the ground floor, not far from the Spring Green Parlor, which Prue had fitted out as a bedroom for Cenda and Gray—and Shad, of course. Deiter went, grumbling, to the Wizards' Enclave, where he spent the hours drinking the meager cellars dry and arguing happily with Bartelm and Nori.

She could no longer doubt Erik loved her. Frequently, she'd feel his gaze on her, and turn to see his eyes a dark, brilliant blue, an almost desperate glitter in their depths.

There were days she left the bracelets off and their lovemaking was slow and achingly sweet. Other times, it was fast and hard and thrilling. But increasingly, Erik asked her to wear them and those were the nights he drove her to the peak, again and again, his eyes wide and wild, his dedication to her pleasure bordering on ferocity. Prue discovered, to her combined delight and dismay, that she'd come to crave the mastery that pushed her beyond her limits and set her free to fly, to long for the security of rope and restraints.

After he untied her, she'd lie boneless, in a stupor of satiation, draped over his chest like a sleepy kitten while he massaged her wrists and kissed the marks of the knots.

But later, she'd wake in the early hours to find the bed cold beside her. Erik would be standing at the window, gazing out at the garden, drenched in the double shadows of the Sibling Moons. Or she'd hear the pad of his bare feet, back and forth, back and forth. If she slipped out of bed and went to wind her arms around his waist, he'd drop a kiss on her hair and hug her close, but he wouldn't speak. Always, his skin was cold and clammy, his heart racing.

He began to lose weight, his face growing gaunt, dark shadows blooming beneath his eyes. The charming smile she loved disappeared as if it had never been. When she asked, he said he was tired, or that his wound still ached. When she pressed, he grew irritated.

At first merely uneasy, Prue became concerned and finally,

truly frightened. Erik was withdrawing before her eyes, behind a barrier she couldn't see, let alone breach. And she was helpless.

One night, he made love to her for hours, staring deep into her eyes, lavishing her with such exquisite care and tenderness she was reduced to tears. Murmuring foolish endearments, he kissed them away, his own voice choked with emotion.

Then he rose and dressed, lit all the lamps and handed over her favorite robe. "Come and sit," he said, leading her over to the couch. He sounded unutterably weary, so grim that Prue's chest tightened and she could hardly breathe.

Forcing a smile, she patted the cushion beside her, but he shook his head. "I have something to tell you."

Prue reached out. "It can't be that bad."

But Erik recoiled. "Don't touch me," he said curtly. "I can't do it if you touch me. You won't want to anyway . . . afterward."

"Merciful Sister, Erik, what is it?" Her stomach twisted. "Gods, you're not leaving me?"

"I don't know. Maybe." His eyes were huge dark pits in a face as white as bone. "When I was seventeen," he said jerkily, "I committed a . . . great crime."

When she leaped to her feet, he held up a hand. "Promise me, Prue. Promise me you will sit and listen. Don't speak, don't stop me, don't even move. In fact, it would be better if you don't look at me."

Abruptly, he turned his back and Prue sank into the cushions, appalled. "What? For the gods' sakes, tell me!"

He kept his head averted. "Promise?"

"Yes, yes! Gods, what is it?"

Erik fixed his gaze on the bed of Walker's dark roses. Even from here, he could smell their exotic perfume. "When I was seventeen," he said, "I nearly died of the lungspasm." He shrugged. "Hell, I *did* die. I saw the gods, the Lord and the Lady, spoke with Them."

He heard Prue shift behind him, but he mustn't turn, or he'd lose his nerve. He was fighting a battle with his roiling guts, his breath coming shallow and fast. Reaching out, he gripped the windowsill. "I see the Pattern now, but at the time, all I knew was that They gave me back the gift of my life—and something else. The Lord warned me. He said everything had a cost." In an automatic gesture, he touched his fingertips to the talisman on his chest.

"It wasn't long after my recovery that I realized what I had. If I set my mind to it, I could sing the birds from the trees. If I spoke a certain way, I could persuade anyone to do anything. I was young, incredibly stupid, selfish. It went to my head."

Fuck, if he didn't breathe, he'd pass out. Erik gulped in air.

"There was a girl. But she didn't want me, she was in love with someone else."

Prue made a tiny noise, and he realized he'd miscalculated— he could see her face in the window, a wavering reflection. She had a hand over her mouth, her eyes huge and terrified.

"You can guess." He slammed his eyes closed, shutting her out. "It was spring, I'd nearly died and she was so lovely, Inga. Oh, gods." Pressing his forehead against the cool of the glass, he forced out the damning words, one after the other. "I . . . compelled her and worse, I made her enjoy it." The laugh was bitter bile in his throat, sour and horrible. "I didn't want to hurt her, I thought I was helping, but she—"

His knees would no longer hold him up. Gripping the windowsill, he slid down, his cheek against the wall. "She had no idea why she'd given her virginity to me and not the man she loved. She . . . she . . ."

Fuck, get it over with. Say it! "She drowned herself in the river. I found her, but too late. Too late."

Frozen silence from behind him. Not even a whisper of movement. He wanted to cry, but his eyes were dry. "So I ran, left Ma, my little brothers, without a word. Out of my head with terror and guilt and shame. I swore I would never use the Voice to compel, only to sing, to bring pleasure. It wasn't easy, I failed often at first. I'm slow." He bared his teeth in a grin that was more like a grimace. "But eventually I learned. Unless it was to sing or to prevent a disaster, I hadn't used the Voice in years. Until I met you."

The silence went on forever. Erik sagged, completely spent. Vaguely, he wondered if he'd be able to sleep now that it was done. His bags were packed. All he had to do was drag himself to his feet and out the door. Fuck, his lips were parched. He'd stop in the kitchen for water. If Katrin was there, he could say good-bye. He couldn't think of Prue. Wouldn't. It was beyond him.

"Why?" The shaky whisper came from the couch. "Why tell me now?" A pause. "Spoil everything?"

Awkwardly, Erik levered himself up. "I've never spoken of it, ever, but the Lady said—"

"Which time?" snapped Prue. "The first time you died or the second?"

Startled, he swung around to face her and nearly fell over his feet. Prue was glaring, two spots of red on her pale cheeks.

"The second," he said numbly. "When I asked Them to take it from me, all of it."

"Go on," she said more quietly.

He swallowed hard. "She said . . . she'd forgiven me, that I'd paid, but that I couldn't . . . couldn't forgive myself. That I needed you for that."

Prue rose and took a few jerky steps, the line of her back stiff and uncompromising. Like a suffering animal, Erik couldn't help but follow her with his eyes, hoping but knowing there was no hope.

"I can't—" She shook her head. "You forced that girl." Slowly, she turned, her tip-tilted eyes huge in her white face. Tears glittered on her cheeks. "Perverted your Magick."

"I raped her," said Erik hoarsely, wanting to die.

"And you raped her mind."

"Yes."

Her lip curled, in exactly the way he'd been dreading. "No excuses? No justifications?"

"No."

She took a tiny step forward. "You've been suffering the tortures of the damned ever since."

It wasn't a question, but he answered it anyway. "I tried never to think of it, but underneath . . . Yes."

Prue tilted her head to one side. "Did you send money?"

"I still do. To Ma. For her and my brothers, and for her to give Inga's family. They don't know it comes from me."

Prue wiped her eyes on the sleeve of her robe. "A lot of things make sense now. Inga was the experience that shaped your life, made you who you are."

"Yes." He clenched his fists so he wouldn't reach for her.

"When we met, I thought you were a challenge sent by the gods, my punishment, but then . . ." He was such a coward, he couldn't take the risk, say the words aloud. Erik dropped his head.

The robe swished and small fingers caught his chin. "Then what?" Prue's eyes sparkled with what looked like fury.

Erik dared to brush her cheek with his knuckles. "I thought you might be my salvation, but I can see I was wrong."

"Wrong?"

"I can smell the anger coming off your skin. You're furious. Disgusted."

Prue flushed. "Of course, I am! How could I be anything else?"

He'd shoved his bags under the bed so she wouldn't see. "All right," he said dully. "I'll get my things."

"How dare They?" snarled Prue, following some incomprehensible train of thought. "A boy of seventeen!"

"What?" he said.

"And people look so shocked when I say I don't believe! Hah!"

Erik's heart flip-flopped in his chest. "Prue," he said, "what the hell are you talking about?"

"Them! The bloody gods! Has it never occurred to you how unfair it was to place such a burden on a boy, a mere child?"

He stared. "But Prue, what I did—"

She gripped his arm. "Was wrong, wicked. Hideous. I don't condone it, not for a second. You did it of your own free will, but don't you see? They *used* you and poor Inga, your precious Lord and Lady." She snorted. "I know grown men who'd go mad with a tenth of the power They gave you at seventeen."

"Prue, you're crazy."

"Am I?" She took a restless turn around the room. "You've hated yourself all these years, locked yourself in a prison made of rules, a personal honor code so rigid you couldn't let anyone close. You told me that yourself."

"*Honor?* After what I did—"

"Godsdammit! Will you get past what you did?"

Dumbfounded, Erik shook his head.

"Think about it." Prue's voice softened as she drew him down to the couch. "The cost was Inga's life, but the result was an air wizard with iron control, a man morally fit to be one Side of the Great Pentacle." She gazed earnestly into his face. "You're the most honorable man I know, Erik. You risked your life for mine." Her lips trembled as she smiled. "It's yours now. You might as well keep it."

Gods, was he going to faint? Spots danced in his vision. "Does that mean you forgive me?"

Prue hesitated and his heart sank. After an age, she said, "It's strange. I've little use for the gods, but there's a piece of scripture I've always loved. The Bridal Gift of the Sister. It's a prescribed text for the religious education of adolescent girls." Pink rose in her cheeks. "I'm not always good with words, not like you. Will you listen?"

He nodded.

Prue took a deep breath. "*Courage is the gift of the Brother*," she began, "*but love is the gift of the Sister. On the night They were wed, the Sister knelt before Him—Brother, Husband, Lord. 'True love is My gift to You, Beloved,' the Sister said.*"

Slowly, she reached out and grasped Erik's hand.

"*She touched Her starry eyes. She said, 'True love sees what is—the good, the bad and all that is between. Because love loves.'*"

Something was rising inside him, something spiky and painful, struggling to be free. Erik tightened his grip on her fingers.

"*The Sister offered Her wrists and cruel ropes appeared, chafing Her silky skin. 'True love can bear anything, endure anything. Love goes on hoping to the edge of forever. It never gives up. Because love loves.'*"

Prue twisted to look into his face. Tears welled up in her beautiful eyes, spilling over her sooty lashes. Her nose was pink. "Do you see?" she whispered. "Love loves. Do you see?"

Wordlessly, he nodded. The spiky feeling had climbed as far as his throat.

Her husky voice was relentless, shoving the beautiful words at him. He was going to shatter, fly to pieces . . . He buried his fingers in the silken mass of her hair.

"*The Sister touched Her sweet breast. She said, 'True love is patient and kind. It seeks not to alter the beloved. Because love loves.'*"

"Stop, Prue, stop. I can't—I'm going to—"

"There's not much more." Her smile shone brilliantly through the tears. *"Reaching out, She took His hand and placed it upon Her head. 'Faith is mighty, Hope is great. But when all else is gone—sense and knowledge, and life itself—True Love alone remains.'"*

Erik shook like a leaf in a gale. A grating cry forced itself out of his throat, hurting all the way. Then another, and another. His vision blurred.

"Let it go, love," whispered Prue, wrapping her arms around him. "I've got you."

Her voice resonated, clear and confident and very, very sure. *"Rising, She clasped the Brother to Her breast and His tears dampened Her hair. 'Because love loves.'"*

Erik rested his head against her sweet breast and wept until there were no more tears left in him, deep, wracking sobs that shook his whole frame. Peripherally, he was aware of her fingers stroking his hair, her voice whispering endearments, her arms cradling him like a child.

The storm didn't last long. Digging in the pocket of her robe, Prue found a handkerchief and handed it over. His practical Prue. It nearly set him off again. His eyes were gritty and he felt so light, so scoured out, he could have used his own Magick to float himself to the ceiling.

"Better?" asked Prue.

He cleared his throat. "Yes."

"Then come to bed." Taking his hand, she led him into the other room.

◦⬡◦

She'd known it would be a hellish night, and she was right. Prue lost count of the times she woke with a start, staring wildly into the dark, her heart drumming with formless horror. And then she'd remember.

Erik lay beside her, holding her tight, as if she were a talisman against the dark, his last and only refuge.

She'd stroke his hair, his arm, his back, and listen to the steady rhythm of his breath. Her heart ached—for Inga herself, for her family and the lover who'd lost her, for Erik's mother and his brothers. So much havoc and grief, all wrought by the actions of a foolish, feckless boy given a burden too great for him to bear.

Who knew who had suffered the greatest pain? How did you measure?

Hot tears slipped out of the corners of her eyes and trickled into her hair.

True love can bear anything, endure anything. Soundlessly, she formed the words. *Love goes on hoping to the edge of forever. It never gives up. Because love loves.*

Prue gave a wry smile. It appeared she was no longer quite so skeptical about divinities. Perhaps one day, she'd meet Erik's Dark Lady. She looked forward to it. Oh, how she'd love to give the goddess a piece of her mind!

In the final analysis, it was simple. Erik Thorensen was who he was, the totality of every experience in his life. The gods had formed his character in a crucible of suffering, honed him ruthlessly for a purpose she scarcely understood.

Faith is mighty, Hope is great. But when all else is gone—sense and knowledge, and life itself—True Love alone remains.

So be it.

Resolutely, Prue closed her eyes, and this time, she slept.

∞

Grumbling under her breath, Prue patted the cold space beside her in the bed.

Reluctantly, she pried her eyes open. It was near dawn. The light had that special cool, gray quality. Rustling sounds and the occasional mumble came from her office and she relaxed, relief making her a little dizzy. He sounded somewhat preoccupied but no longer distressed. Thank the Sister. Rolling over, she buried her head under the pillow.

Tap, tappity, tap. Tap, tap, tap.

What the—?

Crossly, she belted on her shabby robe and padded out into the office.

Completely nude, big and golden, Erik sat in her office chair, scribbling on the back of an unpaid invoice. The Sister knew how she was going to explain to the merchant. With his other hand, he was tapping out a rhythm on the surface of the desk.

Disarmed, Prue took a moment to admire. "What are you doing?"

"Hmm?" *Tap, tappity, tap.*

"I said, *What are you doing*?"

He looked up, the sea blue eyes vague and distracted. "Oh, it's you. Good. Say it for me again." He poised the brush over the paper, oblivious to the big drop about to fall from the tip.

Prue struggled through the mists of sleep. "Say what?"

"The Bridal Gift of the Sister." His eyes shone. "I woke up with the perfect melody in my head. But I need the words."

"You're writing music?"

"Hmm." He frowned down at the blot spreading across her invoice. "It's coming, but only in bits. Driving me mad." When he tugged at his hair, he left ink streaks behind, a smear on his cheekbone. "A boy treble and a tenor, I think. Though a soprano would be good too. Maybe a bass for the Brother. Shit."

With an exasperated sigh, Erik closed his eyes and hummed a few bars of something that rose and fell in an aching minor key. Even to Prue's untrained ear, he sounded completely different, tuneful, but . . . ordinary, the sort of voice you'd hear in any drawing room. In spite of it, her heart lifted. The Voice had gone, but the core of his music, the joyous, healing heart of it, was still there.

Tap, tap, tappity, tap.

"Erik?"

A grunt. *Tap, tap, tap.*

"Rose has a hymnal. Shall I swap her the cuffs you gave me for it?"

The blond head didn't lift. "Hmm."

Prue strolled into the bedchamber and found her hairbrush. With a secret smile, she met her own serene gaze in the mirror. Any second . . . One, two—

"Godsdammit! *Prue!*"

Laughing, she turned to face the door.

Also from
#1 *New York Times* bestselling author

·LORA LEIGH·

Styx's Storm

A NOVEL OF THE BREEDS

When Storme Montague's father and brother are killed
by the Breeds, her father's research is also destroyed—
except for a crucial data chip that both the Council and
the Breeds would kill to possess. Betrayed to the Council, she is rescued by Styx, a Wolf Breed who is different
from most other Breeds she has ever known. Storme
has something he wants too—but it's not a data chip.

There's never been a woman who bad boy Styx
couldn't seduce. But can the charmer of the Wolf Breeds
charm the enemy?

penguin.com

LOOK FOR THE NEW GUILD HUNTER NOVEL FROM
NEW YORK TIMES BESTSELLING AUTHOR

NALINI SINGH

ARCHANGEL'S CONSORT

Vampire hunter Elena Deveraux and her lover, the lethally beautiful archangel Raphael, have returned home to New York—only to face an uncompromising new evil...

A vampire has attacked a girls' school—the assault one of sheer, vicious madness—and it is only the first act. Rampant bloodlust takes vampire after vampire, threatening to leave the streets running with blood. Then Raphael himself begins to show signs of an uncontrolled rage, as inexplicable storms darken the city skyline and the earth itself shudders.

An ancient and malevolent immortal is rising. The violent winds whisper her name: *Caliane*. She has returned to reclaim her son, Raphael. Only one thing stands in her way: Elena, the consort who must be destroyed...

011 33 46 89 00 68

Penguin Group (USA) Online

What will you be reading tomorrow?

Patricia Cornwell, Nora Roberts, Catherine Coulter,
Ken Follett, John Sandford, Clive Cussler,
Tom Clancy, Laurell K. Hamilton, Charlaine Harris,
J. R. Ward, W.E.B. Griffin, William Gibson,
Robin Cook, Brian Jacques, Stephen King,
Dean Koontz, Eric Jerome Dickey, Terry McMillan,
Sue Monk Kidd, Amy Tan, Jayne Ann Krentz,
Daniel Silva, Kate Jacobs...

You'll find them all at
penguin.com

*Read excerpts and newsletters,
find tour schedules and reading group guides,
and enter contests.*

Subscribe to Penguin Group (USA) newsletters
and get an exclusive inside look
at exciting new titles and the authors you love
long before everyone else does.

PENGUIN GROUP (USA)
penguin.com

M224G0909